THE METHUSELAH GENE

THE METHUSELAH
GENE

Russell Husted

This book is dedicated to my bestie Erin who listened and inspired this story and to Deidre, my English teacher who saw in me What I couldn't. Thank you both.

I n my life as a scientist, I have only encountered this mutated gene a handful of times. It is called the Methuselah gene. It is a recessive gene that allows for super-aging. I have yet to meet an offspring of two such parents, and perhaps that is best. We would call that person an immortal because they could live a thousand years or so.

I should introduce myself, as you now are clearly intrigued by my study. I am known simply as Dr. Carl Omega; yeah, I've heard all the jokes, thanks. I call myself Doc. Carl wants to avoid those precious moments. But I digress. I'm a five-foot-five, overweight, 38 y/o man. Thank God I have a full head of hair. That would be cruel, even by Karma standards. I smile through worn-down teeth due to a bad dental plan; being a scientist doesn't really pay well. I do have a sense of humor; if you don't believe me, please refer to the aforementioned stats.

My studies are my life because I became seduced by the idea of immortality in comic books. You know the ones with vampires and eternals that seem to continue living through the centuries. I wanted to find that shred of truth that most people believe is contained in the myths. I named it the Methuselah gene, thinking it to be a cute acknowledgment of the man of history.

I first started looking at long-lived animals and plants and took samples to compare their DNA. I couldn't find a link. Next, I tried with supercentenarians. Again, luck was not on my side. Undaunted, I turned my attention to the origins of my quest, books and texts from ancient times. Five continents, 140 cities, 14 years, and increasingly more powerful reading glasses later, I found that small glimmer of hope in an obscure text written on papyrus in an Egyptian museum. Great, you say, yes, after 14 long years, I found a clue, a hint, a whisper in the wind.

Tears came to my eyes, not joy but rather frustration. How long was my tenure to be on this now quest?

Did I mention that it's 2005 and that I'm almost middle-aged? I started the search in my twenties, right after college. Now thirty-plus (please don't ask me to repeat my age), I have some real information and a handful of samples. Enter stage left, a wild card enigma on two legs by the name of Stephan Orion. I know what you're thinking, but you can't make this stuff up. To describe him, just say he's everything I'm not: tall, handsome, young, thin, wealthy, and with killer eyes. Eyes that can make men look twice. He came to me as an intern, to assist me for the summer in response to an ad I had in the local paper. It was all I could afford. After the interview, I decided he was perfect for the job; he was the only applicant who would work for the money offered. Did I say I was financially challenged?

We started the first week together by acclimating him to the field work I had accomplished. I won't bore you with the tedium of the book work reading. Suffice to say, he proved to be everything I wanted had I the unlimited funds of important scientists. This made me wonder why he chose me, not that I'm complaining, given his talent and backing. He drives a new Porsche, and I drive a 1995 Honda Civic winter rat. Thank God I have a $50,000 grant. Okay, so I fudged a few facts to garner it, but everyone embosses a little, or in my case, a lot.

Again, I digress, but it is my story to tell. I tried to get background on him by casual conversation, but he proved to be a politician in that area. He dodged every question and made me feel good about it. The wild card. I began looking elsewhere for his life story. Nights were spent snooping instead of sleeping. I came up empty and very tired. I should have slept. He was this enigma to me, and I had to solve it. However, I also had a grant to serve, if I wanted the money to keep flowing. As I was burning through the grant money quickly, I put his past on the back burner.

Stephan showed up on time, as always, with two coffees in hand and that perfect smile on his face. I think they're Lumineers. (How much money has this kid got anyway?) Two months into our collaboration, Stephan confided a tidbit of his life. Another whisper in the wind, another hint, another clue, my entire life so far. The hint came in the form of a question, "Carl, I must confess this study intrigues me, but what has this to do with any reality? I enjoy theory as well as any man, but where would I fit in?"

Bells and whistles went off in my mind, and wild imagery took over. A long sip of coffee and a finger to my lip allowed me the seconds needed to compose myself and regroup enough to answer. "Stephan, all of my studies are theoretical by definition. You wouldn't fit into my model." This was when he revealed that clue; it came from those perfect eyes. His expression changed, and those eyes darkened. It felt cooler in the room, and I felt as though he was searching me for the "other" information I was holding back.

I've had enough exposure to clues and thin hints to know when something does and doesn't feel right. In fact, it felt surreal and uncomfortable. Time slowed down, and everything took on new dimensions. I felt dizzy, for real this time, I swear. Then, as soon as it hit me, Stephan's eyes reverted back to beautiful, and my chest unclenched. He actually smiled that perfect smile as if he got the joke. I feigned fatigue and then asked if he could finish up for the day, to which he nodded and turned away too busy himself. He acted as if I were already gone.

I ran out with my coat in my hand, too hurried to put it on. Mistake number eleven, as it began to rain as soon as I got too far from cover. Did I ever say I was lucky? Wringing wet and chilled to the bone, I arrived at what I will call home (a one-bedroom walk-up apartment). I forwent dinner, changed into my comfy clothes, and sat down at my computer to find something out about Stephan. The last name Orion was sort of unique; it had to have a Google entry somewhere. "Let's see, O, R, I, O, N, enter." Two nano seconds later, three million, four hundred-eighty five thousand, one hundred and thirty-one entries. Joy and rapture; another lifetime project. It doesn't get better than this. "Okay, let me try Orion family history." Twenty thousand or so entries, things are looking up.

I click on a good-looking article, the history of the Orion dynasty from 5AD to 1500AD. Four hours of reading later, the family dies out in the plague. Back to square one. I went to bed, knowing that sleep is better than frustration.

I called Stephan the following morning to stay home as I had a 'cold' and returned to my research on Orion. "Orion family myths looked interesting, click." And what to my wandering eyes did appear? Nonsense and foolishness; strike two and counting. As breakfast yearned, I found a small site near the end of the entries; Yes, I scanned all twenty thousand, well, almost, but I did find an article titled "The Mediterranean Orion Family." Color me happy, actually ecstatic. I grabbed an apple and sat to read. Could I have caught a break at last?

Another two hours of reading and a connection. One sentence put me on the path, "it is said that not all the Orion bloodline was lost in the plague of the 1500's. One branch of the family was in exile, but continuing records were lost over time. The only surviving information was the Patriarch's name, Stephan Orion." Could it be, was it possible, were there coins in my Karma bank? Did I need to pray to someone, God, Nature, a Pagan deity? I thought it easiest to start with my God, less work and more comfort, should I have gotten it wrong, and the scholars were right. (for once).

I literally bowed my head and said thanks for the break, if indeed it was one. I printed out this article and made note of the author and publisher, should it prove out. Breakfast tasted like ambrosia, and I walked to the store for a diversion. I deserved it.

I finished the walk more invigorated than when I started. Borders Book Store is only eight blocks away and downhill mostly, but my mood was up. The in-store computer had a listing of articles by the author, and it was near the coffee clutch, a bonus. If I told you his name, you'd laugh and tell me I was joking with you. His actual name is, are you ready? Steven Noiro. Yes, it's Orion backwards, I told you it would make you laugh. So far, the names seem like a fiction novel gone awry.

The coffee was good; I bought the books, went back home, and had a night at home reading intently. Morning came, and it was Saturday, what do you know, I gave myself a long weekend, happy. More reading and note-making filled my next two days. I had to be ready for Monday. I didn't want to ambush Stephan; actually, I did, but didn't want to come across as such.

A year's worth of study done in two days. I felt confident in my decision that I now knew how to broach the subject with Stephan. But would he continue his ambiguity or come clean about the knowledge that I possessed? Only time would tell. I entered the study lab to find he was already there. Knee deep in study with books akimbo about him. He looked up with a mischievous smile and said, "The coffee is hot and on your desk." Did he know the game was afoot?

I started slowly, and that dizzy feeling returned. My control was waning as fast as my fear was growing. I had wanted the upper hand and felt as though I was holding deuces. Stephan approached and held out a text he had been reading. It was the same book I had picked up at the bookstore on Saturday. "It may calm you to read this passage, Carl." He pointed to the paragraph I had intended to cite to him. He was either reading my mind or was a better intern than he let on.

When I finished reading it, I handed it back to him. He looked at me intently with those eyes, those beautiful eyes, and said, "Now let's talk. Ask the questions you've been wanting to ask." An intense calm came over me, and I felt a part of a whole new world, as when you finally figure out the answer to a particularly difficult problem.

"Why did you join my study? Are you the descendant of the lost Orion dynasty? What do you actually want with me? How, at your age, do you have such assets?"

"Let's start with the basics, Carl, then I'll fill you in completely. First, let me say I'm a big fan of your work. You sense what others can only dream about in literature. You have touched on the subject that I actually know far more about, longevity. What you call the Methuselah gene, I call immortality. Actually, I can die as easily as you, from disease, wounds, or accidents; I am only immune to old age. My parents both carried the recessive gene for this trait. I had two siblings, a brother and a sister. He died from a disease, and she died from an accident. Only we received the trait. My family lived in the 1500's. I was born in 1512. The passage from the Mediterranean Orion family book, which I'm sure you brought with you, and that I had you read from, contains the accounts of my life. I wrote it using the pseudonym Noiro, believing no one would make the connection. It's like the drinking water Evian, spelled backward is Naive. Catch my drift."

With those simple words, Stephan began his dissertation on the history of the Orion family. My family hails from the early 500's in a region now known as Greece. I can't relate the entire lineage, but suffice it to say that it's long. We, as a family, realized something amiss around 600AD. When a few of us were still living, not many, but enough to suggest a difference, that was when we decided to move from region to region and country to country to avoid suspicion.

Things went well until around the 1500's (around the time of my birth). My family had the most living relatives, and the rest of the tribe wanted to put down roots. My folks made the decision to keep the family secret and keep moving, a good thought considering the rest of the family ended up dying out from the plague. (Did I tell you that we are all susceptible to disease?)

I sat down with a plop, not completely understanding my good luck. I sized up my 'young' friend to catch any tells of deception. He seemed even more at ease with the telling of his 'secret'. "Even if you were to go public with this information, Carl, I hesitate to say that no one would believe you." I nodded and grinned as though I had been admitted to an 'Illuminati' type society. My life's work was now on the fast track, and I had my own living example. Stephan winked, I fell back into the chair, and he asked if I wanted to hear more. I acted like a crack addict, and he was my only dealer. "Of course I want to hear it all, every juicy bit. You've lived nearly 500 years. I can't wait to get the real stories from the 'horse's mouth."

"Where would you like me to start, birth, youth, or history?" "Yes, yes, and yes, don't leave anything out. Hey, can I record this so I don't miss any details? We can edit it later, and I'll let you have last say." "Okay, buckle up" was all he said, and I almost kissed him.

"The year I was born, Michelangelo finished the ceiling of the Sistine Chapel, having the first viewing on November 1st. My folks happened to be in Rome at the time, so they were the first people to see it. I wish I had been older; I didn't get back to Rome until some years later. 1512 saw many battles around Europe, and my parents had to stay in the countrysides to keep us from being conscripted and involved with the violence. We left Italy because of Giovanni De Medici. He headed the sack of the city of Pratt, using the papal troops to destroy the entire town. I was told later that it was a blood bath. We journeyed to France, assuming it would be better, but no, we had to keep going as the battle of Prato was raging, and it led to the death of Gaston De Foix, the famous French Commander. We kept going to Spain, but it was the same story. King Ferdinand II of Aragon led the conquest of Navarre on the Iberian Peninsula.

My parents took us to Lisbon, Portugal, a port city, and we stayed there until it was time to move to avoid suspicion. I could have stayed as the wine and women, and, yes, men were all to my liking. Youth has a way of allowing for experimentation.

By this time, it was 1546, and we sailed to England right after my 34th birthday, thinking it safe. However, six months later, Henry VIII died on January 28th, and the monarchy went berserk. Prince Edward took the crown at 10 years old in 1547 and reigned until his death in 1553. Then, Mary, I took the throne. She only ruled the queendom for 5 turbulent years. Finally, Elizabeth I ascended to the throne in 1558.

Things were again quiet until it was moving day. My parents were yearning for Italy again, and the artistry of the Renaissance. Age had come to both parents, and they barely made it to Italy before passing (they, now being in their nineties). It was sad, but they had been given their final wish. We had them interred in 1580 at the Cimitero Acattilico in Rome, their favorite place, and yes, I still go there when in Italy and place flowers.

I finally got to the Papal city to see the Sistine Chapel in all its glory, and happened to get an audience with Pope Gregory XIII (born Ugo Boncompagni in 1502). The audience was to have a profound effect on me, though I wasn't to realize it until much later. I found out that it was he who promulgated the Gregorian Calendar and who passed five years later.

I was staying in Calcata, a town in the province of Viterbo, about 29 miles north of Rome. A quaint little town where the villagers took little notice as I wandered about. (having had to learn 7 languages – Greek, Latin, Italian, French, Spanish, Portuguese, and English as a youth). I have to admit the local food was divine, almost sinful, and drinking wine daily was no chore either. I was noticed in 1585 by a visiting artist who wanted me to pose for him. I was flattered and agreed (Although I think the wine had a little to do with it). His name is Caravaggio. If you know of his paintings, look for the painting "Narcissus," and you'll see me on the canvas. He wanted me as his boy toy lover, but didn't realize that I was actually 83 (old enough to be his father). He was a thoughtful soul, and I could have stayed there and lived forever (literally), but I thought better of it and prepared to move on.

I left with heartfelt memories and a teary eye, the place that so entranced me, and headed to Greece to reaffirm my heritage.

By the time I got to Greece in 1590, the Ottomans had conquered the region, and I had to be a Crypto-Christian or secretive Greek Orthodox and Greek "Muslim" to the powers that be at the time. I decided then and there to 'sight-see' other places and return later (as I had all the time in the world, haha). So off to Russia, to find Ivan the Terrible had ascended the throne as Emperor of all Russia. (joy, another language to learn). The summers there were wonderful, and the people were welcoming. The food, however, was bland and tasteless compared to the cuisines I had become accustomed to. The language was insane, and writing almost impossible, but I finally conquered it after 4 years studying under the clergy. I became good friends with another student, Mikhail Romanov, not knowing that he was the grandson of Ivan. This was about the time Tsar Ivan died, and Tsar Feodor became emperor. Russia devolved into turmoil, and being so vast, I continued east and learned more about the country, and its 10 time zones' worth of wonders. Southern Russia was by far the best; the climate was reasonable, and the food was influenced by China and India (spicy, can you say spicy). I was able to avoid most of the turbulence of the Time of Troubles, which ended in 1613, which coincided with Feodor's being replaced by Tsar Mikhail Romanov. I was called to Sankt-Peterburg by the now Tsar Mikhail, the founder of the Romanov dynasty."

"I hate to interrupt you, Stephan, but I need to change the tape and eat something." It was then that I realized to what depth I had stepped. I needed to slow down this tale as I had about four hundred years more to go just learning about Stephan. How many people of history had he met? How much inside knowledge had he received? I wanted more, much more, and he was at my service (an audiobook, if you will). I felt like I had just orgasmed, and I needed a cigarette badly. However, I set about getting together a meager meal to share and put out my fanciest paper plates. Two bologna sandwiches and a handful of chips later, we sat to eat. "I can't believe that you actually knew these people." To which Stephan said, "You have no idea, but stick around, and you'll find it gets juicier and way more interesting." Carl asked in hushed tones, "Can I ask a real personal question?" "Shoot, and maybe you'll get the answer you seek."

" Did you ever marry or have children? Did they get your genetics, or were they normal? Did you keep moving or did you settle somewhere while being a parent?" "One question at a time. Yes, I married after I got to Russia, around 1614, at the age of 102. My wife was of common birth, but her family was introduced to royalty (you'll never guess how), and we soon were called to court. It seems that my friendship with the Tsar was more involved than I remembered. Court life didn't appeal to me, but my wife thrived in it. As minor courtiers, we weren't subject to scrutiny like most of the gold diggers and social climbers. Ours took a more casual approach, and soon we were being invited to dine at the most elegant dinners. The affairs were awe-inspiring, as they say, and I couldn't have been happier. Svetlana, my wife, gifted me 2 children, a son named Gregor and a daughter named Natalia. Sad to say that neither got my recessive gene, and their lives turned out much different. Gregor moved away with his wife in 1635, never to be heard from again, although I did try to stay in touch. Natalia followed in her mother's footsteps and became a lady's maid to the Tsarina Tatiana. She passed due to pneumonia in 1640."

"What happened to your wife?" "I have to say that was the hardest blow, as I needed to move again, and she wanted to stay. By now, we had been titled and had become landowners with our own servants. I had to leave her behind, so I concocted a story about doing the Tsar's business abroad, knowing I probably would never see her again. I never did. I returned years later only to find a grave that had been engraved 'Svetlana Orion, devoted wife and mother died 1660'. I laid a wreath of wildflowers on the grave, wiped the tears from my eyes, and walked away, not wanting to think how she felt about my abandonment in 1645."

We finished for the night, and Stephan took his leave. I couldn't sleep, trying to absorb all that he had told me. The characters and people, places, and scents drifted in and out of my mind, replaying as a record on repeat. I knew that I was in for the long haul, and no one would believe this tale. I would lose my grant, but I had to see it through. I finally forced myself to sleep (albeit with some assistance from melatonin). Tomorrow couldn't come fast enough.

Stephan showed up the next day as chipper as a Boy Scout and just as ready to continue. Coffee in hand, a smile on his face, and again those eyes, shining in the morning light. "Are you ready for today's talk?" All I could do was nod as the melatonin hadn't worn off yet.

"By now it was around 1660, I journeyed back to France and found King Louis XIV, or the Sun King (Le Roi Soleil), sitting upon the throne. I went to court and handed my papers as minor royalty (which Mikhail had written for me) to the king's secretary and requested an audience. I was offered rest and repast and given sanctuary as a guest of the king. I didn't expect to actually see Louis, but the papers must have impressed him (now I wondered what Mikhail had written) for within a week, I was taken to an informal brunch with the king. Louis in the garden struck a grand visage, plumes, satin, and lush jewelry. He stood and welcomed me as though he had known me his entire life.

Louis was at the peak of his power and had many women vying for his affection. He fathered 19-21 children, but only 7 were with Mary

Therese. We talked about architecture (which ignited his passion) and lovers and men talk. He invited me to stay, and thanking him, I agreed to an expanded visit. I knew that I would need to leave at some point, so I explained that I was only visiting and had matters to attend to in other countries. He acknowledged this and asked where I would be traveling so he could write to them asking favors for me.

I finally decided to read the parchment from Mikhail and became humbled. It read, 'I, Tsar Mikhail Romanov, Tsar of all the Russias, hereby request that my ambassador Stephan be treated as my brother and voice in this new land. It is my wish to hear of his gracious welcome.' Below was the official seal and his signature." Hey Carl, would you like to see it? I brought it with me today." I nodded, and I almost fainted as he produced the parchment and placed it in my shaking hands. "Stephan, are you kidding? How many relics do you have? Would it be alright to take a picture of it for my archives?"

"Needless to say, I have warehouses all over the world filled with such artifacts, and yes, you may photograph them if you wish." I almost pissed myself and ran for my camera. Seconds later, I had the snapshot and tried to read the parchment. It was all in Russian script, so Stephan took it and read as he let me follow his finger as he interpreted it into English. "Do you know what this would be worth to the Louvre or the Prado, the Smithsonian?" "As I said, Carl, I possess many more such items. Might I pique your interest in Louis' letter? I have it here also."

I have to admit, I felt faint (and fainted from holding my breath too long). When I returned to consciousness, Stephan was sitting laughing and holding a letter from the Sun King. I opened it, and not speaking French (or any other language but English), he sat next to me and read aloud, "To his holiness, Pope Clement X (Emilio Bonaventura Altieri), please receive my friend and ambassador, Lord Stephan Orion of Greece and Russia and now France, as envoy to your council. I hold him in the highest regard, as should you. All glory to God. With my blessings and good tidings, Louis XIV, King of France." Needless to say, it had all the pomp and official seals of Louis. Little-known fact: Clement X was dedicated to pursuing European peace despite Louis XIV's warring to expand France's footprint in the world. (That's why I keep this particular document, as it contradicts their stances at the time).

Stephan took a few moments, as if in meditation, before continuing. "The year was 1685, I was now 173 and looked 23. I thank the stars no one questioned me about my age or the amount of time in any one place, as that would have proved embarrassing. Italy looked slightly different now, and the roads were better.

I, as usual, went to the resting place of my parents to lay a wreath. Something was amiss as there were other flowers there that I had not placed, beautiful and fresh. I thought for a few moments and decided that this mystery needed to be solved before I left Rome. Not only that, but now Louis was warring and, in 1688, crossed the Rhine to seize additional territory and was pressuring the Holy Roman Empire to accept his land claims. It didn't go well, and Leopold I, the German princes, and the Dutch united in an alliance and forced Louis back. I know this sounds like a history lesson, but being in Rome at the time was no picnic. In 1688, I was called to the Vatican and brought to the Pope. He was firm but eloquent, telling me to use my powers of friendship to convince Louis to give up his efforts. I told him I'd take any correspondence to France for him, and that I could leave on the morrow. My mystery had been put on hold, but my life was assured, traveling as a diplomat for the Pope and King of France."

We decided to call it a day, and Stephan packed his parchments away, preparing to take his leave. "Hey Carl, are you up for a museum field trip tomorrow? I felt like I'd been given an all-access pass to the Metropolitan Museum of Art. (And I could touch without being arrested). Sleep eluded me, having scenarios bounce around in my head. More melatonin and induced sleep came, if only for a few hours.

I slept through the alarm, almost peed myself before getting to the bathroom, jumped into the shower, cold (this time on purpose), and dried off, trying not to look in the mirror, and failed. I looked old at 38, and Stephan looked like the Greek god Adonis at 493 years old. How much more depressing could it get? But I put on a brave face, dressed in my Sunday best, or Friday casual to others, and waited for Stephan to arrive. He showed up about 20 minutes later, a living picture of wealth, health, and beauty. He suggested that we take his Porsche, and I kindly said yes (did you think I'd pass that up?). He opened the moon roof, asked what music to play, to which I said 80's alternative, then off to his 'museum'.

The ride took about 15 minutes (I was sad because I was enjoying myself in the simple luxury of a nice car) and arrived at a common-looking warehouse on the edge of town. It looked usual and had only a couple of guards on duty, "I rent them from a security agency, so I don't worry about vandalism." I had to learn more about Stephan's worth. This 'kid' was flush with cash and now rented guards. He said he had warehouses around the world, which meant guards at those places, too. I thought of asking him to marry me, but it's not legal yet. Yes, I'd marry for money at this point, even if it meant 'playing wife'.

We walked up to the guard, who was surprised to see Stephan with a guest, unlocked the gate, let us enter, then re-secured the gate and led us inside. He wandered back to the security office, and we continued through the first floor. I started taking pictures immediately and thought if this was just one floor of the building, I hadn't brought enough film. To the left were cars (in pristine condition) from 1903 through 2005. Not just any cars, but high-end luxury cars, hot rods, special editions. I wanted to cry. This guy was a billionaire. He said he kept the artwork on the second floor. I knew I was in for a shock and was not disappointed as he had masters of every era from Raphael, DaVinci, Michelangelo, Caravaggio, up to Rembrandt, Picasso, Dali, Gauguin, Matisse, then onto Warhol and too many more to list. I shuddered to think what he stored in the vault on the third floor. He told me that is where he stored the more precious items (more precious items, you mean more than the billions in art and car collections).

He did ask me to turn my back to him as he dialed the code for the entrance to the vault. He also asked that I not take any pictures inside the vault. (That made me want to all the more, but I reluctantly agreed and put the camera away). He opened the vault door, and as it swung wide, my jaw dropped. It was like Dorothy opening the farm door and stepping into Oz, magnificent, stupendous, beautiful, secretive, unbelievable. Well enough with the superlatives, suffice to say, it took my breath away. Statuary, scrolls, books (most were first editions), and even a Gutenberg bible. He told me he had a Shakespeare handwritten script for Romeo and Juliet and Twelfth Night. I perused the documents, saw the lettering, realized that I was looking straight into history, and again had to ask, "This script alone is worth millions; does anyone else know of its existence?" "Only me and now you." I had to sit. Of course, it was in a Louis XIV chair, straight from Versailles.

Stephan motioned to the surveillance camera for the guard, who appeared about 10 seconds later. "Please send for some lunch for 4, thanks, Arnie." "What are you in the mood for?" I said anything, so

Stephan told him good Italian, and Arnie disappeared just as quickly as he had appeared. We made our way back to the security office, although this took a while because I kept asking to sit in his car. This guy had as many cars as Jay Leno. Lunch arrived, and the 4 of us dined on calamari salad, gnocchi, antipasto, pasta bolognese, real meatballs, and chicken Parmesan. For dessert, we had cannoli and gelato.

We waved goodbye to the guards and sped off in the Porsche. Stephan dropped me off with my doggie bag and continued on. I went inside and pigged out on the leftovers. I had not had this much fantastic food since childhood. I couldn't imagine the food Stephan had enjoyed in his last 500 years.

The next morning was a mixed bag of sadness and excitement, knowing I was not going to be among all that lush life but knowing I was to get another taste of his life, his history, his loves. (wait, did he have others? I had to ask him. In strode Stephan, coffees in hand, those Lumineers shining, those eyes enduring, and that wardrobe beyond compare. Boy, did he have good taste in clothes.

"Where were we? Oh yeah, returning to France at the Pope's request. I got to court around 1690, handed Louis the documents, and said I had to travel back to Italy on a private matter. Being involved with matters of state and a war ongoing, Louis bade me well and allowed me my leave. I traveled back to Rome to try to identify the flower person. It had to be a relative, as people didn't go around placing flowers on random graves. It didn't take long to get word from the locals about the mysterious person. I bribed the cemetery caretakers, and they sent word to me about a woman, beautiful, young, always veiled, expensive clothing, leaving the wreaths. They told me she came in the morning about every 4 weeks and placed fresh flowers on that particular grave.

They told me she was due in a week, so I went back to Calcata, rented a villa, actually hired the great-grandchildren of my original servants (I smiled about this but was reticent to say anything), and prepared for the 'meeting'.

The morning she was due to lay the wreath, I also took a wreath and waited. Thankfully, many of the graves had benches to sit and reflect, so I sat at one close to my parents' graves. She walked gracefully to the grave, knelt, and started praying as I approached. "Pardone me, signorina," she looked up, and I froze as I knew this face and yet didn't. It couldn't be, but here she was, Svetlana, my beloved who passed in 1660. She finished her prayer, stood, and faced me. Speaking in Russian, she told me these were her grandparents and that her mother had told her about Greek ancestors living and dying in Rome. She left Russia in 1660 because she was to have an arranged marriage to a man she didn't like. She inquired as to who I was, and I hesitated before simply saying, "a distant relative." She sat with me and told me that her father had been called away before her mother had known she was pregnant. She figured her father hadn't survived and left after selling off the family property, and her mother had died. She decided on Rome as she heard that it was breathtaking. "What is your name?" to which she said, "Natashia." I asked her age, and she said 45. I wondered if she had the recessive trait, but failed to mention it. I told her I had rented a villa in Calcata and invited her to visit with me. She thanked me but said she lived in Rome with her husband and 3 grown children. Then she invited me to her abode. I was intrigued and said yes, got the directions, and parted with a simple hug. I couldn't help but wonder what she thought about a man looking twenty, saying he was her relative, albeit distant. I took it in stride and went home to pack for a few days with my daughter.

I wandered the streets of Rome, remembering the times with my parents and the music. The sound of Arcangelo Corelli, a famous violinist of the time, and Domenico Scarlatti, a composer and collaborator on about 300 pieces. I realized as I approached the house that she had said that she had 3 grown children, and that made me a grandfather. (that took the wind out of my sails). I continued to the address and saw a mansion with gates. I approached the gates, called out to the servant in the portico, and stated, "I am here to see the Mistress of the house. It is at her request." The servant opened the gate and said he had been anticipating my arrival. I was ushered into the lush inner garden and asked to wait for his Mistress. I looked around and was astounded that she had married into such wealth. Natashia appeared and bade me follow her into the house as she gave instructions to the servant to have my belongings brought to my room.

Taking me by the arm, she led me into the solarium, then she shyly asked, "Forgive my ignorance, but I never asked your name." "Stephan Orion, of the Mediterranean Orions." Natashia was taken aback by the answer, "That was my father's name, what a coincidence. I don't remember mother ever mentioning that we had more family anywhere." Now it was my turn to scramble for an answer. "There were many of our ancestors, according to the family history. They seemed to live extremely long lives and moved all through Europe." Again, she pressed for more information and was getting close to the real truth. I asked how much she knew about the Greek heritage she had received, and she simply shrugged. "By the time I was old enough to inquire of mother, she had passed, leaving a gaping hole in my knowledge."

I felt a pang of guilt creep over me and decided to help her in this way. I was about to give up the goods when 3 adults came into the solarium. "Good day, mother, how are you today?" It was my grandkids.

"May I introduce you, children, to Stephan Orion, a relative. Stephan, these are my children – Lucius, age 27, Marcus, age 25, and my precious daughter Claudia, age 20." I said, "Good tidings to you all, and thank you, Natasha, for the introductions." I noticed that Claudia was pregnant with what was my (Ugh) great-grandchild. We sat at the table nearest the reflecting pool and prepared to feast on good Italian fare.

Questions started pouring like the fine wine we were drinking. The kids were bombarding me, and I had a hard time keeping up. Finally, Natasha put a stop to it as I had hardly taken 5 bites of food in between questions. I breathed a sigh of relief and chowed down. I asked the children about their young lives, and centered on Claudia. "I see you are in the motherly way, may I inquire as to if this is the first?", she replied, "Actually, I was married to a patrician, as was mother, and this will be my 3rd child. I lost the first, a girl to pneumonia, but my boy, Antonius, lives, and he will be 3 by the end of the month."

So now I had knowledge as to how they lived so well. (as well as being a great-grandfather). Lucius had gone into the military and was now a praetorian guard. He had not married yet, as he traveled frequently and for long periods of time. Marcus said that he was married and had fathered 2 children, Julia and Fausta. He said they were home with their mother in the countryside while he attended the Senate. It seemed that my grandchildren had fared well also.

The time came for them to ask how I was related. My mind spun with lies, fictitious stories, and fantastical tales, but I tried the truth (which would be stranger than fiction). I asked for my satchel, and the servant laid it next to me. Undoing the leather strap, out fell some scrolls and a few journals. I set them on the table and asked them to read the material. Since most was in Russian and French, I had to interpret for them.

Natashia read some of the Russian documents and saw that they were real. She recognized the signature of Tsar Mikhail from some of her mother's decrees. The astonished looks on their combined faces were priceless. "Natasha, I am your long-lost father. I know I look too young, but I have an immunity to aging. That was why our family moved around in my youth. The graves you visit monthly are my parents."

When the shock wore off, the 'boys' came and shook my hand. Claudia waddled over and hugged me deeply and teared up. Natashia was the last to come over and hugged me while crying. "All these years, and I never knew you existed. Where were you?" I showed her the documents Louis had given me and the papers of the Pope, Clement X. "I was busy traveling and didn't know of you. Had I known, you would have had a father. You seem to have done well, marrying up above your station." Natashia wiped, "Father, I sold the lands and house back to the Tsar, took my dowry, and my mother left me, and I came to Rome a woman of means. It was my husband who married up. I am responsible for his success. I married a handsome man of no means, and he thrived and ascended to his position through hard work (and the bribery money to the right connections). All that you see, I built with the Tsar's money."

Stephan took a breath, paused, and I suggested a pause for the night. Stephan agreed, put on his overcoat, cashmere of course, and bid me good night. Wow was all I could think. He was not only a father, but a grandfather and, yes, a great-grandfather, all by 1690. A lot can happen in 76 years. Stephan hadn't mentioned Natasha's last name or Claudia's. I made a note to ask Stephan the next day. I was now wishing I had a secretary to transcribe the notes and tapes, but that wasn't possible until I had Stephan's approval, another note for tomorrow. I disrobed, showered, and took to the bed for yet another fitful night of catnapping. The tales were fantastic, but knowing they were real and backed up by documents and journals made me smile. Okay, yet another note for tomorrow, ask about the journals; there had to be hundreds by now.

Morning came, and with it the myriad of questions percolating in my brain. I hastily ate, dressed, and headed to the office. There he was, in all his splendor, Stephan. Today he brought bagels with the coffee. "I thought maybe a light snack for later, so we can go a little faster." I had to remember to ask him where he got that coffee, as it was always hot and tasty. I thanked him, took a sip, then set about getting the tape ready to record. "Stephan, I made myself some notes to ask you today, do you mind answering them before we start?" "Of course not Carl." "I had a thought about hiring a transcriber if that's okay. I think I can work it into the budget. It would make the workload lighter for me." "Carl, let me take care of that, you can't afford it. Besides, I'd like to interview the people and choose the candidate."

With a sigh of relief, I asked the second question, "Do you happen to have the journals and diaries that you mentioned yesterday?" "Of course, although most of them aren't local, I can send for them as requested." Stephan settled into a chair and asked, "Are you ready to continue?" I replied yes, started the machine, then asked him, "What were Natasha's and Claudia's surnames after marriage?" Stephan smiled, thought a moment, and said, ' I believe Natasha's was Julia and Claudia's was Cornelia. Yes, yes, my mind gets fuzzy after three hundred years. Where were we? Oh yes, the year 1690, and the kids found out about their grandfather. Lucius and Marcus had to leave for their respective jobs, and Claudia returned home to care for her family. They all invited me to their homes in the near future, and I accepted. I left it up to them as to the itinerary. They waved, said ciao, and took their leave.

This left me alone with my 'new' daughter, Natashia. I asked her if there was anything she wanted to know about me, and I told her I would answer as well as I could. 'Father, mother never stopped loving you to her last breath. She prayed with me every night for your safe return and even beseeched the Tsar to inquire on her behalf as to your well-being. It pains me to know you could have returned to her. Why didn't you? Through glassy eyes, I finally said, 'If I had returned to her a young man, she would not have understood. Times were different then. How could I have made her not scream witchcraft? My only consolation was to keep traveling. Claudia fell into my arms, just as another man walked into the solarium. 'Natasha, what transpires here when I am away? Who is this man? Stand and announce yourself, or else I'll call the guards and have you taken away.' 'Antonius, meet my (father) relative. He has surfaced after many years (can you say 76 years), come and meet Stephan.'

"I am Antonius Julia, Natasha's husband. Welcome to our home. I rose and went to this man, strong of body and short-tempered, shook his hand with the strongest grip I could manage, letting him know I was no pushover. He must have understood my position because he stared at my eyes straight on, then relinquished his grip and bade me sit. We talked as Natashia ordered the servants to bring the repast and wine for the master of the house. I was able to put him at ease (after Kings and popes, he was easy). Natashia ushered us to the table with the two men sitting at the ends of the table and Natashia between us. 'I have asked Stephan (she later told me she had hated calling me Stephan instead of father) to stay for a month. The children stopped by today and have offered him lodging there also.'

I took Natasha's cue and allowed the ruse to continue so as not to give up my 'secret'. Antonius put his best foot forward (when it wasn't in his mouth) and we had a cordial visit. Natashia asked the reason he was home and simply said he lived there. The day ended after Antonius drank the wine vessel dry. Natashia followed him to their chambers, and the servants ushered me to mine. Needless to say, I couldn't wait for this ogre to depart. I had hoped for better, but this brute and my daughter had made an impressive duo. Thankfully, he only stayed a few days and departed for the Senate and his other duties. The parting was short and curt, and I almost wanted to take him down a peg, and would have except that my love for my daughter was growing minute by minute, and I didn't want to hurt her, ever.

The time came to visit the grandchildren, starting with Claudia. I sent word of the impending visit, and she graced me with a most precious welcome. A young boy ran to the gate and hugged my thighs. 'You must be Antonius, ' as I lifted my great-grandson into my arms. He smiled as he called for his mother. 'I was told you'd be here today. As I set him down on the ground, he grabbed my hand, leading me forward into the garden. Claudia came out of the manse with her husband in tow. 'I can't say how happy we are that we got to have your visit first. Please meet my husband, Cassius. This is Stephan, the relative I told you about.' 'Greetings, I am Cassius Cornelli, head of the house. Welcome. This time, I felt a different atmosphere, as he genuinely liked me. We got along well, and I couldn't contain my exuberance at having a great-grandson so entranced by me. I noticed that Antonius looked amazingly like me in my youth, which led me to wonder if…

I almost cried when the time for my departure arrived. I had come to love my new family, especially Antonius, whose features made me wish Caravaggio were still around to immortalize him in oils. I made a note to have him painted through his youth (I sent word to Louis to see if he could send Hyacinthe Rigaud, one of his portrait painters, to assist me in this). My next stop was to visit Marcus.

He was not at home when I arrived, but was well received by his wife, Serafina, and their 2 daughters, Julia and Fausta. The girls were shy and hid behind their mother (as she was a buxom woman, it wasn't hard). Serafina escorted me into their humble abode and shooed the girls away. It seemed that Marcus hadn't fared as well as his sister. At least it didn't show. She prepared a simple meal of mutton, bread, and some wine. Marcus came in around sunset and shook my hand before hugging me tight. This seemed odd to his wife, but Marcus said nothing, just shrugged it off.

Nothing was out of the ordinary. Marcus had a striking resemblance to my father, and I smiled inwardly. My stay was warm, and the girls came to know me. By the departure time, the girls had come to sit on my lap, listening intently to my 'stories' and gushing, thinking they were just tall tales. Onto the home of Lucius, but before I could pack, he sent word he couldn't accommodate a visit. Maybe next time."

I stopped Stephan, let my mind calm, and set out the bagels. Stephan excused himself as he said he had to make a few calls. As he left the room, I chowed down on the bagel, an everything bagel with locks and cream cheese, which had to be half an inch thick. He returned to find my mouth crammed full and a white rim of cream cheese on my lips. I tried to say something, but Stephan hushed me and laughed as he prepared to eat his.

We returned to the afternoon session with him jumping ahead in time. "I left my beloved family and Italy to go to France to visit Louis, as I heard he was aging and was in bad health. I found he had acquiesced to my request and sent his painter to Italy for me. I was given an audience, and we spent days together when he was feeling good. I told him of my plans to return to Russia, although now Peter was Tsar, and requested papers for the journey. I left with documents in hand, knowing that my time with Louis had drawn to an end. I got word that Louis passed 1 year later in 1715. Russia welcomed me with open arms, but I missed the food and wine. The vodka helped, but it couldn't compare. I was surprised when Peter accepted me and my papers. (Thank God I had taken those 4 years to learn Russian). Saint Petersburg was better than when I left, but being winter, it chilled my bones. Peter brought me to his counsel and intrigued me with his vision for Russia. He started the modernization of Russia by switching to the Julian calendar, establishing the first Russian newspaper, and doing other things. I later learned that he came to be known as Peter the Great, though he only lived until 1725. I left for Greece in 1720, wondering what my homeland would be like now. I journeyed back to Piraeus, the port city and birthplace. Trying to remember my native tongue has been difficult (having been born in Rome), and it took me a while, but mastering Greek was nothing compared to Russian; it only took about 6 months. The alphabet was the difficult part. The food was superb, the wine splendid, but the culture was overtaken by the Turks. I decided not to spend my time there and headed to Germany, as I heard the music was marvelous, and Handel was coming into his own. I asked about artists (to send to Italy), and one name kept coming up, Kasten Fur Violoncello. A decent artist and reasonably priced. I commissioned him to paint Antonius. He packed that day and started for Italy. The food was heavy, the beer stout and warm, but overall pleasant. I stayed about a year, but my heart was in Italy. I returned in 1725 and went straight to Rome looking for Natasha. I arrived at her estate only to be told that she had died (she would have been 80). I instinctively knew where to look for her interment. Back to Cimiterio Acattilico and to my parents' graves. Nearby was my dear daughter's grave (at least Antonius had been generous with her tomb). I teared up, having known her so little, laid the wreaths, said a prayer, turned and walked slowly into the town.

Next, I went to see Claudia, who would be 55; chances are, she was still alive. I went to the gate unannounced and called to the servants. The old man came to the gate and recognized me, though he looked at me quizzically as I hadn't aged. He beckoned me in and turned to the girl cutting fresh flowers, telling her to get the Mistress. She and Antonius the younger ran to me, hugging me and yelling, " Grandfather! " Antonius looked like I was viewing myself in a mirror. We entered the house, and the servants took my bags. Supper was served, and I relished the food of my youth. Wine poured, stories unfolded, and I told Claudia of my conversations with Louis of France and Peter of Russia. Antonius listened intently and wondered how I had come to know all these important people. He was astonished to find that I could converse in French and Russian (English, Portuguese, Spanish, Greek, Italian, and German).

I inquired as to her mother's passing, ' Mother died in 1720, and father followed this year.' I was about to make a remark about Antonius the elder when a young woman bounded in saying, 'Sorry, mother, I didn't mean to interrupt you.' 'That's alright, Felicia, come and meet your great-grandfather, Stephan. Grandfather, meet your great-granddaughter, Felicia.' She had to be 35 but looked much younger, like her older brother Antonius the younger. She came to me, looking quizzical, but hugged me and stood back beside her brother. They looked amazing, like a marble tableau. The thoughts I had were racing around my mind. Could they both be like me? Did Cassius have a recessive gene, too? Time would tell.

The servant walked in, announcing the arrival of Felicia's husband, Aurelius, and her son of the same name. (great, now I have a great-great-grandson) I started to feel old (I mean, I was 213 by now). To change my mindset, I asked Antonius if he had the portraits I had commissioned. He nodded yes, and I asked to see them. I now wish I had done the same for Felicia. I stated, 'Felicia, would you like to have your family portrait done as I have connections. I offered to have Canaletto (Giovanni Antonio Canal) brought to Rome as he was becoming known around Italy. With that, off I went to Antonius' chamber. I had to say that the artistry was beyond my expectations. There was a group of about 12 paintings, and he figured prominently in each. French and German painters, and now an Italian, a nice collection. If it proved out that he was normal, at least I'd have his likeness in oil.

We returned to the common room and sat as one large, happy family. Aurelius junior came over, felt my face, and asked if he could sit with me. How could I say no to that cherubic face? About 2 months passed, and I talked to Cassius about his family history. He said that his parents were both born in Rome, but he believed that one distant female relative was thought to be born abroad, possibly in Greece (the missing link).

I figured I would have to wait as they were still under the control of the Ottoman Empire. I stayed in Rome and inquired about Lucius. Claudia sent for word as to Lucius' location and was told he was in residence. I sent a letter requesting a visit and was delighted that he would send travel arrangements for me. I set off after a final meal with Claudia and family. I traveled across Rome and saw the Villa of the Papyri (mansion) come into view. Lucius waved from the balcony and came down to the courtyard to formally welcome me. It seemed unusual to have this much family to call my own, and now that they knew me, I felt comfort."

Stephan asked to take a lunch break, seeing that the tape had ended. I agreed, and he ordered a huge lunch from the local restaurant. I didn't object nor offer to pay when I overheard the price, 'That will be $150.27'. Stephan seemed to be rather generous, and believe me, I started liking it. This time it was French cuisine, and truth be told, I wasn't prepared for what he set before me. Croissants, real butter, Bleu cheese, grapes, foie gras with capers, baked capons, French baguettes, lightly seasoned roasted vegetables with a finish of crème Brulee, and macaroons. How on earth did this guy stay so thin on a diet like this?

After lunch, I stored the leftovers in the fridge for later and went back to set up the tape again. I almost asked Stephan why he kept offering to pay for such expensive food, but thought better of it and said nothing. He finished his phone call as I entered my 'study' or work alcove as it was. He started again as I hit the record button. "Let's see, I was just meeting Lucius as we ended the last tape. He was entirely euphoric to see me again, although it had been 35 years. He looked amazing despite having been in the praetorian guard. Being 62 now, he still maintains his statuesque presence. He had silver flecks at his temples, so I assumed he would be like his and my parents, simply normal.

We chatted long into the night, and he regaled me with stories of his years abroad. I, preferring not to name-drop, let him continue with a look of amazement on my face. (I didn't want him thinking I was jaded after all these years). He told me that after his father and mother died, he took up residence and ended his military career. Not many were that lucky. He had married, but she died a few years later in childbirth, and that finished his family life. These days, he feasted, drank, and hosted parties for his comrades.

My time with Lucius came to an end, with me getting the wanderlust again. I explained that time waits for no man, and the road beckoned me to travel once again. He promised to keep in touch, as did I, and turned in for the night. Tomorrow would come too soon. By now, Catherine sat on the throne of Russia. Louis XV sat on the French throne, George I was now King of England, and King Frederick William I was in Germany. I knew none of these people, so I decided to try to get papal papers to travel, but I didn't know Pope Benedict XIII either. I went to the Vatican anyway and used my letters from Clement X to seek an audience; it worked. I was ushered into his chamber, where he asked how I came into possession of the letters. Being resourceful, I told him that these were my father's papers. This must have satisfied him, and he bade me sit. I requested traveling papers from him, and he granted me this boon for 'my father's sake'.

I traveled around Europe, corresponding with the grandkids and their families during my travels. I just meandered while taking in the cultures, the food, and exquisite wines and liquors. I let time get away, and soon it was 1750. I heard that A new museum had opened in France and went to visit. They named it The Louvre. The artists were mostly contemporary, and the exhibits were sparse, so all in all, disappointing. I traveled to England, now knowing George II was sitting on the throne. He was a member of the Hanover clan from Germany. I thought about trying again to push my old documents, but I thought that the papal seal would do me more good. I reached England in 1755 and went to Hampton Court seeking out the King. It took some prodding, but with searchable titles and papal backing, I got to see George. He had such an entourage that I barely got to talk with him besides civility. Times were much different now, and I needed to adjust.

I garnered a few minutes alone with George, knowing his Hanoverian background, and addressed him in German, meeting with a smile from a withdrawn man. He started chatting me up, loving having a fellow he could talk with in his mother's tongue. It put him more at ease as the 'ears' of the castle couldn't understand the Germanic language. Finally, I noted that for future escapades. He beseeched me to stay, gave me a new title, Friend of the Realm. How could I refuse? I stayed another year before requesting my papers for traveling, including my new title and knighthood. I was now Lord Stephan Orion, Duke of Yorkshire. (Boy, did I get good use out of that.

I headed back to my beloved Italy and arrived in Rome in 1757. I went immediately to Claudia's house. Hoping beyond hope that she was still alive (being 87 by now), I found her there, albeit frail and elderly. I gently kissed her forehead, embraced her, and asked about Antonius and Felicia. She said that Antonius had succeeded his uncle Lucius in ownership of the family estate, and Felicia was with her husband and had her own grandchildren now. (My granddaughter was now a grandmother)

It seems Aurelius junior got busy. She called her attendant and bade him send word to the kids that their great-grandfather was in town. I asked about Marcus and was told he and Serafina had died, but Julia and Fausta were around. I wanted to see them again, but that could wait; I wanted to see Felicia and Antonius. The anticipation was killing me. I wanted to see young people to confirm my suspicions.

The days dragged by until the arrival of my beloved Antonius (he had to be 70 by now). He entered the room, and I saw myself; he was dashing and as youthful as I was. We embraced and sat as bookends to his mother. She blushed, having this much affection heaped upon her, and we lavished her with love. Now to see Felicia, Aurelius Sr., and little Aurelius (Felicia now being 67). Until Felicia arrived, I talked endlessly with Antonius, inquiring as to his life. 'Dear great grandfather, I believed that we had many things in common, so I chose a solitary life, not wanting my beloveds to keep leaving me by passing. It has served me well, and I'm not lonely as the maidens flock to me for my youth and resources.'

With a wink and a nod, we rejoined the group, and I was confronted by a new group of descendants. Felicia Massimo (looking her age), Aurelius Sr., Aurelius Jr, his wife Olympia, and their offspring, Aurelius III, age 20, and Lucius, age 18. Lunch was a grand affair; all the delicacies of the age were represented, a primo platter featuring pasta, gnocchi, wild rabbit, and roasted vegetables. Antonius smiled as he enjoyed the repast, and I nodded to him to join me away from the family. Once alone, I entreated him to give family life a try; I wished for him to have an extended family as I did, and he said he would consider it. "After all, I was 102 when I married your great-grandmother Svetlana." He laughed until his sides ached. "I guess I've got a few years then." It was my turn to laugh. I tousled his hair and, hugging him, returned to the courtyard.

I stayed with Felicia for a few years and visited the great, great, great grandkids, Aurelius III and Lucius, and even got to see Lucius get married. The year was 1760. The wedding was called the event of the year. He married a socialite by the name of Maria Amalia (Duchess of Parma, Piacenza, and Guastalla), daughter of Emperor Francis I, Grand Duke and Empress Maria Theresa. (talk about marrying up). Later, I found out he sired 5 children with her. (Yes, that made me a 4x great-grandfather). Aurelius III didn't marry till later, and I had left by then.

I heard of the industrialization of England as James Watt had invented the steam engine. I went but was disappointed because it darkened the sky and made the once pristine cities a dark gray and the streets soot-covered. So I left to tour around Europe again. I reinvented myself as my grandson with family titles and headed to France. There, I read of the troubles brewing in the Americas; the English subjects were revolting. It was 1773, and the 'Sons of Liberty' dumped tea into Boston Harbor dressed as Mohawk Indians. It almost made me want to visit this new land, but I thought better of it due to my minor royal standing. I returned to my beloved Italy just in time to catch a young musician, they called Mozart. I have to say I was impressed by the music he produced.

Of course, I returned to the Villa of Papyri to visit Antonius, who was thrilled to have me join him. We decided to tour Rome together and visit the old haunts. We did go to the cemetery as Antonius said that Felicia had passed away in the last year at the age of 82. We laid many wreaths and somberly went into town and toasted to their lives. I inquired as to Lucius, Aurelius III, and found that Lucius had a couple of kids by now. He then told me that Aurelius III had died of pneumonia at the age of 34 in 1771. I asked about Marcus's 2 daughters, Julia and Fausta. He said they had faded into the countryside and were lost to time."

The time was near midnight when Stephan stopped his remembrances. I bade him goodnight and turned in myself. I left the leftovers in the fridge for the next day. Saturday, and I almost frowned that I had to wait 2 more days for the next chapter of Stephan's life. I arose sleepy and smelled fresh coffee, but it was Saturday and Stephan was supposedly away for the weekend. I stepped into the living room in my shorts and got a chortle out of Stephan. He pointed, and I almost dropped my coffee. "Dude, you need a better wardrobe, at least some appropriate underwear." I blushed a deep red and turned to slip on my tattered robe (not much better, but still something to hide my morning wood)

"What are you doing here? I mean, besides deriding and humiliating me. I thought you were away this weekend." "It didn't pan out, and I thought I might bring a few of my journals for you to peruse, but now I think that should wait, and we should go shopping, my treat, there, lumberjack." "Are you sure you want to be seen in public with me, Lord Stephan?" Stephan fell into the chair and started that guttural laugh as I went to put my 'clothes' on. Soon we were on the way to a shopping spree. It warmed his heart to do this for me, and I felt like his 'kept boy'. But I let him since it brought him such joy. I saw him using his credit card, and it was black, only one of about 100 in existence. I guess it meant he was in an elite group of people. When the salesperson saw the card, he acted as though I were royalty and treated me much better. Leaving the first store, I was carrying bags like Julia Roberts in Pretty Woman. Again, he smiled, and the embarrassment left my body. He suggested we stop for lunch and went to one of the most exclusive restaurants in town. I told him they were usually booked 4 weeks out, and he shrugged and ushered me inside. The maitre'd saw him, asked if he wanted his usual table, and Stephan winked and led on. Of course, the food was beyond compare, and I really wanted to get a doggie bag, but I ate the entire entree before finishing with a baked Alaska.

Stephan tipped the waiter a cool crisp $100 bill. All I could say was I was glad I had Stephan as a new friend. We sauntered out into the street and returned the Porsche, offloading the purchases. With the packages secured, off we went to the next store. I sat back and looked sideways at the face of this extraordinary man. He was confident, humble, and most of all generous. I wished at that moment that I was gay, or at least bisexual, because I would have asked for his hand in marriage. The thoughts one has, but suspending disbelief, I followed him like a puppy dog into the store. The clerk almost hurt himself getting to us, as he obviously knew Stephan. "What's your pleasure today, sir?" Stephan grinned at me and said, "I need your assistance in getting him into some proper underwear. May we go in the back to the dressing room as you pull some samples for him to try on?" The clerk just nodded and pointed the way, and we were moving again. "But he doesn't even know my size," to which Stephan replied, "He's really good in that department, now disrobe and let's get those atrocious shorts off." I tried to object as the clerk came bounding back with an armful of styles. "I believe that these will fit the bill, Sir." "Just leave them here, and I'll call when he's done trying them on; he's a bit shy." "Yes, sir," was all he said, and disappeared from the room.

I assumed (wrongly) that Stephan would follow him out, but there he stood. "Ahem, aren't you leaving too?" "Why. I've already seen most of what you have, just try these on." He threw me a pair of silk boxer briefs as I was shedding the last of my clothing (along with my dignity). Standing there au naturel, I was at least thankful I couldn't see myself in the mirrors. I slipped into the briefs, and they fit as though I had been measured and these were tailored to me. The texture was a new sensation, and I started to get embarrassed again as it felt sensuous against my form. I turned to let Stephan see the result, and he seemed pleased. "How do you like them? I fell in love with silk undergarments since my time in England." I blushed, looked down in shame, and knew my body was betraying my thoughts.

Stephan told me to look at myself in the mirror, but all I could think of was an old line from Priscilla, Queen of the Desert, 'A cock, in a frock, on a rock'. I looked, and to my surprise, I looked kind of good. I even turned a bit to see about my butt. It made me feel giddy, looking good in my shorts. I asked how he knew I'd look and feel better in these. "I was you many centuries ago." I forgot my surroundings and started trying on more pairs without a care. I got lightheaded after trying them all on. Stephan called for the clerk, and 2 nano seconds later, he was standing there admiring this semi-old man with the extra pounds. Stephan said I was going to wear this pair and to take the rest to the counter and to bring the selection of pants and shirts he had picked for Carl. This went on for a couple of hours, and the time flew as I felt like the proverbial princess before the ball.

The clerk had me suited up, looking incredible, even for me. He took the rest and, seeing the number of packages, asked if Stephan wanted them delivered. Stephan said yes, gave him my address, and we left the salon. "That was great, but you didn't have to do that, Stephan. Besides, I can't afford to even try to pay you back." Stephan waved me off and said, "Just get in the car." I said no more and waited for the next chapter of this escapade. This time, he pulled into a beauty salon, simply saying it was time to address that mop I called hair. Again, the stylist knew him and readily seated me at the shampooing station. Then to the chair where he placed the apron around my neck and body. He addressed Stephan as to how he'd like me to look. That was weird, as I was sitting there (I guessed my opinion wasn't needed). The scissors started whirling, hair started falling, and the chair started turning in all directions. This guy really knew his trade. The cutting stopped, and the hair blower began. I knew better than to move, and soon the chair whirled around, and I saw this different person in the mirror. It was me, but not me, I mean, a much better version of me. I smiled (which completed the conversion), and the apron was removed. I stood, fully looked at the person in the mirror, and words failed me as Stephan proceeded to pay the stylist. A hug and a handshake later, we were out into the street. I passed a few women on the street, and they did a double-take of me (that freaked me out; they looked at ME) just as we got back in the car. Stephan took me out to dinner to finish the day, and I could have died then and there, knowing my life was complete.

What a Saturday, lunch, shopping, dinner, and a return home to find that Stephan directed me to carry in the purchases as he took the journals from the car. I had forgotten about them, too ecstatic about everything that happened to me today. I recognized that Stephan and I had morphed towards partners (although I knew it would be bittersweet when the other shoe dropped). Stephan got me settled in, and he took his leave, letting me peruse the journals over Sunday. I decided to sleep before peeking at the journals, for fear that I would read them all night and never sleep until I had finished.

Sunday started as I awoke, wondering if yesterday was real or just a dream, then felt that my undies were different, soft, silky, and hugging my thighs, and realized I wasn't dreaming. I could wake this way every day. I stumbled into the kitchen and, not smelling that delicious coffee Stephan usually brought, ended up making my version of it. (mud water with creamer and sugar). I ate the remaining bagel with my coffee and set out the journals for a cursory look. I arranged the journals by date. What I didn't take into consideration was that it was written over 3 hundred years ago and in several languages. "CRAP," I could manage to say, thinking now that Stephan had known that all along and had pulled a fast one on me. I got up, went to the bathroom, and decided it was time to take a shower. I put on new underwear (which took no time to become accustomed to) and stepped into the steamy water. I got out after 15 minutes (the water felt sooo good on my body) and toweled dry. I looked in the mirror, tried to remember the style of my new cut, and actually got pretty close to the same (put a notch in my belt for the attempt). Stepping into the briefs was a new and exciting feeling as I had never been so comfortable (although it was gonna take some time to adjust to the silky feeling). I waited for the appearance of my 'feeling' to subside, and pulled on some PJs (I couldn't wait for the packages to arrive with my new wardrobe).

I settled in, opened the first journal, and to my amazement, found that he hadn't started his journals until after he was in England, and I could make out most of it. I engorged myself with the writings and had to reread some of the passages as they were so astounding. It basically retraced the narrative Stephan had already told me, so I just took notes to add to the tapes when they got transcribed. I made a note to ask the secretary to add them as addenda. The first journal took me around three or four hours to peruse. Time for lunch, crap again, I had finished off the leftovers from Saturday morning. Oh well, bologna sandwich again. I almost felt bad for the bologna after tasting the assortment of food from yesterday. Now to journal number 2. Back to Italy, France, and Russia. However, my luck had run out, and the language barrier got to me. I would have to wait another day. I went for a walk and started getting those double-takes again. That put the hitch in my giddy-up. I smiled and whispered a quiet thank you, Stephan, under my breath.

After an anguishing day of anticipation, Monday finally arrived, and with it, my coffee, his smile, and my interpreter. He walked in and noticed I hadn't bothered to dress beyond those wonderful undies. He couldn't help himself and put down the coffee and laughed. "What, haven't you ever seen a grown man in his briefs before?" He continued to smile and handed me my coffee. "I knew you'd love them. You look purty too. Who styled your hair?" We both laughed at that and settled down to work. "How far did you get in the journals, Carl?" "I got through the first journal, and then some a**hole started writing in tongues." Stephan looked at me, held his sides, and rolled around laughing, realizing that I couldn't read different languages. "Poor Carl, let me see if I can help you out there. I am sorry, I didn't think about that before." He grabbed the second journal, opened it, and started reading to himself. I told him I couldn't read minds either, and he said he just wanted to remember the journal before reading aloud. "Get the tape started, here we go…"

"I won't bother you with the material we've already covered, but there are a few bits I'd forgotten. I didn't tell you of my affair in 1690 with Antonio Canova, artist and sculptor. He begged me to pose for his sculpture 'self-portrait,' but if you look, you'll see my naked body in full splendor. I even got him to do a portrait of Antonius. That cost me several nights of companionship (if you know what I mean), and the sculpture cost him the same. He was a decent-looking man, slender of build and explosive in the bedroom. He was obsessed with self-portraits throughout his whole life, and I believed him to be narcissistic. That turned me off, so I stopped posing for him. I didn't realize until much later that Antonius posed for the statue of Perseus. Yeah, I know, it runs in the family, but times were different, and as long as it was kept low-key, it was allowed."

Another tryst was with the Italian opera singer Angela "La Giorgina" Voglia. She was sweet, young, pretty, voluptuous, and available to pretty youths. She apparently figured me for a man of means and thought I would take her hand in marriage. I took her hand and other parts, but stopped before marriage caught us. I left her a woman, wiser but no wealthier. I don't think she ever forgave me.

Next, I'll jump to 1714 when I visited Louis for the last time. I met the son of a painter, Jean-François de Troy. He was 35, and I was 'older'.

I never posed for him, but we partook of a new wine he had procured, calling it 'champagne'. It was sparkling, came from the champagne valley, and made us quite intoxicated. That led to him trying to take advantage, and I ended that affair by finding out who the man in the room was. (he took it like a man, though). Stephan had to stop, and we both laughed, though I believed I shouldn't have. I mean, what kind of people were these Europeans, just randy animals. "It did set my preferences for better wines, though. Next, in 1719, 5 years later, I was in Russia visiting the new tsar, Peter. I gifted him a few bottles of my precious champagne, and we talked as I learned about this new Russia. He was making it modern (for 1719). Peter held a dinner for me and invited his Archbishop Stefan Yavorsky (born Simeon Ivanovich Yavorsky). He was a man of the cloth and a Russian Orthodox, which supposedly meant a man of God. He talked politics with Peter, religion came up, and seeing I was uninterested, he changed the subject to his literature, being an author also. That piqued my interest, so as the dinner came to a close, he issued me an invitation to visit his rectory the next day to continue our discussions. I decided to go against my better judgment and found I was right. The conversation quickly turned to his private literature, and it made me blush. This man was more than a man of God; he was a pervert. He plied me with vodka, thinking I would succumb to his 'charms', but didn't realize I could drink him under the table. I let him please me, then left, he was left wanting, the bastard."

I looked at the clock, lunch time was upon us, and I offered my 'world famous bologna sandwiches'. Stephan shook his head, called the secretary, asked her what she wanted to eat, she said Bavarian, and he asked her to attend to that while we finished up and prepared the kitchen table. The meal arrived about 30 minutes later, and I was ready to gorge myself. It got laid out, and we set about to dine. I put out my best paper plates and napkins for the feast of Rouladen with buttered noodles, sauerbraten, sweet and sour red cabbage, pumpernickel bread, and stout beer. I would need a week to recover from that meal, but the secretary (did I mention her name, Trudy – short for Gertrude) got up, stored away the leftovers, and went back to work on the transcription.

Stephan closed the second journal, put it and the first journal back in his briefcase, and got up to leave. "Sorry, Carl, but I forgot about a meeting I have this afternoon. We can pick back up tomorrow." I didn't question him, but watched as he left and felt a pang of loneliness fill me. How was I going to feel when this was over? I had come to rely on his friendship a bit too much. Could I be developing feelings beyond just friends? I sat, meditated on it, and decided I needed to allow a certain amount of distance to happen. It would be the only way to cope with my new feelings. (keep it at arm's length).

That almost brought me to tears, thinking of me alone again. I almost wished he had not entered my life. I was miserable and lonely, and I think this made it worse. To have a taste of his life and then have it taken away. A walk to the liquor store was in order. Let the pity party begin. Maybe tomorrow will give me a better perspective.

Tuesday arrived, and my new wardrobe arrived. I almost didn't want to put them on, as it would be a reminder of yesterday's thoughts. But being the weak man that I am, I put on the pants and shirt, styled my hair, and went all the way to the living room (20 big steps) and prepared for Stephan. I smelled that enchanting coffee before he appeared at the door. He entered, sensed that I was slightly off, didn't mention it, and handed me my coffee. "You look sharp today, Carl. I hope you like the clothes." I nodded but said nothing. Stephan removed his coat, sat down, took a sip of his coffee, and asked the fateful question, "What's bothering you?"

I almost burst into tears, but controlling myself, I said, "Stephan, you know how grateful.

I am about everything, the food, clothes, the talks, the journals, and well, everything. But what about when the story ends? What happens next? You leave, continue your journey, and I remain behind, having had a taste of the high life only to be thrown back into my pitiful existence." "Carl, I wouldn't do that to you. You've become more than a friend. A confidant of sorts. Just enjoy the time we have and remember that your life before me is over. Please trust me, that's all I ask." "OK, Stephan, I really don't know what to think, but I trust you completely." As I said this, my body relaxed, and I slumped into the couch as Stephan reached for the third journal.

He opened the journal, read a few lines, realized that it contained mostly his thoughts from his time with his family, and told me not to bother with this one. Placing it by his side, he grabbed up the fourth and last journal he had brought and started rereading it. "Let's see, this journal lands us around 1773. By this time, Catherine the Great was Empress of all the Russias, and Louis Phillipe I had just taken the throne of France. But I was in Italy and had been introduced to a landscape artist, Claude-Joseph Vernet. He was charming, young, and exceedingly alluring for a man. I had the pleasure of his company for a time, and he had a fetish for wearing lingerie when we were alone. The music would play, and he would dance around, acting like a fae creature. I let him sit on my lap like a lady and treated him accordingly. He felt flattered, and I caressed him to his delight. Our nights together were spent pleasurably, and the days were pleasant. He sobbed heavily when I decided to leave, but understood and found another man to take my place."

"This should bring us up to where I left off in my story. I decided to travel to the new world by now and landed in America in 1803 (I was now 291 y/o). Thomas Jefferson was in the White House and had purchased the Louisiana territory. I headed north after learning about the slavery issue in the South. This landed me in New York City. It was becoming heavily populated as people kept coming in as migrants. By now, the musician I knew as a newbie was being recognized as an idol, Wolfgang Amadeus Mozart. The music scene was alive with the music of Beethoven and Chopin. The artwork of William Russell Birch created the 'City of New York' for the city, and George Catlin was heading out west to paint the indigenous tribes of the plains. I traveled up the Hudson River and got to Albany, the state capital. I stayed around for the fall colors I had heard so much about and listened to the tales of the region. It was easy and relaxed to be in the city and the surrounding areas. I headed to Boston for the winter as I was told it was milder."

I sailed back to England the following spring and found out that the British had burned the White House down in 1814. Thank God I had left. George III was still on the throne, but it was his wife, Charlotte, who was actually in power. I didn't bother with London, but went to my properties in the suburbs of the city. The estate was still there, but someone else was in residence. I knocked on the door and was received as a guest in my own home. I asked as to the lord of the manor, and to my happy surprise, out popped my mirror image, the imp Antonius. He hugged me tightly and said, "Great-grandfather, I took your advice and, using your papers, came to England to settle down. Please let me introduce you to my lovely wife, Sarah. We married in 1810 but have yet to produce children." We dined on venison and roasted vegetables.

We drank mead as was the custom for the times. Antonius bade me stay with them for an extended period. I could not refuse the offer (as I had nowhere to go anyway).

Tuesday came to a close as Stephan finished his tale of reunion with his great-grandchild. He got up, stretched, and asked what I had to eat. "Sorry, but the menu is still the same," Stephan called for Trudy and asked if she could get groceries on Wednesday morning before coming to work. She said yes, and he handed her a wad of cash and said, "Go crazy. You know our tastes." Trudy nodded and left with a huge smile on her face. It seems she was tired of bologna, too. Stephan followed not long after and said, "Get some sleep, it's going to be a field trip tomorrow." Then he winked and left, making me wonder what was up his sleeve. But I knew better than to question his motives; they always came out in my favor.

I took a hot shower and slipped into my satin pj's (I was getting into this new me) before spreading out in my bed for the night. Sleep came as a welcome friend, and I dreamed sweet dreams. Tomorrow could wait, and I fell into a deep sleep. It seemed like 10 minutes when the alarm awoke me. I had slept 7 and a half hours. I got up, disrobed, and took another hot, steamy shower. I wanted to look my best for Stephan (I'm glad I didn't have to make-up or I'd probably use that too). I was more than ready when the doorbell rang. I ran to the door and flung it wide only to see Trudy standing there with bags of groceries. I looked disappointed, and she saw it, saying, "What were you expecting, a date?" I quickly ushered her in, took some groceries, and followed her into the kitchen. We barely got them stored away when the bell rang again. I fussed a bit as I went to the door, refraining myself this time. Stephan walked in, carrying his valise, and set it down in the corner. He noticed Trudy in the kitchen and asked her how she was doing. She said she had his change, but there wasn't much left as she had to buy nearly everything. Stephan told her to keep the rest for doing him this favor, and she asked him what he wanted for breakfast. "A simple repast, Trudy, as we'll be traveling a bit today." "Eggs with hash browns and toast, it is then." Off she went. I think she liked this job more than she let on.

After breakfast, Stephan told me to grab a coat and get ready for a busy day. I suggested taking my car, knowing his response, and he didn't let me down. "Nonsense, get in the Porsche. I want to get there today, and a Honda won't cut it where we're going." Okay, he piqued my interest. "Do I

get to know the destination, or are we playing games again?" "Fine, I'll tell you. We're heading to the shore, and it's going to take a few hours. I have a camp there and some other relics I want you to see." Well, it was something to ponder, although I now knew as much as I did before, bupkus. He played classical music on the radio, explaining the movements and the composers and how he knew most of them in person. I started to learn the enjoyment of simple and complex compositions as we slowed to a halt. We had come to a big iron gate. Stephan hit the buzzer, and the gates opened. He entered, hit the inside buzzer, and the gates closed as we rode on through the windy, tree-laden road. I asked who owned it, and Stephan just looked at me as though I was clueless. "I do, who did you think owned it, The Kennedys?" I felt small and shut up in fear I'd misstep again.

Just then, we came into the clearing, and I saw the 'camp' or his version of one. It had 3 stories, had to be at least 5000 square feet of living space, and a guest house that was as large as my apartment building. It led down to the gardens and a boathouse, again much larger than my apartment. I could only look on and try to keep my jaw from hitting the floor. We pulled up in front, and Stephan shut off the motor. I stepped out onto the driveway, all paved and just took it in, and WOW was all that came to mind. He tossed me my bag and led the way to the door. He turned the key and then stood back, allowing me to enter first. I felt like I was in Oz again, turning 360 degrees to take in the foyer area. Fresh flowers were spread about in all the nooks and crannies. It looked spit-shined, and the chandelier was crystal and exquisite. If this was the entrance, I couldn't wait for the tour. He led me upstairs and showed me my room. I told him I hadn't packed to stay the night, and he quipped, "My dear Carl, that was taken care of by the clerk at the clothing store. They dropped off your wardrobe yesterday. I told them to duplicate the last order." (This Stephan was too much.

"I believe the water is warm enough to swim, so change and I'll meet you in the entrance way." Getting cheeky, I shot back, "Not staying to watch me change?" "Oh, Carl, I already know what you look like. Get ready." He blew me a kiss and left. (Gotta love this guy, he's such a dick sometimes). Well, I got dressed, put on my kimono, and went downstairs. I saw Stephan in a sleek Speedo, and I had to admit, he was a specimen of beauty. A beautiful blond in a bright red Speedo, rippling six pack, and as always, a smile to live for. He led the way, and to the dock we went. I followed him like a puppy. He went to the end of the dock and just dove in, no prep, no toe in the water, just that confident. I edged my way to the end, tried to dip my toe in, and got splashed by the lord of the manor. "Just dive in, Carl, the water's fine." So in I went and came up like a buoy, shivering, to the bone. "Stay under the water line, and you'll be fine." Away he went, swimming around like a porpoise. We swam around for a few minutes, and then he launched himself up onto the dock. I used the ladder as I knew I didn't have it in me to make that leap. He threw me a towel, set his towel out, and began to sun himself. I tried to grab my kimono, but he told me to leave it off and get some sun (as I could glow in the dark, I was so white). I placed my towel next to his and reclined. I noticed Stephan's endowment and had to look away quickly, as even this was perfect. I could only wish I had a bit of his looks.

About an hour later, he arose, grabbed his towel, and said, "Let's head back to the camp, I believe lunch is ready." I got up, turned to grab my towel, and got a swat from the other towel. I turned back to see Stephan grinning widely and saying, "What, let's go." I tried to twist up my towel, but he was too far ahead, so I ran on and planned my revenge. We decided not to change before lunch, and went into the dining room where a huge lunch awaited us. Stephan handed me a mimosa and grabbed a celery stick and munched on it. I drank the nectar of the Gods, sat down beside Stephan, and went to town. Fresh vegetables, fresh fruit, a slice of prime rib, smashed potatoes, au jus sauce, various cheeses, fresh-baked bread, and a sparkling wine to go with it. We finished, left the dining room to the attendants, and went to the library (yes, this place had a den and a library). We sat in front of the fire, and Stephan handed me a relic.

It was a small statue, just a simple ivory one, but the story I heard made me stop in my tracks. Stephan started, "It looks like a simple articulated artist dummy, but it is worth about $7200 in today's market if you could buy it. It was in Claude-Joseph's studio, and he presented it to me as a farewell gift. I brought it with me to America and actually forgot about it until after we met." I looked around at the camp artwork, real paintings that I had to assume were originals. "The artwork alone here would make any man wealthy. Is there a reason you keep it all hidden away from the public?" "Yeah, actually, there is a reason, Carl.

If word got out that these works existed, it would turn the art world upside down, and my private life would be no more." I felt more ashamed in that moment than ever before and begged to be forgiven. Stephan tousled my hair and said, "Get dressed, more to see." Then he took his leave, and I got to see his perfect butt walking away. (This guy had it all, and why was I checking out his butt?) I shook my head and went to change.

We toured the manse and then went to the guest house. Again, awestruck and amazed, I entered the 'cabin' and took in the view. I knew better than to speak, so I just enjoyed. Stephan pointed out the artwork, the painters' names, and the year painted. The statuary was no less impressive. He opened the side French doors, and we stepped into the lush gardens. Flowers in bloom all over, Black Eyed Susans, Lilies, Hydrangeas, Roses of every variety and color, azaleas, and lots of green and red leaf plants and bushes to fill in the gaps. The path was cobblestone and snaked through the entire side yard. One could get lost in the unseen areas of the garden. Stephan bade me to close my eyes and take in the scents. (I could almost taste them). Then back to the house for dinner. I ate with the same lust as the first time Stephan took me to dinner. I didn't know where he got his staff, but I wasn't complaining. They prepared the meals like 5-star chefs. After dinner, we lounged in the den and had bourbon in fancy snifters. The fire was a bit warm, and Stephan removed his shirt (I really didn't want to stare, but couldn't help myself). Stephan didn't say anything, but I caught that insidious smile.

I excused myself and turned in. 'My' bedroom was a dream, masculine but not overly done. My clothes had been laid out by the shadow staff (all satiny pj's and silk briefs). This might pose a problem while trying to sleep. But sleep came easily, and I luxuriated in the comfort of the satin sheets. Tomorrow could take its time.

Thursday seemed to arrive too quickly, as they all did when I was with Stephan. I found him in the dining room, reading the paper. "Pope John Paul II died yesterday. I guess Rome will be buzzing for the next few weeks. I never got to meet this Pope." I took my seat, and the servant appeared with my breakfast. It seemed that they always knew what I wanted before I asked. The hot coffee smell made me stop thinking about other things, and I took that first marvelous sip. (the one that says, 'wake up'). Stephan put down the paper, looked at me, and said, "We should get back to the city as you have to send in your quarterly report to the grant people. You did write it, Carl?" "Well, I know what to write, does that count?" Stephan tried to scowl at me, but couldn't keep from busting out laughing. "That means we need to hurry up, drive back, write the damn thing, and get it sent in before the end of the day. I'll drive as you scribble notes, you know, the ones you thought of so far." Still laughing, we packed up and left, only telling the staff via the intercom.

The wind was calm as Stephan drove. I scribbled as best as I could, and we soon got back to my depressing apartment. It seems that the apartment shrank after having been to the 'camp'. Having 3 people in it didn't help either. Ever faithful Trudy was waiting with iced tea and finger sandwiches when we arrived (how did these people coordinate with our timing?). I guess that goes along with my now surreal life, everything is orderly, on point and timely. Perfect to a fault. I was definitely gonna miss that. Stephan opened the conversation, "Let's see the notes genius. Maybe we can have Trudy type them into a reasonable report and send them electronically today." Trudy appeared on cue, took dictation, saw the scribbles, and was typing before we finished our sandwiches. Trudy asked questions as to format, details, and what to leave out. About 2 hours later, the report was done, I reviewed it and Stephan ok'ed it. I hit send and Stephan ordered takeout as Trudy had been too busy to cook. I don't remember when Trudy crossed over into secretary/domestic but I was glad. Even Stephan noticed and gave Trudy a substantial raise. One happy, if not entirely odd family unit.

We decided to wait until Friday morning to continue. Trudy and Stephan left, leaving me to my thoughts. That was a bad thing as I really wasn't up for the mental back and forth I was having. Pros and cons about this 'at arms length' situation. I didn't think it a bad idea but the reality of having such a good friend and confidant (did I mention the perks?) were holding me back. I wanted to be able to say so long when the inevitable day came but it also made me want to cry just to think of my life after Stephan. I told myself not to but I came to like this way of living to which I had become accustomed. I dragged myself into the bathroom and hurried into the hot rushing water. Maybe a few minutes would wash away my issues. I stayed under the shower head until the water ran cool. Begrudgingly I stepped out, dried off, decided against blow drying my hair, put on the oh so pleasing pj's and sank into my warm bed. I tossed and turned as though I was on a spit and kept waking up in a sweat. Friday was gonna be a long day.

Friday started as usual with Stephan arriving with those enticing coffees in hand. Over his shoulder he carried his leather valise. I could only wonder what goodies he had brought for show and tell. It took some persuading but he finally opened the case, and let me peek inside. As I reached in for an article Stephan slapped my hand away and pointed his finger at me. "I'll hand them to you in order, Mr. Nosey." I feigned disappointment, frowned and that only made Stephan laugh harder. He handed me a leather bound book and said, "This is my diary from about 1850. Let's start there." I received the diary as though it was the gutenburg bible and handled it with care. I almost suggested white gloves as it was 155 years old.

It was written in Italian so I assumed he was back in Italy. "Okay, let me see, yes, I found myself in Italy, in the midst of civil unrest and fighting. The Pope had been exiled, the country had become unrecognizable. I heard that the Ottoman Empire was out of Greece and they had installed a King, Otto I. I decided to go there and visit my real ancestral home. I took a bit to reacclimate to the Greek language and writing but it came back quickly. I didn't know the cuisine and put about to try it all. The grapes and the olive oil, different from Italy but still wonderful. Stuffed grape leaves, Souvlaki, Ouzo, and many more delicacies. I trekked around the countryside until I returned to my family's birth city, Athens, now the capital of Greece. I went to the libraries and churches in the area and found out about the lives of my ancestors, actually pretty common folk and hardworking. I went to Agia Triada Sotira Lykodimou, the newly restored church in Athens and happened to be there when the King and Queen visited. King Otto, resplendent in his royal togs and Amalia in her royal raiments cut a beautiful image as they entered the church. I bowed to show my respect and they noticed. They approached me and asked as to my position. I replied that I was only minor royalty from France and England and Russia. This piqued their interest and I was invited to the state dinner that week. I prepared as one does with the protocols of court, and found a tailor to ensure that my clothing would meet with their approval. The night approached and the coaches started arriving in the city. I figured that I would also need a coach, so I rented one for the evening. I dressed in my finest fare, seated myself in the carriage, and off to the Castle. I made myself arrive fashionably late for effect but not too late. I saw that almost all in attendance had an entourage but it was too late to create one so solo it was.

I spoke little, listened a lot and was surprised as to my reserved seat, very near the King, and quite visible to the Queen. She nodded to acknowledge me and the King side winked at me. I was taken aback as the King was a very handsome man and the Queen very pretty. Either I was clueless or was getting mixed signals. I decided to let it play out. The affair was grand, the food wonderful and the conversation engaging. The evening ended when the king and queen turned to leave. Boy did I misread the room. I was ushered to a side room and the servant handed me a tray with a note on it. "You are requested at the behest of the King and Queen to stay and be received in their private parlor." Signed, King Otto I with a wax seal. Maybe I hadn't read them wrong. I followed the servant to a wing of the castle and double doors opened as I was announced. I entered, saw the king and queen as the doors closed almost silent. Otto beckoned me over, had me sit near Amalia and motioned for the server to pour the ouzo. I waited for them to begin to state the reason, and Otto said, "We appreciate that such a statesman as you grace us with your presence. Amalia is intrigued as you speak Greek well but are foreign royalty. Pray tell, where were you schooled?" I, trying to think on my feet, said, "I became an ambassador for the King of France, The Italian Pope, The Russian tsar, and the King of England. I am also fluent in Spanish and Portuguese." Amalia piped up and said, "That's quite the accomplishment Stephan. I knew as I sensed it when we noticed you in the church." By this time, Otto had come to sit on my other side and I felt like the meat in their sandwich. They sent the servants away and started with their seduction of me. I laid back and allowed this couple their dalliances as I believed it would serve me well in the future (I was right). I have to say, it was a wonderful time had by all as they were quite the assertive pair of lovers. I don't know why I was chosen, but I wasn't about to question it. Menage a troi I believe they call it. I called it fun (and satisfying). They called me to court. I stayed for about a year as their personal play toy. I found out later he was deposed in 1862. Oh well, I had moved on."

Stephan took a breather, I got up and stretched, Trudy brought us lunch and we all dined on china plates (were had they come from I wondered). Trudy removed the used plates and Stephan sat for a few more minutes before continuing. "It was now around the summer of 1853 when I arrived back in Russia and Nicholas I was Emperor. I went to my old home and visited the cemetery, placing flowers on my dear Svetlana's grave. I couldn't believe it had been 208 years since her passing. The new owners were gracious and provided me a meal and lodging for the night. I left soon after and pondered my next move. I didn't think about visiting St. Petersburg and seeing Nicholas I. I decided to just head west and let the winds take me on another adventure. I made it as far as the Ukraine.

It seemed bad timing as the Crimean war had just started between the Russians and the British, French, and Ottoman Empire. It lasted until 1856 and I had been conscripted by the tsar's army due to my ability to speak as a poly linguist. I didn't fight on the front lines but provided much in the way of translating documents captured by the Russians. The tsar Nicholas II sent word to have me join him in St. Petersburg after my assignment ended. Well, I went although I had not intended to stay even this long. Tsar Nicholas II was formally introduced to me at the victory dinner (Russia had defeated the Ottoman Empire). I had to say he cut a fine figure but he was married (so I behaved myself). I was getting rather comfortable floating between the guys and girls.

I waited about a month, staying in the royal palace, then asked for traveling papers and headed west again. Yes, back to Italy in 1859 to see if any of my descendants still lived besides Antonius Julia. I visited the old neighborhoods and made inquiries as I feasted on the delicacies of Rome. I found out the Julia name had died out but a descendant still existed. I sent word to the master of the house to who the descendant was. To my surprise, a young lady answered my note and invited me for dinner. The lady had a resemblance to my great great great granddaughter but I thought that line had passed. She greeted me as she announced her name, "Great grandfather, it is I Fausta, Marcus' daughter. I married after we had departed for the countryside. I'm so happy to see you again."

I intended to question her more after dinner, but the evening sped by enjoying everything about her and the tales of her life. I guess listening was better than questions and I learned more than if I had talked. I turned in, knowing she was widowed (after all, she was 130 actually) but happy. I thought if Antonius (now 170 y/o) knew he had a second cousin, maybe he'd return from England to visit her. I made a note to send word to him. I loved being around her and she me. I could have stayed forever but as usual, the road beckoned me. I sent word ahead to Anthony (as he now went by) of my arrival and word came back when I reached Portugal that I was expected.

I walked up to the gates of my former home, gained access and was told the master would receive me at dinner. Until then, I would be shown my room and allowed to settle in. It couldn't come soon enough for my liking. Dressed in my finest silk garments, I presented myself at the dining hall and saw myself standing there, laughing. It seems we could only be told apart by our raiments. He stepped forward, shook my extended hand and then hugged me (as only a masculine man can) making me feel at ease. "Great grand father, I've waited so long for your visit. Was everything to your liking?" "All was fine, but this made it worth while. I tried to return to you sooner but was conscripted in the Russian army for 3 years and then went to visit your second cousin Fausta. She resides in the family house in Rome.

"I'll send her a letter later to firm up arrangements to visit." I couldn't believe that I now had 2 descendants aging like me. I followed Anthony into the room and sat near him to dine. "Did you hear grandfather, that the Prince, Albert built a marvelous crystal palace and is dedicating it to the Queen next month. Would you like to attend? I can get Albert to send the invitations." "I didn't know that you knew the Prince?." "More than you'd like to hear. I met him when traveling to London on some business. I took your advice, married well, assumed the wealth upon Sarah's death. Now I'm a prominent businessman. Anyway, I met Albert when he wanted to build some other building around London. He and Victoria were at odds about making decisions concerning their children (they had 9 by then, the youngest, Beatrice being 3). Albert and I met at the local Pub, got talking about intimate times and he told me about his 'Prince Albert' piece of jewelry. I prodded him until he took me aside and showed it to me. I'll tell you that I was highly impressed by it and knew now why Victoria had such affection for him. I was curious and asked to touch it (Not very subtle). Surprisingly, he let me and things got wild afterwards." (Stephan just smiled as the apple didn't fall too far from the tree).

Anthony smiled nervously as though waiting for a reaction. I smiled back, setting him at ease. I told him that I had tales that would make him blush. We finished dinner, took a brandy from the tray, and settled in the den. The tape ended and Stephan stopped by closing the journal. I asked if he wanted anything to munch on as he now had plenty to offer. "Anything besides your 'world famous' bologna sandwiches." I stuck my tongue out as I passed Stephan, he turned quick and kissed my cheek.

(my turn to blush, not because it was a man kissing me but the fact that I liked it). Stephan had Trudy create a sandwich board for us to pick at, was told she could leave and she bid us goodnight. Alone together, we put down about 3 sandwiches each. I reset the tape, and Stephan asked to just talk. I turned off the machine, sat down and looked at Stephan quizzically. He motioned for me to relax, he just wanted to talk. My heart settled down, and I sat back in my chair awaiting the conversation.

Stephan took a deep breath and started, "Can I speak plainly Carl?" I just nodded, now more curious about what was to transpire. "I wanted to say that I've come to really enjoy our time together…(here it comes I thought, the other shoe was about to drop) and was wondering if you felt the same way?" I couldn't talk for a few seconds, then said, "I have come to rely on your visits, field trips, and journal readings. I even regret that your not here on the weekends." Stephan crossed the room, leaned down, kissed me full on the lips and asked to spend the night, I was surprised (not really), shocked and having that come from left field, uncertain what it would mean. "I just want to feel the warmth and intimacy of another person Carl." With that, I had no choice, I reached up, cupped his handsome face and kissed back, a warm moist lingering one. It had been far too long for me and I welcomed it. The only question was, "Why me though when you could have anyone you wanted?" "Because you know me intimately Carl. You see me for me, and if you'd stop being self shaming, you'd see yourself for the beautiful soul you are. There are too few people that see me for more than a wallet and a good time. You're not just another notch in my belt Carl, you're special to me. I want to give that back to you. Let's get a hot shower and turn in." I followed behind blindly and let him take the lead. It actually felt pretty good letting someone else be assertive for once. The shower was hot, welcoming but 2 guys at once was a bit close. Stephan washed me (and I mean ALL of me) and then turned so I could do the same for him. It was weird, but sensuous, and it somehow felt right. We exited the tub, dried each other off and put on the pj's Stephan had gifted me. Well, time to turn in and Stephan asked which side I wanted. "I usually sleep on the left side, you?" "I sleep on the right, so far, so good." Stephan disrobed down to his silk boxer briefs and I stayed fully dressed as we got into bed together.

Stephan rolled over, kissed my cheek again and let me settle in. I guess I was more into it than I wanted to be because within 5 minutes we were spooning and I actually wanted to be the little spoon. Stephen being the experienced lover, took his time, letting me set the pace, the level of intimacy and finally the lovemaking positions. I couldn't believe that I was allowing this masculine, beautiful man to have a part of me that up to now was virgin. It felt wonderful, and he made sure I was satisfied also. I almost didn't want it to end, but we were both tired now and cuddled falling asleep in each other's arms. I didn't remember sleeping so well. I woke up with his manly arm over me and I reminisced about the night before. I smelled coffee and started to panic knowing Trudy was here. I quietly left the bed (and my new lover) and dressed for the morning. I crept out of the bedroom only to see Trudy pouring 2 cups of coffee. "Will Stephan be getting up soon? (she said with a wink)" "I ah, I think, ah, ah." Trudy just smirked, and I now knew we had formed a tight, loving family unit.

I had to hug Trudy and she smiled, "Tell lover boy breakfast in 30 minutes, now here, take sleeping beauty his coffee." With that, she shooed me back into the bedroom. I found my prince charming in the bed, spread out and beautiful in his nakedness (I now know why so many artists immortalized him in oil and marble). I felt lucky to have shared him with the many before me. Stephan stirred, looked at me through those eyes, swiped the hair out of his face and whispered, "Is Trudy here?" "Yes and she said breakfast in 30, she sent this coffee for you." Stephan took the coffee, set it on the side table, grabbed me, pulled me back into bed and playfully planted kisses all over my face. I pushed him away, "Your mouth smells like a dick, go brush your teeth and gargle." We both laughed and made sure we were ready within 30 minutes.

Trudy went to transcribe, Stephan got dressed as did I, and he asked me on another field trip. How could I refuse. This time I dressed much to Stephan's approval (I wanted to look especially good today) and we set off in the 'family car'. We headed east, the wind in our hair thinking it was toward the mall. I was right, Stephan said if he was going to spend another night in my apartment, we needed new bedding (how rude). We went in and soon were leaving with a trunk full of bedding I couldn't buy if I had spent the entire grant budget. I don't know why but I wanted to hold Stephan's hand to let the world know how I felt about this unique human being. He must have read my mind because he held out his hand and I immediately took it. Stephan smiled that million dollar smile and I for once smiled from ear to ear.

We went to eat at the best restaurant, Indian food as he had a hankering for it and I knew nothing of the culture or cuisine. I had to say it was less spicy than I was led to believe and the rice pudding dessert was light, airy and surprisingly delicious. Onto the next escapade. Stephan took me to a men's specialty shop where they had exotic (I say erotic) bed clothing. He made me try on (and model) a LOT of the merchandise and I won't even tell you what he bought there. (Can you tell I'm blushing again). Why does he always make me feel this way, special, shy, overwhelmed, but happy all at the same time. I felt like we were on our honeymoon (and maybe in some ways, we were). When we returned home, Trudy had finished her work, left a meal in the oven with instructions for reheating, and taken her leave. Stephan took advantage of the situation and asked that he get a private showing of the new 'undergarments' (if you could call them that). I hemmed and hawed about it until Stephan said ok and pouted his lips. I just grabbed the bags and headed to the bedroom. Stephan tried to follow but I stopped him saying I wanted to make an entrance. He pouted again but I held firm and turned him to the couch and patted his butt and sent him on his way.

I think we got through about 4 articles before Stephan got too worked up to continue. I felt him caressing my calves, then thighs and well, you know the rest. I was acting the wife and really had no problem with it. Only one who has had an experienced male lover knows how it feels to surrender control and enjoy and I did (enjoy I mean). It was only Saturday night, and Trudy wasn't due back till Monday so we ended up acting like drunk frat boys, loud, funny and silly (and mostly naked all night). I could only think about having missed out on this while in college.

Sunday, we got mostly back on track, but you know what novelty brings to a relationship. Stephan got out another journal, titled 'years 1880 through 1900'. I knew better than to reach out, besides, I thought it was probably in foreign languages. I settled on the couch between his thighs as he started to read and translate, "By now, the United States (as it was calling itself now) had settled down from it's civil war, and I heard about this young Serbian-American inventor (who was strikingly handsome). His name Nikola Tesla, and I was intent on meeting him, so I traveled to the USA, New York City to be exact. The history books say that he was celibate and only loved a pigeon. I can tell you, they left out a few chapters. I was eating al fresco in Manhattan in 1889 when I spotted him. Or should I say, he spotted me. He came right up to me, asked how I had been and sat right down. I looked stunned, then he said, "Anthony, how marvelous to see you again. Are you still single?" Okay, mystery over, he mistook me for Anthony, my great great grandson. I played along saying, "Of course, I was waiting for you." Nicola stared at me for a second, then said, "You're not Anthony, but the resemblance is eerie." I knew then he heard me speak and Anthony has a heavy Italian accent. "Okay, I'm Stephan, Anthony's relative." (I didn't want to spook him by saying I was 377 years old).

He relaxed, asked if he could join me for the repast and I accepted (he was strikingly handsome). We talked and he explained that he and Anthony were quite 'close' friends before and was surprised when he saw me, thinking Anthony had returned from England. The lunch turned into a dinner date and we dined at the Russian House. He regaled me with his newest interests and ideas for inventions. I listened intently and informed him that IF he needed funds to get started on his newest invention, to count me in. I guess the wine got to him and he moved closer to me as his inhibitions left him. I didn't stop the seduction and then he asked to walk me home. Of course I said yes and we had the best night of pleasure. The next morning he must have had a pang of guilt, as he said his goodbyes and hurried away. Too bad, but I still feel a sense of fondness when his name comes up." Stephan zoned out for a second, obviously remembering that night and I got a little jealous (leave the past in the past lover). Stephan looked at me then realized what I was sensing. He leaned down to me and said, "Don't worry babe, but you have to realize that I have a lot of history before you." Stephan set his journal down, hugged me tight, then rolled me over his knees and swatted my butt. (that's for your thoughts). Wrestling followed with me ending in a downward dog stance. Somehow that's how we spent the rest of Sunday. Monday arrived, Trudy saw that we hadn't accomplished much and asked for grocery money, shook her head and said, "You boys must have worked up a massive appetite as there's nothing left in the fridge." We all laughed, we two boys kissed Trudy on her cheeks, and she smiled and left. "I guess we better get to work or Trudy will have nothing to transcribe." Stephan grabbed the journal, flipped ahead a few pages and started again, "It was now 1893, I don't know how it happened or why but people started runs on banks causing a panic that led to a deep depression that lasted 4 years. I decided to leave the USA and departed for Europe and my beloved Italy. I visited Fausta (Now with a wealthy young man) and spent the better of a year. (I'll bet he was glad when I left). I continued on to Greece as I heard the 1896 Olympics were about to begin. I stayed in Athens enjoying the food and culture. The events of the Olympics were limited to 43. I enjoyed the gymnastics, swimming, wrestling and field and track. There were 280 athletes (all male) and some of them made my mouth water.

I received a letter from Anthony, back in England. He wanted to know if I'd be returning soon and having seen the Olympics, headed his way. I got there in 1900 and Victoria was still on the throne. Anthony had his own knighthood now and he was massively wealthy. He had changed up his name to Sir Anthony Julius (instead of his birth name Antonius Julia). It seemed that he knew better than I how to adapt to longevity. The very next year, Victoria died, leaving the throne to Edward VII. Anthony and I journeyed to London and gave our final goodbyes to the Queen. The papers were telling of the Boer war in South Africa (when not posting about the newly departed queen) and a stretcher bearer volunteer was hardly being reported on, his name, Mohandas Ghandi, later to become the Mahatma or "the great souled-one." More on him later, as Sir Anthony and I spent days and weeks in the countryside charming the women (and men) sometimes calling ourselves brothers or cousins and laughing about it later. We returned to the estate and he showed me his collection of portraits (he had kept having them done after he 'grew up'). I had to say he kept up with the times and the portraits proved it. He found landscape artists willing to take on the task, including: Teresa Copnail, Helen Edwards, and Eleanor Hughes. He winked at me saying, "These ladies weren't much in the looks department but they were easy to charm and much less costly.

I loved my time with Anthony but the road called my name. Anthony was feeling itchy too as he said he'd like to accompany me around Europe. He wanted to see the old place, see what was new and get into 'trouble'. I guess that meant Italy but I told him, I wanted to see Portugal, France and Spain also. He readily agreed to my plans and said, "Let's go." He left the instructions behind, finalized his business in England and we took the ship across the channel. He found that the Portuguese food was a bit spicy for him. The culture didn't much appeal to him either, so we moved on to Spain. We visited the Prado and saw a new painter in their collection, Pablo Picasso. I can't say I much liked his current pieces though. I told Anthony I hoped it was just a phase. The Paella was spectacular to eat as I loved all the fresh seafood it contained. We stayed about a month and then on to France. Ah, the food and wine poured freely as we literally spent a small fortune on a good time. The ladies set upon us like locusts, as they were not of means. We showed them a decent time and surely tasted their 'wares'. That lasted approximately 2 months before leaving. We circumvented Germany and got to Italy by 1903. We read that the Wright Brothers had flown a plane at Kitty Hawk, North Carolina. We arrived in Naples before heading to Rome as I hadn't been in the countryside for ages (try 300 odd years). Anthony and I dallied with the local 'talent' spreading ourselves thin. The ladies were voluptuous and curvy and knew how to cook. The food kept coming, the wine kept pouring and we kept the ladies happy in their turn. That did not exclude the men, we had them also. I sent word to Fausta as to when to expect us."

Stephan was getting tired so I suggested a break and we headed to the kitchen nook. I think Stephan was a little perturbed because the nook was barely big enough for me let alone the both of us. "We have to do something about your living arrangements Carl." "What do you suggest, given my pay grade? I can barely keep this place and it's at the low end of the scale." Stephan backed off a little, asked me to sit down and said, "I want to keep this 'family' unit together and you do realize I have the means to live anywhere I choose. Let's talk to Trudy, as I'm sure her commute is taking its toll. We'll find a place closer and big enough to stretch out and give her a real kitchen and office to work in. Don't sweat the cost, I'll take care of that and no, I won't have to sell any of my collection of things." With that, he kissed me, turned on his heels, swatted my behind and literally danced into the living space. The thought of 'movin on up' sounded very enticing, even intoxicating but I threw up my hands and said, "But what happens later, after the novelty of me wears off and you get that 'wanderlust' again." "I told you Carl, you'll have to trust me. You DO trust me, don't you?" I hung my head like a red headed stepchild just having been disciplined. "Of course I trust you but listening to your history, I have to wonder if you still get that feeling. Yes I trust you, I gave something I never even thought of using in my life, me and my most intimate parts." Stephan returned to me, bear hugging me and smothering all my doubts.

About that time, Trudy came back, we assisted in bringing in the groceries. Due to space, we allowed Trudy to work alone storing all the goodies. She then started to make lunch and I suggested that we order in, her choice, and to join us in the living room to talk. "Take a seat

Trudy. I promise this is a good thing, don't worry. I or rather we, would like to propose a better living space closer to your home, as in walking distance. We'll make sure you have an office of your own, big kitchen, dining room, and at least 3 bedrooms, in case you work late. How does that sound?" Trudy smiled and said, "I was hoping you'd say that. It seems all three of us are on the same wavelength. I know a house, three doors down from mine and it's exactly what you're describing. I even know the Realtor. I can call him later if you want. He hasn't even listed it yet. You wouldn't get into a pricing war. But can you afford it and my salary?" "Trudy, of course I, I mean we, can afford it. Please set it up, thanks."

Lunch appeared, Trudy joined us in the Italian affair (bless her heart, she tried and said it was as good as being in Italy, believe me, it wasn't). We ate it, Trudy and I thoroughly enjoying it and Stephan letting us go on about it's merits and taste. (how he wanted us to have the REAL thing). We boys returned to the readings and Trudy set up the meeting. About 2 pm, Trudy called us from the journal to say Henry (the Realtor) would be waiting so we packed ourselves, all three of us, into the family car and sped away, Trudy acting as our GPS. We got to the house and it was everything Trudy said it was, charming, well landscaped, and most of all, large. Henry stepped to the Porsche, opened the door and we poured out like from a clown car. I had to say, both Stephan and I eyed this tender morsel but said nothing. I knew we'd be buying this home.

He went up the stoop, placed the key in the door, and opened the door as Stephan had to me at the 'camp'. We entered and tried to look nonchalant but at least my insides were bursting. Trudy went immediately to the office and then kitchen. We took our time in the living room and den. The main hallway led to an atrium with a reflecting pool. You could go to all 4 wings of the house from there, the walls being glass just added to the grandeur. The plants were in bloom and the foliage were multicolored. Can you say heaven, and we didn't even get to the second floor yet. The grand staircase made me think of the Tara plantation in 'Gone with the Wind'. I completely forgot to say where I lived, in South Baltimore and we were in Riverside now, near the inner harbor. Stephan walked up to Henry, pulled him aside as I meandered into the kitchen to see Trudy just caressing the stove and marble counter tops. I interrupted her dreaming and said Stephan was talking to Henry (and I was a bit jealous I have to admit). We joined them as Stephan said, "Welcome home, We can move in immediately. Carl, when do you think we can get the movers to pack you up? I'll have mine brought Wednesday. (he had a lot to pack). "I'll toss a match and walk away, I can stay the night, I'll even sleep on the floor until the furniture arrives." We all got a big laugh out of that, decided a day later for me as Stephan had most of his stuff packed or in storage and the movers were on retainer. Trudy hugged Stephan, then me and ended with Henry. I guess Stephan was right when he said my past life was over and my new one about to begin. Trudy showed us her residence and it made me wonder why she was working. This neighborhood wasn't one where the ladies worked aside from chairing committees and having charity events.

Stephan allowed Trudy the rest of the day off saying we had stuff to do. I mistook that to mean an afternoon of pleasure but we went to the car lot instead. Stephan quipped, "We can't have us looking like paupers driving up to our new home in just a plain Porsche. And you definitely have to have a new car." What, my winter rat parked outside a mansion was no good now, humpf. Stephan walked in, a salesman walked up, and Stephan told me to pick out a car. I looked around and couldn't find one less that $100,000. I gasped, sat down for a second as Stephan looked at the Bentleys. He chose a regal shiny black one, I couldn't even guesstimate the cost. I saw a car that caught my eye, but it was out of my league, it was a Maserati, blue metallic. Stephan made me sit in the driver's seat, closed the door and said, "We'll take this one too. I sneaked a peek at the sticker price, $139,900." (my car was lucky if it had a scrap value). The salesman, grinning ear to ear, took Stephan into his cubicle to work out the details. I just sat in this 'once in a lifetime' car. I couldn't fathom the depths of Stephan's pockets but I wasn't going to deny him his pleasure. The steering wheel was bound in leather, the seats crushed velvet, the accessories too many to count. It was going to take months to realize the true talent of this car (but I was willing to suffer for my man). Stephan was coming out of the office as I came to my senses. "Okay, we can pick them up Thursday, let's go. We have a busy week ahead of us." Note to self, if this was just Monday, I was moving in Thursday, then throwing away my old car and getting this one the same day. By Friday I was going to be a rich bitch, pardon the expression.

Stephan dropped me off, asked if I needed my car any more, removed the plates and called the Salvation Army to come get my car. I acted as though it was going to be a hardship but was secretly touching myself at having a new car. (actually any car newer than this one, but a Maserati, heck yeah!) I almost slipped up and regressed to my old self. I had to wonder, where did he live, I never asked. He had to live somewhere close, now I felt like a schmuck, I didn't even know that about him. I found out Tuesday morning when he arrived with that wonderful coffee, actually 3 cups as he now included Trudy on everything. (I didn't know anything about Trudy either. What an idiot I was beginning to think). Before starting our session, I asked both of them to clue me in on these basic pieces of their lives. Trudy started by saying that she had married a gentle man, had a couple kids, they grew up and left home. Then she became a widow after 30 years of marriage. When this opportunity came along, it allowed her to get back into living and she loved us for it. It made her feel special and needed (and in truth, she was). Stephan only said that he lived in the neighborhood and left it at that.

I dropped the subject and Stephan produced a diary, a far more intimate log of his life. He was letting me further into his life. The diary had 1920 on it. He explained about the lapse in time by saying, "I know there is 10 years missing but those were the years we spent with Fausta and her newest lover. I didn't think you wanted to hear about those escapades. Suffice to say, it was more of a Bacchanalian orgy fest. Anthony returned to England and I to the Americas. Fausta promised to visit me here after her fling ended and I told her not to hurry. Anthony promised to visit when Fausta did. The family reunion, planned and set, I sailed to Baltimore during their build. I couldn't have picked a better and worse time to arrive. They were converting the wholesale trade into retail buildings and offices. The pandemic flu killed off about 4125 people and sickened about 24,000 people. I survived the flu and that was the year I got into baseball, being that the Orioles won the pennant. By then, The tsar and his family had been assassinated, women had been given the vote, and I was 308 years old. I settled in the riverside section of Baltimore. The roaring twenties were good to me, the parties were never ending and the liquor flooded freely at my soirees. It all went well until October, 1929 when the stock market crashed. That was a horrendous sight as people's fortunes evaporated (except mine) and it gave me a unique opportunity to appropriate a ton of 'worthless' stocks. I knew it would recover but most people basically gave their shares to me at bargain prices. Those shares now are worth about 1.3 trillion dollars."

Now I knew how Stephan could afford so much. Stephan closed that diary as Trudy appeared with lunch. We ate and talked about the new house. Trudy asked if we wanted her to move into the house with us. She had wanted to sell her house as it was becoming more of a burden after the kids grew up and her husband died. Stephan looked to me for an answer and I grinned and told Trudy to consider it settled. She had to hug us both and called Henry. We set up the movers to get Trudy moved in by the weekend. It was all coming together, Stephan, Me and Trudy. I wondered how her kids would take the news. It wasn't long before the answer came, they were excited as they had wanted their mom to move on and this was the chance of a lifetime. Wednesday we got the keys, moved Trudy's clothes in and waited for the movers to bring over Stephan's things. I had to stop myself as I saw the things being unloaded from the truck. Why it shocked me I don't know but it did. I don't think the movers knew what they were handling. I guess they thought the paintings were reprints and reproductions of the masters (if they only knew the truth). The guys finished the first trip by 1 pm. Trudy had lunch waiting for us and them. They were famished and tore into the feast as Stephan and I simply ate sandwiches (not bologna ever again). Trudy cleared away the remnants of the feast as the movers went to bring the next wave of furniture. By days end, we were effectively moved in and the boys even set up the beds (for supper which we ordered in).

Stephan allowed Trudy time in her en suite to settle in and then led me to our en suite, a beautiful 20 by 40 foot bedroom complete with fireplace and sofa, king size four poster bed and satin sheets. (let the honeymoon begin). We spent the first night in OUR home canoodling and consummating our affection (to me it was love, I couldn't speak for Stephan). Thursday was a blur as we had so much to do. I bid farewell to my apartment, got in my new Maserati, and headed for my new life, complete with new togs and lover. We parked our cars in the garage as we had to make room for Trudy in the driveway. I asked which car we use as the family car now and Stephan said, "Really, there's more room in the Bentley and what's the good being rich if you can't show it a little bit." Trudy was transcribing when a call came in for her, it was Henry calling to say that he had an offer on her home. She asked us if she should give the money to her kids as we smiled back and said in unison, "Of course, then you're stuck with us." She got up tapped both of us on our cheeks, then hugged us both tightly and went to call the kids. I didn't mean to eavesdrop on her conversation but told each of the kids to expect a check in the mail in the amount of $500,000 dollars each. A gift from their father. The 'family' was beyond my belief and we invited the kids and their families to a housewarming party. Trudy was put in charge of the arrangements and the bounce house and whatever else she could think of for the grand kids. By the following weekend, The party was set and we three welcomed an entourage of 6 young adults and about 9 kids (if my counting was accurate). Trudy was overwhelmed by having her kids and grand kids there and we the doting 'uncles' had the best day with Stephan grilling, Trudy's salads and my being just the silly 'uncle'. I have to say, Trudy's kids were accommodating, helpful and accepting of their mother's new role. A true loving family, a real Norman Rockwell painting family. The kids, now part of our family, allowed us to plan Christmas for everyone.

The move took about a week, the movers pouting that it was over and the free meals ended, took their check and left. We settled into our new home and Trudy set up home delivery for groceries so she could concentrate on her true job, transcribing. She set up her office and bribed the movers on their day off (with her cooking) to get her equipment working. She took over and we couldn't have been happier. Stephan decided to take a week off and we told Trudy to hold down the fort as we went to the camp for the week. She stocked a basket for us and had groceries delivered to the staff for us (gotta love that woman). We spent the last week of summer basking in the sun, swimming, and generally having a blast in the countryside. I don't know when my sexual tastes changed but this felt so right now, easy, unpressured and natural. Stephan was a wonderful lover and I couldn't help myself. I reached over, took his hand and asked him to marry me. He knew we couldn't unless we went to Canada. He said if was legal, he would but it had to be here. The next day he presented me a ring, saying that he would now consider us wed. I melted into him and asked for a ceremony that our family could attend. He acquiesced, and I made mental notes as to what I wanted.

The week went speeding past and we started back on his story. The diary was labeled 1930-1940. I could hardly wait but I really didn't want to hear any more of his dalliances with other people. He flipped through the pages and decided that it was just fluff and sordid affairs. We agreed to set that diary aside. Diary 1950-1960 contained mostly things he wrote in like the Korean war ends, schools integrated in 1954 by the Supreme Court ruling on Brown v Board of Education, Sputnik launched by the Russians. What intrigued me was that Stephan never really got into the new technology, television. I asked him why and he said that he had heard it was just a passing fad (boy did he miscalculate). He did mention that he sent word to Fausta and Anthony about coming to the states. He heard that Anthony lost most of his fortune in the crash and was trying to make ends meet by giving tours to his estate. "Fausta, I found out, died due to the influenza. She left her fortune to her last lover and so that resource was gone. I told Anthony to visit anyway. I paid for his passage, and he arrived looked the worse for wear. He looked less a nobleman and more a peasant. I brokered some stock (the lesser ones) and when he left, he was again wealthy. I didn't care, I had more than enough." Stephan did explain that his love of music and his vast resources allowed him to dabble in the music industry. He came to love the new music, Rock and Roll. He bankrolled many new artists, including some kid name Elvis. He didn't much like Colonel Parker but the kid had talent, and hips, and was also sweet. Stephan put away this diary and started to get the next one. I called Trudy, asked her to get us a snack, and took my leave and returned to our bedroom. When I returned, I was wearing a robe and was barefoot. Stephan pointed to the food but wondered what I was doing. I headed over to the food, disrobed, showing Stephan my new indiscreet wardrobe, and pranced around to show him my intent. He laughed, threw down his diary and joined in the dance. We bumped and ground until Stephan got in the mood and he joined me in my bawdiness.

The diaries could wait, but my need could not, I needed to feel him around me and in me. How could I have become such a wicked wanton white woman for this man, having been a breeder for so long? Oh well, things happen and I couldn't be happier. Stephan teased me and kept edging me until I couldn't take it any longer. We exploded at the same time and both fell into a relaxed sleep. We woke to the smell of fabulous cooking, got up and dressed and followed our noses. Trudy, as always, had the perfect repast for hungry men and we dined in our pj's. Trudy brought us back to reality when she asked if we had finished our quarterly for the grant. We looked at each other, shook our heads no, and Trudy said, "Then it's going to be a long night as it's due tomorrow boys." We hustled to get it done, Trudy pulled an all nighter to get it ready and we sent it in. The response was less than we hoped for and they let me know that the grant would sunset within the month. I looked despondent and worried that my time was up and the other shoe was about to drop.

I hoped that Stephan was as good as his word, I mean he could keep Trudy as he had means, but where would I fit in, now broke as a church mouse. Stephan found me in the atrium, silently sobbing and worried. He came to me, sat as he put those manly arms around me and said, "Don't worry Carl, as long as I'm here, you're safe." I looked up behind reddened eyes and said, "the words 'as long as I'm here' sound like a terminal disease, it's good until it ends. That's what I'm afraid of." Stephan wanted to take away my fear and told me to follow him into the office. He went to the safe behind Trudy's desk and opened it. He handed me papers to read. It brought me to tears. Stephan had plans for me to be taken care of in perpetuity as long as I should live. Trudy too was taken care of. Of course, this was what Stephan had said many times about trusting him. I wept, mostly of happiness but some because I hadn't trusted him as much as I should have. I spent the rest of the night making it up to him. I slept the sleep of angels that night and woke to his arm around me.

Stephan took his shower, appeared in his towel as I was stirring. He 'accidentally' let it slip to the floor and I bent to pick it up. He took advantage and soon we were back in bed. Trudy yelled up to us to "Get you're sorry asses out of bed or I'm throwing the breakfast away." Two grown men, hustling for any clothes we could grab and running down the stairs half naked because we knew she meant it. All we found was a great lady laughing heartily and pointing to the kitchen. It was at that point that Stephan asked Trudy to become the house manager instead of just a servant or secretary. She asked what that entailed and we both blurt out, "just what you do now, only with a better title and more money." She smiled, blushed and wondered how she ended up running this crazy household.

Breakfast ended before she 'threw it away', and we retreated to the den to continue our work. I don't know why I said that as it wasn't my work any more. Just a project between Stephan and I. He wanted to finish anyways so I set up the tape again and he took up his journal titled '1960-1980'. this volume was thicker than the rest and I was curious as to why. It didn't take long to understand as the music scene was buzzing, the Viet Nam War was happening, revolution and unrest was on the campuses and free love was flowing like a river. 1961 saw the Berlin Wall erected between east and west Berlin, 1963 saw the fall of the great man John F. Kennedy, shot in the car in Texas in front of his wife Jackie. The new president Johnson signed the civil rights act a year later. 1965 saw England's prime Minister Churchill die, 1968 saw 2 more deaths, Martin Luther King Jr. in April followed by Bobby Kennedy on June 6. The Beatles, the Rolling Stones, The Supremes, The Who, The Band and too many more to mention bestowed on us the greatest music of the 60's. We read the journal far into the night, only stopping to get a tray of food delivered by the staff (yes, Trudy had hired a staff to tend to our every need, she being the gem of a person we now could not think of being without). Stephan read on about the Singers of the Baltimore area and he brought up a singer I loved, Cass Elliott. She went on to California and made it big with The Mamas and The Papas. He said he heard her with the group at Woodstock in northern New York and again at the Monterey Pop festival. There he heard another of my favorites, Janis Joplin, formerly of Big Brother and the Holding Company.

He told me the story about getting back stage, sharing drinks with Janis and heard her mention about her upcoming album, Pearl. He was sad to hear she overdosed before the album caught on. Her charisma and talent wouldn't be forgotten. The seventies started with the three big deaths that year, Jimi Hendrix, Jim Morrison and Janis. Then the Beatles broke up, disco came in and with it glam rock. Genders bent, Nixon was in office and the world went crazy. Just when things started to settle down, Nixon got impeached and resigned from the presidency, his veep Agnew was forced out of office for bank fraud and tax evasion. He copped to the charge of tax evasion and resigned, making way for Gerald Ford to replace him. Then when Nixon resigned, he assumed the presidency for 2 years. He was never elected to the office having only served Nixon's term. Stephan, having been around politics in Europe most of his early life (about the first couple hundred years) intended to keep a low profile and let the politics happen. It served him well and he used his vast wealth to stay out of the limelight. 1976, the Bicentennial year and bands across America all got in on the act. The best was a concert in Tampa, Florida. Stephan flew down and was introduced to the Eagles, Fleetwood Mac, Loggins and Messina, and Dan Fogelberg. (money has its privileges). He partied for a week with them and never wanted to leave. He grew to love the weather and the culture, especially the Keys. Stephan told me he now owns a condo in South Beach. Note to self, next vacation is Florida.

We forgot to get some sleep, overslept past breakfast and Trudy sent in the staff to see if we were still alive. They caught us snuggling, noticed us breathing and quietly left the room. We had woken by then and looked at the clock. "Holy crap, Trudy's gonna blow a gasket. We showered together (a mistake as it took 10 minutes longer), then into clothes and down the stairs. Trudy just stood there, hands on hips looking menacingly until she broke up laughing. We kissed her as she waved at us to get to the kitchen. Breakfast got microwaved and served on paper plates. Second note to self, don't piss Trudy off. "Where were we, oh yeah, the year was 1976, I had just returned from Florida. I settled here in Baltimore and set up my warehouses. By the way Carl, you and

I should take a visit to the other storage facilities I own. It'll blow your mind if you thought the last warehouse was amazing." I thought why not go now as we had blown off most of the day already and I no longer had a grant to serve. Stephan yelled, "To the bat mobile Robin" and I retorted, "Who said you could be Batman?" we laughed, Stephan pointed to himself and said, "If you're really nice to me, you can drive the Bentley." "To the Bat mobile Batman, now hand over the keys." Stephan threw me the keys and laughed all the way to the car. I have to say, these luxury cars drove much better than my Civic winter rat.

Stephan navigated as I drove, chose the music and generally kept me on my task. We arrived to the new warehouse and what an impression it made. All brick outside with heavy looking ornate oak doors painted bright yellow. The sentry asked me my business and I said, "I'm here with the owner, Stephan Orion." "Please prove it or I can't allow you entrance." (obviously he was new and hadn't been introduced to Stephan). Stephan called him over, produced a license and immediately the guy yelled to the guard, "Let them in", and to Stephan quietly said, "Sorry sir, but I'm new here." "That's okay, actually it's more than okay, what's your name son?" "Eric sir and again my apologies." Stephan scribbled something on a notepad, ripped it off, handed it to Eric. "Take this note to Bobbie, the head guard. You can read it if you want, it's about you anyway." Eric backed away from the car, opened the note carefully and read the contents. Whatever Stephan wrote must have been good because Eric almost skipped to the office. I parked the car, threw 'Batman' the keys and asked when the Robin suit would be ready for pick-up. Stephan looked my way, remembered our earlier conversation and started choking, laughing so hard.

We entered the front door and I was transported to Oz again. I don't think I'll ever get over the amazement I feel when I enter his warehouses. Again, more cars, although newer, were just as expensive and pristine as in the other warehouse. He said he wanted to go to the vault first. We walked to the back of the first floor, Stephan opened the door, and just gestured for me to go in. I think he enjoys the look on my face when I see these things for the first time. Like he's reliving the feeling he had when he acquired them. He had original Warhols, Lichtensteins, Pollocks hanging like garage sale items. If the world only knew. He asked if I liked any of them as he would have the staff pull them for viewing in our home. I pointed out about 3 popular renderings and some classics (I loved the pastoral ones for the bedroom). I asked if we could take a couple statues as well. He nodded and I went to get the staff moving on it before Stephan could change his mind. When I returned, Stephan had re locked the vault, and was motioning for us to climb the back stairs. Floor two was just as entertaining and I saw a fashion show on hangers. Stephan explained they had come from different charity events as auction items and I saw many gowns and suits from the 'Golden Era' of Hollywood. He had some awards sold after the winners' deaths, apparently sold by the next of kin to make money. Stephan confided, "I'll donate these to a museum if I find one I like, or maybe build one if I don't." He then buzzed the intercom and a staff member appeared from nowhere. "We'll be dining on the roof, please order from La Tavola, my usual thanks. And have Eric join us please." The guy disappeared as quickly as he had appeared and Stephan grabbed me, spun me into his arms and planted a juicy one on my lips. He was in his glory and I was there to share it with him. We headed to the roof and took in the view. I could see the entire inner harbor and it was beyond words. Lunch arrived and was set up for the three of us as Eric sheepishly approached us. Stephan calmed his fears, asked if he wanted to join us for lunch (it must have taken him all of 3 nano seconds to agree) and he sat down. "Eric, I'd like to talk to you about a new position. You see, we own a house in Riverside and Trudy, the house manager will be expanding the staff. She will need a security person and I feel you would fit the bill nicely. It comes with a pay bump and a room if you'd like. (did I say Eric was also some nice eye candy). Come to this address tomorrow if you'd like to apply. (again, he nodded like a bobble head). I'll let Trudy know you're coming. Just a note, don't piss her off. EVER." we both laughed but poor Eric didn't take it as a joke. "Yes sirs." We doubled over at that. Lunch was as good as ever, Eric chowed down, and we sent the leftovers down to the troops. When we left, I told the staff to hire a new security guy. The trip home (I still have a hard time saying that, home) was uneventful as 'Batman' drove. I played with the stations until Stephan turned it off. We were 5 minutes from home so I left it alone.

I went to shower and change my clothes as Stephan went in search of Trudy to explain about tomorrow. By the time I reached the kitchen, they were both laughing and I surmised that he had told Trudy about Eric and pissing her off. It made me impatient for tomorrow and his reaction to her. I have to say having another, younger and more handsome guy in the house made me a little nervous but then I remembered about Stephan's words and calmed back down.

Morning came, at last and we waited for the 'victim' to arrive. Just then the doorbell rang and the staff ushered the poor kid in. He was shown to the atrium and was gawking at the house he was to work in. We joined him and called for the now infamous Trudy. She appeared, matronly and careworn with a friendly smile on her face. "Come with me young man as I have some questions for you." He followed like a dead man walking instead of a confident guard. I almost burst out laughing before they left the room. Stephan swatted my behind and said,

"Let's get to work. There's still a couple journals to get to." With that, we went to the den and closed the door. "We didn't finish this journal but I don't think there's much there you want to hear about. Let's get the 1980-1990 journal." Stephan put down the 1970-1980 journal, sitting on it (which meant I was going to read it later). "Hmm, oh yeah, the 1980's started with a new Supreme Court judge, Sandra Dey O'Connor, the first woman on the court appointed by Jimmy Carter. Later that year, I started losing friends to the 'Gay Cancer' or AIDS. Then in December, The world lost John Lennon in an assassination in front of his home, the Dakota. I felt like leaving for Europe again but resisted the urge. I didn't know if any descendants still lived in Europe except Anthony and figured that I could go back sometime later. Later became sooner as Anthony called asking for more funding (he had blown through about $100,000,000 that I had given him to start over). I took an accounting of my available liquid funds, got a cashier's check and flew to Heathrow where my more than eager great great grandson awaited me. "Grandfather, so nice to see you, were you able to bring some money?" I nodded and handed him the check. He looked disappointed but took it and my bags and we got into the rental I procured. "How did you even get to the airport without a car?" "A friend dropped me off." was all he said. He looked terrible for a person. I wondered if he had contracted AIDS but didn't mention it. I later found out it was a drug addiction. He had spent all his money on wasting his gift of a long life. I asked if he still lived at the manor and he said no, he had lost it to taxes. He actually lost it to his addiction. I rented a townhouse nearby London and we went there. Anthony snuck off to deposit the check (I only gave him $1,000,000 this time). Then he must have bought some coke as he sniffled a bit when he came back. I asked to be alone for a few minutes as I had some business to attend to and he was more than eager to continue his snorting. He didn't know I called a Rehab Facility and they said he could be admitted if I could get him there. I rejoined him in the living room and watched as he wiped the residue from his nose. He looked calm and I suggested dinner. He said he was fine but I could eat (the effects of the drug I guessed). After dinner, I asked if he'd like a drive in the countryside and he said sure. I drove him to the Rehab Center. I took him in, he started to balk but I told him it was either this or the funds were over. Saddened, he went with the white coats and I didn't see him again until he got clean. I headed back to the states.

Stephan wiped a tear from the corner of his eye as he finished this entry in the journal. I had him stop reading for a few minutes and sat with him just holding him. No words were spoken nor needed as he continued to process the grief. He said that he knew that Anthony would need more seed money once he got clean to start over. Stephan noted it and went about garnering more disposable income for when the time came. He continued, "Anthony stayed in rehab about 1 year and as I assumed, asked politely if there was a chance he could have a loan to restart his life. I said yes after he apologized numerous times and pledged to behave. I told him to come to Baltimore and see me. (I thought that leaving England would be good for him and it was). He stayed in the area and I gifted him a small amount to invest and he did well. First he bought stock in Microsoft, a young company. Then in 1984 he invested in a start-up company called Macintosh. A couple years later, Apple bought them and marketed their computer worldwide. Needless to say, he became wealthy again. He longed for England and I sent him off a changed man.

1986 wasn't much better around the world. The Space Shuttle Challenger exploded after lift-off killing all seven crew members and later that year, Russia's nuclear reactors in Chernobyl exploded killing thousands over time and leaving that part of the country desolate and deserted. 1988 saw Margaret Thatcher become the longest serving prime minister in England's history. 1989 saw the Berlin wall fall and Berlin was reunited. However, it also saw the Exxon Valdez oil spill leaking out about 10.8 million gallons of oil." Stephan finished the journal and set it down. We went to the kitchen for a bite and saw Eric chatting it up with Trudy. "Well, what you two think?" Trudy looked at Eric, winked and said, "I think I can train this whelp." With that, we toasted to the new security guard and he offered up "I will move here tomorrow if it's alright. All I have at my rental is personal items. About 1 carload, two if you include clothes." We all nodded in unison and I think Eric wanted to kiss us. (I knew how he felt in that moment, having been there once).

The following week we used as a vacation. We left Trudy to handle the house and train Eric. Stephan and I headed back to the camp. We took my Maserati this time and I drove. The drive wasn't long and Stephan kept fondling me to keep me excited. I barely got in the door before Stephan was behind me unbuttoning my shirt. I guess he had needs and wants and desires that needed attention. I gave in. My conversion was complete, I was his man whore and he my love of life. When we finally took a break, Stephan let the staff know that we would be poolside and to bring refreshments and food, lots of food as I was famished. I had drinks in hand as Stephan left the pool. I still couldn't get over this man's looks, statuesque and perfect form. He took a sip, placed the flute on the table and sat down for the meal. I pulled up my chair, teased him until it showed he was interested, then called the staff over to refill my flute. Stephan tried to hide his wares and I did my best to embarrass him but it didn't work. The servant stared at my guy with lust in his eyes. (so much for my revenge tactics). Note to self, stop trying, the only winning move is don't play.

The week zoomed by and we left our playhouse and went back to reality. We got to the gate, Eric was on duty and quipped, "ID please. Are the masters' of the house expecting you?" We laughed at Eric, Stephan said, "It looks like Trudy got you trained." Eric stepped aside, winked at us and let us enter. Our 'family' was growing and soon, the 'grand kids' would be visiting. Trudy was given the day off, and we all partied in the garden with Trudy's kids and grand kids. My life was content and I had everything a man could ask for. Monday arrived too soon (as it always does) and Stephan grabbed the final finished journal. 1990-2000. it seemed Apartheid was abolished in South Africa and Nelson Mandela was released from prison. He was elected president of The country and won the Nobel Peace prize.

The biggest event however came on the 30th of April, 1993. The world wide web became public and access became free to the public. This opened a whole new world for dissemination of knowledge and communication. Websites and then applications starting popping up everywhere. That same year, the USA signed an agreement with Mexico and Canada called NAFTA (North American Free Trade Agreement). It allowed products to be sold between the US and the other two countries without tariffs. The next set of events happened in 1995, Java script was created, windows 95 was released and EBAY was launched. The new world was shaping up in technology. Music was diversifying, Coolio, TLC, Bruce Springsteen, Mariah Carey, and Alanis Morissette took the charts. Brad Pitt was the sexiest man alive (with the exception of my guy). Morgan Freeman starred with Brad Pitt in Se7en. The only scandal being the Monica Lewinsky scandal with then president Clinton in 1998." The only item of note left in the journal was a side note about the scare of 'Y2K'. Stephan closed that journal and looked at me and simply said, "Well, then you came along and here we are." I couldn't believe we had taken a 500 year journey through the annals (no pun intended) of history in the last year and how my life had changed. I still needed to find that darned 1980-1990 journal though. I really wanted to see what he skimmed over but that could wait.

We walked into the kitchen and our constant, Trudy was preparing the newest feast. She was in her full glory, and we were fully enjoying it. We called 'our boy' Eric to dinner and the four of us dined, drank and spent the evening in the living room watching movies and eating popcorn. We were complete. Tomorrow could wait, forever, in my mind. The movie ended, Eric and Trudy went to bed and Stephan and I went to the atrium and sat at the edge of the pool looking up at the stars. Stephan was the first to speak, "Carl, are you happy? I mean the way things turned out, you, me and being here?" I turned to him, looked into those blue eyes and laid my head on his shoulder. "I didn't believe I could be attracted to a man, any man and yet with you, making me feel like this was how it was meant to be. A natural attraction, just two humans falling for each other out of mutual respect and fondness." We stood, held each others hand and walked to our bedroom.

Morning came and over breakfast, Stephan asked if I wanted to start refining the work we finally finished. It made it sound so finite. I nodded and we took our coffee to the den. Trudy had brought all the transcripts, 4000 pages in all, to the den for us. I asked her why she didn't have the staff do it as surely she was too busy and she told me it was too personal for wandering eyes. I agreed and took the first hundred pages to start the arduous process of editing. I called Stephan to my side so he could input his 2 cents. The morning drudged by as we made notes, added and subtracted as needed, and rewrote some passages (Trudy was going to need a secretary). After 4 hours, we took a break and entered the kitchen to find Trudy calling in our grocery order. I yelled over to her, "Don't forget the bologna!" She shushed me and continued although she was laughing a lot. She finished, put down the phone and slapped my hand saying, "Don't do that, I almost lost it." Stephan stepped next to me and asked Trudy to sit. "I know you're duties keep expanding Trudy, do you want to hire a secretary?" Trudy frowned at the suggestion and told him, "I really don't want the staff or anyone else knowing your true age Stephan. You've both been so generous to me and my family that I don't want to jinx it. If this is what you want, I'll see to it but in my opinion, I'd rather go back to secretary rather than let that information leak." I nodded immediately and Stephan pondered the possibilities before continuing. "Dear heart, I know you will need help, I'll leave it up to you to find a new person to assist you in whatever facet you feel necessary. How about a kitchen person and chef and a gofer for you. You'll just manage the heads of the staff." Trudy said she'd get back to me with her needs and called Eric to the kitchen.

We sated ourselves with leftovers from yesterday, grabbed a couple of sodas, and returned to the den. I think we made it through about 200 pages on day one. This was going to take a while. Stephan asked me about taking a real trip and asked if I had a passport. "Do I look like a person who needs a passport?" Stephan laughed, slapped me on the back, and said, "Well, I know what's on the agenda tomorrow. Be ready around 9 am. Robin," Even I had to laugh at that one. We had nicknames for each other, and we were now a real couple (of what I had no idea). I decided I needed a trip to the costume store (can you say cosplay).

At dinner, we told Trudy of our plans, and Stephan asked if she had a passport. "Of course I do, just in case I want to take a cruise. Who doesn't?" They both turned to me, and all I could do was look away as they broke into laughter. "Would you like a trip to England and Italy, on me?" "Consider me packed. Would you like me to have the staff pack for you two?" Stephan pointed to me and said to Trudy, "I'll see if they can expedite the processing for our friend here." Again, raucous laughter, almost cackling. I walked out of the room. Stephan stepped behind me and whispered, "Don't be mad, it's just poking a little fun. You know we didn't intend to hurt your feelings." I tried to look hurt, but I couldn't pull it off and leaned back to smooch my 'Batman'.

We let Stephan make the plans as we had no idea what he had in mind. Eric was to be left in charge of the staff (he had been promoted to chief assistant to Trudy), and he, in turn, hired a new security guard (after Trudy interviewed him). I think Eric wanted to come also, so I told him next time, and told him to get a passport. Life at the hacienda was sailing nicely. Stephan said we would need a new wardrobe for the trip, and I immediately agreed (what did I know about England and Italian fashion) and put that on the agenda also. We started out to the post office, getting my picture taken, and filling out the paperwork. Stephan talked to the postman, and I assume made arrangements for the expedited. Then we headed to our favorite tailor shop. This time, the clerk simply walked to us, told us to follow him to the fitting room, and took Stephan's notes to start pulling clothes. We started with casual and worked our way up to formal. I was the first to try on an outfit and marveled at the fit (note to self: the kid needs to be our personal shopper). I appeared, dapper and with a fresh look, Stephan nodded, and the clerk wrote down the outfit for sale. I was disrobing when I noticed the sizes on the clothes. It was 2 sizes smaller than when I met Stephan. I guess his gastric diet was working wonders on me. I also noticed that I looked younger with my new hairstyle.

Stephan didn't say much as he tried on his clothing, and the clerk was bouncing around like a pinball, getting and taking clothes, appearing and disappearing in the blink of an eye. The shopping done, the clerk totaled up the bill, and Stephan let me peek before paying. The total came to $35,854.26 (probably the clerk's entire year's gross pay). That was the moment Stephan looked at me, and I knew we were hiring another staff member (our personal clothing shopper). He quietly talked to the kid, and he about melted, turned, and put in his 2-week notice on the spot. Our 'family' was growing again. Best to let Trudy and/or Eric know. The clothes were to be delivered the following day, so we left the store empty-handed and went to eat. Stephan wanted something light, and I decided on a salad (now that I looked good). The food was plain, considering what I had become accustomed to (not to mention Trudy's home cooking). We decided to play hooky the rest of the day and headed to the salon. We didn't have an appointment, but somehow they managed to fit us in (with the promise of a hefty tip, no doubt), and we spent the best part of the day with a mani/pedi and trim and reshape. We showed up at the house in time for dinner but were stopped at the gate. The new guard was on duty and didn't recognize us. Eric came running and said for him to let us in. We reminded Eric of his first time at the warehouse, and he calmed down quickly. Another moment of laughter, and we retold his first time to the newbie. That put everyone at ease, and we went to face the Mistress. She 'scolded' her prodigal sons and told us to wash up. She met us in the dining room and discussed her thoughts about staffing.

"I believe I have found a balance of duties and only had to hire 2 more people." "That makes three as we hired a personal clothes shopper this morning." Trudy said, "Well, that brings our staff to an even dozen. If we get more, we'll have to call Henry (the Realtor) and get a bigger place." Stephan was right as usual; my old life was dead (I said a silent prayer for it), and I stepped into my new life. I realized that Stephan had gotten his wanderlust but wanted to share it with us. It took about a week, and the passport arrived in the mail (the postman must have been happy with his fee). The bookings were made, and the day of departure arrived. Trudy barked last-minute orders to the staff, telling them to stay on point as Eric would be checking with her intermittently and reporting any problems. They were told that the den was off limits and made Eric pledge adherence to that rule. He snapped too, received a kiss on the cheek and a wink from Trudy as the limousine showed at the gate. We were whisked to the airport and taken to the lounge until boarding. 4 hours later, we arrived at Heathrow airport and were ushered to another limousine. It took us on a route Stephan remembered, and he asked the driver what the destination was. The driver mentioned that he had been told by Anthony to take us back to his home. I then smiled, as it was my old mansion and estate from 1755. It seemed that Anthony had indeed straightened himself out and reinvested well, allowing him to repurchase his old estate. I was proud of my gg grandson in that moment. We went through the front passage, and the mansion came into view. It seemed that the owners, before and after Anthony made some updates to the old house. The ambiance was the same but with some improvements, modernization without harming the antiquity qualities.

The staff was assembled at the door, and Anthony appeared at the door to welcome us. "Great-grandfather, guests, welcome to my 'humble' abode." Entering the foyer, Trudy and I looked like tourists, and I had the urge to take pictures (but thought better of it). We were taken to our apartments in the east wing, Trudy being followed by her attendant. We freshened up (and other things) before being called to dinner. It was informal, and Anthony doted on us. He was genuinely happy to see his great-great-grandfather, and I was happy for Stephan (this meant that I was a step-great-great-grandfather, holy crap). Dinner ended, we men took our brandy and cigars to the den, and Trudy was taken on a tour of the lush gardens in the back acreage. Upon her return, she explained that we needed a garden like this in Baltimore. I looked at Stephan, and he at me, and we turned to Trudy and said in unison, "Okay, call Henry. Hopefully, he'll have something for us when we get back. Do you think one of the kids will want our old place?" Trudy said, "I'll call them, I think Judy and her husband might want it due to her being pregnant again, if the price is right." Stephan put her mind at ease, "We'll take what they get for theirs." Trudy went to call her daughter with the news.

I got to spend a little time with Anthony and remarked how similar he looked to Stephan. He told me that he had a gallery of original paintings by masters (although they were young and before they were recognized as masters). He bade me follow him to the gallery, and I was astounded; the fashion changed, but he had not. It was a literal walk through history. I pointed, and he described the times and stories behind each. He said he was glad his grandfather had found someone for now (that stung a little). He showed me his painting of himself and his wife, Sarah. Unfortunately, their union did not produce an heir. I told him about our 'family unit'. He said he would talk to Trudy about some trust funds and one for 'our son', Eric. I figured between what he had in mind and what we were setting up for them, the family would be well taken care of. We found Stephan in the library reading a manuscript. Stephan joined us and showed us what he was reading. "This was long before Antonius, I mean Anthony, was born. I'm mentioned here and here." He pointed at the passages, and even Anthony was impressed. I was stunned. It was 1755, and George II was on the throne. I still get chills when I think about his real age, it now being 2006, and he was actually 494 years old. That made me ask what day and month he was born. "Truth be told, I know the year, and I know I wasn't able to walk until late 1513, so probably September or October, something in 1512." Anthony and I decided that since my birthday was October 10th, 1967, Stephan would now have October 10th as his birthday also. That made it easy for me to remember and for him to use. That brought up another question: how did he procure a birth certificate and a birthday to get his passport? "I used my driver's license with a guesstimate on the date; I actually used a date close to yours. It says September 10th, 1893." "Okay, but that wouldn't fly now, you'd be 113 by that date." Stephan laughed and said, "You'd be surprised what wealth can buy. I paid the registrar to change the year, saying the last person mistyped the year, easy peasy." I relented and announced, "Then October 10th it is, which by the way is in a month. Hey Trudy, come here, we have a birthday celebration to plan." Trudy and I left the 'boys' to talk and reminisce, and planned with the staff a proper birthday. I asked to be taken into town soon to shop for the right present (what do you get a man with literally everything?).

The month went by quickly, and the party was upon us. Anthony did the invitation list, and Trudy and I monitored the arrangements. We decided on classical music, violins for me, and chamber music for Stephan. The fare was truly English, which meant hearty and caloric (I needed to watch my figure). The staff decorated the banquet hall, and the band arrived. You would have thought the Queen was coming (maybe she was, you couldn't tell with Stephan and Anthony), as the settings were perfect and expensive. I think the pattern was periwinkle, sedate, and pretty at the same time. The flatware was silver, the glasses were crystal, and I was impressed. The fashion was to be really formal, black tie, and gowns. Anthony was really putting on airs. Stephan helped me dress and stood beside me after we both finished. Looking in the dressing mirror, we looked like the perfect couple, and I couldn't help myself. "Stephan, will you marry me, I mean, if we ever can?" I got down on one knee and presented him with his present, a wedding ring. He swooped me up in his arms and said yes. I placed the ring on his finger, we kissed, and sealed the deal. We had to start over dressing, but made it in time for the music to start. We were announced at the entrance, and people greeted Stephan and me. Trudy was announced, and she entered, in a peach Dior gown, her make-up flawless, looking every part a duchess. We both went to her, kissed her hands, and escorted her to the head table. I wanted her to feel special, and so did Stephan. It seemed that she caught the eye of one of the guests. An older gentleman whom Anthony introduced to us as the Baron (John Stephen Robinson) Martonmere of Blackpool in Lancaster, England. He asked her to dance, and he held her attention for the rest of the night. Stephan and I were introduced to the crowd individually, and it exhausted us. Anthony basically flitted around the room, gossiping, drinking (sparkling water to look good), and dancing with the young ladies, allowing them to swoon, hoping they had a chance to bag this wealthy young man.

The evening came to a close, Trudy was given John's contact information, Anthony took all the numbers of the ladies, and Stephan and I went to rest (or you know). We ended up cuddling, lying together with the fire fading in the hearth, and fell asleep in each other's arms. It was a perfect night. We woke to find a note from Anthony slipped under the door saying he had taken up one lady's offer and would see us later. Trudy met us in the dining room, and we proceeded to have breakfast. She confided that she really liked the Baron and wanted to know if she could invite him to our housewarming party after we moved. "Of course, the more the merrier." We chortled together and prepared for the day. Stephan told us that it was time to get to Italy, and he would talk to Anthony when he returned.

We said our goodbyes later that week and were transported to the airport. Italy came into view, and we landed at the Leonardo Da Vinci – Fiumicino Airport near Rome. It took about 30 minutes to clear customs, but I caught a cab to Calcata and a hotel near where Fausta lived. On the first day, we got a half dozen wreaths and traveled to the Cimiterio to honor the relatives. First was Stephan's parents, then Claudia, Felicia, and Fausta. The last one we placed on Lucius' tomb. The dates shocked me a bit, but we allowed all the time Stephan needed to commune with his kinfolk. He thanked us and then said lunch in a REAL Italian restaurant. He wasn't joking about the food. It came wave after wave, and we tasted about 10 entrees. Most got bagged up for later at the hotel. The rest was distributed among the employees to take home. We returned to the hotel. Stephan said he was going to ask around about the Villa of Papyri. He recounted his conversations with the locals and was told it remained in the Massimo family. That was Felicia's last name. Stephan made plans to find out who was there as he thought the line had died out. Word came back that a young man named Lucius Massimo was in residence. That meant that Aurelius Jr. and Olympia had a son with my recessive genes. Lucius would be his great-great-great-grandson. Stephan remembered bouncing him on his lap. He kept his relationship to his ggggrandson to himself. Stephan said he would go to the villa by himself in case he was mistaken. Stepping up to the door, Stephan requested to see the lord of the manor. Lucius came to the door slightly perturbed until he saw his Ggggrandfather. "Oh my god, is it really you, Grandfather Stephan?" "You were expecting someone else? How about a hug for this old man?" They embraced, and Stephan was taken inside. The manor was as he remembered, except certain things had been modernized. Lucius said, "I was just setting down to dine. Please join me." "With pleasure. You look good for your age, Lucius,

267 if I recall right." "Yeah, but don't tell anyone. They think I'm around thirty-five." It seemed Lucius was a parent as a lovely lady came into the dining room with a child hiding behind her skirt. "Let me introduce you to my wife, Elena, and my son Stephan. Come meet your relative." They approached. Stephan, being shy, stayed back, walked around me, and sat on his father's lap. "This guy was born in 2000, a millennial kid. This is Stephan also, he lives abroad and just returned to Italy." Elena came over, shook my hand, and took her seat next to Lucius.

Stephan invited them to the hotel, but Lucius would have none of it; he said they would have the three of us to dinner on Friday. (that gave them and us 3 days to prepare). Stephan hugged it out with Lucius, bid farewell to Elena, and took his leave. He returned to the hotel, trying to mask his excitement. He doesn't have a poker face. He told us his ggggrandson Lucius lived there with his wife and son. (That makes it a 4x great-grand kid. To those who are counting, that makes 7 generations. We waited cautiously, aware of the partial deception we were about to play. Friday came, and we arrived by limousine. Lucius greeted Trudy and us, and I was introduced as Stephan's traveling companion. We were shown a wonderful time, ate fabulous food, and drank hearty Chianti with fresh-baked bread. I got to tour the villa and was astounded by the wealth of Stephan's entire family. We stayed in Rome a month as Stephan got to know Elena and little Stephan. The time came to go home. I was homesick by then, but Stephan was melancholy about leaving his descendants. I understood and told him he could stay until he felt ready, but he said he needed me (I can't believe he said that, but I welcomed it), and we left. Trudy said her goodbyes, gave Lucius important contact information, and thanked them for their hospitality. We went to the airport and headed home. Jet lag is real, and we 3 travelers arrived home beat and tired. Eric was eager to show how he managed, but Trudy waved him off and simply said, "Tomorrow, Eric, thanks for keeping the place from blowing up." She left him with a smile. I think it was 2 days before we started feeling ourselves again. Trudy was barking orders, and Eric was responding. Life was back to normal. Eric got a bonus for his efforts, and Eddie (the clerk) came to greet us and said he was also the valet for us when we were not out buying things. Trudy really had a handle on everything (okay, so she got another raise).

We finally turned our attention to the papers. I don't even know why I kept this up, as it couldn't be published, but Stephan wanted to tell his story, and I could not refuse him anything. We basically had to start over because I had forgotten where we were. A week went by, and the food actually got better at the house (Trudy must have given the chef a bunch of recipes from Italy). We got up to speed, and the editing got a little easier. Stephan rewrote and added to, and redlined the transcriptions. Trudy was gonna be busy. It was now the end of summer, and we invited the troops to the camp for the weekend. The only people left at home base were the security guards. We arrived with our small entourage and set up for the onslaught. Eric brought the troops to camp by chartering a bus, and 'Camp Getaway' was open for the weekend. Eric became the camp counselor, Trudy was the troop leader, Stephan and I were the hosts. A huge cookout was held, and the chef tossed grillers and hamburgers on the grill. Trudy had the salads and meat trays catered. It went smoothly, and everyone had a great time. We had rented tents and beds for the others. We slept in the camp. Morning brought breakfast on the griddle, coffee, and, for those who wanted, Bloody Marys. I grabbed a Bloody Mary, Stephan a coffee, and Trudy just juice.

It was beach day, and the troops got Stephan and me into a volleyball match. I think I'm too old for this, as I was wheezing after about 15 minutes. Eric was in good form, and Stephan kept up pretty well. Eddie tried besting Eric, and they went at it like warriors. Eric came out on top, and they have had a side bet because Eddie wasn't smiling as they shook hands at the end. (I'd like to know what they bet each other. Later, we found out about the side bet and waited for the performance. In pranced Eddie, dressed in a ballet outfit, too-too and all. He was red-faced but took it like a champ until Eric took pity and said he could go change. Eddie left quickly and swore under his breath about revenge. It seemed Eric had an evil streak but a kind heart. (I had to talk to Eddie about Eric's vulnerability. Yep, I'm evil too.

Henry (the Realtor) showed up, presented some options, and we were taken to about 4 places. Stephan and I reduced it to 2 estates, both with guest houses and 10 bedrooms, 4 baths. We had Trudy, Eric, and Eddie go with us to make the final selection, as we all were living in the house. Trudy liked option 2, Eric liked option 1, and Eddie liked both. I liked option 2, and Stephan didn't care which but chose option 2 (for me, I think, as he wanted me happy). Henry drew up the papers, and Trudy and Eric got busy planning the packing and moving. This was a lot for me, so Stephan proposed staying at camp until it was finished. I thanked him but said I'd like to help (especially packing the transcripts and tapes). I wanted to guard Stephan's secrets, and Trudy agreed with me. So it began.

The new place was about twice the size of the old place, and the price was amazingly low. (The owner's kids wanted to dump it after their father died. Stephan offered cash as a motivator, and the sellers bit. I took the den as my room to pack, as the other rooms got assigned. Stephan agreed to station himself at the new place to arrange our stuff as it arrived. This allowed me time to hunt down Stephan's journal 1980-1990 (it had to be in there somewhere, and no, I hadn't forgotten about it). I had to pack nearly the entire den before it surfaced; he didn't want me reading it. I put it away with my box of things and had the movers remove the box. Trudy and the chef took the kitchen, and the staff handled the rest. It took about 3 weeks to effect the move. It took another 4 weeks for us to decide on the new places to place the accent pieces. We finally settled down into the new routine, and Stephan and I christened the house "Chateau Orion-Omega." I know it was cheesy, but what the hell.

Stephan left me alone in the chateau to conduct some business and went straight to the box to do some reading, but the box was empty. I asked Eddie about unpacking, and he said Stephan had taken care of that. So he knew about my little indiscretion. I wondered how long he'd take to mention it, and I was a little afraid of the conversation. I tried to act nonchalant, but it weighed on me like an anchor. Stephan returned, asked me to come upstairs, and led me to our room (the scene of the crime). We sat on the bed, and he popped the fatal question, "Why did you take my journal? Please be honest." I started to speak, broke into tears, and sobbed while I replied, "Stephan, I'm sorry, but I really wanted to find out about those undisclosed years. I'm sorry, truly sorry (and I started crying again)." "Thanks for being honest. I knew you'd be upset if you found out, and I wanted to spare you that. You see, there was another woman that I loved before I knew you, and the romance lasted about 9 years before she died from AIDS." He asked if I still wanted to read it and produced the journal from his nightstand. He tried to hand it to me, but I pushed his hand away and tried to conceal my disgust at myself (I should have known better, as Stephan was never anything but loving to me). Stephan replaced the journal in the nightstand and reached out to comfort me. I shrunk into his arms and wept quietly. We spent a while until Stephan got up, suggested that I freshen up, and left me alone with my thoughts. I didn't know if it was a test or not, but I wasn't going to fail this one. I rose, disrobed, headed to the shower, and started spraying myself down. It took a bit to cleanse myself of my sins, but I felt better after I finished. Eddie laid out clothes for the evening, and I hurried as Trudy yelled up about dinner.

Stephan never mentioned the incident again (and I was glad). As I entered the dining room, Stephan was just finishing a call. "We will be expecting visitors next month. Lucius, Elena, and little Stephan will arrive on the 5th. I think I'll call Anthony to see if he can make it. It will be good to get us all together around Thanksgiving." Trudy then asked about our other 'family'. "I think that would be great, let's do it up." Eric was going to be with his fiancée's family, but Eddie couldn't wait. Our Eric was growing up, but we still had our little Eddie, as our family kept evolving. The chef was put on notice (actually, he couldn't wait to show off his skills), and the house became a situation room. Stephan and Trudy wanted everything perfect, and I do mean perfect. The poor staff were jumping and running in all directions to get things ready.

Trudy had invitations printed, and Eric set up transportation from the airport for our guests. Lucius and family flew in on the 5th as expected, and Anthony the next day. Introductions and revelry started, and we made like tour guides for the next few weeks. Shopping (of course) was Eddie's department (which he relished), and Trudy loved baking with the chef for her grandkids and Little Stephan. He loved playing with them, and they loved him. I stayed in the background watching my love and his reactions to his family. The sure pleasure and simple joy was what I would never have, but it was enough to see Stephan so happy.

Thanksgiving was in a few days, Little Stephan became comfortable with his 'uncle,' and Stephan held his 4x great-grandson. Stephan ordered a portrait for Lucius and the family. Anthony reminded Stephan that portraits were photographic now, but Stephan got his way, and the family sat for placement and photos. That way, the artist could leave and paint in his studio. The portrait would be their Christmas present.

Thanksgiving day arrived, and the house filled with people, kids, adults, staff, and a few friends, about 30 in all. The chef prepared a feast to be remembered, the wine (and sparkling cider for the kids) poured freely, and the dessert table brought cheers from the youngsters. All in all, it was the most grand affair I had been to. Exhaustion set in (I think it was the tryptophan), and folks dropped like flies. The staff was given the night off to recuperate, the family waved goodbye to the guests, and when our 'family' was left, we collapsed in a heap, sated but tired. The morning after (and it was in all respects), I found Lucius talking to Eric as we descended the stairs. Lucius greeted us and let us know that he and the family would be leaving for home on Saturday. Eric left to make the arrangements. Stephan and I made the most of the time with Anthony and Lucius until departure time. Stephan asked, "Do you want us to see you off?" to which Lucius and Anthony said no. The limousine arrived, got loaded, goodbyes given, and hugs all around (I even got one from little Stephan). We stood in the driveway as they disappeared from sight. Stephan turned, wiped a tear from his eye, and went into the house.

I followed as he continued up the stairs. I caught up to him as we entered the bedroom. I closed the door, paging Eddie to say please do not disturb for a while. It was my turn to comfort him. He went to the nightstand, withdrew the journal, opened it to the halfway point, and started reading softly, "I met a young director today. He said his name was John Waters. He was hawking some scripts for a new movie he wanted to make called 'Pink Flamingos'. I had heard it was a B-movie, but I liked his avant-garde style, so I invested. He invited me to the set during the filming and introduced me to the cast. Among them was an actress named Cookie Mueller. The star was a 'woman' named Divine. I became friends with him/her. I started dating Cookie, and we fell for one another. We dated, but she wanted to pursue her career, so we didn't marry. Later, she married and then died. She is the one who died from AIDS in November 1989." I said nothing, held Stephan, and set his journal down on the bed. He looked at me, and I could see the pain in his eyes (I never wanted to see him like this again). I put him under the covers and said I'd return to get him up for dinner and left.

The next few years went by quickly as we worked on the manuscript. Eric married his fiancée and left the house, but stayed in our employ (the money was too good, and we did buy him a house for his wedding present). Eddie was dating a cute guy, but I don't think it was serious. Trudy finished the corrections and edits, and Stephan was ready to present it in its entirety. We traveled more and let Trudy manage the camp (after all, she had lots of her brood and they needed a 'camp getaway'). Stephan wanted me to see his actual homeland, so he booked us a trip to Akkadian, Greece. His Greek was rusty, but he quickly adjusted. We toured the region, and I was surprised when he showed me the now ruins that were his ancestral home. "Here is really where my story begins. The Orion name was formalized in the 1300's. We adopted it as we were already using the moniker since 500 AD. The name means 'heaven's light'. My name means 'crown of heaven's light,' and that always makes me think of the love my mother had for me. We even have a family shield." He pulled it up on his phone, and it was impressive. The food took some getting used to, but I found I liked most of it. The ouzo took about 3 seconds to enjoy. The view (young men) was intriguing, and the beach plentiful. I stared a bit, and Stephan said, "Go ahead and leer, I am." We started laughing and went to eat. The month went by casually with shopping (I wish Eddie were here to assist), dining, and touring. We headed home after having some of the items shipped. I think we arrived home just in time because Trudy wasn't looking good. She said she was alright, but I called the doctor. He treated her, made her comfortable, then nodded for us to follow him out. He said she was exhausted and needed rest. He also said she needed a physical because he thought there might be something else causing her fatigue.

Stephan set the appointment and went to see if she needed anything. He called Eric to arrange an attendant for her and to let her rest. Upon entering, Stephan saw Trudy in the light, and she looked old and a little ashen. She was sleeping, so he left and went to call the kids to inform them of their mother's condition. Her daughter, Judy, came right over. I forewarned her about her mother, and she left me and went upstairs. When Judy returned, I saw her face and explained my strategy going forward, which seemed to calm her down. "I intend to elevate your mother to the position of head of household, so she needs only to coordinate the staff responsibilities. Eric will do the day-to-day responsibilities, and Eddie will get us someone good to attend to your mother from now on. We love her almost as much as you do, and if you'd like, you can assist Eddie with the decision." Judy asked, "What if that person is me? I could do it, and who knows her better?" "Only if you'll accept a stipend to do it. I couldn't be happier if you did." Stephan and Judy came to an arrangement on salary, and she agreed to start the next day.

I had Eric get another key to the house for Judy so she could come and go as she needed. Eric returned with the key and then asked Stephan and me to join him in the atrium. We sat steeling ourselves for bad news, but Eric excitedly blurted, "We're pregnant. Nancy is 3 months along." We breathed a sigh of relief and asked the staff to bring champagne. Judy came in as we were toasting and asked, "What's the occasion?" "Eric and his wife Nancy are expecting." Judy hugged Eric and left to tend to her mother. Stephan slapped him on the back and said, "I guess this means more responsibility in your household, and then you'll need a pay raise." Eric, as always, looked at his shoes as though he was going to bring it up and squeaked, "I was kind of hoping..." Stephan said, "How's $10,000 a year more sound?" Eric beamed and left to make a phone call (I assume to Nancy to let her know of his 'negotiating skills').

Stephan called his accountant to set up the raise in pay and also a college fund for baby Eric. I went upstairs to check on Trudy and found her on the balcony with Judy, taking in the afternoon sun. I bent over, kissed her cheek, and asked how she was feeling. "I'm okay. I don't know why you asked Judy to care for me. I'm fine." I told her that the doctor had ordered rest, and by God, she was going to do it. "Eric has everything in hand and, if needed, can ask you about the particulars. Now rest and don't give Judy any grief." She blew me a kiss, and I left. Judy met me downstairs a little later and explained that the doctor told her that Trudy indeed had more wrong. She had the beginning stages of Parkinson's disease. It wasn't bad yet, but it would get worse over time. How long, he didn't say. I told her that we would just have to make plans for long-term care for her mom. You could see her stress level ease at that statement, as she was wondering how the siblings were going to handle their mother if we terminated her employment. "Trudy has been our 'mother' too, and since we have the funding, we'll handle the finances. And we wouldn't think of making her leave our house. This is her house, too." Judy ran over, hugged me, and whispered a simple, "Thank you, Carl."

Stephan returned from his call, told me everything was set for Eric, and I told him about Trudy. I couldn't even get out what I told Judy as he said, "We've got to tell Judy and the others that we'll handle everything. I don't want them worrying about Trudy." I told him that I said the same thing to Judy. "That's my boy," Stephan said, and he kissed me before finding Eric to inform him about his 'new' position and how many more staff to employ. I told Stephan about asking Judy to assist in the interviews, and he agreed. Our 'family' was morphing again, and I started realizing how much Stephan must have had to adapt over the centuries. I felt more compassion for my lover.

The months flew by, and Nancy presented Eric with a bouncing baby boy. They named him Nathan after Eric's father. Trudy had relinquished her duties and became the 'house mother', Judy and her kids were always around, Eddie was in love again (For sure this time, lol). Stephan finished his tweaking of the manuscript. I read the final draft, agreed it was good to go, and he actually sent it to the editor of his old publishing company. I believed that it would come back as too fantastical, but Stephan received an advance book and a huge down payment check for his original 'fiction'. We agreed to a shopping trip and another trip to 'our' beloved Italy by way of England. This time we invited Eddie and sent in for his passport. It came just in time as we were leaving the following week, and he had just lost his 'true love'.

Eddie went with us to shop (yes, we bought some clothes for Eddie too), and he had a field day. I won't bother to tell you the cost, but my car cost less than this spending spree. We even had enough for lunch (no, we didn't eat bologna sandwiches). I thought I was going to die laughing when Stephan asked Eddie to drive after lunch. He drove the Bentley like a little old lady; he was so afraid of an accident. We let Eddie take care of the deliveries, and he didn't disappoint. We packed, left the house with Eric and Judy in charge, and headed to the airport. We arrived at Heathrow and went to the hotel in London. Stephan called Anthony and said we were in London and to join us. He made arrangements, and we all had lunch (the food hadn't gotten better). He invited us back to the house, and we accepted. Poor Eddie had stars in his eyes when he saw Anthony. Anthony was warned not to string Eddie along, as he was on the rebound from his latest romance. He flashed his pearly whites at Eddie, and he fell like a rock. Well, we tried. We spent the next few days around the estate, walking in the gardens, and Stephan mentioned the differences from his original design. Anthony let his new 'toyboy' Eddie feel like aristocracy by sharing his fancy wardrobe (that he kept from the last 400 years), and Eddie was flying high. I was sad thinking about when the time came to leave and how Eddie would take it. But, in the meantime, we let him have his fun. About a week later, we went to visit the Baron that Trudy had a shine for. He welcomed our visit, and Stephan clued him in to Trudy's condition. We assured him that all was taken care of, and John Stephen (the baron) asked if he should and/or could visit her. Again, we assured him that all that was possible and he would be more than welcome, and it might boost her spirits. Stephan encouraged John to call her directly and ask her permission (to make her think it was with her blessing). He asked us to join him for lunch, and we did. The afternoon whizzed by. We returned to the estate for dinner and were surprised when the 'dynamic duo' showed up in Edwardian garb. "You two look amazing for 1910. Hey

Carl, do you want to join them? We can suit you up in about 10 minutes." I shook my head and said, "I'll pass; they look fancy enough for us all."

Laughter rang out, we toasted our 'fancy pants kids' and went into dinner. I think Anthony and Eddie schemed with the chef, and we were served French cuisine, a much better menu. Another week passed, and Stephan mentioned the dreaded end to our visit as we wanted to get to Italy. Eddie frowned until Anthony agreed to join us. At least the shoe dropping could be delayed. They trotted off to Anthony's private wing of the mansion (to 'freshen up' and pack – whatever that entailed), and we prepared for the trip. Stephan is making add-on reservations for Anthony (I almost forgot about worrying if we had enough money for one extra). I sat and reflected on who I was now, so different from the man that Stephan met. Our (or should I say my) journey into the environment of the wealthy and worldly, where nothing or nowhere was above our ability to procure or travel. Uber wealth beyond imagination, quiet and private but pervasive. Stephan 'woke' me from my private thoughts, got me back in the game as Eddie (flushed-faced and walking as if he'd just dismounted a long day of riding) asked if we wanted him to pack now. We nodded and barely let him leave the room before looking at one another and falling down laughing. Onward to Italy and our usual haunts. Of course, we contacted Lucius, and he met us at the airport. Little Stephan saw us first and leaped into his 4x great-grandfather's arms. Lucius came over, shook my hand, and led us to the waiting limousine. We reached the Villa of Papyri, and Elena came to the door waving as we arrived. Little Stephan took Stephan's hand and literally pulled him from the car. It seemed he had an urgent need to show his grandfather something important. It turned out to be a tree he planted in the back yard with the assistance of his parents. It was an olive tree, and it was actually a mature tree that could produce fruit within the year. We finally got into the house after everyone oohed and aahed at 'his' accomplishment. Eddie and Anthony took the bags and instructed the staff as to where the others went. I think they wanted to unpack their own bags because of the contents within.

Being late, the nanny put Little Stephan to bed, and we adults made reservations at a restaurant close by. We rented out the restaurant for privacy and bribed the staff to stay very late for us, and they were happy to do it (I believe that between Anthony, Lucius, and Stephan, the tip was about 200% of the bill). The next day was planned out with our usual trip to the Cimitero. The solemnity of the day was not lost on Little Stephan, and he asked a hundred questions, and Stephan fielded them all until Little Stephan was finally satiated and went looking at the other tombstones. The rest of the day was spent at the beach, and we all had a relaxed day. Little Stephan fell asleep in the car for the return ride, and Lucius carried the sleeping beauty into the house and to bed. Everyone went to their respective bedrooms, and the house fell silent. My beloved Italy had changed somewhat, but the charm never faded. Our time with Lucius and family went by too quickly, and we found ourselves getting ready to leave. Eddie was at a crossroads about love and loyalty. We left it up to him to decide, and he chose Anthony. Stephan and I wished them well, told Eddie we would forward his personal items, and headed to the airport. Stephan and I were discussing our options about hiring another valet/shopper and decided that we would wait six months in case the novelty wore off, and Eddie wanted to come home.

Home sweet home, and Eric sent a car for us. Customs was a drag, but we navigated it like champs, and soon the car was pulling into our driveway. Judy and Eric met us, exchanged greetings, and then asked about Eddie. We informed them that he had found love in England and decided to stay. Eric just nodded and said, "Anthony got him, didn't he?"

"Yep" was all that needed to be said. Eric asked about a new staff member, and we told him to wait. He shrugged and had the staff bring in the bags. We took Judy aside and asked about our dear Trudy. Just then, Trudy came around the corner and announced, "See for yourselves, boys." We raced to her and hugged her tight. Kisses to and from her and tears all around. She had settled nicely into her new role in the house (and having a letter from John Stephen didn't hurt). She mentioned him in the next sentence, "Oh, by the way, I hope it's alright if I happen to invite a guest for a few days." Stephan and I played dumb and asked, "Do you mind letting us know in case your mystery guest has special needs." Trudy blushed a bright red and whispered to us, "It's John. You know the baron we met at Anthony's house." Stephan held it together for another few seconds until Trudy caught our side glance to one another. "You guys talked to him, didn't you?" I replied, "Actually, Anthony invited him over for dinner, and he asked if he could, and we just said yes (did you think we'd say no to Trudy's man). She tousled our hair and said to go get freshened up. The jet lag took the wind out of our sails, so we just showered and dressed for dinner. Trudy must have had the chef practicing for us before we returned because dinner was perfection, and the wine had to be imported from Calcata, Italy (God, I sound like a snob; the money was getting to me). We prepped for our titled guest (was a baron above or below a Lord in the ranking, I wondered). Note to self, Google title ranking. John arrived, and we sent our limousine to fetch him. We even went as far as to have a placard made up to wait for him to clear customs. He arrived about an hour later to a formal greeting from the household, Trudy, Eric, and staff, and us in the entrance way. He went to Trudy, kissed her hand, asked her how she was doing, and she just planted a big smacker of a kiss on his cheek. "That should let you know how I feel." He blushed, and they entered arm in arm. We followed the others and closed the door. He was taken to his room, and the staff brought up his things. Judy stated that she would be five minutes away if needed, and we saw her off. "Sure wish Eddie was here to unpack for us", Stephan said, and I had to stop myself from agreeing (I was getting too used to this lifestyle). We unpacked for about an hour, then got a little frisky and started throwing clothes back and forth. We were called to dinner, and the room was a mess (oh well, add it to the agenda for later), so we dressed in our closet clothes and left the room (hoping a clothes fairy would notice and pick up). The dining hall seemed abuzz with activity, and Trudy was giving last-minute instructions to the staff. We entered without fanfare, but when John appeared, Eric announced him by title, "Announcing Baron John Stephen Robinson Martonmere of Blackpool in Lancaster, England. We all rose, nodded in his direction, and he strolled to his seat near Trudy. After the appetizer was served, John rose from his chair and proposed a toast, "To friends new and old, may your troubles be few and your joys plenty, cheers." We toasted, but I noticed that Trudy was shaking a little while holding her flute. I think I was the only one who noticed, but I made a mental note to myself to talk to Judy the next day. The meal was flawless, and we called in the chef to acknowledge him. Eric mentioned for us to retire to the den for brandy and cigars. John asked Trudy for permission, and she waved him on, "Go, I know you'll be around later." She winked and smiled her devilish smile. "We won't keep him long, promise." We headed to the den, where John told us he saw the shaking and asked how to handle it. "Just keep it in mind when you're with her so as not to put her in a noticeable predicament." "Gotcha, don't worry." said John as he finished his brandy and waved goodnight. We stayed behind to relax in front of the fire. Two hours later, as the embers died down, we remembered the mess in our bedroom and dreaded the effort to clean it up. I entered the room first and saw a clean picked up room (thank you, fairy godmother), and Stephan followed. He didn't bother with any thanks but took it for granted. Note to self, never take things for granted. Sleep came easily, and I personally wondered where John slept. Morning would tell. We got up early, took a joint shower, dressed for the day, and went to the kitchen for a light breakfast. The two love birds were already there, and she was feeding him a bagel with lox and cream cheese. We got a cup of coffee, had the breakfast sent to the patio, and left the folks to their moment. I set my coffee on the table as the food arrived, and Stephan started giggling at the 'old folks' canoodling in front of us. I started giggling also, and it took a few minutes before we started eating. Eric showed up with a young man and asked if we had time to talk to him. "What's this about?" asked Stephan. Eric said, "I thought maybe you could use a temporary guy to take Eddie's place for six months. That way, if Eddie stays in England, he will be trained to take over, and if Eddie comes home, then he gets a good reference from you for his next assignment (which we know as somewhere in our 'family' employ). "What's your name?" to which he replied, "Devon, sir." "Best let Trudy know and be ready, Devon, she's a tough interviewer." He looked shocked, and we had a hard time keeping a straight face. Eric took him away, Stephan felt good, and I silently thanked Eric for doing this, as I hated housework (even just taking care of clothes). I believed that Eddie would return, but Stephan noted that Eddie and Anthony were good for each other, and I couldn't disagree. So our family was morphing again. The next thing I knew, thirteen more years had gone by, and Eric's son Nathan was now a teenager, having turned 13. Trudy was doing well on her medication, Judy was still stopping by, Devon was proving indispensable, and John Stephen kept visiting on a more regular basis (we told him to come any time he wanted and that the door was always open for him). Stephan's book made the fiction best-sellers list. I retired from the college, and Stephan kept me in his business affairs in case something happened. The year was now 2019, and Christmas was upon us.

John was coming in, Eddie and Anthony were due any day, Judy and the siblings and their families were coming for the day, so the house would be full. Devon was sent to shop for new clothes for us, and we gave him a budget to get some attire for himself (Stephan set a limit of – drum roll, $10,000 for Devon). I let him drive my new Maserati as we were driving our new Bentley.

What I didn't know was that Stephan had given Devon specific instructions on what to buy for us. The house was abuzz with activity. Eric, Trudy, and the chef led the charge, and the poor staff (who were gonna expect a large bonus this year) went off like firecrackers in all directions, taking care of preparations. This year saw a deviation from the regular decorations. This year's theme was a white Christmas. We managed to fit everyone in the 10 bedrooms we had available, doubling up where possible. Christmas Eve found us all in the atrium, and Stephan clinked his toasting flute, announcing that tomorrow, after breakfast and presents (for the kids and staff), he had a surprise for everyone. That drew a round of applause from our guests. Even the Baron made it in time for the festivities. Evening was abbreviated, and we each went to our repose, Stephan and I to our room, Trudy and the Baron to their suite (yes, we had an apartment suite made for his visits), Anthony and Eddie went to their en suite, and the others to their assigned bedrooms. Breakfast was rather light (I think the kids just wanted to attack the gifts under the tree), and the staff were called singly by name to be rewarded for their service to the house. Then came the time for Stephan's surprise. He led everyone outside to the garden, where chairs, an aisle strewn with flowers, and an arch were erected. Stephan repeated his words to me, "Carl, will you marry me on this day, December 25, 2019?" Of course, I repeated yes. Everyone took their seats, the minister stepped up to the arch, Trudy stepped forward, grasped both our hands, and led us down the aisle (I think Trudy was in on it), and Eric appeared on Stephan's side as his best man (they were all in on it). We met the pastor under the arch, and the ceremony began. Stephan had a speech written, and I spoke from the heart. "You may now kiss the groom," was announced, and the group applauded us as we turned to greet our assembly. Poor Eddie was in tears with utter pride and emotion. Even the staunch Trudy wiped a tear from her eye.

Back to the atrium, where the staff had it changed into a reception area (these folks were good). The band was seated and started playing the classical music Stephan so loved. He whispered to me, "They're playing from the original musical sheets." I whispered back, "If they only knew." A cake appeared from the kitchen and was set in the corner, 4 tiers, simple yet masculine, with the marble articulated human form that he had taken from the vault. We were ushered to the dance floor, the music started, Stephan took the lead (and I was glad), and we spun around in grand fashion. I couldn't have asked for a better day. The guests presented us with wedding gifts (I'm starting to think I was the only one not aware of the event), which we set aside until later. Then the chamber group left the area, and another band took the stage. Current music rang out, and the troops came to the floor to 'boogie down'. I took a second to whisper to Stephan, "You rascal, you planned the whole thing." He laughed and said, "I had a lot of help." The day ended as it had begun, joyful, and everyone turned in. Stephan had our wedding night wardrobe set out for us, and it was white. Risque, sexy, and almost transparent, but white. I went to the bathroom to change, and when I returned, my 'Batman" was sprawled out on our bed, ready for consumption. I tried to act shy and coy, but that only lasted about 2 seconds. I jumped onto the bed, and Stephan pretty much ripped the clothes from my body (that's about $5000 worth of clothes destroyed), and I let him have his way with me. I could have died completely. Morning found us very tired until we heard that familiar voice, "Get down here before I give your breakfast to the dog." It's amazing how motivated you can get if you're hungry. We hit the stairs 4 minutes later. "Good thing, I was about to have Eric go adopt a dog." It took a kiss on the cheek to turn Trudy's frown into a smile.

We said our goodbyes to the guests, and we noticed Eddie sporting a new piece of jewelry. "Oh yeah, by the way, Anthony surprised me with an engagement ring this morning. I'll be sure to get your invitations ready soon enough for you to plan on attending." We hugged it out, and they took their leave. The Baron was the last to leave, and Trudy escorted him to the airport. Devon asked what we wanted to do with our scraps of clothing, and we just told him to dispose of them. He turned with the heap of scraps and left us. I got a weird feeling and asked Eric to do me a favor. A simple request, but my 'spidey senses' were tingling, and it made me feel ill at ease. Eric told me not to worry, he'd find out for me. I let it drop. I didn't want to bother anyone if I was wrong.

Stephan started work on another 'fiction'; he had been put under contract for one more 'fiction' as the last one had been so successful. Yes, he wrote it under the name Noiro. I couldn't believe the millions he made from his story, but I was glad to be his ghost writer. We decided to donate the proceeds of this new book to Trudy's heirs, Judy and her 2 brothers and their kids (don't worry, we already took care of Eric and family, Eddie and the others). We were dropping cash like crazy, and I made mention that Stephan might have to sell a painting or 2. He laughed and asked, "As Ephraim Levi would say, what good was money if it didn't get spread around, encouraging young things to grow." I laughed it off. Eric came into the den, asked me to join him as he needed my help, and we left Stephan to work.

"I think I have some news for you. Did you send Devon into the den for something? I've seen him in there alone a few times." "No, you of all people know it's out of bounds for the staff. Only Trudy, Stephan, and I are allowed." "That's what I thought, then your suspicions are right. What do you want me to do? Nothing right now. When does he usually go?" "Around 10 pm, after everyone else is in bed, my staff keep track of those records." "Thanks, Eric, I'll take it from here." "Okay, just give me the word, and I'll take care of that little creep." I left with a knot in my stomach. We had vetted so many good employees; this one bad apple made no sense. I went and talked to Stephan, and he, in turn, hired a private eye to find out what Devon was up to. We started locking the den after that.

It wasn't long in coming as we found out he was trying to sell a couple of original music sheets to collectors. We worked to set up a sting on the kid, and it worked in spades. He had a bidding war on the dark web and hadn't sold anything yet. He had stolen about 4 sheets and wanted to sell them together, an amateur mistake. He also wanted to sell locally, another mistake. We bid through a shell corporation, Noiro Inc. He bit, and we set up the time and place. He actually showed with the sheets in his possession (another amateur mistake; the kid was pathetic). We took possession, fired him on the spot, and informed Eric to allow him just his personal possessions at a time and place to be determined. Devon cried and said he had gotten in deep with a gambling debt and needed quick cash to stay in good graces (meaning beat up if he didn't come across with the money). Stephan took a little pity and asked how much he needed. "He wants $5000 by Tuesday, or he'll wreck me." Give me the information, and I'll see what can be done. I wish you had come to me first; we could have avoided this unpleasantness." With that, Devon gave Stephan all the information and, with his head down, left, walking slowly and looking back, hoping Stephan would cave, but he didn't.

I asked Stephan what he had in mind, and Stephan said, "Carl, this isn't my first rodeo; I've been here many times before. You do remember my exploits with the king of France and the Pope. I played diplomat, friend, and gossip. I also played them against each other when needed. Leave it to me." I felt bad for the kid, but I was worried for Stephan. "Can Eric and the guards back you up at least?" "I told you, sometimes it takes one to know one, and I find dealing one on one is usually better." ok, but at least take Eric, pretty please, dear." "Ok, ok, worry wart." We went home and requested that Eric join us. "Eric, 'Robin' here, wants me to have backup, and he'd like you to do it. Are you up for it? It's up to you." Eric nodded and said his job had become a cake walk, and he'd welcome some action. "Ok, Carl, satisfied?" "Yes, dear," and I sidled up close and kissed his cheek.

The time and day were agreed to, and the boys left under the pretense of checking out a warehouse.

I have to admit I held my breath until they came back. When I laid eyes on them, unscathed, my breath returned and rushed up to Stephan. "Tell me everything." "Let's go to the den, and I'll tell you. I'd like you to tape it for later, as I'd like to use it in my book, it's that good." We walked to the den, asked Trudy to join us, and unlocked the door. Stephan noticed that her Parkinson's was getting worse and made a mental note to have that attended to (by now she was 64, as she told us she was born in 1955). I started by setting up the tape, and Trudy and Stephan took the seats near me.

"Let me start when Eric and I got there. The place was neutral, as I demanded, the mysterious 'guy he owed money to' man appeared, and we stepped up to him. He had a couple of goons with him, but they stayed back as did Eric, and we sat to discuss terms. I told him I would 'buy' Devon's debt, but that he had to end it there. He agreed, and I asked the price without interest. He said $3500, but with interest, it was now $5000. I told him I wouldn't pay that interest but would offer to make him whole with a little more. 'How about $4000 cash and we shake on it.' 'Deal, and I laid the envelope on the table, let him count it, and got up to leave. He made the mistake of grabbing my arm to ask who I was. I waved Eric back and just said, 'A nightmare if you don't just go'. He released me, waved for his guys, and they left out the back door. Eric came to me and asked if I was alright. 'It seems my bluster is still up to par. I don't know what I would have done if it didn't work.' 'That's what I came for, boss man.' Let's go, but take another route home in case we're followed.' Eric led the way to the car, looked around, noticed a man in a running car, and said, "One moment, boss." He went over, knocked on the window, and the guy in the car, one of the goons from earlier, rolled down the window. As soon as Eric saw his face, he cold-cocked him into unconsciousness. Took the keys, flung them, and returned to me. "That felt good, boss, thanks for bringing me."

"We did take the scenic route, but those guys were local talent. So much for my eventful night." Trudy said she aged a decade just listening, and I looked pale. We all took a stiff shot of brandy, and Trudy left us for the evening. We talked more, but Stephan assured me it was over.

Now to get another valet. "Just sick Trudy on them from now on." We talked about a scooter for Trudy (when the time came) and decided to ask Judy to assume most of her mother's duties (yes, with a pay raise. Get ready to sell a couple of cars, also, Stephan. Lol). We went to bed, and I hailed my conquering hero.

2020 arrived without fanfare until we heard about the pandemic from China, and it was spreading to Europe. We sent word to our friends and family, and they said they were fine (I hope they find a cure). They called it cov-id 19 after the year they found it. We locked down the estate and told the staff to stay home on pay. Eric was told to stay home with the family, and we only allowed Judy in to help with Trudy. Many wanted to stay, but we insisted for their safety, and they finally agreed. With everyone gone and Trudy incapacitated, we had to rely on ourselves and Judy for meals. Needless to say, we ate a lot of sandwiches and simplified meals. I suggested my famous bologna sandwiches, and Stephan said he'd rather chew the leather chairs first. By June, they kind of had it figured out, and Andrew Cuomo led that charge (I was glad someone took the lead, since the federal government was sadly lacking in that department). I mean, bleach injected or a black light up the ass, hydrocloriquine or horse medicine, really, quacks were coming out of the woodwork. We were fine, and the reports coming in from abroad were encouraging from the family and friends. We as a unit had made it until 2021, and the vaccine became available. Some said they didn't need it or want it, and Stephan and I begged for them to get it. They all acquiesced and got it, albeit begrudgingly. Things started getting back to the new normal, and we gave a collective sigh of relief. John Stephen was cringing while he waited for clearance to travel and get back to his dear Trudy. Anthony let us know that Eddie had indeed contracted the dreaded disease. Fortunately, he had no secondary issues, so he recovered after about 3 weeks (it was touch-and-go for the first week, though).

We finally heard from Lucius, and with God's blessing, they avoided the scourge that happened in Italy. They wouldn't be able to travel for a while, but we were still thankful they avoided the plague that took so many from their loved ones. Eric got around to finding us a suitable replacement for Devon. The kid who had taken Eddie's place at the clothier. We decided to take a shopping trip to test him out before we sent him to Trudy, the inquisitor. The Bentley parked near the door of the shop, and we hopped out. We entered the store, and he stepped over to us (Stephan and I both gasped at his beauty, black curly hair, 6 ft 4, 210 lbs of muscle, robin's egg blue eyes, that rivaled Stephan's, and clothes tailored to his body like a second skin). As we both undressed him with our eyes, he inquired as to our needs. We said we'd like a new wardrobe, and he (unaware of who we were) simply took us to the back of the store as though we were special. Impressed, he asked what we wanted to start with so he could start pulling pieces. "From undergarments to formal wear and everything in between." He turned, not asking our sizes but just a simple scan of our torsos, and left. Before we had fully disrobed, he was back with what he assumed we'd like. I will say my taste is all in my mouth, but he hit it out of the park with his choices. Stephan asked for assistance with his boxer briefs (I assumed to make me jealous, and it worked) and then sent him over to me and let him adjust me also. The clothing fit as though he were tailoring the clothes before bringing them in. We casually brought up topics such as his interests, hobbies, and the like, and he gladly answered without hesitation.

We spent the better part of the afternoon there, and when the last of the clothing was set aside, we asked him if he knew us. "I'm sorry, but no" was his answer. We thanked him for his time, asked if he could arrange to bring the parcels to our home, and he said he would attend to it personally (this guy was a dream doll and professional at the same time). We gave him the address and told him to bring it after his shift. He arrived on time, assisted the staff with bringing in the bags, and we called him to the atrium. We called Trudy to join us, and we asked the newbie to sit. "Thank you for the assistance you provided today. We'd like to hire you as our personal shopper and valet, if you're interested." He said, "I'd love to, but I'm now the owner of the store and need to attend to it." Both of us were broken until Trudy took over. "If you could keep the store and work here, would you?" "Of course, but I don't see how?" "Come with me, my boy. Let's work out the details. My son happens to be very good at business affairs. You see, Stephan and Carl have been my employers for 15 years, and they have seen to it that I, Eric, and everyone they employ have not only been rewarded financially but also nurtured and protected. They treat everyone as 'family,' and if they like you, as I see they do, you'll never want." Trudy led him away, and we knew he would start within the week. Trudy returned about 30 minutes later and told us to expect Hunter in the morning. All we could do was kiss our dear Trudy.

We asked the chef to take the day off and ordered in from our favorite French restaurant. Stephan called in the order for the entire house and sent Eric and a couple of the staff to bring it home. Stephan got a return call from the manager to ensure that the order was legit because the total came to $1432.96. He was assured that it was real (and, given that the restaurants were suffering, it was ecstatic) and said that we could call anytime and he would personally see to it that we were taken care of. Of course, Stephan rounded it up to $2000 for the restaurant staff.

Halloween is coming up soon, and we decided to have the troops in and have a costume party. I secretly went to a tailor with Hunter and had 2 suits made to order, and Hunter decided on playing along, so I added his costume to ours. Next, I snuck out to a body shop and requested a special car made (as Stephan had made me a second user on his black card). I swore Hunter to secrecy, and he was all in. The family came in, and the baron arrived. We were prepping for the party, and Stephan asked what I wanted to be for the party. I told him I had him and me covered, and he said great. Trudy finished the rewrites on his second 'fiction'. He sent it in after Trudy gave the thumbs up, and the editor even called and asked if Trudy wanted another job, as it was perfect. Trudy let him down easy, saying she was happy here and couldn't think of leaving (especially since she had a salary of $300,000/year).

Halloween day came, and I told Stephan I needed Hunter to go shopping and pick up our costumes. We left as the troops started partying in the garden. We got the costumes, tried them on, and decided to wear them home. I had the car timed to arrive at six o'clock. We got home, appeared in the garden as Robin and Superman. I had a box for Stephan and ushered him upstairs to change. We came down together, yes, Batman and Robin (in suits exactly like the TV series). Stephan loved it, and then he said, "All that's missing is the Batmobile (as the clock struck six and his car arrived). The crowd erupted in laughter and applause as I handed him the keys and whispered, "To my hero, my one and only Batman." We took it around the block for a spin and got appreciative looks from the neighbors.

Superman got googly eyes from everyone, looking amazingly like his character. We even got him to have that single curl on his forehead. He had eyes for one of Trudy's granddaughters, and she blushed and flirted back heavily. With that, we nodded to each other and knew we'd be planning another wedding soon. We ended up planning a wedding, but with the baron and our dear Trudy. We took care of everything, but had reservations about our family situation. Would she leave us for England as Eddie had? Only time would tell. The baron asked us for a private meeting, and we feared the worst, as did Judy. We asked her to join us, and we all went to the Atrium. "I want to marry this wonderful woman, and I can see the concerns in your collective eyes about the future. My plans, if you'll allow me, are to give my estate and land to my son and move here with Trudy in our apartment." Stephan only objected to one part, "You can move in, but we'll move you two to the guest house, so that you'll have more privacy and space." Everyone relaxed, and the preparations were made for the following month. We gave the baron a walk-through and asked if there was anything he wanted changed. He made and gave us the notes, and we handed them off to the architects. They were told that the modifications needed to be done within the month (and to make sure, Stephan sweetened the pot with unlimited funds to make it happen).

Judy went shopping with Trudy for the dress. The baron had us try on tuxedos and went with the simple black tie ones. Class exuded as the affair started, and we walked our Trudy down the aisle to her new life with John Stephen (what a way to start 2021). "Introducing the Baron and Baroness Maronberg of Blackpool" was announced as they walked into the reception room. We spent the rest of the reception with our expanding family. The couple (having cleared it with Trudy's doctors) headed for the airport on their honeymoon, to Stephan's house in South Beach, Florida. We chartered a private plane for Trudy's sake and had extra staff go with them for John's sake. One last kiss, and we saw the plane lift off.

Back to the house and more goodbyes as the Boys left and Judy and the gang headed home. We were left semi-alone for the first time in a while. Bed awaited us, and we cuddled and slept soundly. The morning would be an adventure. As we had the house to ourselves (mostly), we took our time before going down to breakfast. Eric was in the kitchen with Tony (the chef), and they were discussing the topic of the day and the expected rally at the ellipse in Washington, D.C. We watched as the crowd grew, the reporters opined, and people milled around. I asked to have the channel changed, but Stephan was interested in it, so it stayed. Stephan mentioned that something bad was about to happen, and he wanted to be clued in. By three in the afternoon, Stephan's suspicions became a reality as the mob sacked the capital. Even I was glued to the TV, disbelieving what my eyes were seeing. The vice president's life being threatened and the calling for the Speaker to 'come out, Nancy' to face her detractors. The National Guard finally arrived, and the crowd dispersed. The election got certified, and the new president announced (with finality).

Stephan relaxed and told the staff to prepare for a week at the camp. We all needed a break and some sun. I think they had read Stephan's mind as they were ready within the hour. We loaded the cars and the caravan headed to Camp Getaway. We called Judy to join us or take the time off, and she opted for the latter. Eric, wife Nancy, and son Nathan (now 14) arrived about 10 minutes after us, and the new 'family' unit was together. Tony barbecued for half the afternoon and presented us with a real down-home cuisine. I think I forgot myself and gorged on it, the pork was sooo juicy and tender (I sucked the meat off the bone and then sucked the bone). Nathan was not far behind me in this attempt, and when Eric tried to rein him in, I quietly asked him to let the kid be. "When do you think he'll get to stuff himself like this again?" "Eric whispered back, "Every time he's with his 'favorite uncle,' but okay for today." We laughed all the way back, and Eric signaled for Nathan to go wild (within reason). Nathan smiled in my direction, and I simply nodded back.

The week went by as we wanted, no problems to solve, but we knew coming home meant coming back to reality. I had taken over the bills as Stephan requested (He wanted me to feel as though I was in control of some part of my life, and I stepped up for both of us). Stephan took charge with the construction crew and was behind (because Stephan required much higher quality items than the estimate stated). Stephan called the owner of the company (smoothed it over after making arrangements to pay a premium and doubling their estimated budget). The owner called the lead worker and even authorized overtime. The construction made up time, and the job finished 2 days before the return date of the newlyweds. Stephan said, "I think this place needs some finishing details. Call Judy, as she knows her mother's taste. We'll take a trip to the warehouse and pick some stuff out for their home." She came over, we took the Bentley, and 30 minutes later, we arrived at the warehouse. The attendant waved us through as he now knew us and the car. We waved back and parked near the side door. As I opened the car door for Judy, Stephan unlocked and opened the door and stood back. Taking his cue, I did too and let Judy enter first (I wanted her to have that experience I had the first time and see it through her eyes). We were not disappointed, Judy's eyes lit up and enlarged at the many objects de arte she saw. We let her and a guard pull all the artwork and statuary she wanted for the guest house. We told her to send word to us on the roof when she felt satisfied. We went up into the sunshine, ordered lunch for the group (staff and guards included and had it delivered. It arrived, we set it out and had a picnic al fresco.

The guard was given instructions for the delivery, and we left them at the gate and came home. The panel van appeared about an hour after us and was parked near the guest house. Judy took a couple of strong staff members and directed where she wanted everything placed. Satisfied, she called us to get a second opinion. "It's flawless, Judy, truly remarkable. Maybe we should have you redo our place, it could use your touch." Judy said, "But I don't really know your taste." Stephan swung around with his hands outstretched and said, "This IS our taste. I couldn't have done better with a decorator." She blushed a bit and gave us the thumbs up. "Okay, but I'll need at least a couple of trips to your "boutique." No sooner said than done. We gave her permission and Stephan said, "Carl will go with you the first time so the boys don't bother you (by this I now knew I had Stephan's complete trust).

The lovebirds landed at the airport, and the limousine was waiting. We all met them at the door and went inside to hear all about their days in South Beach. Then, to introduce them to their new home (of sorts). We gave them the keys and simply stood back. Trudy let John unlock the doors before taking his hand, and they walked across the threshold together. They stopped quickly, and we worried if they liked it. Trudy started weeping, and John looked stunned. They turned in unison and said as one, "HOW? We were only gone a couple of weeks. Did they work 24 hours a day? This is beyond beautiful, and the artwork is astounding." Stephan nudged Judy forward and said, "Thank Judy for the décor, she is the real heroine. In fact, we asked her to redo our house since it came out so well." Trudy beckoned her over, hugged her, and smothered her in kisses. John joined in the hugging, and Stephan and I backed out quietly so they could have family time.

About six months later, we got a gold hand-lettered envelope in the mail (we assumed from Eddie) and opened it after breakfast. The boys had finally set the date, and we were invited to the wedding. We found out that the entire household, Trudy's kids, and their families had also been invited. Thank God the kids gave us time to get everyone passports and reservations in England near the estate. I reworked the budget to include the 'family' on our trip (how was I gonna tell Stephan this would set us back north of three hundred thousand dollars). I waited till we were in bed and Stephan was comfortable when I broke the news. "Oh well, we can start by selling the Maserati. Then maybe the Batmobile." I looked at Stephan, waiting for him to say he was joking, but nothing happened. I tried to sleep, but was worried that this time I may have gone too far, and my thoughts of our life together were finite. Morning arrived, and I had contingency plans whirling around in my head as to how to make it happen without any of Stephan's funds being used. We got up, showered in silence as I tried to figure out how to explain my new plan for arrangements. I figured on selling jewelry, my car, and a few items that Stephan had bought me to cover the cost. "Stephan, please sit down. I need to talk to you about this trip. I figured a way so that it doesn't have to interfere with the budget." I told him about the fire sale, and when I finished (downtrodden and depressed but relieved that it was out), he looked at me seriously. "Carl, you would do this for me and the others?" "Of course, don't worry about anything. I'll handle it from here on." Stephan took my hand, "Carl, I thought you knew I was joking, but this just proves how devoted you are to me and 'us'. I will never try to prank you again. I'm so sorry, Carl. Do you forgive me?" He pulled me in close, smothered me with sloppy kisses, rolled on top, and started getting aroused. Needless to say, Trudy was getting a dog today, as we didn't get downstairs until noon.

The passports came early and got distributed, Hunter (the valet) went clothes shopping for the entire entourage (with Judy in tow), and the arrangements were finalized. We were to stay at the estate, John and Trudy were staying with his son at the homestead, and the rest were at a nearby hotel. All in all, we felt chartering a 747 would be cheaper than buying individual tickets. We arrived at the airport and were taken to a private hangar where we all boarded. We nearly filled the seats with merry old England. The plane arrived at Heathrow, and again we were taken to a private departure lounge. We all went through customs (except John), and it took the better part of the afternoon. All clear, we headed to our respective cars and set off to our homes away from home for the next week, and got settled in. Stephan and I got out of our limousine at the estate, and the guys greeted us in the driveway. Eddie had matured a bit since Trudy's wedding, and it looked good on him. Anthony looked the same (as always), and after greetings, we all went inside while the staff took our belongings to our room.

We freshened up before dinner and were treated to American cuisine (I think our Tony must have gotten a call because this meal tasted like our usual fare). We went over the festivities with the guys, and we decided to take the troops sightseeing first before the 'grand finale'. We rented buses for our 'army' to get around, and they got to see Buckingham Palace, the changing of the guards, Piccadilly Circus, and the British countryside. John had us all out to the homestead for picnicking, and we were introduced to the new baron. He was most accommodating, although a little overwhelmed by the barrage of people in our entourage. "Don't worry about John Jr. He actually loves showing off 'his' new estate and title." Lunch done, we packed the buses and returned to our designated sleeping quarters. We got back to the estate late and dropped from exhaustion.

The guy's wedding day came, and we got dressed in our tuxedos. Stephan was to be the best man for Anthony, and I guess I was to be the 'Matron of honor' for Eddie (oh well, it could have been worse, I would have looked foolish in a gown, lol). Trudy was given the place of honor as Eddie's 'mother' (as his real one had died previously). The garden was filled to the brim (mostly from our troops) and dignitaries from England (Anthony's friends and contemporaries). The ceremony was simple, short, and over the top (As Anthony would later tell us, it was at Eddie's request). From the looks on the assembled group, it was rather expected, and they had a 7-tiered cake rolled out with 2 guys kissing as the cake topper. The exchange of cake came, and everyone expected it to be smeared into their respective faces, but Eddie poo-pooed that idea, and they lovingly fed each other. (Eddie, as we found out, didn't want his make-up ruined).

We ended the night partying as the guys made their way around, saying their thanks and acknowledging everyone in attendance. Then they made their way out and left the partying up to us. We took full advantage and made merry. The guests left, and we were left alone in the house. We went to our room, placed a 'do not disturb' sign on the door, and drank champagne on a bearskin rug in front of the fire in our 'birthday suits'. We woke around 4 a.m., cold as the fire had died out, and we finally took advantage of the warm bed. We tried to get back to sleep, but Stephan had a stiff reason why he couldn't. My man needed assistance, and who was I to neglect him in his hour of need? We didn't get up until about 9 am (by which I mean, we showered and dressed after Stephan was tended to). We grabbed a croissant with butter and a cup of tea and headed out to the grounds. Stephan showed me all of his favorite spots and the private areas he so enjoyed in his time there.

We packed for our journey back home. Stephan rallied the troops, and the bus met us at the airport. The trip home was uneventful, and we landed in Baltimore around 4 pm. The cars were there for pickup, and our limousine was warmed and waiting. More hugs and waves, and we left. Home never looked so good (although I wasn't missing my apartment). We spent some time recovering from our jet lag. Trudy was in the kitchen when we came down, but she was moving slowly. She blamed it on the trip, but we knew it was time to get her the mobile scooter. We told John about our plans, and he agreed. Trudy fought us until we explained she only needed to use it when she wanted to. She took it for a spin, then decided we were right. "Careful, boys, I could get used to this." We nodded as she took off for the guest house.

Life continued, and Trudy's condition degraded. Judy gave us the news that she wouldn't be joining us in the main house anymore, as she had enough trouble navigating the guest house. Thankfully, Judy and John had thought ahead and had a bedroom made on the first floor. No more climbing stairs. Judy had transitioned into her mother as house manager, Eric had literally taken over the other parts of managing things, and Stephan's second book erased all the family's debt. Trudy's kids and grandkids would never have to worry about money issues (although Judy's daughter started going down the wrong path). Judy asked for a little extra financial help, and we gladly gave it to her. She sent her daughter to a rehab facility in California, away from temptation. At first, Dahlia (Judy's daughter) fought the help, but in the end, she overcame her addiction and decided to stay in California and was offered a position as a recovering counselor at the facility. Judy was slightly depressed by losing her daughter to California, but we told her that she and her husband, Jeff, could visit her any time. That comforted her, and she went to tell Jeff.

It was now 2024, and the cursed cov-id was just something we had to live with, but the nation had recovered. I was getting ready to celebrate my 57th birthday and was dreading getting older. That meant that my time with Stephan was narrowing, and mortality (and my personal pity party) was setting in. I tried to keep in shape, but I guess my warranty had expired as the physical determined I was living a bit too "richly." My sugar and blood pressure levels were too high for the doctor, and he suggested drugs to manage them. I asked if I could do it by diet and exercise, and he said yes, but he didn't know many who could be that disciplined. Stephan told him that he would personally see to it and allowed us a trial period to prove him wrong. We hired a personal trainer (actually, it was Hunter with a pay raise) and started. Hard was over-simplifying my feelings when it started. I was ready to become a pill popper, but Hunter persisted, and Stephan cajoled me into keeping at it, and my return to the doctor three months later proved their point. My blood work acknowledged that my efforts (or should I say Hunter's) worked, and the results came back astonishingly good. I even impressed the doctor. He asked if he could recommend my trainer and diet to others, but I told him it was just hard work and determination (I certainly wasn't going to share my trainer/valet with anyone but Stephan). The doctor didn't push and let it go, although he really, really wanted to know my secret.

So 57, in better shape than when Stephan entered my life. He wanted to celebrate with something elaborate, but I said no. Stephan was going on 512, so what was the big deal at my age? We had known each other for 19 years, been married for 3, written a book together (with Trudy, of course), and seen our family grow and prosper beyond our dreams. Then we received a letter from Italy. It was from Stephan (Lucius' son and now 24), I couldn't believe it. The kids kept aging. We opened the letter with trepidation, but it was heartening because he was told to ask before just coming to see us. Stephan grabbed the phone, and we both yelled, "Stephan, of course you can come. We'll have a limousine waiting for you at the airport. When should we expect you?" He gave us the details, said goodbye, and went to tell his father.

Stephan, the elder, looked at me and wondered how his 5x great-grandson looked. Would he take after his father or take after his mother? Our answer walked through customs as the young ladies did double takes and got all flirty as he appeared from the bag retrieval. I almost mistook him for Anthony and Stephan. The three could be brothers. You should have seen the look on their faces as he addressed Stephan, "Great-grandfather, so good to see you again" (it was priceless as they looked the same age). We walked past the onlookers and whispered, "Good genes," and laughed all the way home. We asked what brought him to the States. "I wanted to see you guys. Sheesh, maybe I shouldn't have come." We both punched him and said, "You listen here, poophead, we want to see you whenever we can. It's just out of the blue. That's why we asked." "Okay, I'll come clean and tell you. I didn't want Dad to know I've been conversing with a girl online and wanted to meet her. I want it on the QT, so please keep it between us, okay?" A typical youngster, we nodded yes with a caveat that it be in a group and in neutral territory. He nodded (and we knew it was just a gesture to coddle us). "Please be careful and let Hunter come with you as a chaperon."

Stephan told me that now he had lived to see 8 generations below him, and it made him start to feel old. I quipped, "You don't look a day over 300." He told me he'd get me for that, and I told him, "To the bat cave." He grabbed my hand and headed upstairs. I paid his price (all the while egging him on). Batman even wore the mask and cape while exacting his 'revenge'. Stephan 'the younger', as we now had to call him, asked where we'd gotten to, and we said rest as we were much older than he was. He winked in his grandfather's direction and called out to Hunter. They left for his rendezvous. He took the Bentley with Hunter driving (praise God). We waited for the report when Hunter got back. Judy, in the meantime, came to us with her ideas for freshening up the main house. We both green-lighted her plans and went to see Trudy. John came to the door and said she had taken to her bed and didn't feel up to company today. I asked if the doctor had been called, and he said Trudy nixed that idea, so he left it alone. I took Stephan aside, and he agreed that the kids needed to be told. He sought out Judy, and I called the boys. We made up a schedule, and they came in turns to visit their mother so as not to overwhelm her. Her time was coming, and we grieved her illness in our own way. Judy was there almost constantly, her brother Tom took time away from work to relieve Judy when she needed it, but Allen (the oldest) couldn't accept it and stayed away. Stephan sent Judy over to get him there, and he finally appeared, hesitant, but there. He went in to see Trudy, and he made her day. She smiled more brightly and actually sat up. He stayed about an hour, kissed her (I think for closure), and took his leave (at least she saw him one last time).

John waited outside, stoic but on the verge of tears as his glassy eyes betrayed his inner feelings. We went to him and he let loose a torrent of pent up tears. We shared his emotion and wept. Judy interrupted our sob fest and called us in. Trudy was fading fast as we entered. We gathered around her bed and Asked to have Tony and Eric brought in. They about ran when they heard and arrived as Trudy was losing consciousness. She saw us all assembled, told us she loved us all, closed her eyes and entered eternity. Our dear Trudy was no more and the house grieved her loss. Judy called the Funeral home and took care of the arrangements. He arrived, removed the body (I hate when they call someone a body after death) and prepared her for the wake and funeral. I called the guys in England and Stephan called Rome. The services were set for two days hence to allow for the arrivals and the house went into hyper drive to ensure it was 'Trudy perfect'.

We gave her the royal send-off as she deserved and returned to the house for a reception. Stephan asked for a few private moments and left us. He wouldn't allow me to see his full grief, and although I protested, I gave him his space. He returned to the group about 15 minutes later, red-eyed and ashen, but stoic. I went to his side and let him lean on me. Stephan the younger stayed beside us while Eric, Nancy, and Judy took care of hosting. We allowed the family to stay, and we went with John to the guest house. "I guess I'll be leaving soon. You'll probably want to use your guest house again." We staunchly said, "John, you're like a dad to us. You can stay if you'd like, or leave if you wish. The choice is up to you." He looked at us as if seeing us for the first time. "I'd like to stay if you'll have me." We went to him and hugged it out. We may have lost Trudy, but we still had her family. The days after proved sad, but we put that grief energy into our work and projects. The house was never more productive. Stephan got a contract for another book, and he literally threw himself into it. I assisted when I wasn't busy with household issues or paying bills (gratefully, we had an accountant). Judy got promoted to her mother's position and salary. That allowed Jeff to retire, and he took up driving for us. We patched together a cohesive, albeit strange, family unit. Stephan and I were the uncles, and the rest of the kids were nieces and nephews. Eric had become an uncle, too. Nathan was getting ready for graduation and college. Eric came to us, and we knew he'd be asking for funding for Nathan. We handed him the account book we had been adding to since Nathan was born. He opened it, closed it, and asked if it was real. We nodded, and he left as usual, happy as a clam. I asked Stephan if he thought $200,000 was enough, and he let me know that there was more where that came from.

Stephan asked me if I wanted to go to Rome with him due to him needing some things from his warehouse there. I tried to be coy (it never worked) and finally nodded yes. Hunter was sent shopping (as though we really needed more clothes), and he took the Maserati (which by now was the utility car), and we assembled our necessities and passports for the trip. Stephan chartered us a plane (for ease of traveling), and I worked out the specifics. 2 days later, we decided that since we had extra space on the plane, we invited Hunter to go with us (and Stephan wanted him to shop for us in Italy). Hunter accepted but said he would pay his own way. "Don't be daft, the plane's been fully prepaid. Now enough talk, go pack. Besides, you'll be working part of the time (but Stephan liked this guy's class)." Once that was settled, I privately wondered what that stud looked like in a Speedo. Note to self, make plans for a beach day and let him know after arriving in Rome.

Lucius was notified, and he sent 'the younger' to fetch us at the airport. He appeared at the customs desk as we were finishing up. The Stephans greeted each other, and people stared (as always), and then he came over and hugged me, too. I really had a family I could call my own (if only through marriage). We were escorted to the waiting limousine and off to the villa we went. The Stephans chatted as we weaved through the traffic and winding roads to Calcata. Those 29 miles seemed like 5 as we entered the gates of the villa. Lucius and Elena trotted out from the garden as they heard the stretch limousine approach. I couldn't wait for the food I knew would be available as we went inside. Hours of chitchat ensued as we caught up. Dinner was announced, and I jumped up (a bit too anxious) and got a laugh out of the relatives. Antipasto, calamari salad, gnocchi in butter sauce, Chianti, fresh bread (toasted on the grill and rubbed with garlic with extra virgin olive oil on the side), balsamic vinegar drizzled over the oil, then the pasta (farfelli or bow ties to us foreigners) with a huge meatball and whole day sauce with fresh basil torn (never chopped) with a brick of parmesano reggiano (of course) ready to shred. Black pepper grinder on the table if preferred. Needless to say, I thoroughly enjoyed myself (chef-approved). I finished my plate and had no room for dessert (until I laid eyes on the cannoli. I made room). I stood after trying twice, said goodnight to our hosts, and went upstairs. Stephan was left to finish up the conversation with his family. Stephan walked in quietly and crawled in beside me, allowing me this one indulgence.

The day started with a light meal (I was still full from the night before). Hunter met us in the kitchen, munching on a roll and drinking an espresso. We followed suit and soon took a rented car to the shopping areas. Hunter was impressed and loved the fashion. He pulled the attire himself, only asking for help if he didn't see the exact article he was looking for (in perfect Italian, I would add). I have to say, his taste was excellent, everything fit as though tailored. I had to ask where the Italian speech came from. He simply said he was taught it in school. Stephan noticed Hunter looking at an Armani suit and said, "Hunter, go try it on, I want to see how it looks on you." Obedient as always, he took the suit in the back and appeared minutes later, a vision that even stunned the manager. "Boss, it looks great, but the tag says put it back on the hanger." "Nonsense, add it and whatever else strikes your fancy to the bill. By the way, get a swimsuit for the beach this week." I was secretly hoping he'd try that on too, but alas, I'd have to wait a couple of days. Stephan worked out the payment with the owner (who was willing to sell us the store at this point. He told Stephan and Hunter to count on him any time and from anywhere to outfit us all. Stephan said something to the manager, and the manager beamed (so I suppose it was flattering, not knowing Italian). He turned to Hunter, still speaking Italian, and Hunter replied. Stephan gave me a wink but said nothing. We returned to the villa knowing that our new wardrobe would be waiting for us when we got home.

The following day, we finally got to the warehouse, and it did not disappoint. Stephan started pointing to statuary and paintings, and Hunter directed the staff to pack them up for transportation to America. As usual, we bought and provided lunch for the staff and ourselves. I was a little frustrated as they all spoke Italian and rapidly. The food was perfect, and I settled for that. They returned to the business as I strolled through the warehouse. I was shocked when I saw a painting of Stephan in all his glory. I pointed to this painting and motioned for the staff to box it up, also, and I guess they finally realized what I wanted. It got whisked away, and I continued my walk. The historical value alone had to be astronomical, but I didn't ask; I just enjoyed. Hunter was sent to find me, and we took our leave. The deliveries were going to put Eric and Judy to work for a while. The villa came into view, and I admired the tableau (classical Italian countryside landscape). No wonder Stephan loved it so much. Having accomplished our goal, we made our usual visit with the family to the Cimitero. The last day, the younger put on a feast for us, complete with classical music, for his grandfather and me. We went to bed, but Stephan couldn't sleep. "What's wrong? Usually, I take longer than you to sleep." "It's just that something is up with Hunter. I spoke in old colloquial Italian, and Hunter caught the meanings. It just makes me wonder a little about him." I told him I'd watch for any clues and put Eric on high alert (I didn't want another

Devon affair). We parted from the kids and went to the airport. Our plane was fueled up and waiting for us on the tarmac. We lifted off and settled in for the 6-hour flight.

Eric met us at the airport in Baltimore and helped us once customs cleared us. The ride home was a quiet one, and I put it down to jet lag. Hunter excused himself, and we told Eric to join us in the atrium. "Do us a favor and watch for anything out of the ordinary with Hunter. Just don't let him know." "Gotcha, boss. What in particular should I be looking for?" Stephan told him to look for unusual phone calls or messaging. Any letters being sent out or a change in his disposition. Stephan went to the den, and I followed like a puppy dog. He had piqued my interest now. Stephan had me pull a few books as he read another. Suddenly, Stephan yelled to me, "Carl, come here. I think I just solved the mystery." He showed me what he had found. On the page was a picture of Hunter, but not Hunter. It was a picture of Gioffre Borgia, the illegitimate son of Pope Alexander VI (Rodrigo Borgia) and brother to Lucrezia. "Look, he had children, and I believe our Hunter is a descendant of his kid Geronimo Borgia III." I had to ask, "That doesn't make him bad though, does it?" Stephan conceded, "Not necessarily, but just in case, we'd better be sure."

"I don't know why there would be any bad blood between our families, as he died 2 years after I was born, but who knows." Stephan kept looking, and I googled the family and found out there were many descendants living in America. Holy family feud, 'Batman', just what we needed, a 500-year-old vendetta. I hoped it wasn't true. I really liked Hunter, and he exuded class and beauty. We kept it under wraps as Stephan continued his research. When Stephan finished his research, he called Eric, Hunter, and me into the den (which was highly unusual). He ushered us all in and then locked the door (this didn't bode well). "I guess you're all wondering about the secrecy but I'll explain. Hunter, what's your last name?" to which Hunter smirked and said, "I thought you'd never ask, it's Borgia." Stephan simply blurted out, "And how old are you?" "Normally I'd have you guess but since the cat's out of the bag, 203. I was born in New Jersey in 1821. I read your book and had a good laugh as I knew it wasn't fiction. When the position became available, I jumped at the chance. I played it cool, as you have all these years. How did you think a young man could buy out a store and still want to work for others? I just wanted to be around others like me. Am I being fired?" Stephan arose, went over to him, and said, "Of course not, Hunter. It's just that you understood my old Italian dialect. It made me curious." Poor Eric, his jaw dropped to the floor and stood looking back and forth between the three of us. I stood also and pointing to myself said, "Not me, I'm just normal and 57." Eric formed the word how but nothing came out. I went and got the copy of Stephan's first book with me and handed it to Eric. "Read this, actually it's all true. No more secrets, Eric. Trudy was the only one in our employ that knew, and now she's gone." He took the book from me and sat to read it. Stephan asked if he would be comfortable working here after the revelations he just received. "I'm sorry, boss, it just took the wind out of my sails for a moment. I'll be alright and don't worry, all your secrets are safe with me." Trudy had taught him well. So now I had two immortals to contend with. One was married to, and the other was in our employ (I now wanted to know what Hunter's wealth was). No wonder he had style and class; it stemmed from his family background and personal wealth.

Another mystery solved, everyone relaxed, and we toasted to their health, and Stephan unlocked the den door. Eric took his reading assignment and went home for the night. Hunter had been admitted into our inner circle, hopefully strengthening it. Saturday morning, I woke early and decided to let Stephan sleep in. I went into the kitchen, made myself a bowl of cereal (how long had it been since I 'cooked' for myself, I couldn't remember). I took the bowl with me onto the patio overlooking the pool and saw what I had been waiting for, Hunter in a neon blue speedo. I almost frothed at the mouth when he launched himself out of the pool. WOW! Stephan was gorgeous, but Hunter was no slouch, and he was packing. He saw me, waved, and came to the table. It took a lot of willpower not to look, but he seemed nonchalant about his near nudity. I swallowed quickly and said, "Stephan slept in this morning. I guess I should get him up." "Stay, Carl, I have to change anyway. Why interrupt your breakfast when I'll be passing his room to mine?" It made sense, but I hated the thought of Stephan seeing this Spanish/Italian god as I had.

I hustled to finish and get upstairs under any pretense. I got to our room as Stephan stepped from the shower. I told him I had heard the shower and came to dry his back. He knew I was lying (but I keep trying to get one by him) and said Hunter had stopped and awoken him. He smirked, and I knew he knew why I was there. He said, "Carl, you jealous man of mine, it's truly heartening to see you like this, even though you don't have to worry. Always remember one thing, 'Batman' will always need his 'Robin' and I hope the same goes for you." With that, he dropped his towel to the floor, and I went to the closet where the mask and cape awaited.

Our deliveries arrived, day after day, as they cleared customs, and the poor staff went bounding around the house as we redecorated the main and guest house with the new items. Judy was in her glory, John was happy for the change, and I had my special painting placed in our bedroom on the wall opposite the bed. Stephan moved some of the items and asked for one crate to be delivered directly to our den unopened. I knew better, but I loitered near the den waiting for the reveal. Stephan shooed me away, and I left while looking back with a pouty face. He just pointed and turned his back. Into the den, door closed, and I heard the click of the lock (I thought he said no more secrets). It was like that until dinner. We ate, mostly in silence. Stephan let me go the entire meal before asking me to accompany him to the den. Finally, the suspense was killing me. He handed me the key and stood back, a shit-eating grin on his face. He had a satisfied look on his face, and I relaxed, knowing he was trying to impress me. I opened the door and couldn't move. The place had been converted into the Italian library from the villa of papyri. Well, a recreation of it. I turned, gave him the thumbs up, and he hugged me as he placed the music on the Victrola. Violins filled the air, and he took me into his embrace and whirled me around the room. I was complete.

Christmas 2024 came, and Stephan and I were missing our dear Trudy, but time passes, and life must go on, so we put on our brave faces and got our new 'family' together. Eddie and Anthony couldn't make the trip, but Lucius and his family made it. Judy called Dahlia, and she made plans (at our expense) to come home. John Stephen and Hunter assisted in decorating, and Eric, Nancy, and Nathan (almost 18) said they would attend after morning presents. The family had morphed many times over 19 years (and I, for one, was grateful). The chef outdid himself; the staff was invited (if they had no other plans), and the total came to about thirty people for dinner. I gave Stephan a portrait of me (I had one made to place by his and yes, in the nude as his was). He was starting to open it when I whispered in his ear. He quickly stopped and placed it beside him. We both laughed at the inside joke, and the others looked at us strangely. Presents and bonuses were distributed, and the look on the people's faces told me that Stephan had been extremely generous this year. We got John a present he didn't expect. He received a message from his son about a gift left at the door. John opened it to see John Jr. there. They hugged, John Sr. cried, and they joined us in the atrium.

Stephan and I decided on a quiet New Year's Eve, so we sent the staff home early, took ourselves up to our room, and lit the fire. The chef had left a charcuterie board there with enough champagne for 4 people. We got comfortable in our pj's, laid the board and champagne bucket near us and played Stephan's favorite selections on the sound system. We rang in the new year, kissed, toasted each other, and went to sleep not knowing our future.

Eric gave us an invitation to Nathan's graduation in June (I assume because Nathan was hoping for a big gift). We accepted on the spot, and Nathan grinned and left with dreams of anticipation. It started seeming that 2025 would be a quiet one, but alas, life throws curveballs (and usually hits its mark). February came, and John Sr. fell ill. The doctor came and told us he had pneumonia. We called Jr., and he made it the following week. Sr. held on about three more days before falling into a coma. The doctor had him transferred to the hospital (we sent Jr. with him and followed behind). John left us as he held Jr's hand. It didn't get any easier, but we pulled it together, made arrangements for Sr.'s final journey home to the home of his ancestors. We asked if any staff wanted to join us to honor our surrogate 'father'. I chartered another plane, and the entire entourage assembled on the tarmac. We would send our John off in style, and Jr. arrived a day ahead to plan our arrival. Twenty staff, Stephan, and I made it to the estate a day before the ceremony. Eddie and Anthony invited everyone to their home for dinner (to give Jr. and his staff time to finish up the reception plans). The next day, we listened to the eulogy, a sermon fit for a baron, and then from the adjacent hill, the outlaw pipes at sunset. That did it. I was okay until then, and had to lean on Stephan as I silently cried into his shoulder. We sent the staff home as Stephan wanted us to stay in England another week. Eddie and Anthony begged us to stay with them, and I couldn't say no. The boys pulled out all the stops, and we recovered from our newest loss.

We returned to the States to find our home in one piece (Eric and Judy kept it going, and we decided on a big bonus for them). We gave Jeff two tickets to anywhere and Nancy the same. The instructions in the envelope simply said: "Give us a few days' warning before you go." We gave Eric and Judy some spending money (we agreed that $50,000 apiece would do it). They left to make plans. Hunter stayed with us (he had time and money to go anywhere at any time). Stephan 'the younger' sent us a request to come, and since the guest house was empty, we said yes. He arrived a few weeks hence and took up residence in John Sr.'s place. I found the Stephans at the pool and decided to join them (I opted for board shorts as I had not received the 'good genes'. They and Hunter had Italian cut speedos on, and I had a problem. I tried to appear uninterested, but my body had other ideas, and they all pointed and smirked. The elder stepped over to me and said, "Carl, you know it's just harmless fun. Besides, it proves you still have the urge." I blushed and accepted the compliment. We left Hunter and the younger to play at the pool and went inside to ask the chef for lunch (yep, I had crossed over to a wealthy mindset, crap). We peeked out at the pool and discovered the boys missing (were all the immortals gay?). We turned and ate the 'simple' sandwiches the chef had whipped up.

The younger went to the elder in the den and they closed the door. Obviously they wanted privacy but I knew the elder would tell me later during our 'pillow talk'. Stephan didn't disappoint me and I found out that the younger wanted to break away from his father for just a while.

He wanted to find himself without the condemning eyes over his shoulder. I told Stephan the younger to consider this his home while he was in America and he kissed my cheek. He then whispered to me, "Thanks grandma" and I almost swatted his butt and then thought, why not and smiled. These nicknames were getting a little out of hand but they meant we were definitely family.

June arrived, the younger was still here, he and Hunter had an on again off again affair going on, Eric and Nancy got plans made for Nathan's graduation. We were in the market for new cars so we gifted Nathan the old Bentley. His parents were furious with us, setting up unnatural expectations, but we did it anyway. It seemed that Nathan liked the gift. We smoothed it over by saying the car's ashtray was full so we HAD to either trade it in or get rid of it. Besides, it had reached a full 20,000 miles on the odometer AND it was used. Eric frowned and smiled at the same time and Nancy finally broke up laughing, saying, "Only you two can make this sound plausible, men." We gave Nathan an envelope and demanded he say nothing about the card (which had several thousand dollars in it). Everyone was growing up, maturing, marrying, having kids (at least the straight ones). Now we were sending those kids off to their futures.

Life did give us a few months of respite until Thanksgiving. Chef told us he was thinking about retiring finally. We were taken by surprise (as we forgot that he was aging like me). We decided to let him retire after Christmas and prepared to try to replace him. He said he would take care of the interviews and send us the top three for final selection. That eased my mind somewhat but Stephan worried about the candidates. Would they be like Devon or Eric? Only time (and a private eye would tell). We feasted with staff and their family for Thanksgiving and prepared for Christmas. Hunter assisted Judy in decorating the main house and he and the younger decorated the guest house. (Hunter had moved in with younger and they set up house. It seems they 'ironed out' their differences). I noticed Stephan the younger had taken to wearing more 'fancy' and lighter colored clothing while Hunter took on the very masculine look. Note to self, ask my new 'granddaughter' how it feels. The day came for our last meal with chef and we invited the staff to see him off. We talked to everyone around him quietly and found out his plans. He was thinking of going on a cruise with his wife and touring Europe. His wife and family were there and when the meal had ended, we handed them an envelope. He opened it, dropped it to the floor and put his manly hands over his face as he broke down in tears. His wife picked up the envelope and its' contents. It contained two all expense paid reservations on board a cruise ship to dock in England, then a plane to Europe and Viking cruise tickets for two to tour Europe by boat.

Our beloved chef was leaving us and we wanted him to know his worth to us. Champagne flowed like a river and so did the tears. I shook his hand and he hugged both of us and told us it had been his honor to cook for us all. They left and got the royal treatment as the staff lined up one last time to say their goodbyes. We had little time to recover as the new chef we had picked, Andre started the next day. Chef had left a cookbook full of recipes and instructed our newbie about how we liked things. He took up residence in Hunter's old quarters. Our first experience with Andre was okay (I think I was partial to chef) and it went well. He had big shoes to fill and I think he knew it.

Andre was a good cook, a decent baker but not much to look at. He reminded me of me when Stephan appeared at my door. We had Hunter and the younger go get him a new wardrobe and they Jumped to it. I got the bill two weeks later and called them both on the carpet about it. "Care to explain this bill? How did you guys spend $15,000 on a chef's attire? What do you think we are, made of money?" I frowned my best frown (as I already knew the answers). The guys gave me puppy eyes, pouty lips and I caved. "At least let me know before you do this again, okay?" They both kissed my cheeks (knowing they had just gotten away with it as usual). I checked the account, making sure we had enough to cover it (we did of course) and wrote the check. Thankfully, Stephan the elder didn't bother with these 'trifles'. I reconciled the account and burned the evidence before Stephan saw it.

We stayed around the house as Stephan had more finishing to do to put his latest fiction to bed and the secretary and he basically lived in the den. We sent in food, and he emerged after a week triumphant. "Eureka, another masterpiece. He stretched and I got a peek of his midriff. I couldn't help myself and yelled, "Holy midriff, to the bat cave." I grabbed 'Batman' and led him upstairs. I hoped the cape was cleaned from last time, oh well, if not the mask would do.

2025 arrived, and so did the new presidency. It seemed that America decided a convicted felon was better than having a woman president. Oh well, buck up and get on with it (besides, we were wealthier than Bezos, Musk, and Buffet combined). Stephan asked if maybe I wanted to relocate to England or Italy. I told him no, although the thought had crossed my mind. But I was turning 58 and was starting to feel my age. This convinced Stephan, and he went looking for 'cures' for my 'condition'. He researched for months, and I became his personal guinea pig. Facials, peels, vitamins, extra niacinamide, quartz rollers, and gimmicks too numerous to mention. Next came meetings with top geriatric doctors and 'blue zone' experts. He was going to crack the secret before I got much older (I guess he wanted his current partner around for a while).

When the genetics guy got called in, I confided in Stephan that his secret could get out, and they would use him for experiments. Stephan had to agree (I mean, we had three specimens in one residence). Although I gave him my blood, we neglected to mention the others. He saw good blood but nothing out of the ordinary with mine. He went away empty-handed, and I was back at square one. Stephan set up a quasi-lab in the den. He had requested the notes from the genetics guy and set about trying to engineer his own answer (using his blood sample). It seemed we were compatible, and he asked if he could infuse a pint of his blood into me. I knew it would do no harm, but I was hesitant. Was I ready if it worked? After much cajoling, I agreed for this one time.

I lay on the couch, and Stephan started the infusion. It felt funny as I could feel the fluid enter my system. I sat up after and drank some juice. We went about our normal routines as usual, but Stephan took notes. He was looking for even the subtlest changes. I didn't notice anything, but it seems Stephan did (well, he was writing a lot on that notepad). Days went by and then months. The fall was upon us, and we decided to travel to Rio (as my personal interpreter knew Portuguese). Hunter and Stephan the younger wanted to go also, so we 'invited' them along. It was too bad we'd be leaving Rio before Carnivale, but at least it wouldn't be crowded. The guys went shopping (on Hunter's dime, we weren't playing that game again). I chartered the plane, made sure the passports were still good, packed for the trip (well, Hunter packed for us), and got ready to go. We arrived and saw Christ the Savior extending his arms above the city as though welcoming us.

We were taken to the hotel and, having deposited our things in our suites, sought out the ambiance of Rio. The food was good, the music was intriguing, and the street fare was colorful. We indulged for what seemed hours, and then something caught Stephan's eye. We went into a curio shop and Stephan sorted through the odd items. He bought some exotic herbs and powders (I didn't know he could cook). He asked to have the items boxed and shipped back home. I managed to keep up with Stephan all day, but crashed around supper time. Four meals a day were getting to me. Breakfast was light, lunch was salad and fresh fruit, dinner was the main affair, and supper was about 10 pm (too late for me to eat without heartburn). I turned in, and the guys went to eat in the restaurant in the hotel. The following day, we went to the beach, and the guys wore their new Speedos. Three magnificent bodies on the sand and me, grandma glasses and floppy hat (all I needed now was a moo moo to complete my look). They tried to coax me into the water, but it wasn't going to happen. They frolicked around for about an hour and took pity on me, and we went to eat. I seemed to be less hungry as the days went by, but I blamed it on the activities and spicy food.

Our vacation came to an end, and we returned to 'the grind' of everyday life. Hunter returned to his duties, and Stephan the younger decided to introduce Hunter to Lucius and Elena as his fiancée. Since we really could do without Hunter, we said okay, and they left for Italy. Our 'boys' were becoming jet setters. Judy and Eric kept things running smoothly in the house, and Stephan kept working on his project in the den/lab. Stephan handed me a smoothie for breakfast and said I needed to start eating a little healthier for my age. I flinched at the comment but slugged down the gruel-tasting mixture. He added an apple for flavor, but it didn't help much. I will admit it gave me more energy during the day, though. He continued this ritual every day for a month. I felt much better and put it down to 'clean living'. I joined Stephan in the den and found he was concocting the mixture in his pseudo lab. "What exactly is in that stuff? It tastes barely drinkable, but it does work." Stephan said, "Remember the spices I got in Rio. Well, they assist with the rejuvenation of the body. With the other herbs I had sent, I was able to come up with this elixir. Would you mind if I had you go through a physical to test my theory?" "Yes, dear, if it will satisfy your curiosity."

Stephan set up an appointment for the doctor to come, and he took blood samples and gave me a thorough going over. Stephan talked to the doctor before he left, and the doctor nodded to him. Note to self, ask Stephan what's happening. The boys got back home to Baltimore about the same time that Stephan got my test results. "Well, Doc, what's the lowdown?" Stephan asked me to sit down in the den next to him. "To be honest, I've been working with ingredients to help you age more slowly. The results show that it's working, see here." With that, he explained the results that were (and I must say I was impressed) what he had hoped for. "You seem to have the physiology of a man about thirty-five. If you keep going, you should live to 100 or more." "Thanks, I think. Whatever happened to the infusion you gave me?" Stephan said not much and left it at that. Who was I to question him after that? What we were to find out was that the doctor, seeing my results, had copied the notes for another reason. Stephan got the latest issue of Modern Medicine and found out our good doctor Eugene Harmon had published his findings. I was exposed all through the article, and Stephan told me immediately. "We need to lay low for a while and may need to travel to Italy to get away."

"The guys and staff can handle the house while we're gone, and I need to handle one good doctor." Hunter and Stephan Jr. (as we started calling him) asked if we'd like them to make him disappear. "Guys, as much as I'd love that, we need to be discreet, and Stephan is best at that, I mean, if he can handle a tsar, a couple of popes, and some kings, I think he can deal with an unscrupulous doctor." They nodded and left to batten down the hatches. Security was elevated while we got ready to leave, and with the calls to Lucius and the airport to get our newly acquired private jet ready for take-off, we left the States for Italy. Stephan made a few more calls, which I was not privy to (the good doctor was about to become a bad smell in New Jersey), as the plane left the ground. "Don't worry about that doctor. I think he's about to retire and disappear." I knew better than to ask and watched as the 'boot' came into view. Rome felt more homey now, and we arrived at the villa around dinner time. Lucius came out, ushered us in, and got the staff to tend to us. He said food was available in the kitchen and he would see us in the morning. "Something's wrong. Elena wasn't there to greet us, and now he's leaving us as soon as we arrive. It doesn't look good." I nodded, and we went to the kitchen.

The morning greeted the horizon in the east as we woke, and we went down to find Lucius at the breakfast bar with glassy eyes. Stephan went to him to comfort him, and Lucius looked up with red, puffy eyes, and he collapsed into Stephan's arms. "It's Elena, she contracted that damned disease and now she has what they call long COVID." We did our best to empathize, but he was inconsolable. I left them to call Jr. and let him know to get here. Then I called Judy, Jeff, and Eric to let them know. By the time I had returned, Lucius was slightly better. He thanked us for coming, and I let him know that Jr. and Hunter were on their way (I had the jet return to Baltimore). We left Lucius with Elena and visited the Cimitero. It was dreary and clouded over, so we just sat and communed with the ancestors. Stephan took a walk around the Cimitero to see and talk about other graves and tombs of people he had known over the centuries. The 'boys' touched down around dinner time, and I had the limousine go fetch them.

We instructed the staff as the boys went to see Jr's mom. She rallied when she laid eyes on Jr. it seems it was better than medicine. Color returned to her face, and she smiled. She raised her hand to stroke his face as the tears appeared. We quietly left the room as a courtesy. They joined us in the dining room, and we ate a somber meal. Hopefully, she would pull through. We told Lucius that we would leave the following day so that the boys would have their time and so that he wouldn't have to entertain guests. "Nonsense, there's plenty of room, and you're no imposition. I need your grandfather and Carl. I'd feel worse if you weren't here and something happened." We agreed and told the staff not to bother packing our clothes (after they had already packed our clothes). I felt bad and decided to do something nice for them (although I really didn't know what to do yet). Eric called me in a slight panic as he read the paper over the phone. "Headlines in the paper about a missing doctor by the name of Harmon. They suspect foul play and are investigating. Isn't that the doctor you had, Carl?" "I believe so. Keep me informed, will ya?" "Will do, boss." I let it go, but whispered it in Stephan's ear that they believed that he had met his demise. Stephan nonchalantly said, "Pity, maybe he should have had better scruples. Probably ran afoul of the mafia."

We ended up staying the month as Elena regained her strength. I was elated as we had lost so many good people lately. Our departure day came and we four guys left for England. Eddie met us at the airport hangar and whisked us off to the estate as the pilot reset the jet. Anthony was busy with business and joined us for dinner. Eddie was flourishing in his role as housewife. He said Anthony had him knighted by the Crown Prince William, and they were now both lords. I know it was meant to impress, but it was still just Eddie to Stephan and me. Dining with four immortals and two normals was something, and the Cognac after dinner in the den with a roaring fire was just what the doctor ordered (no pun intended). The stories from hundreds of years and many countries held us in normal attention till late into the night. I crawled in next to Stephan and fell asleep almost instantly. I got updates over the next few weeks from Lucius and Eric and touched base with Judy to see if she needed me for anything. "Jeff and I are handling the house duties and staff, and Eric is handling the security." Eric came to the phone and said, "There were some detectives here asking about you, Carl. I told them you have been out of the country for a while. They asked about details, and I told them you had left to attend to a sick relative living in Rome. They wanted as specific an answer as I could give them, and I think they were satisfied with the information. "Very good. Let me know if something comes up." "All over it, boss."

I confided in Stephan about the detectives and he said not to worry. "Just enjoy the vacation, Carl." I did. We decided to return to the States and headed home. We arrived at the door around 10 pm and headed to sleep. We arose around 8 am, and as we descended the stairs, we heard the doorbell. Right on cue, the suits appeared ready to ask me questions. Stephan started to join me in the drawing room, but was asked to leave (the suits apparently didn't do their homework, nor did they know my guy). "Pardon me, you want to tell me where to be in my own home. I think we're done here. I've called my lawyer, and you can talk to THEM. Good day, gentlemen." He had Eric show them the door unceremoniously. "You know they'll be back, right?" "Carl, you worry too much. Let me take care of this, will you?" "Yes, dear." Stephen led me away from the drawing room and to the pool. On impulse, he grabbed me and jumped into the pool. Coming up totally wet and a mess, Stephan looked into my eyes and landed a sloppy kiss on my lips. I had to laugh and got water up my nose. Towels were folded on the chairs nearby, and we utilized them. I wiped Stephan down and wrapped him up in the towel. He fell into me, and we laughed again as we fell to the ground. That night, I took a shower and went into the bedroom where I found 'Batman' all suited up. I slipped into the wardrobe and reappeared as Boy Wonder. What a way to end a night.

Breakfast was light, I slugged down another smoothie and felt like a million bucks. Our lawyers called and said that the suits wouldn't be bothering us again, as they had been put on notice about their inappropriate behavior when they paid us a visit (it's amazing when you have unlimited funds, who you can hire). Stephan took a small blood sample from me to test in the lab. I tried to ask why, but he pressed his finger to my lips and said, " Shush. I left the den and my mad scientist. I went to the kitchen and noticed Nathan at the counter. We shook hands, and he thanked me again for his 'used car'. "It made quite the impression on the girls on campus. "I bet. Remind me, where did you end up going?" Nathan said, "Well, my boards weren't outstanding, but they were good enough to get me into Johns Hopkins University." I congratulated him and asked Andre to feed my hungry adopted kid. He laughed and thanked me for the lunch invitation. Eric rounded the corner as I was leaving, and he saw his child. I left them and went in search of my 'Mr. Peabody'. I found him near a machine that reminded me of 'the way back machine ' (yeah, from my cartoon days). He actually motioned for me to join him. "See that, wow." I shrugged as the numbers meant nothing to me. "Enlighten me, oh wizard." "Well, the numbers mean that the infusion I gave you a while back kinda worked. It seems my blood has changed your blood anatomically. You're now part me, so to speak." I freaked out a little until he said, "Sit, and I'll explain. The makeup of my recessive gene allows your blood to live longer in your body. This means your aging process has begun to slow down, or in other words, keeping you younger longer. Right now, you have the blood properties of someone 50. "Thanks, so I'll be an old man longer." Stephan shook his head no. "It means that if you were to get regular injections, you would actually get younger as you get older, 'Benjamin Button'.

I sat back, thought of the implications, and said, "Do you think that was what Harmon was alluding to in his article?" "I believe so. I think others may try to get samples from you, so we'll have to be careful about your next general practitioner." Oh great, I thought, other people are trying to drain me because I happened to fall for an immortal (you could write a great fiction novel about me. Wait, he already did). Well, I already 'drank the kool-aid', so why not keep going? I agreed to the injections, so Stephan set up the schedule, and I prepared myself for 'immortality'. I hope that Stephan realized that he made the vows of 'till death do us part' a lot longer.

We got on with our lives, and we welcomed 2027 in with a bang. We got the troops all together, and Judy's daughter Dahlia came as a surprise (and I know Stephan had a hand in that). She really surprised us when she showed up with a man and a baby boy. "I'd like you all to meet Allen Jeffery Thomas Halstead and my husband, Aaron Halstead." We congratulated them, passed the baby around until Grandma Judy hogged him to herself. Anthony and Eddie (or should I say Lord and Lady Julius) mingled with Hunter and Jr., Nathan was home from college, Eric and Nancy were fussing with baby Allen, and the staff was busy handing out champagne. The fire was roaring, and I could only stand back with Stephan and admire our extended family and how thankful I was to have it all.

The new year's banquet was Andre's crowning achievement (he had come a long way), and we feasted, toasted, and made very merry.

Stephan asked me quietly to get a college fund started for Allen, and I told him I had already thought of it (I was becoming Stephan in more ways than one). By spring, Stephan and I had gotten his wanderlust and decided on Russia (Putin was dead now, and Democracy had finally arrived there). We got there and headed to St. Petersburg. We settled into a rented estate and planned a visit to Svetlana's grave. We went and were greeted with an overgrown and deserted field. A few of the stones were apparent, but not many. We finally found Stephan's wife's stone, and he gently cleared the weeds and twigs away. I helped, and it took an hour, but we left it with new flowers and a promise of moving her to a proper cemetery. We returned to the estate, and Stephan brushed up on his Russian. We got a newspaper (hieroglyphics to me), and he read it to me, nothing interesting. He showed me the culture, and we ended up drinking a lot of vodka. The food was unique but nothing like what I had become accustomed to. I kept up with Stephan much better than I thought I would.

I secretly couldn't wait to leave, but I wanted Stephan to have a good time, so I went along with anything he wanted. He must have come to that conclusion as he asked if I wanted to go to Greece. I nonchalantly said, "Ok, if you want to" (my lying got no better over time), and we packed up and left the next day. Greece appeared on the east side of the plane's window, and we set down early in the morning. We rented a villa near the beach and went in search of some Greek cuisine. Calamata olives, feta cheese, artisan bread, extra virgin olive oil, balsamic vinegar drizzle, lamb meat, stuffed grapes, and baklava for dessert. Fresh fruit, dates, figs, and other delicacies kept coming, and we finally stopped so we could take in some ouzo. We visited his old haunts (and now they were haunted). My tour was more complete than most, as I had an actual Greek leading me around. Most of the people were typical Greeks, but some were like Stephan, amazingly so. I tried to point them out, but Stephan said nothing.

With our wanderlust satiated, we headed home to Baltimore. I was so happy to be home and to get back to normal (or at least our normal). Eric and Judy let us know everything was fine, and we retired to our room. A hot shower and comfy PJs, and we slept soundly until the alarms rang out. We ran out of our room, descended the stairs, and met Eric and security. "What the hell is going on?" Eric stated, "Someone set off the new alarm system. I think they tried to gain entry to the grounds. Security is all over it. Sorry for the inconvenience, bosses." My heart sank thinking about it. Stephan told me to go back to bed and turned to Eric and gave him further instructions, to which Eric ran off without looking back. I waited for Stephan to come to bed and then turned to him and asked what he had said to Eric that made him literally run out. "Carl, I just told him to conduct a security check on the warehouses also. It's a big order, and so he opted to go instead of calling the guards." That didn't make me feel any better, nor did the call we received about 2 hours later. Warehouse number two had been attacked. The cops were on the scene with Eric, and one of the guards was missing. Needless to say, we were dressed and arrived at the scene about twenty minutes later. The officer tried to stop Stephan from entering a possible 'crime scene'. Stephan calmly said, "I own this warehouse, you'll find my name on the paperwork. Now let me in before this gets ugly." The officer began again as Eric whipped around the corner of the building screaming, "Let him in, he's my boss. Sorry Stephan, I didn't realize that they would be such jerks or I wouldn't have called them." Stephan stepped past the officer, noting his badge number and name, and then went into the building. That left me with 'officer friendly'. He asked me why I was there, and I decided to get cute (it was worth a try), "I'm the boss's wife." The look was priceless, and I walked past him and wiggled my butt and winked (it worked, mark today down, it finally worked). I joined the guys in the warehouse and waited for the bad news.

"Well, it's not really bad, but it looks like Eric and I have some work to do investigating the guards. It looks like an inside job." I wondered what they got and looked around. It seemed that they got about three of the cars from the collection (thankfully not the really expensive ones, amateurs). They never made it to the second floor before the cops got them. Stephan was asked if he wanted to press charges, and he just looked at the cops. "Are you kidding me? Of course I am. Now get out there and find my cars before they chop them. They're worth more than you guys will make for your careers, and if I don't get them back, I'm going to see to it you'll be walking a dog beat before week's end. Now go." I believe Stephan got his point across as they hurriedly left, talking to themselves. Eric returned and said the upper floors were secure and called for a couple of reliable guys from warehouse one to come and take over operations. Stephan got the names of the possible offenders and decided that New Jersey needed a couple more unidentified smells. It's a good thing he doesn't hold a grudge.

We went home and asked Andre about breakfast, nothing heavy, just some croissants and homemade jam. And maybe some huevos rancheros (you know, something simple). We drank coffee until Andre called us to breakfast. Stephan looked a little worried, and before I could ask why, Eric appeared, handed Stephan a paper, and he was asked to sit and have breakfast with us. "Nancy will be worried. I should go for a few minutes, boss." Stephan waved him out and read the paper. He handed it to me to peruse as he stood and paced. He must have been thinking about retribution for his generosity because he kept gesticulating and cursing under his breath. He hated unfaithful people (note to self, NEVER be unfaithful). The paper had the names and pertinent information about them. It also contained a few business names and stuff, but I didn't understand why it was on the paper. I was about to find out. I handed it back to Stephan, and he placed it in his pants pocket. By then, Hunter came in, followed by Jr. "What's up? What were the alarms about?" Stephan looked at Jr. and Hunter, said, "Hunter, I want you to get internal security for the guest house. I want you both protected in case anything goes down." Hunter didn't question him and went to call for an installation. Jr. grabbed a croissant and followed Hunter out.

The cops called and had us come to the station to identify the perps and to press charges. Stephan took care to identify them and then turned and asked about the cars. "We got there and saved two intact. The third one had been dismantled. Stephan asked where the dismantled one was so he could have his restoration staff rebuild it. "That's evidence, you'll be lucky to get it back this year." That was officer friendly, or as I'd call him, dead meat. Stephan signed the charging papers (and made a mental note as to where the evidence was). We turned, Stephan all smiles and respectful (which meant dead meat was toast). Stephan got in the passenger side of the Bentley, and I knew he was up to mischief. He whipped out his phone, hit one button on it, and I heard it ringing (that's a real bad sign; the other person was on speed dial).

"Here's the address, go get it." He simply hung up and replaced his phone in his pocket as though he had just ordered a pizza. "You hungry? I could go for something Italian (no kidding, crime boss). We ate Italian antipasto and went home; this time, Stephan drove. We arrived at the house and found a flat-footed detective there. The day was not shaping up to be a good one. "What can we do for you detective?" He started, "We're investigating the break-in…" Stephan stopped him there,

"Detective, I've got my own security working on it, and I believe your talents could best be used elsewhere." "Be that as it may, I've been assigned by the captain and so please indulge me." "Okay, but make it quick, I'm a busy man." The detective (and I swear his name was Richard) started the questions, and they didn't seem to be about the crime but rather about Stephan and me. Stephan gave succinct answers if he gave any and asked for 'Dick's' card in case he 'remembered anything else'.

My cagey husband was gonna eat these people if it took him a lifetime (and he had more than enough of that). The security guards went to jail, Officer Friendly is now guarding a port-a-potty on the docks, and "Dick' never got his report written. (I think he said insufficient evidence to continue). We took a trip to Warehouse Two and, after meeting the new guards, went inside, where I found all three cars back in place, looking pristine. "I'm not going to ask how you managed the dismantled one." "Good, don't. Let's go to the gallery before we have lunch." I took his hand as we went up the stairs. The art was either becoming better with age, or I was getting more appreciative of it. We literally had to be called and told the food had arrived. We ate downstairs with the crew and left most of it for them.

I'd like to say that the year ended in a calm state, but I started getting requests for a follow-up interview from the medical journal (that damn Harmon was haunting me from the beyond). The requests came more frequently, especially from one doctor who wanted to test me again (like that was gonna happen). Stephan took another sample of my blood and came back smiling. "It seems that you're now about the same age as when we met, well, physiologically speaking." Well, I felt better, and now I was actually looking better (the body matching my hair). I snuck upstairs to try on a Speedo in private. The mirror gave me a compliment, and I turned around and, of course, got caught by Stephan, who stepped into the room, closed and locked the door. My day was shaping up nicely.

We decided on a quiet Christmas (but that didn't work out as the boys went overboard yet again). It was worth it, though, seeing everyone, and it got us back in the spirit. New Year's Eve, and we finally got our wish, an intimate affair for two. We held up in the den and drank champagne on our bearskin rug. A crackling fire faded as we covered over, hugged one another, and fell asleep in each other's arms. 2028 started out the best as we awoke refreshed and hungry. Note to self, get the rug cleaned. Andre was waiting in the kitchen and asked what we'd like for breakfast. We told him to take the day off, and we treated ourselves to the abundant leftovers. The boys joined in on our raid of the fridge and nearly succeeded in emptying the whole thing. The boys made Bloody Marys, and we celebrated each other. All good things must come to an end, and the summer arrived early, and with it, business and appointments became the rule of the day. I started getting overwhelmed, even though Eric and Judy cared for everything house-related. They had become indispensable to us. I usually took about 3 hours just writing the checks, and that didn't include the register entries. I went to Stephan in the lab/den and asked if we could maybe simplify our lives somewhat. "We could downsize to a one-bedroom apartment if you'd like. We could even go back to your infamous bologna sandwiches." I took that as a no, punched Stephan in the arm, and had to smile (I now knew there was no going back). He got up, tugged me along, and said, "Let's go swimming. I think I hear the boys at the pool." I actually didn't mind as I put my new suit on. The boys turned their heads and started whistling to show their approval of my choice, red to match my complexion. I dove in right after Stephan and reached the far side easily. I felt great, the water caressing my entire body (the heated pool might have some part to play in that).

Eric approached me and said, "There's a person here to see you. His name is Dr. Charles Tidwell, associated with the Academy for Longevity Studies. What do you want me to tell him?" I told him I'd talk to him, and Stephan got up to go with me, but I waved him off. I put on some cargo shorts and went to the sitting room where I had him wait. I greeted him, and he said, "Thank you for receiving me. I'm here because I've read a lot about your studies, having taken your place at the university when you retired. I was wondering if you had continued your research post-grant." I had to think quickly and said, "I appreciate your interest, but I put my studies away after leaving and have been traveling abroad since marrying my partner. Good luck in your pursuits. I wish I could be of more help." I turned to usher him out when he said, "I see you have an amazing physique for a man of what, 61 years. Do you have any tips for the common man?" I quipped back, "Get 8 hours of sleep daily, eat right, and exercise. Drink little, except water, take 60 ounces a day. Now you have my secret, good luck." I almost pushed him out the door and closed it. Stephan came up behind me, put his arms around me, and said, "You know he'll be back. I guess Trudy's notes were a bit too good." I agreed, and we prepared for his return. I took to reading up on this guy. His papers were interesting to read, and he put forth some noteworthy hypotheses. I almost caught myself wishing he had collaborated with me; he was that good. Stephan said, "You really want to pick his brains, don't you?" "Yeah, kind of. Look here how he describes my work and acknowledges me in the footnotes." "You can be a real nerd sometimes, Carl." I laughed as he kissed my cheek. Stephan and I talked back and forth for about a month before I was prepared to reach out to the good doctor. I invited him back for a lunch date and had Andre prepare a light fare. Jr. and Hunter asked to be there also, so I made it an event, and Stephan said he might stop by. We met him at the door and took him to the atrium. I made the introductions, and Dr. Charles was surprised that we all looked so 'young'. We let him talk about his work, his research other than mine, and his new hypotheses. He seemed eager to indulge us without getting into the weeds. Stephan got a good vibe and actually invited him back for a follow-up meeting. The boys were intrigued but weren't very interested in continuing (they knew the material pretty well). After he left, I asked Stephan why he had changed his mind about this guy. "I genuinely think he is a disciple of yours. I think he could use our help to advance his career. That way, people will focus more on him and his studies instead of us." "If you're sure, I'll set it up."

Dr. Charles Tidwell started coming on a regular basis, and I fed him information (Stephan-approved information). He ate it up, and we only asked for final say before allowing him to publish it. We filtered out our personal information. He told us to call him Chuck, and we agreed. He called me after getting published. It seemed that he was getting quite the following with his knowledge of the aging process. He did ask for a blood sample, but Stephan declined, as did everyone in the house. Chuck seemed disappointed but respected our decisions. With our resolve intact, we went about our business. Chuck said he was going to take a hiatus for six months to research abroad, but would keep in touch with us and send his findings also. That made Stephan want to travel, and I simply asked where. "I don't know, actually, where would you like to travel?" I thought about it for a moment and said, "Why not start in England and try France? I hear Paris is nice, besides, you should see the Louvre now, it's gotten much better with age." I called to get the jet ready, and Stephan asked Hunter to purchase us some nice clothes for the trip. I advised him to limit his spending, to which he said, "Of course,

I'll even take Jr. to make sure (that I knew meant a big bill coming). We gathered our bags and headed to the airport, where the jet was waiting (I kinda like saying that and like it more having it). Eddie had been notified, and Anthony waited for us at the hangar. We got through customs easily and headed to the estate. Eddie was showing signs of salt and pepper hair, but was still the energetic kid we remembered. We told Anthony that we'd only be staying about a week until we were jetting to Paris. Anthony asked if we wanted a couple of chaperons, and we both said yes. So four gents, looking pretty good, hit the streets of Paris.

Eddie hadn't been there yet and was totally awestruck. I was a little less stunned (having traveled so much with Stephan). We got a hotel suite just off the main thoroughfare, and the view was inspiring. We dined that night in the hotel dining room, and it was par to Andre's cooking (as that was where he studied). We planned to visit the Louvre in the morning. Anthony wanted to shop, and Eddie wanted to go to the museum, so they split up, and Eddie went with us. Stephan became our tour guide and told us stories about the artists (Eddie thinking that Stephan was reiterating something he had learned. I knew better). We stayed the week, did some fashion show buying, and then the guys were ready to leave. They chartered a plane to go home, and we said our goodbyes (I wondered when Anthony was going to have 'the TALK' with Eddie). We stayed a couple more days, then followed suit. Baltimore, calm and serene, and back in the USA. Judy had Jeff pick us up, and I asked about Eric. "Oh, he tripped over his laces and fractured his arm. Doc says he'll be fine, but no driving for six weeks." That was good to hear. We took a day to recover before catching up on bills and correspondence.

It was around January 2029 when Chuck got back. He wanted to catch us up on his findings, and I was nervous. Stephan took it all in stride (as always) and welcomed him at the door. He was loaded with documents and books, so I sent the staff to assist him. We set him up in the sitting room, and he spread all the literature out on the tables. We (or should I say I) were intrigued with the presentation and thanked him for catching up. Stephan perused the material for any particular information and was grateful to find it missing. I asked Chuck if he wanted something to eat, and he immediately said yes as he was tired of (you guessed it), bologna sandwiches. I almost doubled over as Stephan smiled broadly. I led him into the kitchen and requested a brunch for three. We drank an expensive wine as we waited for the feast to begin (have I become a show-off now, yes). I rationalized that I wanted Chuck to have a taste of the good life. Stephan joined us in the kitchen as Andre finished up. He told us he was having the pool area set up for us, so we led our guests to the patio. The look on Chuck's face when he saw the appetizers alone was enough to make me think about my past life and how I'd feel in his place. After the meal, I asked if he'd like Andre to box some up for later and nodded (with vigor). We returned to the sitting room and continued with the information. Chuck had me intrigued, and I delved into the material, noting things I had missed back then. This guy was thorough, and I almost missed a page about the Mediterranean Orions. I was about to turn the page, and Chuck stopped me and asked Stephan a blunt question, "Stephan, is there any chance that you're related to this family?" I looked to Stephan to answer, and he simply said, "No, they died out in the 1500's." At least I knew that if he went down that rabbit hole, he'd be searching for the one obscure book that I had found by Stephan (probably out of print now). Still, it was probably worth looking for any miscellaneous copies anywhere and scooping them up. I set the boys on that mission. Hunter was eager, but Jr. was not so much. When I told them it might include travel with an expense account, Jr. came around. Stephan smiled as I told him, saying, "It looks as though you're starting to think like me. Quick, what am I thinking?" I sauntered to the stairs and nodded upwards. "I'll race ya to the closet, loser gets the suits cleaned." I literally ran as though my butt hung in the balance, but Stephan was quicker. Oh well, what's another trip to the cleaners (I'm starting to think these guys at the cleaners are getting suspicious about us). The next day, Chuck reappeared, and this time he brought the infamous book. Darn, darn, darn, we weren't quick enough, or he was that darn good. I played it off, and Stephan wanted to know how much Chuck actually knew or assumed.

Stephan casually asked what Chuck was reading, and Chuck came back with, "It seems that according to this book, some of your ancestors may have survived Stephan. Even the author's name is intriguing. Would you like me to try and find out more?" Stephan decided on intuition to take Chuck into our inner circle, nodding to me and then saying, "I've made a decision, Chuck. How much do you want to know about the Orions? I wrote the book you're reading from." It wouldn't have taken a feather to blow Chuck over, but his eyes grew twice their original size, and he simply nodded yes and made the grand circle with his arms. "Can you really tell me more about your family? I mean, you can, but how much? This book tells a lot, but there's a lot missing." I leaned in and handed him the first and second books that Stephan wrote. "As you'll note, the author is the same. It says fiction, but as you'll research, it's not."

It looked as though Chuck had won the lottery. "If this is real, why would you tell the world. I mean, wouldn't it be dangerous? Won't there be people looking for 'the goose that laid the golden egg'? Stephan looked deeply into Chuck's eyes and said, "Yes, but those people never got to tell anyone of consequence." Chuck got the inference and gulped and choked on his spit. "Why would you say that? I almost crapped myself just thinking about it. Now that I know it, they might come after me." "Exactly, that's why I told you. I never have to threaten anyone, they end up with the risks." "It's one thing to be inside the circle, but somebody always messes up the salt, and evil always gets in. But since I'm knickers deep now, might as well know it all. Let the learning begin." Stephan brought Chuck in, and he proved as adept as Stephan and grew more passionate about the subject matter. Over the next month, Chuck learned as much as he could absorb.

Chuck came by as often as possible, and we planned a trip to the warehouse with him in tow. He had a three-day weekend upcoming, and we sprung the 'trap'. "We're planning a trip to check out our warehouse, care to come?" Chuck didn't really grasp the monumental experience that lay in wait for him (but we did. He was about to go to 'the candy store'). We told him we'd pick him up at his apartment (not knowing he had actually taken my old place), and he begged off. Stephan said, "We're picking you up, sorry, but your car might not make it there and back." That stung a bit as I saw him flinch, but he gave us the address and went home. I felt really bad for Chuck as I'd been there. Stephan hadn't actually realized until I told him about it, and he said he'd apologize in the morning. Saturday saw us in the Bentley (the newest one, 'black beauty'), and we pulled up to the building. He sprinted down the stairs but stopped short when he saw the chariot. I waved him to my side, and he cautiously got in. I assured him he could relax and give him credit; he tried, but it wasn't working. We arrived at the gate, and the guards approached the car until they saw Stephan, then they snapped to and let us in. I was thinking that Chuck was about to have a peek at the goodies inside, and I wanted to feel that feeling again, that awestruck feeling of being a part of something bigger than oneself. Kind of like looking out at the ocean for the first time near sunset and seeing the sun set as the first star becomes visible. A perfect twilight made just for you.

Stephan unlocked the door and stood back as I did, Chuck wondering what was happening. I prodded him to the door and whispered, "Welcome over the rainbow, Dorothy." He entered slowly and stood glued to the floor as he caught a glimpse of the car collection. He turned, all flushed and said, "Where did you get these cars? You'd make Jay Leno jealous. Could I get a closer look? I promise to be careful and not touch." I led him to the cars, newly back in place, and he looked like a person on uppers; euphoria sprang across his face as he came to realize it was all real. "Should we take him to the gallery?" Stephan nodded and let me guide him up the stairs. Chuck rounded the final step and saw the gallery before him. "Please tell me these are reproductions. No one could possess this much real art. Wait, I recognize the signatures and the individual styles, but not the subjects. Are these undiscovered renderings?" I nodded as Stephan came around the corner. Chuck looked at Stephan and said, "These paintings would be worth billions if not trillions of dollars if the world knew about them. Why do you have so many?" Stephan led him to 'Narcissus' by Caravaggio and asked him, "Do you recognize anyone?" He looked at the painting and back at Stephan, shacking his head no as he couldn't put it together in his mind. "Yes, Chuck, that's me in the 1500s, and it's real. One of the few that's actually been in the world. You see, it came up at auction and, being I had the money lying around, added it to my collection for totally personal reasons." Chuck got his mind blown and stuttered out the next sentence, "But you're the same age as when the painting was made. That's impossible." Stephan referred him back to the book and said, "Then the book's not possible either. Read the publishing date. Chuck came to me for any advice, and I said, "Welcome to Oz, you just met the wizard." We headed up to the roof as our lunch arrived. The fare was Greek, and it didn't live up to my expectations, but Chuck seemed to like it. Note to self, take Chuck to Greece to taste real Greek food. We sent the leftovers downstairs (to Chuck's disappointment). We went back to the house and later sent Chuck home in the limousine. Stephan explained that Chuck was a good guy and we wouldn't need to fear his loyalty.

The days flew by, and Chuck seemed to show up a lot around meal times. Stephan was gracious as usual, and I found a new pal who more than shared my interests (as we were closer in age). Jr. asked about our newfound acolyte, and Hunter asked if he was going to need a new wardrobe (hoping for another shopping trip). Chuck arrived as if on cue, and Stephan called Hunter to ask his opinion on Chuck's attire. "I see you, Chuck, in a more upscale wardrobe, though more casual than formal. I think tweed and cotton outfits. What do you think, Carl and Stephan?" We looked at each other and nodded. "I can call the shop and have them pull together something if you'd like. Let's see, 5 foot 6 inches, approximately 185 pounds, size 34 or maybe 36 waist, depending on style and give, 15 inch neck, and 29 inch sleeves. I'll have it delivered tomorrow." Chuck just looked at Hunter, mouth agape, and asked me, "How does he know my size by just looking at me. Those are my exact measurements," Carl explained that's why we hired him all those years ago. "I can't afford anything like what you're talking about. I have to plan to buy a shirt or a pair of pants. I don't want you to bother if I can't afford it." I sat him down, explained that I was in his shoes (so to speak) and felt the same way. "What if I said that Stephan and I wanted to treat you and support Hunter's shop. Would that make it better?" Chuck nodded hesitantly. "Good, now that that's settled. Let's see what else you found while digging." Chuck showed me books he had gathered while in Europe. We browsed through one that was hinting about the same time line and events, but as I later learned, had been written by one of Hunter's ancestors, a Pietro Garibo (anagram for Borgia). Chuck asked how I had garnered it from the name. "Simple, they must all have been doing it to protect themselves. You really can't blame them, I mean, could you imagine going around with people knowing you're about 2 or 3 hundred years old? You would have been burned at the stake," Chuck said. "Point taken. It's mind-blowing. But you look young for your age, do you mind giving up your secret?" I told him about the injections, and he asked if Stephan would mind if he looked at the journals of Stephan's research. "I think that instead of injections, I could synthesize the ingredients into a pill form that you would only have to take once weekly or so. What do you think of me asking Stephan?" I didn't realize that Chuck minored in chemistry as well as longevity studies. "That's actually how I got started in longevity studies, through chemistry." I led him into the lab/den and asked Stephan for a few minutes of his time. I let Chuck present his proposition, and Stephan looked intrigued. "The only thing I would ask is that if it works, that I be allowed to take it also. I will sign any NDA's you want, in blood if you want. What do you think?" Stephan asked for a day to ponder it all. "Of course, but in any case, I'll honor your decision, Stephan."

Chuck left that day, and Stephan convened a meeting with Hunter, Jr., me, and himself. He spelled out the ramifications and problems associated with allowing someone into our inner circle, more inner than even some of the staff. We went around the room, and the decision was made. Chuck appeared the next day with trepidation but hopeful. Stephan came and took him to the den alone to give him the answer. He didn't appear again until dinnertime, together with Stephan. "We have come to a deal. Have Andre make a winner, winner, chicken dinner for our new partner." Andre shook his head, shouted from the kitchen, "I hope he likes duck, as that's what I made, and that's what's for dinner, boys!" We all laughed as Jr. and Hunter simply came to see how Chuck took it. "Your new clothes are in the guest room, or should I say, your new bedroom, if you want it. I realize it's not the one bedroom that you're used to, but it might be okay." Chuck almost lost his appetite thinking about moving in here (no more cold bologna sandwiches). Let's eat first, I think he'll be staying. Then a fashion show, okay Chuck?' Chuck nodded, grinning ear to ear, and thanked Stephan and Hunter as Jr. and I looked on (I wondered how he would look in his new silk briefs, and how he would try to hide his excitement).

The fashion show started slowly as Chuck was having a bit of 'trouble' adjusting his body into the clothes (not that the clothes didn't fit, but rather that they fit too well). He came out, flaunting his new look, looking like he used too much rouge. We all noticed his 'problem' but said nothing, not wanting him to get too embarrassed. Chuck looked great as we knew he would, and he kept thanking us (wait till he tries on his new pj's). We all retired for the night and waited until the next day to ask if Chuck had a good night's sleep. He came down the stairs and headed to the kitchen as we caught up. Chuck started the conversation with, "You didn't quite prepare me for the night. Yes, it was wonderful, but I kept having a 'problem' because of the luxurious textures if you know what I mean." I nodded, and we all broke out in laughter before having morning coffee. Chuck went through the same learning curve as I did, but adapted more quickly. Chuck asked about his apartment, and I said that if he wanted, he could take a couple of the staff, box up what he wanted to bring, and leave the rest. He basically said he'd head over, box up his research, and leave the rest as it was valued at less than a

Happy Meal. After Chuck left, Stephan looked at me, and I said, "Yes, Stephan, we'll get him a new car tomorrow. I'll redo the budget to accommodate it. What were you thinking about a car?" Stephan grabbed a set of keys from the hanger and motioned to the garage. "How about this one (pointing to my Maserati), after all, it is 2 years old, and it doesn't match your status anymore." I think I might have bruised his side as I hugged him tight. I knew what that meant, a matching pair of gentleness. Screw the budget, we'll give the old Bentley to Jeff as he likes to drive. I don't think Judy will mind. Stephan told me he received an envelope this morning and asked if I would go get it. It was from the publishing company. He asked me to open it, and it was a cashier's check for $1,000,000 for royalties. "Do you think that's enough or should I get a loan?" I decided he needed a lesson in humility. "May have to let Hunter and Jr. go shopping. Better go get that loan."

Chuck came back, and I went to meet him with a for sale sign in my hand. I handed him the keys to the Maserati and put the sign inside the windshield. He just looked and stood there. "Well, we couldn't have your car here permanently now, could we. What would the HOA say?" Chuck was beyond words at this point. "You really mean it, don't you?" I nodded, and he went to sit in his newer car. "Careful, the ashtray might be dusty." I think he was going to like it here. Lunch was festive as Chuck settled into the daily routine. He took his books from the apartment to the den and set up a station with Stephan in the pseudo lab. He toiled endlessly as I read more about the Borgias in the book Chuck had brought. Stephan was working just as hard, and they spent more time together than with me. They came out about a month later with a pill. "Would you like to try it out?" I asked if maybe Eddie would be a better test subject, and Stephan thought that was a brilliant idea. "We haven't been to see the Lord and Lady in a few years. Chuck, do you have a current passport?" "Of course, who nowadays doesn't?" Stephan just smiled as the memories came flooding back. "Oh, Hunter, could you do us a favor and shop for England for Chuck? He'll need more formal clothes." Hunter almost ran out the door (my poor budget, how did Trudy manage).

I had the jet prepped, and the staff packed lightly as they knew we'd be buying more. Hunter asked if he and Jr. could visit the folks while we were in England. "Sure, send Lucius and Elena our best and tell them we might stop in if we get the time." Chuck still had chills as he boarded the jet. He was used to economy, not this level of luxury. He even weighed his bags to make sure they were within limits. He saw our luggage and gasped. The steward got us settled, and we prepared for lift-off. Ten minutes into the air, the steward popped a bottle of champagne and filled our waiting flutes. The hors d'oeuvres were served: caviar on toast points and prosciutto, olives, and mozzarella slices. Andre had prepared in-flight food for dinner. He chose French cuisine as he knew what we'd be facing in England. Dinner done, we slept the rest of the way there and were awoken as we were preparing for landing. We cleared customs pretty easily and got into the limousine Eddie had sent. Chuck was looking around as we neared the estate. The manse came into view, and the 'Lord and Lady' came to the door. Chuck asked where the lady was. I whispered in his ear, "The lady is right in front of you, Eddie is 'thready', affectionately speaking." Chuck shook his head and was trying to keep up. "Did you get the package I sent?" asked Stephan. Anthony said, "Yes, but you sent a letter with it saying to wait until you got here before opening it." Stephan began, "First, let me introduce you both to Dr. Charles Tidwell, or Chuck as we know him. He has been helping me with formulating a pill from the injections that I've been giving Carl. I wanted to help keep Carl around longer, and it seems to be working, but injections were getting a bit too laborious. Chuck came to us following in Carl's footsteps, and now he's a part of our extended 'family'. Chuck, this is my 4x great-grandson, Anthony, and his partner, Eddie, who used to be our clothier before Hunter and before he met Anthony." Chuck looked at the assembly and noticed that the only one aging was Eddie.

"I wanted to try the pill out on Eddie, if he'd like, because he hasn't had any other medications or injections. What do you think, Eddie?" Eddie looked to Anthony and got the nod, so he said," I'll do anything to stay with Anthony. I never dreamed that I would be living this life before you and Carl came into mine." "Good, Chuck and I will set up in the atrium so as to keep things apart from the daily living." Chuck looked at me as though to say, how do you know the house so well. Stephan winked and said, "I lived here in the 1750's. Anthony took it over later. George II was king then, and he appreciated that I knew German as he was a Hanover prince." Chuck was flabbergasted, just thinking about knowing a king, any king, but from the 1700's was astounding. "Better brush up on the books he wrote, Chuck. Remember, it's all true. Wait until you read about Nicola Tesla or the Russian tsars. It'll knock your socks off. Anthony got his title from me, and when he and Eddie married, Eddie ascended to a lord."

We started by getting a baseline on Eddie and his vitals. Chuck entered all the data and then came up with the biological age of 45. "But I'm only 44. How can that be?" "It's a biological age based on your history and living conditions. Obviously, you're living a bit too much of an indulgent life now, and it's accelerating your age. That makes you the perfect subject for our experiment." Eddie was a bit put off by that statement, but shrugged it off as he knew it could only get better, and looking at me, decided that it would be worth it. Chuck started the log journal, 2030, and the test subject is starting his daily pill regimen. I consoled Eddie by saying it took about a week before I started getting more energy and about 6 months before I noticeably looked younger. Since Chuck was dealing with the daily journalism, Stephan and I decided to go to Italy and join the boys, Lucius, and Elena. Besides, Italian cuisine was sooo much better than English. We lifted off later that week and arrived in Rome, and headed to Calcata and the villa of Papyri. Lucius received us and said that Elena was stricken again. The boys went visiting the beach friends they knew, and we spent the day seeing Elena (poor thing, she looked so old and careworn). Lucius led us out of the room as Elena dozed off. We went to the patio to enjoy an al fresco meal. It was so welcome after the English cuisine.

The days passed as we kept checking in with Lucius and Elena. The boys were respectful of our time with Jr.'s parents. We still had to return to England and gather our newest member. We packed up and headed to the private jet. Hunter saw us off and asked if I could possibly send back the jet (now affectionately called 'the airbus') for them when they were ready. I said yes as I knew it would be cheaper than letting Hunter and Jr. fly first class. We lifted off and headed to England. Heathrow came into view as we prepared for touchdown. The limousine was waiting at the hangar, and so was Chuck. "I need to talk with you both, and I didn't want to let Eddie know until you did." That sounded ominous, and so we listened intently. "I have some good and bad news. The bad news is we will need to adjust the formula for each individual as it affected Eddie differently than Carl. It seems the injections differed Carl from a normal person starting out on the pills. Carl handled the dosage much better than Eddie. He has had some unusual side effects. It seems to have dropped his testosterone levels and (if you can believe it) has made him even more effeminate. He hasn't noticed, but I have. He gets more emotional, and his gestures are definitely female." Stephan started to ask as I said, "What's the good news?" Chuck laughed and said, "Well, it works, maybe too good. Wait till you see Eddie. Can I video it for posterity, pretty please?" Stephan nodded, as did I, and we entered the estate.

The moment we saw Eddie, we immediately saw what he meant. Eddie (never the athlete) came flouncing out like there was helium in his shoes. He looked great, though. (I could only think that Anthony finally got the wife he wanted, and chuckled to myself). We greeted Eddie as Anthony came to the door. We went inside, and Chuck ended the video. The evening meal was a decent one. We sat in front of the roaring fireplace with snifters of brandy when we got the call from Jr. that Elena had passed. I told him that we'd gas the jet and be there the next day. I informed Anthony that he and Eddie also wanted to go, so we made room and had the staff pack us all for the trip back to Italy.

The trip back was somber but quick. We cleared customs and headed to the villa. Hunter received us, noting that we were not alone and took care to inform the staff to assist us (It seems that Hunter had taken charge so that Jr. and Lucius could grieve in private). We went to them in the great room (where Elena had been laid out. Hugs and greetings all around, and then a small ceremony before we said our last goodbyes. We left Hunter with Lucius and Jr. The funeral director and Hunter prepared the final closing, and the hearse came around to the front door where the entire house assembled to send her off. Tears enough to carry the coffin downstream were shed as Elena was beloved by all. We followed the hearse to the family plot at the Cimitero. Prayers said, we watched as she entered eternity in the family mausoleum. The flowers were placed before all the family, and Stephan described all the relations, starting with his parents and finishing with dear Elena (As long as you say their names, they will never die). We headed back to the villa but decided to let the staff have the rest of the day off to grieve in their own way. We went to our favorite restaurant and had a full 7-course meal. Stephan and I offered Lucius to stay with us for a change of scenery, as did Jr. Lucius thanked us all for the invitation and said maybe later. He still had the villa to run. Jr. offered to come home for the time his dad was visiting, and Lucius agreed to it for a later date. We just said come at any time.

We left Italy on a sad note, but realized that Elena was normal and it would come to most of our friends. We arrived at home to find Eric and Judy at their posts running the show, and decided to raise their salaries. Hunter asked if that meant it also to him, which we said, "Definitely not, remember you're family now and we don't pay family, especially someone who 'shops' us out of house and home." Hunter laughed and said, "Okay, but clothes are getting more expensive if you know what I mean." We all had a good laugh knowing exactly what he meant (which meant throwing out my budget again). The boys went to the guest house, and we retired to our suite. Sleep came, and I was thankful. I started Monday with a new budget plan, we informed Eric and Judy about their raises, and asked if anything interesting had happened while we were gone. For once, all was quiet, but Chuck had gotten a notice that he had missed his report to the grant committee, and he needed to call them. Chuck went pale as he realized it might get him canceled. I told him not to sweat it, as I had been canceled and I had delivered mine, but they just wanted to conserve money. I worked with him on a resignation letter, and he thanked the college for their patience (all the while getting his papers out so no one else could use them), something I hadn't thought of.

Chuck relaxed as I told him he was here as a 'family member' now. I did ask him if he wanted Andre to add bologna to the shopping list, and he punched me lightly on the upper arm. I laughed as I rubbed my sore arm (I couldn't help myself, though). Chuck fit in nicely, and I asked when he would start with the pills. "I want to get the dosage right as I really don't want to turn into Eddie." All I could do besides smirking was nod in agreement. He went to the lab, and I went in search of Stephan. I found him sitting poolside. "I'm gonna have to get a 'bat signal' if you keep disappearing. That way you'll know I want you." Stephan turned and said, "Listen, you are Robin, not Commissioner Gordon. Stop changing characters. Pretty soon, I'll be calling you Batgirl." I pouted until Batman decided to make up and then led the way to the 'lair'.

Our lives went on as Chuck got the formula for 'normals' right and decided it was time to start his conversion. I took on the job of note-taking and observations while Chuck went about his days. It was now 2035 when Lucius finally decided to visit, so I told Jr. about his father's coming, and he wanted to stay, but a promise is a promise, and I made him take the family 'bus' home and told him to have Lucius fly back the same way. Hunter asked if he could accompany Jr. to Italy and chaperon Lucius back. We both nodded as one. While Jr. was gone, Eric turned fifty. Nancy wanted to give him a big party, and we turned the house over to her (with Judy's approval, of course). The whole troop was invited, as well as friends and others. I asked Nancy what her budget was, and she said $1000 was not even enough for the band. I gave her my black card and said, "Nancy, make it really nice. Eric is like my son, and he deserves only the best. Besides, Nathan would never forgive us if he couldn't brag a little." Nancy retorted, "You mean like showing off with your 'used car' at college? You spoil him too much." Then she grabbed the card and kissed my cheek. I guess that meant she forgave me or that my budget should be written in pencil.

The affair went exceptionally well, and everyone had a great time. Anthony and Eddie came, and they looked better than ever. I took down Eddie's statistics, and Chuck did the examination to compare them to the baseline. Lucius stayed for the party, and Hunter live fed it to Jr. Judy's daughter Dahlia, husband Aaron, and son Allen (now nine) flew in, and it more than made Judy and Jeff's day. The house was bulging at the seams with all the guests, but we managed. I had to step back and see what Stephan had built (with a little help). I was living a life far beyond what a mere mortal should experience. I realized that I could still be impressed, and it touched my soul with gladness and appreciation.

The time came for Lucius to return to Italy and for Jr. to come home. We made the same arrangements in reverse, and the 'bus' lifted off. We waved goodbye, and we were left to our own devices. We headed to the beach in the Bentley and spent the rest of the day relaxing in the sand. We got home late, Judy scolded us (like mother, like daughter). "If you're looking for food, the dog ate it. Maybe Andre can fix you guys a sandwich." She turned and left for the night. Oh well, a cold sandwich and a beer, and then to bed, it was worth it. I gave Chuck the results, and he compared his results to his baseline and his to Eddie's results, and made me come to read them. I got excited as they were incredible. "Are you sure of these results?" Chuck looked at me with that smirk of his and nodded. "That's astounding. Welcome to forever, or at least a long time. Let's go show Stephan." We skipped to the sitting room and gave Stephan the report. He perused the document with a poker face. "What about long-term effects? Have you considered that? Let's keep checking with Eddie, yourself, and Carl. If it's that effective, it will be worth an outright fortune."

Now I sat and pondered the ethics of what Stephan had just said. I kept it to myself, though I wondered about the shared results with Chuck. Here was a guy who had nearly nothing getting in on the ground floor of an eternity drug and who now had the formula. Would he quietly sell off the formula for a fortune or keep his loyalty to us? What about Eddie and his inability to keep secrets? He might inadvertently spill the beans. I tossed and turned all night. Should I voice my concerns to Stephan or let it play out? I decided I'd speak to Stephan and ask his opinion, as he and the family had the most to lose. Morning found me looking like a crash survivor, and I saw it in Stephan's eyes how I looked. Stephan said nothing, but rather just came to me in the shower and sponged me down. Then a kiss, letting me know whatever I was overthinking, he would assist with, and we'd face it together (only true love can express that much by saying nothing). We dressed and headed downstairs following the scent trail of our aromatic coffee. The coffee put me right, and I asked that Stephan ride with me to the warehouse. I needed a safe talking place, and I wanted to do it in the gallery, my favorite place.

We arrived, noticed nothing out of the ordinary, and headed to the gallery. I started by sitting, taking Stephan's hand, and saying, "Stephan, I've had many thoughts on the conversation from yesterday, and I'd like to bounce them off you if you don't mind." Stephan looked deep into my soul and saw my desperate need, so he simply nodded. "I have been wondering about the temptations and misplaced loyalties or even simple misstatements that could hurt you and our family if it gets out. I don't care about the money, but rather our safety. Do you really trust Chuck with that amount of temptation? What about Eddie? I have no doubt about his loyalty, but he is a bit flighty and says things he really shouldn't." Stephan looked calmly at me, leaned in, and said, "Leave all that to me. I've dealt with worse things over the centuries. I'll be damned if I'll let any harm come to the family or us. Eddie is harmless, and no one would believe him anyway. Chuck knows too much to talk, and I think the idea of living long enough and having everything he wants will satisfy him. Remember that he gets hurt also if he talks." I hadn't considered that. I guess Stephan was right, and I leaned over, gave him a peck on the cheek, and lay my head on his shoulder, knowing it was going to be all right. We sat in the gallery for about another hour, then headed home.

A couple more years sped by, and it was now 2040. Nathan was now 33 and a top surgeon at Johns Hopkins. Eric was celebrating his 55th birthday, I was 73, and Chuck was 72. Stephan would be celebrating his 528th birthday. Eddie turned 54, and Lucius would be 301. Anthony turned 353. The numbers were staggering, and we just had cakes with a single candle (for safety's sake). Andre was getting to retirement age, and so we took on an apprentice chef named Harold something, wait, I mean Harold Garibo. It seemed Hunter had more relatives than he knew (I guess after 2 or 3 hundred years, it gets difficult following the descendants). The world had changed, morphing into a world that Stephan (having seen it over the span of his life) could only shake his head at why people kept making the same mistakes over and over again instead of just learning from their misjudgments. The United States was just now recovering from its choices in the 2024 election. The rest of the world was beginning to dig out from their 'conservative' (meaning dictator-led) times. We are still trying to regain our leadership role in the world, having been left behind because we couldn't be trusted in the continuity of principles. At least President Trump is no more, and Trump-ism is dead in politics (silver lining, always look for the positive).

Our lives weren't much different (as we prepared for the inevitable). Chuck decided to join our 'family' and leave his old life behind. I helped him start up a business that dealt with life-enhancing drugs (keeping our private pills to ourselves). He gained national acclaim for his work on those items, and he became very wealthy. He was taking longer to evolve than I did to this life, and I, for one, was happy about it. Chuck kept me grounded (I suspect Stephan knew it or at least felt it when he chose Chuck). Stephan called Lucius to just check in on him and found he was in a bad way. The death of Elena was taking its toll on him. Stephan told him to expect us within the next few days and to keep in touch daily (Stephan was genuinely worried about him but tried not to let on). I talked to the boys, and they chartered a private jet and left the same day. We followed behind the next day and got to the villa to find him in poor condition but alive. The boys greeted us, and we immediately sought Lucius out. He was in the atrium, looking pale and gaunt. The boys took over the running of the villa, and we were free to set our own agenda.

We decided to visit the Cimiterio and took Lucius with us. He needed more closure, and we were determined to have him achieve it. We stood back as Lucius told Elena how angry he was that she had left and cried outright, knowing it was natural. We consoled him to any extent we could, and Stephan let him know that he had gone through the same feelings and events. "I'll be here for you always, we will be here always, and Stephan Jr. would be there as much as he wished." I think realizing that he would never be alone, it comforted him, and he asked if we could stop and get something to eat. We basically ran to the nearby restaurant to get him fed. He revived before our eyes (and I knew Stephan would let the boys know what we had said). The menu was never-ending until Lucius cried out, "I'm stuffed, and I don't think I could eat another bite", so we packed up the cannolies and went home (you didn't think I was leaving dessert behind).

The boys talked to us and said that they would be moving to Italy for the foreseeable future. We concurred and said our goodbyes. Packed and ready, hugs, kisses, and tears done, we lifted off. Stephan told the pilot to detour to England, and I smiled (Lord and Lady, here we come). Stephan made a phone call, and when he hung up, said, "It's all set, the car will meet us at the airport." Heathrow came into view, and we left our purchases in the plane (easier to get through customs) and set off to the estate. It was an easy ride, and the estate never looked better (Lady Eddie must have taken over that duty, as it was perfect, the way Stephan recalled it looking way back when). Anthony and Eddie met us at the door, and we waved out the limousine window. Eddie looked amazing (considering how he started out), and Stephan was glad that we found Anthony in such good shape, also. The house greeted us as a friend, and Stephan felt at home (after all, it was his home to start with).

Dinner in England, mm mm average (they really needed a new chef). We discussed the 'elephant in the room' situation with our anti-aging pills, and it is not getting into the public realm. Eddie must have felt the direction in which the conversation was taking as he said, "Please don't worry about me, I promised Anthony and I would never break that vow. I happen to be one of the luckiest men alive, having found a loving man, a great family, and a home I can be proud of. There's nothing more I could want." That settled, we took our after-dinner bourbon in the den and sat in front of the roaring fire talking about our current events.

Morning came, Stephan and I went to the kitchen and surprised the staff. "Sorry, but we are used to having to serve ourselves (Just ask Judy). They smiled and left us to it. The lord and lady came down and were aghast at us in the kitchen. It seems they were really enjoying the life of privilege.

We stayed about a week and told them we were heading home soon. They understood and had the staff attend to it. We were shuttled to the hangar and belted in for the flight home. I will say that flying in a private jet was a privilege that I thoroughly enjoyed, even if it meant I was spoiled. Stephan sat beside me on the ride home, and we dozed off and on. We got home and found everything under control. Eric, Judy, and now Jeff were handling everything but the outgoing bills, or so I thought. Judy simply said, "Jeff and I decided to take that on so you two wouldn't feel flustered after your trip. We used the house account and put everything on the card so you could peruse it at your leisure. I hope you don't mind." I simply kissed Judy on the cheek and took the one bill and reviewed it. "It's marvelous, Judy, Jeff, and you, too, Eric. You've saved me mountains of hours. I'll see to it that you're all compensated for thinking of us." I turned, walked to the den, and explained the situation to Stephan. He agreed and planned a car shopping trip for the 'family'. The following Monday, we had Jeff drive us to the export car lot and took them to the showroom. Stephan said, "Okay, kids, go pick out a car for yourselves, and I mean one each." After their jaws came up from the floor, they meandered around the showroom and decided on their choices. We called our usual salesperson over and told him to box them up (I think he just realized he was about to make a year's salary today and get his picture for 'employee of the month' put on the wall).

We were told that they could deliver them the following day after they were gone over, registered, gassed, and polished. We told him that would be fine, and we left to go eat (as that always made us hungry). Our restaurant offered to close to the other customers when we all popped in, but we shook our heads no to that, and we were seated at the corner table (the biggest they had). The ambiance was great as always, and the food was exceptional. We left it up to the chef, and he delivered in spades. Antipasto (a charcuterie board on a plate), fresh Italian bread grilled and rubbed with garlic, extra virgin olive oil with a drizzle of balsamic vinegar on the side, angel hair pasta with a delicious marinara sauce and grated Parmesan cheese over the top, and calamari salad as a side. Dessert was figs and a dessert wine of Muscato and Prosecco, grapes, and a lemon wedge to cleanse the palate.

The bill came, and Stephan handled the bill (it came to $789.31, but Stephan rounded it up to $1000 and gave the chef his own tip of $500). Needless to say, they welcomed us and any of our 'family' any time to return, and they would accommodate us. We left stuffed and completely satiated. Jeff drove us, and we retired for the evening. Just spooning, Stephan and I fell into a deep sleep. We awoke to Eric calling us downstairs for a delivery (he wanted us there to join in the merriment). He and Judy handed us coffees so we could wake up, and we went out to the driveway as the cars came down from the carrier. "Please check them out to ensure they are alright", said the delivery guy, and then told Stephan to please sign off. He asked the guys into the house for a moment and they looked at him quizzically. "it's okay, I just wanted to tip you two for your service and then handed each delivery guy a crisp hundred dollar bill, "Take your significant other out to dinner on us and thanks for the careful delivery, it was perfect and I'll let the dealership know too. Expect some repeat business." The guys waved as they left, and the smiles were infectious. I looked at everyone in the driveway and felt content that they were genuinely happy with their gifts.

Our lives were now meshed and intertwined in the best way, and Stephan was satisfied. That alone made me happy. Chuck came to visit with us at the main house (having moved into the guest house) and found us in the kitchen drinking coffee and munching on Harold's croissants. Chef Andre decided that Harold could take over and was now confident in his abilities. We needed to plan a send-off party for him and had Judy set it up. Chuck told us of his intentions to retire and enjoy his life and said he'd move after the party (he wasn't stupid, as our parties are pretty epic). We agreed, and he grabbed a cup of coffee and returned to the guest house. It seemed that the family was morphing again, and Stephan just took it in stride. I asked him how, and he said I'd get used to it. "When you've lived and loved this long, you see there is an ebb and flow to existence and realize you need to enjoy the good times as they arrive and know that the bad ones are only temporary." I'm glad I have a lover, friend, husband, protector, and mentor all rolled into one.

The day of Andre's retirement came, and everyone who could make it came as well as his family. We presented him with a card that simply said, "Have a great retirement, use this token of our esteem wisely. Good luck." With it was a cashier's check for $2,000,000 dollars. He blushed, showed his wife the check (and she put it in her purse), and came to thank us. "You two have been more generous to my family and me than anyone else. It has been my honor to cook for you. Harold has all my recipes, and I feel confident you're both in good hands." His eyes welled up and glassed over as he turned to leave. His wife hugged him, and they left arm in arm. We walked into the kitchen as Harold was finishing up. He asked if there were any apartments near our house for rent, as the commute was starting to get to him, and we suggested our guest house. He said he couldn't afford it until we told him it was free for an employee. He almost cried as he asked when it would be available.

"Chuck is moving out this weekend. You can move in Monday. Do you need help packing and moving?" Harold shook his head no and said, "Hell, I can pack my clothes and burn the rest, it's yard sale stuff." We told him to go pack, come back, and stay in the guest room until Monday, and he almost bowled us over getting to his car.

I guess not everyone in the Garibo (Borgia) family made a fortune. Boy, did that statement take me back. Then that made me crave my old bologna sandwich (but that craving passed quickly). He was back before dinner time and cooked as though his luck depended on it. He fussed over everything and tried so hard that he was exhausted after the dinner was done. He finished up the dishes and went straight to bed. I heard him talking to himself about breakfast tomorrow and trying to mentally make a menu. Stephan looked at me, smiled, and said, "See what I mean about ebb and flow, some leave, and others enter our lives, and it will continue for a long time." Right again, Stephan nodded to me and whispered, "Are they clean?" I nodded, and we raced upstairs, and I won (no dry cleaner for me tomorrow).

Over coffee, Stephan told Harold that he would need to upscale his ride if he was going to stay in the guest house. "But I can't afford it, that would cost me a year's salary. Not to mention my FICO score is in the 600's." Stephan handed him a card with an address and a note that said: "See John in sales, tell him I sent you, and put it on my account." This is an export car dealership; those cars are insanely costly. I nodded and said that I would accompany him, and he calmed a bit. More memories like blasts from the past kept coming, but this time I was on the other side of the equation, and it felt good that I could do that for the kid.

The next day, we had Carvana pick up his car, and went in search of his first luxury car. We took my Bentley, and he was nervous but liked the ride. We pulled into the dealership, and John came running out. "So glad to see you back so soon. What can I get for you today?" I told him that Harold needed a car befitting his new position as head chef in our home (Harold almost broke his face smiling so wide, hearing him being elevated to a position of title). John took Harold over to the Audis, Mercedes, but I mentioned that my first luxury car was a Maserati, so we headed over there. John excitedly went over all the bells and whistles of the car (hoping Harold would bite). Harold looked at the car, sat behind the wheel, and then noticed the price. He almost jumped out of the car. I asked if he liked it and to disregard the price. He gasped as he said he would cherish it, but it was too much. I motioned for John to write it up and gave him the account number. John ran to the office and came back with the keys. "We can deliver it by the end of today." I nodded, told Harold to give him the plates, and he'd tend to it. We returned to the Bentley and waved goodbye to John. Heading home, Harold kept thanking me, and I said, "Welcome to the family."

Stephan asked Harold what he chose, and he blurted out, "a Maserati, but Carl told me to get it." Stephan said, "Good choice, that was Carl's first car when we got together." I think Harold was as stunned as I was when that happened. Too many deja vu's as I remembered the past. Harold left to start lunch, and we requested a salad and a sandwich. We told Harold to have it sent poolside, and we went up to change into our Speedos. I chose a blue one, and Stephan opted for red. We lay on the chaise lounges and sunned ourselves until the meal arrived. The repast was just what was needed, and we finished as they came to collect the dishes. I just sat and thought back to the times in my apartment when I had almost nothing. It surprised me as to how far I had come in life and as to why I was searching for this so much. Maybe it was reincarnation, and my past life was like this. However it happened, it's best to leave it in the past and start living in the now. It was now my duty to inspire the upcoming kids and to get them ready for their lives. That would suit me better than relying on Stephan to guide me along.

My thoughts were interrupted by Stephan as he said that I was looking like a strawberry. Crap, I got a bad sunburn and had to go through that burning and itching as it healed. I went into the kitchen and retrieved the vinegar. Stephan said that if I was going to smell like a salad, I was going to sleep in the den. I showered in tepid water and hoped that it would be sufficient. Stephan waved past his nose but let me in bed anyway (now that's true love). My night was filled with random thoughts and memories, and when I finally fell asleep, I dreamed of my life – from a dumpy middle-aged straight man with a grant and a crappy apartment to a stud muffin gay young man with a husband and a life of unlimited wealth, jet setting around in a private jet to any place in the world. Gifting heavily to many close friends and family. I awoke almost as tired as I went to sleep.

Stephan let me sleep in, and when I finally appeared, he was dressed as though attending to some business. I asked if he needed me, and he waved me off. "I'll be back in time for lunch, see you later, sweetie." Stephan left, and Judy told me he had gotten a phone call earlier and then went to dress. I wondered all last night, and now I'm wondering about today (I should have stayed in bed). Now I had heartburn and hadn't even eaten yet. I was overthinking it, but I am a worrywart. I guess there will never be a day when I won't need Stephan. He was my fixer, the one to make everything okay in a world that couldn't care less if I lived or died. I waited until he came home, and the look on his face made me queasy. Those beautiful eyes were blankly staring, and I knew right then that it was way beyond my ability to help. I let him take his time to collect himself, and he asked for a stiff drink. I got it and handed it to him, bracing for the bad news. He started the conversation with, "Junior called this morning. He and Hunter found Lucius dead in bed, an empty bottle of sleeping pills by him. The death of Elena was too much. Junior wants us to come as soon as possible." I took Stephan in my arms, held him, and we cried it out together while I directed him to the den for privacy. I asked Jeff if he would handle the arrangements, and he came back about an hour later just saying, "You two leave tomorrow morning." He left us quietly, and I just held Stephan tight, wishing I could take the pain from him into me.

We arrived in Rome around dark, and Jr. had the limousine waiting. We got to the villa and went inside to be with Jr. and Hunter. They were on the phone with the funeral director, and when Jr. spotted Stephan, he gave the phone to Hunter, hugged Stephan, and broke down. "I'm now officially an orphan, both of them are gone. I thought dad was okay, but mom's death cut him to the core, and he never healed." Jr. continued to cry into Stephan's shoulder, and I went to Hunter to ask how he was coping. "I'm okay, but I'm really worried about Junior. He's virtually inconsolable." "Don't worry, Hunter, Stephan will handle Jr. Let's handle the funeral arrangements as they talk. The funeral was held a week later so that Anthony and Eddie could arrive and attend. We six had Lucius' service private (although we allowed the staff to attend). I told Stephan to stay, and I'd send the jet back when he wanted to return. Hunter said that they were going to keep the villa and live there (which I thought was an excellent idea).

The idea of returning alone was awkward, and I felt that it was necessary, though (I needed to grow up a bit). I kissed Stephan goodbye, shook Hunter's hand, and headed to the airport. I landed in Baltimore as usual, but was stopped by customs. I wondered what was wrong, but they just took me to a holding area without a word. I asked the reason, and they simply said that they got a tip that I was trying to smuggle something into the United States that was illegal. They were searching the plane now and handed me the search warrant. I read the warrant and found out that it was about an antique stolen in Rome. That was news to me, as we had more antiques in our possession than the Louvre and the Prada combined. What did I need with anything else?

Before I could ask to phone my lawyer, they said I could go, saying they found that the plane was clean. I took the limousine home and collapsed on the sitting room couch. Eric asked why I was so late, and I related the story to him. "Who could have sent in the tip? Can I see the warrant? Maybe there's a clue as to the informant." Eric took the warrant, scanned it for any clues, and asked if I wanted him to get to the bottom of it. "You don't have to, as they found nothing." Then I remembered that day when he took out the thug. "Well, go ahead if you want. Just leave it between us, as I don't want to upset Stephan, especially now." That made his day, and he kept the warrant, but I didn't know why. Oh well, a good stiff drink and bed. The mask would have to do tonight.

Eric checked in for the next few days, saying he'd found nothing yet but had some leads. "Let me know before you do anything." He assured me and left to get back to it. He was like a man on a mission. I knew if anyone could find out, it was him. I didn't have to wait long. Eric came to me with some pretty specific information and a name. I didn't recognize the name, but allowed Eric to lay it out for me. "It seems there is someone jealous of your life and knew you were flying solo this trip. "He wanted to give you grief, and that's what happened. Should we pay him a visit or just return the favor and get him in trouble." I thought about it and said, "Can you get me all the information on this guy? Time to see how it feels to him to be on the receiving end of an allegation." Eric grinned and went on his way to hire a private investigator to get the goods. I looked at the name, and it began to make sense, then I remembered he was a colleague of mine. I had gotten the grant he wanted, and he must have had me followed to get some dirt he could use to bother me. Well, now to figure out his issues. Eric came back to me a week later and laid out the pictures and paperwork the PI had developed.

"First, Eric, he was a colleague of mine, but why he did this is in question. What have you got? Let's see." Eric smiled again as he showed the guy in compromising situations and enough paperwork to have him convicted in any court (the guy was that dirty). "What do you want to do now, boss?" I looked at all the stuff and said to have his guy leak it to the press and the authorities, and let them handle it. "I really would like to see you 'strike a blow' for justice but this is longer lasting. Eric simply nodded and left. The following day's newspaper had a lead story, "Educator found having sex for grades and offering illegal drugs to students." I showed Eric and he pounded his hand with a satisfying grin. "You got him boss, and no one will be the wiser."

I was glad that all got taken care of before Stephan got back. He called and asked for the jet to be sent. I called the hanger and set it up. Come home to me, lover. I couldn't wait. I went to the airport and waited for the plane to arrive. Stephan stepped out of the plane and into my waiting, outstretched arms. "I've missed you terribly, but I also knew it was important for you to stay. How's Jr. doing?" "He's okay now, and Hunter is with him, so he has someone. I've missed you, too, slugger. Please tell me everything's good here." I nodded and let it go at that. I held Stephan's hand all the way back (I couldn't believe that I could love a man the way I loved this one). He walked in, and Eric greeted him. I shook my head, and Eric got the message, nix the issues we had while he was away.

Harold saw Stephan, asked what he'd like for dinner, and Stephan said something light as he wanted to get some good sleep (mask up tonight, and he can sleep when he's dead. That should let him know how I felt about his absence. We went upstairs, and the poor guy, silently pouting, I let him sleep. Tomorrow would be better.

I woke up sleeping beauty around 7 am the following morning, and he realized he was home. We didn't make it to breakfast, and Judy didn't even ask why. I caught Stephan up on most of the events while he was gone, and he seemed relieved. "I want to go to the beach, what do you think?" I asked if he wanted to be just us or the troops. "I want everybody and everything. I need to be surrounded by my family." So be it, I told Eric of our plan, and he got everyone on board. The beach was going to be busy this week. The caravan made it to the beach, and the kids ran for the sand. We went into the house and got ready, too. Tents, canopies, chairs, and assorted other things dotted the beach, and food was set up closer to the house. Camp Getaway was in full vacation mode, and we settled in like the grandparents we were. Stephan coaxed me into volleyball, and Eric beat us badly. Harold kept bringing snacks until we waved him off. It was wonderful and quiet.

The week came too quickly, and we all headed home. Stephan started writing again, so I let him have his space. He encouraged me to keep a journal so I could go back and reflect on my time on Earth. "What a good idea. I wish Trudy were here; she always took care to be a good editor and transcriber." Judy heard those words and said, "Did I mention that I did half of the typing when mom was feeling under the weather?" "No, but now that we know, you'd better get some under staff to free up your time." She laughed and nodded that she had it covered. Diligently, I started my journal. First, it was fluff, but as I got into it, it started to resemble something Stephan would have written. I asked him at dinner about how long it took for him to start writing meaningful items in his journal, "I started the same as you, but you have to understand the times were different then and writing was the thing to do. We were taught to express ourselves with flair and elegance." I thought about that for a moment and decided to let it permeate my brain. I had read Stephan's journals, and I studied them again to get the rhythm and cadence. My writing began to look more professional and touching.

Judy let me know how she felt about the new transcription and said she noticed the positive change. I began to feel better about the entries and almost let Stephan read them, almost. I was intimidated by his natural ability to describe the event or set the scene. His flair with the written word was a wonder to behold. I kept the journal until the end of the year (which was 2042, by the way). I had Judy transcribe the final draft and then asked Stephan to read it. He took it into the den and emerged hours later for dinner. I almost couldn't ask if he liked it, and he was as poker-faced as always. Judy finally broke the ice and asked, "So what do you think of our newest writer?" Stephan said nothing but came over to me and hugged me tight and whispered, "I think it's wonderful. What say we discuss it further upstairs? I may want to re-create some of the passages in real life." I nodded to Judy that he was pleased, and then we basically ran upstairs and wrestled the closet for our suits. Tonight was going to be special. 2043 was going to start well. We were in the third year of the Buttigieg administration, and the markets were doing excellently. Costs were down, salaries were up, and the MAGA movement proved to be a failure and had been diminished to a few conspiracy theorists and crazies.

Harold proved to be a good, bordering on a great, chef. Judy and Jeff were now heading up the household. Eric and Nancy had welcomed their second grandchild, a girl named Rita (after Nancy's mom), and a boy, now six, named Nathan Jr. Nathan had married an RN named Anita during his residency final year. Our family was growing exponentially and yet Stephan and I were looking the same. Thankfully, no one ever questioned it, and Judy fully assumed her mother's role as protector of the family secret.

Hunter and Jr., or should I say Stephan now, checked in saying that their life was wonderful, and we had an open invitation to visit. I asked Stephan to accept, as we hadn't been to Italy for a few years now. He nodded, Jeff hopped on the line and set up the 'family bus,' and the staff prepared the bags that we would need. We were in the air hours later and saw the 'Boot' coming into view. Italy opened its arms to us as we landed. Customs was a breeze (although I had to admit I had angina after the last time). Our car was waiting, and the boys welcomed us at the door. Stephan and Hunter asked if we wanted to go shopping (as they knew we didn't have a personal clothing shopper anymore), and we decided to try the new fashions on for size. It happened to be fashion week, and we took a trip to Milan for the shows. Just let me say that September in Milan is incredible. The scents and sounds, the models (both male and female), the food (of course), and people in general. I was even learning some Italian to impress my guy.

Hunter led the way, and with his influence (and lots of bribe money), we were treated to the best seats and backstage passes to do meet and greets. I had to sit back a little and take in my life and how this one beautiful man changed the entire trajectory of it. Love finds the one not looking, and I certainly didn't believe I'd be married to a man, let alone Stephan. We had Hunter make the shipping arrangements for the purchases, and Stephan assisted, as he wanted to expand his life with Hunter. Stephan and I hit most of the sights, and especially the restaurants of Milan. I almost asked Stephan to get a home here so we could come any time we wanted, although I decided against it because I wanted to keep the costs down (even though I conscientiously knew that we were worth close to a trillion dollars if you included all of Stephan's collections of art). Stephan took me to a winery, and we had a private wine tasting. I think we purchased half a vineyard worth of wine. So much in fact that the Vintner invited us to a dinner at the estate. We accepted, and the food literally blew my mind. How they took such simple ingredients and made such sumptuous delights was above my pay grade, but I was glad they knew. The antipasto was unique, the Chianti flavorful, grilled garlic bread, spinach-flavored gnocchi, lightly seasoned grilled asparagus, medium-sized meatballs with marinara sauce, farfalle with garlic butter sauce and Parmigiano Reggiano, finished with a tart of pears with apricot glaze and some Prosecco.

I had a hard time leaving the dinner table, but Stephan dragged me to the car, and the Vintner (or Tony as we found out his name) gave us his card and told us to please visit on a regular basis and stay at the estate (and I knew we would). We bought a couple more cases to take back to the boys and waved goodbye to Tony. Back at the hotel, Hunter was finishing up the final shipping details and said that the purchases should arrive before we got home. Stephan called the house to warn them of the deluge of stuff headed their way. We presented the boys with their cases of wine, and the boys got them ready for the trip back to Calcata. I asked Hunter if he had any receipts for the purchases, and he just smiled. I told him not to worry, and then he handed them over (well, it was better than most of the other times; he only overspent by five grand).

Calcata, although having its own charm, was nothing compared to Milan. We stayed with the boys for another week and headed to the 'bus' for a trip to England. Calls were made, and Eddie said come ahead and he'd have transportation waiting. England welcomed us as always, the limousine was waiting, but Eddie was in the car when we opened the door. "Surprise, I wanted to see you as soon as you landed. I hope that's alright." "We love having you here. How's Anthony?" Eddie smiled and said, "He's been heavily invested in stocks and day trading, so he's home making us sustainably wealthy. He never wants to be in the position you found him in before. Stephan, you are his mentor as well as his x amount grandfather. He just wants you to be proud of him now." Stephan wiped a tear from his eye as he entered the limousine. I noticed, but let it alone. "Home, James, to the manse." We arrived about fifteen minutes later, and the estate looked fabulous, which we mentioned to Eddie. "This will be my legacy to Anthony." I didn't know what to think about that statement, but let it lie there also.

We walked in, and Eddie went to summon the lord of the manor. I looked around and saw that Eddie had restored the manor to its former glory. I, for one, was impressed. Stephan said nothing, as was his way, but I noticed him touching and fondling the furniture, taking in the artworks and tapestries, and walking from room to room. Anthony appeared, and the two men hugged, Stephan smiling at his grandson and letting him know he was proud. He had the staff take our suitcases to our room, and he led us into the dining room. He told us he had hired a French chef to assist in the kitchen and to prepare for a feast as he had been cooking all day (I prayed for French cuisine). I was pleasantly surprised as the feast was indeed French, starting with French onion soup with Gouda cheese and crouton topping, a garden salad with Bleu cheese dressing, steak grilled to medium with butter melting over the sear, potatoes Au gratin, baguettes on the side, wine, of course (a good pinot noir), and fruit with a glass of Muscato. I was in heaven, but I must have put on twenty pounds this trip due to the luscious food. Stephan picked at his, but enjoyed it though.

Eddie wanted to show us the million-dollar tour, and we went. Anthony went back to work and told us he would join us in the den later. We started in the gardens and ended the outside tour on the patio. The newly restored patio caught Stephan's attention as he looked at the Terra cotta tiles. "These look like the original tiles but newer. How did you find them?" Eddie proudly pointed out, "I had a mason test an original tile and sent him to salvage others from updating homes. I wanted it as authentic as possible. If you look, the windows are the same, and I tried researching to try to find anything that Anthony had sold off during his 'lost years'. "Well, bravo, Eddie, you've gone far and above with the restoration. I can't wait to see the rest of the house." With that, we entered, and Eddie led us from room to room, pointing out the items he had retrieved and some new antiques. It fit in perfectly, and I patted Eddie on the back. We ended in the den, and Anthony was there having a cigar and a drink. I looked at Stephan, and he looked at Anthony. Anthony noticed and said, "Don't worry, Grandfather, it's sparkling water with a lemon twist. All the look but none of the alcohol. Eddie has seen to my needs, and I couldn't be happier. I've been sober for years now, and I credit Eddie for that." Eddie blushed at that statement and cuddled up to Anthony and pecked him on the cheek.

We spent the next hour discussing events of the day and new topics about their life in England. We told them about the boys living in Italy and how our home was morphing again. It was time to turn in, and we all went to our respective rooms. Tomorrow would be interesting if my guess was right. After breakfast, Stephan asked me to go with him to the warehouse he had there, and Eddie asked to accompany us (of course, we said yes). We took a pickup and a panel van to the warehouse. The guards were wary about letting us in until Stephan proved his existence. That done, we roamed the warehouse with our guide Stephan, pointing out things to pack and things offered to Eddie for the manor. We spent nearly four hours browsing our personal boutique, and Eddie went straight for the wardrobe area. He picked out many of the antique clothing pieces and promised to restore them also. We picked out paintings and statues for the house in Baltimore. All in all, we packed the panel van to the door, and Eddie loaded the pickup to the hilt.

We called Anthony to meet us at the restaurant that Eddie approved of and settled in for more French cuisine (it seems that he loved to eat). Anthony appeared and came to our table, sitting across from Eddie. He told us that he made a small fortune today on trades (having taken profits from the recent boom). Eddie couldn't wait to tell him all about the things he found in the family heirloom section of the warehouse. Anthony was happy for Eddie, but not impressed, as he had seen most of it all his life (which made me realize how much different he and I were). I fawned over the items Stephan picked out. We decided to call the shipping company and let them handle the arrangements. Then we settled out on the patio as the weather was perfect for a fire in the pit. Stephan, Eddie, and I sipped wine, and Anthony had his sparkling water. The sunset over the valley was spectacular, with the clouds tinted red, the sky turning from light blue to azure to navy blue. I leaned into Stephan, and Eddie leaned into Anthony. The perfect ending to a perfect day.

We stayed a few more days and then packed for our trip home. The 'bus' was readied, we said our farewells, and lifted off. Coming home meant facing the reality of how to install the new items into a packed house. What I didn't know was that Stephan had commissioned an addition to our local warehouse for the items leaving the house. He always knew the best for us and was forward-thinking. I dreaded thinking about getting the budget back in shape after a month away. The limousine and Jeff were waiting at our hangar as we pulled in. He had staff take our personal things to the car and got us sorted with customs (our necessary evil). Home never looked so good, and the shower and cuddle session that followed was euphoric. Sleep overtook us, and we relished in the sweet dreams that came our way.

Stephan took the next day, getting his bearings by talking to Judy. She let us know that our spending spree had arrived and was waiting for us in the garage (she told us we shouldn't be surprised at that, as she wasn't going to handle that mess). Stephan and a troop of guys went to the storage place to unpack it all as I talked to Judy about the budget. She said, "I believe that you'll find it in order. You see, you didn't send anything for me to transcribe, so I took on the budget. I saw that you two were trying to bust it wide open, but I manipulated a few payments and made it work. However, if you could see to finding a few thousand to buffer the account, that would be nice." I couldn't help myself and kissed her on the cheek. She blushed a little, turned her head, and went back to the kitchen. I decompressed in two seconds, happy in the knowledge that she had handled it all. I knew who was getting a fat bonus this year (not that she ever got a small one). I took my journal out and got back to writing about our newest adventures in Milan.

Dinner at the house was good as usual. Harold was on point, and we asked Judy, Jeff, and Eric to join us. We shared some of the wine, told them all about our time with the boys, and then came the presents for the ones gathered. Judy got some haute couture and perfume, Jeff got some wine, and Eric got an original painting by Claude-Joseph (which

Stephan told him to keep quiet about as the public didn't know of its existence). I dared to take an estimate and put it at around three million dollars in value. If he only knew about its value, he might be tempted to try to auction it off. We spent the winter at the manse in Baltimore. The holiday craziness was in full swing, and people were coming and going, tinsel and glitter exploded in the house, and the electric usage was about to burden the grid. So it went, and we were never happier. The 'family' gathered and the guest house filled with visitors, so much that we had to put up a schedule so as not to clog the house too much. Dahlia and her family came in for the holidays, Nathan and his tribe stayed at Eric's house. Christmas dinner was actually a brunch that lasted five hours. Presents around the tree in the foyer reached half way up the twenty foot tree. We payed an actor to play Santa for the kids and he and a few elves distributed the presents (budget be damned). That could wait until the new year. Stephan and I looked at our extended family with a sense of pride that I never thought I'd experience.

New years came and we decided to celebrate quietly (fat chance as England and Italy descended upon the house). I have to say having our true nuclear family was better than enjoying our extended family and seeing all the boys rallied Stephan to even crack a smile. New Year 2044 came with little surprise and a calm that was much welcomed. Stephan and I took a week at the beach house to compose ourselves for the year ahead. We only took Harold to cook for us, and he left us to ourselves most of the time. I loved my time with Stephan, and he seemed to open up more. I was going to be 77 this year, and Stephan 532. Looking back, we had now been in each other's lives for 39 years, being married for twenty-five of them. My appreciation for my life was being poured into my memoirs, and it showed. Judy was busy with her editing and corrections as I just emoted in writing.

Stephan had finished his new 'novel' and had sent it to the editor. He received a healthy check in the mail, and we went about trying to decide what to do with it. Fate, however, had different plans, and we received a notice that we owed thousands in land taxes for properties I didn't even know Stephan owned. Stephan got on the horn and talked to his lawyer in England, who stated that Anthony never paid the back taxes for the estate (during his lost years). Being that the estate was still in Stephan's name, he owed the money. "Well, there goes my royalty check. I'll see how much more I'll need to come up with and talk to Anthony to get the estate transferred to his name going forward." I asked Stephan to talk to Anthony first, but Stephan took responsibility (as usual) and said no to my idea. To my knowledge, the royalty check was for two million dollars (how much did the kid owe?). I simply told Stephan to let me know so I could adjust our budget for the year. "Don't worry, I'll just sell some art pieces." With that, Stephan went to make a few more calls and set up the payment to the crown.

The auction was set, and the pieces were put on the block. I felt a pang in my soul as I felt something bad was coming (I was right). After the auction, the pieces were authenticated, and the buyers wanted to know how Stephan had come into possession of unknown masterpieces. He tried to be obtuse and ambiguous about his answers, but the questions kept coming. Now the auction house got in on the act, and that led to the crown checking in. Stephan had had enough and decided to tell them the simple truth. "I told them they were painted for me by the artists." My jaw dropped, and my complexion turned pale. Stephan started laughing and said that the critics accused him of stealing them, but Stephan told them to prove it by naming the original owners of the previously unknown pieces. When they couldn't, he laughed in their faces and told them he was going to bring a suit against them for slander and false accusation. They finally found out who they were dealing with. He also told them to drop the back taxes before he let it go (my man, got to love him).

It seems that they caved, and Stephan left with a clean slate and all his money back (did someone mention a trip to Milan?). I hugged my guy and headed to the cleaners to ensure a good night. Why do things like this happen to good people? I guess it comes with the territory. At least I was going to get a trip to the vineyards out of it. We waited until September, as it is the best time for travel to Milan, and called our vintner to set the arrangements. He stated that the yield wasn't as good as the year before, but we decided to go anyway. Jeff called to get the 'bus' ready, and we packed (or rather, the staff packed for us). Lift off was uneventful, and the flight was an easy one. Da Vinci airport came into view, and we landed softly. Customs was a breeze as we hadn't brought anything but our credit cards and some lire with us. We called the boys and told them we were in the area, and told them to visit, as we pretty much had the vineyard estate to ourselves. Our host had his guest house ready (a five-bed, 3-bath house at the end of the patio). We settled in and informed him that our two kids would be joining us. Hunter drove, and Stephan navigated. They arrived two days into our stay. We introduced them to Tony, and he welcomed them warmly. We spent the week and got in many tastings. Tony let us know that we could purchase the entire stock if we wanted, but we only had room for about twenty cases to take back home. Hunter agreed to buy the rest as he and Stephan needed some for their house. Tony smiled as though he had won the lottery. Invitations were being handed out like confetti. We welcomed Tony and his family into ours. Tony took Stephan aside as we ate dinner, and Stephan grabbed Tony's hand, waving it in the air and stated, "We have a private vintner now. Tony has agreed to produce only for us. He will also get an infusion of funds to help with his fields and new varieties. He will make a special wine for the Yule tide for us." Tony blushed but knew his legacy was assured.

The time passed too quickly as we spent the days at 'our' vineyard. Hunter and Stephan went into the city to shop, and we spent the time writing and sending the transcripts to Judy for typing and editing. We were saddened to learn that we were needed back in the states, so we bade so long to Tony with a promise of returning soon, fueled the 'bus', and took our leave. Hunter and Stephan remained to enjoy the culture of Milan. They sent us pictures of their adventures, and we promised to check them out on the next trip. Judy welcomed us back home, and Eric took us to the office to discuss why we were needed back home. It seemed that the events in England had piqued the interest of the art world and that it was growing as they were asking for interviews and inquiries (I privately prayed that they hadn't found out about the warehouses). Stephan, ever stoic, took it in stride and said that he'd handle it. I told him to count on me, and Eric pledged any support he could provide (and he meant it, lol).

The first step was to find out the source of the problems. Eric contacted his PI and got the information flowing to us. In the art world, the auctioneer stirred the pot, so Eric assigned the PI to handle it. The PI, or Bob as he was known to us, found out where all the bones were buried and threatened exposure if the auctioneer continued. The report came back that the auctioneer suddenly lost interest in continuing his search. We rewarded Bob (Randolf was his last name and our new PI, as we put him on retainer) with a sizable check for his efforts. He promised discretion in all our dealings. The second to stop the inquiries. Eric took care of that by, let's just say, his methods, and we didn't question it. All we knew was that the inquiries stopped rather quickly. I knew some of the methods, and seeing Eric smiling led me to believe he had relieved some of his frustrations constructively.

Situation avoided, we sailed into winter quietly and got ready for the holidays. Stephan, for his part, had moved many of the better artworks to his warehouses in Europe so as to escape detection. He also contacted both Anthony and Stephan to do the same. They hopped to it for their grandfather, and that made me feel a lot better about the holidays. The invitations went out, the acceptances poured in, the staff went berserk, and Harold hired an apprentice for the season. Basically, holiday as usual. We rented an Airbnb for some of the guests and got the guest house set for the boys (Hunter, Stephan, Anthony, and Eddie). We invited Tony and his family, but they had their own traditions, and we sent our good tidings. Bob Randolf (the PI) and family were invited to the festivities, and as they lived locally, they said they'd come at the appointed times to join us all.

The wine flowed freely, the food was never-ending, and the budget went out the window as we presented a flawless event. Eddie assisted Judy and Jeff in the decorating (I had shown Judy the results of Eddie's restoration of the manor to ease her mind). Eric added extra security to allow the events to go off without a hitch. I was in a quandary as to what to get my man (who literally has everything) and decided to write him a poem, simple, profound, and touching (and something I had no idea how to do). I sequestered myself in the office for a few days to try to write this masterpiece, only to come out empty-handed. It was way out of my league. Determined to do it, I studied a few YouTube instruction videos and came away amazed as to how simple they made it out to be (they lied). I still couldn't get a handle on it. Then I heard my guy singing in the shower, and he sounded so poetic, I scribbled the words down and left for the office.

Christmas day came, and my time came to present my gift to Stephan. I handed him a scroll that I had hand-lettered, and he read it to himself first, then asked me if he could read it aloud. I nodded, and he started, "You came into my life as an enigma, beautiful beyond compare. You saw something in me that I couldn't, and allowed me to be me. You took this man, ignorant of your world, and molded me into the man I am, thankful and metamorphosed. I have no words equal to your love, but I will, until my time expires, try to express my gratitude. Thank you for coming into my life. All my heart, Carl (aka Robin)." Stephan never read the final two words, too immersed with emotion to continue. I saw in that moment a man totally exposed and raw with emotion, and I was content knowing I had decided to write it. He came to me in a public display of affection and teared up as he hugged me tight. He whispered in my ear, "I will love you always, Carl. Thank you for the best gift I've ever received. I'll have it mounted for hanging in the den." Then he kissed me deeply and wiped the tears from his eyes.

True to his word, the scroll was placed in the den above the fireplace in its place of prominence. Needless to say, I had to go out and order new suits after that night. New Year's came quietly (finally), and we greeted 2045 with a toast and a dinner delivered to our room. Let the year begin, and it did. I don't think we were prepared for the events, but they rushed to us like moths to a flame. First, we heard that Stephan had broken his arm trying to fix the chandelier and had fallen twenty feet onto the marble-tiled floor. Hunter was perturbed beyond words, knowing they could have had contractors do the work. I think Stephan got the idea from Eddie to assist around the house. Then we heard that Anthony lost half his fortune in the stock market, betting on a risky stock instead of betting against it. Eddie kept him from regressing, though, and Anthony was able to recoup his losses on his next foray. Our household was next, as Harold's apprentice 'hurt' himself about two days before his contract was up. When we heard that, Judy went to him and said, "It's too bad that you hurt yourself. I was about to offer you a permanent job at the house, but we need adept personnel." At that, the guy told her it wasn't bad and that he could continue. Judy admonished him and sent him packing. Stephan advised Eric to watch out for any retribution coming our way. That made his day and set him about calling Bob for a new mission.

Next came a call from a news reporter requesting an interview with Stephan. He denied the request, and that started a banter back and forth with each other. Stephan finally refused to speak with him again, but the reporter, one Nick Delaney, wouldn't let it go. I employed Bob to get him to stop, and unleashed hell by mentioning it to Eric. I don't know what happened next, but the reporter's column stopped being published, and that nosy reporter simply faded away (pity). We got a respite for about two months, and then summer brought its own flurry of doodoo. This was going to go down as a year to forget as Jeff got into a car accident (thankfully, he was driving his pickup, and that saved him from injury) and totaled the truck. I took him to our dealership and got him a better truck than he had, so we weathered that storm. They say bad pennies return, and so did Nick Delaney, the reporter. This time, he tried extortion, a bad move on his part, as Eric stepped in and paid him a visit. The cover story was that Eric was going to pay him off, and the ruse worked. Nick let Eric know where to take the money. He made the fatal mistake of being there when Eric arrived (with 4 assistants). New Jersey was about to get a new resident, or more precisely, another bad smell.

Fall came, and we made plans to head to Italy, this time stopping in England first and bringing the boys to Italy with us. That went well, and we soon landed in Italy. I called Stephan, and he and Hunter said they could come, but it would be a few days. Tony greeted us all and was happy to meet more of the family. We settled in, took a tour of the winery, and got to taste the new wine Tony created for us. The yule wine had a full-bodied taste with a touch of sweetness, perfect for dessert. We shipped it out to Baltimore with more of the stock. Tony welcomed Hunter and Stephan when they arrived. Together, we looked like college frat boys on holiday. Shopping, led by Eddie and Hunter, turned into a competition, and they one-upped each other into infinity (for once, I was glad we weren't footing the bill). Boys will be boys, though, and we would have a lot to laugh about during dinner. Tony's wife prepared an authentic Italian spread, and we ate to capacity. I personally consumed a bottle or two of wine with dinner. I believe the final count was a case of wine between us. Anthony drank his sparkling water, and Tony seemed shocked at that. I took Tony aside and explained the situation, to which he asked his wife to add it to the shopping list.

Two weeks is simply not enough time to spend in Milan, especially when it's fashion week. But the time came for us to leave. Anthony asked Tony if they could extend their visit (surprise, he said yes), and they chartered a jet home. We arrived back in the States, hoping for a peaceful autumn and winter, but no, more crap was on its way. Almost no one could make it to Christmas due to other obligations, so we decided on a locals-only, small, and intimate gathering. We ended with Eric and Nancy, Nathan and family, Judy, Jeff, Harold, Bob, and us. This year's budget was minimal (compared to other years), and Harold did the entire affair himself. He asked to bring a plus one, and we agreed (I was more than curious about his love interest). Turned out that he found an online date that turned into a full-blown love affair. Her name was Ellen, and she was as pretty as a picture. She was well-mannered and blended in almost immediately. Judy took her into her protective custody and led her through the proceedings with ease. During the evening, after dinner, Harold surprised her with an engagement ring. She said yes, and the planning got started. Guess who was moving into the guest house? At least we ended the year on a happy note (and that darn Harold got his raise to help out).

New Year's Eve couldn't come fast enough for Stephan, and I decided on another candlelight dinner in our room. Champagne popped open, drinks in hand and satin jammies on, we settled into bed. Midnight came around 10 o'clock as we slept in each other's arms. 2046 came and went easily (thank God), and New Year's Day 2047 appeared on the calendar. This was going to be the year I turned eighty (where did the time go?) I had just started my new journal. Eric came into the office talking about something, and I looked at him, realizing that he was now 61 years old and looked it. Then I realized that his son Nathan was turning forty this year. I had stopped counting the years because I wasn't aging anymore. What a huge difference Stephan had made in my life. Eric brought me back to reality with a blunt statement. "Boss, I need to ask a favor. Nancy wants to visit her mom in Seattle. Do you think I can take a couple of weeks off?" I told him to take it and the 'bus' as well. I told him to leave as soon as Nancy wanted. "Tell Jeff to get the jet fueled. Call ahead for a limousine to pick you two up. Use my card for any expenditures and have a good time." With that, I handed him my card and left him to get things handled. Eric left me with a hearty handshake and a hug.

I thought it was going to be a little hard trying to get along without Eric, but he left me a note containing a name and a number: "If you need anything, call Bob at 410-555-4321." Well, I knew (or hoped I knew) who Bob was and how efficient he proved in past dealings. I began to relax, having an ace card in my pocket. I explained the situation to

Stephan, he nodded his consent, and asked for the card. I didn't question his request, but it did pique my interest. At dinner, I tried a soft approach as to why he wanted the card, but he shrugged it off. Now my overthinking brain went into hyperdrive at the idea of a problem looming on the horizon. Stephan finally noticed my fidgeting as we headed upstairs, so he tossed me in bed, cuddled up, and said, "I assume that brain of yours is working overtime to try to figure out my intentions with the card. I wanted to check out the guy to see if, in fact, it is the Bob of Eric's past dealings. Well, it is, and he checks out. Here, take the card back and relax, Batman's on the job." I giggled as the lights went out.

Eric got back after two weeks in Seattle. It seems he was reluctant to use the black card, and he only spent a couple of grand for the whole trip. Nancy was relieved and sent us a beautiful card thanking us for our generosity and concern. The surprise came in the form of a letter from Nancy's mom, expressing her long-distance thanks to us at her time of need. We decided a fruit basket was in order and sent it with our affection. I have to admit, I liked taking these kinds of actions. That being said, we heard that Harold and Ellen had set the date for that summer, and the plans were okay but not lavish. I asked Harold why, and he said that they wanted to save money for a house (not that the guest house wasn't nice), but they wanted to start a family and wanted a house of their own. I asked him to envision what he really wanted for a wedding of his dreams, and he said, "What I'd really love is to have a location wedding in a castle or villa and invite all our relatives." I told him that Hunter and Stephan could help him out there in Italy, and we'd foot the bill for the entire event. I think he was about to break down and cry when I reminded him that Hunter was his cousin after all.

Harold must have told Ellen because she ran into the house, found me, hugged me tight, and kissed my cheek. She composed herself until Stephan walked in, then attacked him, too. Stephan looked at me and mouthed, "We're paying for this, aren't we?" I nodded, and Stephan hugged her back and said, "You're more than welcome"(as though he knew all along). Summer came fast as the nuptials took form. Harold and Ellen went house hunting in the area and settled on a 3-bedroom, two-bath house (quaint but certainly not very large and the price was ungodly; they'd be paying for it most of their lives. I mentioned it to Stephan, and he said, "Well, it's their choice (by which he meant for me to rewrite the budget to include the mortgage or worse, the entire cost).

The week of the wedding came, and the 'bus' was busy with trans-Atlantic crossings to get everyone to the villa and surrounding hotels. We stayed at the villa with the boys (why I keep calling them the boys when they're old and middle-aged respectively). Ellen got her final fitting (with her mother in tow), and Eddie was uber busy with the details to ensure that it would look perfect for the couple. He flew in flowers from Italy and America (as that was where the couple hailed from). The pillars were re-creations of the original Doric style ones that were found at Anthony's estate (adorned with wisteria). Eddie must have planned these items out for months, as they were in full bloom, and it ended looking like the hanging gardens of Babylon when he finished. Harold was kept busy with the guys to keep him from seeing Ellen before the wedding.

The day of the wedding was epic. Eddie had hired a full orchestra to play live, the back garden had been transformed into an open-air chapel, gauze cloth curtains flowing in the breeze with mini light strands glowing to set the mood. Anthony got a bishop to officiate, and we were asked to be in the procession as ushers. The parents of Harold and Ellen were impressed, to say the least. The photographer was imported from England (at Eddie's request), and the photos he took ensured that Harold would be proud of the memories. Champagne (from Champagne, France) was shipped in and flowed like water during the day. Of course, we had Tony ship some cases of 'our' stock to enhance the ambiance. The chef was local (our restaurant friend, of course), so the meal was top-notch. It started with antipasto boards containing ham, salami, chicken, pepperoni, Gouda, Bleu, cheddar, mozzarella, Parmesan, and provolone cheeses, calamari and green olives, grilled bread, and assorted sauces. That alone would have been enough, but that was just for starters. The next course was pasta (angel hair pasta) in garlic butter sauce with Parmigiano Reggiano, followed by the main course of meatballs with a bed of penne pasta and red sauce. The dessert was simple, though, with fruit drizzled with balsamic vinegar and Prosecco to drink. The music started again, and the plates disappeared. All the usual traditions were observed, and the cake sharing went off without fanfare. Ellen threw the bouquet, and her cousin caught it. However, the garter was snapped by Hunter (I wonder what he had in mind for that as he placed it on his arm). The event wound down, and I was glad we were staying in the villa and didn't have to go far to repose.

We presented Harold with his gifts (a paid mortgage and a check to cover his honeymoon and set up for his new digs). I used some of my money to assist Stephan, but as usual, I ended up finding it back in my account. Stephan led the way to our boudoir, and we settled into a cuddle sleep. The day and the event had been without blemish. Breakfast time came, and the four of us (the lucky ones) had a simple meal of eggs Benedict and toast, steaming coffee, and some apple slices. We welcomed the remaining guests in the garden, and the chef set up a big lunch for the troops. We offered up a trio to provide music, and they played classical Italian music during the afternoon. The guests started departing for the states, and the 'bus' got busy again. We took the last flight as it was only the two of us and the crew. I was never so happy to see the airport as we prepared for landing. Customs done and the bags in the car, we set off for home. Jeff drove us and let us know that Judy had everything covered. She greeted us but made us remove our shoes as she had just had the floors cleaned (she's so her mother, and I'm so thankful). Jet lag being real (I never got used to it), I collapsed into the bed, and Stephan allowed me to sleep (well, until he came to bed).

2047, the year I turned 80, I had so much going on that I forgot to celebrate it. Stephan had other plans in store, though (he's always surprising me). I received an anonymous card in the mail, and when I opened it, 2 tickets to Milan fell out, and it said it was for fashion week. I knew then that we were about to have another adventure. What I failed to mention to Stephan was that the pills were sunsetting, and I once again realized I was a mere mortal. The sands of time would run out, and my only comfort was that Stephan would have a large family to help him through it. I figured that I'd be entombed in Italy, my new home from home. But until then, bring it on, Milan, here we come. We called Tony, and he set up for our arrival in September. I was secretly determined to make the most of the time I had left (God had given me extra time, and I wasn't going to squander it). I did make a call to Eddie and told him my findings, and he said that he had also noticed. I swore him to silence, and he agreed.

Well, Milan came into sight, and a car was waiting after customs. We were herded into the car and whisked away to the vineyard. Tony and his son greeted us at the house, and Tony Jr. was given the task of taking the suitcases to our room (or suite, as Stephan had commissioned and built as a surprise for my birthday). We went to the dining room and beheld the feast Tony's wife had created. When Jr. had stowed the bags, he joined us in the dining room and sat to the right of his father. We began with a grand antipasto, then came the stuffed manicotti with medium meatballs and a robust red sauce. A salad with a balsamic vinaigrette was set beside the pasta and a glass of Merlot. For dessert, a simple dish of lemon sherbet to cleanse the palate, and then to the den for a bourbon and a smoke. We spoke of the plans to travel to Milan the next day, and Tony just nodded his acknowledgment. The car awaited us for the trip, and I noticed Jr. driving. "Did your father ask you to drive us?" Jr. turned and said, "I asked him to let me drive you because I wanted to see Milan and maybe some of the models at the show. Don't worry, I'm paying my own way as I have saved some money for the trip." Stephan said nothing but looked at me as if to say, in a pig's eye, he's paying. I just nodded back and let it go. We were about to give this kid the adventure of his life.

The road trip was short because we were talking so much. I asked Jr. if he minded us calling him that or if he preferred Tony. Tony said that his family nickname was Skipper, and we could call him that if we liked, or just Tony. We decided on Skipper, so we went to the hotel. Skipper got the bags out as he deposited us at the door of the hotel. By the time he had secured the car and entered, Stephan handed him the key to his room (which was adjacent to ours with a pass-through) and told him that it was fully paid. "I told you not to bother and that I'd pay my own way." I whispered in Skipper's ear, "Trust me, Stephan wants to pay, and you better let him. Either he pays, or you go home. I've learned to just let him, I think he gets off doing it." Skipper shrugged his shoulders and inwardly smiled as it gave him spending money in the new city.

The next day was shopping, as Skipper didn't bring much of a wardrobe. We took him to our favorite men's shop, and the proprietor saw our faces and smiled (he knew he was about to make his profit for the month). We started from the skin out (talk about deja vu), and Skipper blushed the entire time that he tried on underwear. Next came the trousers and shirts. Then onto accessories and watches. Skipper hadn't seen the prices (but I did, and the kid would have fainted had he seen), and Stephan just waved his black card at the owner. We had the packages set for delivery later that day at the hotel (the bill coming in at a staggering $17,847.27 – that kid needed a lot of things). We purchased a few items so that he wouldn't feel too bad. We took him to the hotel dining room and had a simple dinner. By then, the clothes had arrived, and Stephan asked for a fashion show. Skipper blushed again, but I told him to get used to it, I did. He did ask how much he owed, and I couldn't resist teasing him, so I produced the receipt. I think the kid was going into shock, so I told him it was a gift from Stephan and that he owed nothing. He immediately stopped shaking and thanked Stephan with a hearty handshake. Stephan shooed him into the adjoining room and started the show. I will say that working the vineyard with his father had produced a wonderfully chiseled physique. He trotted out in his underwear and made a show for his benefactor, then retreated to the other room to continue. The show went on for about an hour, and then Skipper went to bed. I closed the pass-through and locked our side, seeing the kid did much for our libidos (too bad I left the suits back in the states, I guess we'll have to make do with our imaginations).

The fashion week went on, and we showed off our new family member to society. Skipper caught a great many double takes as women and men drank him in. Some agents asked him if he was looking for work, and he smiled and said no (but I told him to take their cards in case). His enthusiasm and confidence grew, and it showed. By the end of the week, he had accumulated a handful of cards and just as many numbers (I don't know his preference, but he certainly had his chance at both sides of the aisle). We packed to return to the vineyard, knowing Skipper would be taking us to all future fashion weeks. Skipper couldn't wait to tell of his adventures and show his mother the new clothing. Tony asked how it went, and we extolled Skipper's value to us as an escort. But as always, the time came to leave, and we made arrangements for wine shipping and package delivery. We waved goodbye to the family, and Skipper hurried over to hug us as a family member and said thanks again for the adventure and everything else.

We flew home, and the jet lag hit earlier than usual. I think Stephan was noticing a slight change in me, and I feared he'd find out why. I know that I looked much younger than my true age, but the signs were beginning to show, like my temples were graying and a few crow's feet were forming in the corners of my eyes. I did my best to mask the aging, but Stephan noticed. He took me into the den and asked directly, "Carl, why didn't you tell me that the pills stopped working? Do you want to age or should I call Chuck Tidwell and ask what can be done?" I told him that Chuck could be called, but I didn't think much would come of it. "You know I will move heaven and earth for you, and I will accept your decision, but it will tear me up if you pass. I never thought that I could love another as I did Svetlana, but then you came into my life. At first, I took it as a challenge, converting a straight man to gay, but our love blossomed over a year, and trust and loyalty built our extended family. All I could give you was a better life, but you gave me family and purpose. My life was wild when I was younger, but now it's whole. Trust me when I say, Batman needs his Robin and hopefully Robin wants his Batman." I noticed tears in his eyes for the second time since I met him, and it strengthened my resolve. I told Stephan to call Chuck and see if there was anything new he could do.

Chuck was not to be found, so we put Bob on the case and received encouraging news two days later. Bob hunted down our elusive doctor in his villa in Belize. He was living the life as a Bohemian recluse. Stephan called Chuck, and he said he wasn't practicing anymore, but he would come to us and see what he could do. I think Stephan was happier than I was at that announcement. Chuck said the arrangements would take about a week, so Stephan told him to fly back via our Airbus. Stephan wanted him there, and within 3 days, Chuck knocked at our door. We greeted him and had the staff care for his bags while Stephan shuffled Chuck into the den with me in tow. The door closed, and the physical began. Chuck and Stephan had me unclothed and lying on the examining table in about 2 minutes. Stephan looked concerned as he viewed my body critically. Chuck took blood samples and checked out all my orifices. Then he examined my body. He finished his initial exam, and then I was allowed to dress. He took Stephan aside as I dressed, and that meant bad news to an overthinker. He said he'd have more for us after the blood analysis. I was stressing out as I couldn't read my husband's face (never could by the way). The next day was another meeting in the den with Chuck, Stephan, and me. I told them that Eddie was having the same problem. Chuck said that the blood samples were actually great and that that was not my problem. The active ingredient in the pill was the culprit; it was made for a younger person, and the strength needed to be improved. Stephan relaxed at that statement, and Chuck set about correcting the pill efficacy. He also called Eddie and told him that was what he would need.

Chuck stayed for about a month and redid the blood samples. The next day, the new pills were ready, and he started me on them. He stayed another month to ensure that the pills didn't have any side effects. Then we called Eddie, and Chuck said he would be sending his new pills in the mail. We celebrated that night, and I let Stephan know that he would have his Robin for a while longer. That night, we went to bed, and a much relieved Stephan held me tight into the night. I felt silent tears on my neck as he released his fear of loss.

Morning found us late for breakfast, and we heard the usual cry of feeding the 'dog'. I shouted down between pauses that she should feed him then. I heard a hearty laugh and then heard a dog barking. Well, looks like we have a pet now. When we got downstairs, we found a medium-sized mutt of mixed origins wagging his tail and asking for petting from everyone. "What's his name, Judy?" to which she replied, "Batdog." We about pissed ourselves at that, and everyone had a good laugh. Then Judy told us she actually called him Alfred. The dog did get our breakfast, so we made ourselves some brunch and took it and Alfred to the poolside. Shopping was in order as we had to make our sidekick comfortable, so we finished our meal (or most of it, the dog got the rest). We put him in the Bentley and headed to Petco for some much-needed supplies. Coming home, Alfred barked, took in the wind, and then farted in the car (note to self, stop feeding him rich foods as they cause stink bombs). Alfred was shown all his new items, like beds for most rooms, leashes, collars, coats, booties, toys of every description, and toiletries. I would try to describe his joy, but it would be inadequate at best.

I did notice he took to Stephan more than me, and that was alright with me (I'm not much of a dog person or cat person, actually, I don't much care for pets). That night Alfred snuck into our room and got on the bed, thankfully at the end and not on us. However, in the morning, I found him being spooned by my husband, so much for boundaries. I almost forgot, we had him tested for his DNA and found out our new mutt was a mix between terrier, poodle, and pit bull. He looked more terrier and had a poodle tan or buff coat, but had a pit bull attitude. I found out when Anita tried to discipline Rita, aged 4. Poor Anita (Nathan's wife), she yelled at Rita to stop and made the mistake of raising her hand to slap Rita. Alfred jumped between them and bared his teeth at Anita. Stephan called Alfred off, and no more was said, but I think that's when her love affair with Alfred started. She gave him treats and shared her food with him all the time.

2048 started quietly as always, and I was feeling the effects of the new medication. I had more energy, but the fading of my looks didn't change (Now I wished that I had been more active in my health. I wasn't getting older, but alas, no younger). Stephan would joke about dating a 'daddy,' and I would play pout, but I knew it was all in fun (now Robin looked older than Batman). I was blissfully unaware, but the time had come for our beloved Eric to retire (being 63 now). I helped Judy and Nancy to prepare for the party and make it a blow-out affair (how do you say so long to such a devoted 'family employee'). I invited England and Italy to join us, and of course had pleas to use the 'bus' to travel. I told the boys to coordinate between themselves, and Eddie offered to handle that part. I took Eric aside and explained that the party was going to happen (as I knew he hated surprises) and told him to look surprised. He thanked me and then added, "Trying to replace me with a newer, prettier guard?" I looked intently into his eyes and said, "No one could replace you, Eric, and I wouldn't try. You've been better and braver than even you know, and as for loyalty, no words can describe yours. If, however, you know someone in the ranks to recommend, I'm all ears." We discussed a couple of current employees that he particularly thought could take his place, and I asked him to handle the interviews.

The day of the party came, and everyone was having fun. We raided the wine cellar (Tony was going to be happy), and Nancy brought in his retirement cake. He kissed her, and we toasted him in grand fashion.

Stephan stepped forward with an envelope, and I think everyone knew it contained a fantastic trip and a voucher. We asked Nathan about his parents' dreams and made them come true. They wanted to sample wines in Italy and stay in a villa (you know where this is going), and we said that we thought we could handle it (hello Tony, can we ask a favor?). We set up the bus for the next day's departure to Rome, Italy, and then to the vineyard. Before the end of the day, Eric handed me a note, and on it was a name, Bob Randolf P.I. He whispered that he thought Bob would be his best choice, and the other two he thought about couldn't hold a candle to Bob, besides Bob was only 48 and would be around for a while more. I tucked the note in my shirt pocket and went back to the party.

Eric and Nancy took their leave and headed out in the limousine around 9 am. I took my coffee to the den and brought one for Stephan. Alfred greeted me at the door and allowed me entrance (after I bribed him with a treat). I saw Stephan in deep thought and just handed him his coffee and sat down in the nearby chair. He smiled and took a large sip, enjoying the flavor before swallowing. "Eric's retirement made me think about Judy and Jeff. They must be getting close to retirement, also. What will we do without them, Carl?" I looked over to Stephan and, for once, noticed the concern in his eyes. "They have kept our secret, and they have run the house for years now." I tried to speak, but the words were hard to say, "We're going to have to rely on Judy and Jeff to recommend their successors. Are you okay with that, Stephan?" He looked back at me and slowly nodded. We called the pair into the den, a first for Jeff, and asked them about their intentions. Judy looked at Jeff, he nodded, and she started, "I see the concern in your eyes, and we have talked about it and decided to continue until we can't. Dahlia has voiced her wish to move back to Baltimore, and this might be good for all of us.

Aaron got laid off last month, and he could use the employment. Since Jeffrey Allen is now a freshman in college, he won't be much of a consideration. What do you say, should we pursue it?"

It took all of a nanosecond to respond, "Yes, that would be great all around." Judy took over from there and said that the kids would be driving in after graduation day for Jeffrey. So a third-generation family member was to be our new house couple. I felt old knowing that Jeffrey Allen Halstead was attending college, having known his grandmother as a child. Aaron flew in early to check out the accommodations and set up for the move across country. He was impressed with the guest house (their new residence) and flew back west after making all the appropriate changes. The moving day arrived, and Jeffrey got an envelope from his 'great uncles'. His mom and dad moved the following week and set up house in their new digs. Dahlia got with her mother, and Aaron got with his father-in-law to make the transition seamless. It was calm until Christmas, and we sent out the invites to bring the clan together. The boys came in and stayed at a local B&B. Harold prepared the meals with the staff and set out a great feast. During the pre-Christmas festivities, Harold and Ellen announced that they were expecting. Drinks of champagne and wine flowed even more as toasts were being raised.

It seemed that Christmas lasted a month, but time came for farewells and trips home. I have to say that Stephan and I (while being happy with our 'family' around us) were glad to have the house to ourselves for a change. 2049 rang in with Stephan, and I sequestered in our sanctum santorum enjoying a quiet night in our satin jammies, sipping champagne, and eating a feast of tapas (Harold was getting really good at cooking). We fell into each other and slept until Alfred licked our faces the following morning. We stayed upstairs until we heard a familiar phrase. We laughed because we knew that since Alfred was with us, the food would be waiting, no matter how long it took to get downstairs. Coming out of the shower, we realized Judy had let the dog out and that the food would be gone by now (Que sera sera). Jeff let Aaron take over the chauffeur duties. We introduced him to our new security guy, "PI Bob." Eric had chosen well, and besides, Bob had done a lot of work for us in the past.

It took Dahlia somewhat more time to become accustomed to delegating responsibilities and handling deliveries, not to mention the paperwork. Judy proved to be an effective teacher, though, and Dahlia came around. It was almost time for our annual trip to Milan (also England and Rome). It seemed September crept upon us. It was Hunter who reminded us, and we sent Tony our agenda. Arrangements made and the 'bus' fueled up, we set out for the airport. It took a while, but we lifted off and slept until the Isles came into view. Our transportation was waiting at the hangar, and we sped away to the estate. Anthony and Eddie (looking good, the medicine must have been effective) greeted us at the door, and we dined Al fresco on the patio. For England, the meal was fabulous, consisting of pate with capers and toast points, a garden salad with mixed greens and a balsamic vinaigrette reduction, and spaetzle with a grind of fresh pepper and butter. Fresh sourdough rolls, grilled t-bone steaks (medium rare as though there's any other way to serve it), wine of course, a new Tony blend for Anthony and Eddie, and followed with a light dessert of cheeses and fruit. I couldn't help myself as I indulged. We discussed Rome, and the boys wanted to go see their Italian counterparts, so we prepped the 'bus' for two additional bodies. We stayed about 2 more days and then headed for our beloved "Eternal City." It took most of the next day to get us to the villa. Hunter and Stephan asked if we got lost when we finally arrived. "The darn airport added security and having a private plane with Americans and

Englishmen on board, not withstanding four gay men, it twisted their minds. But here we are, safe and sound." Stephan took Eddie on a tour of the villa (trying to show he had taken Eddie's inspiration and improved the villa). Hunter showed us to our rooms and said dinner would be in an hour. I wondered how I would spend the next hour, but the plans had been pre-destined by a masked man (yes, he packed his suitcase well).

We ate a light meal as we knew that dinner was only the third meal of the day, and we still had supper at ten. I picked at the antipasto as did Stephan, then we ate a meatball (the size of a tapas plate) and drank Chianti. A small dish of chocolate gelato finished the meal. Stephan feigned tiredness after the meal and, with a side wink to me, said he'd be turning in for the night. I, being the dutiful husband, said I'd tuck him in and probably read for a while (before running up the stairs to change into some 'other' night clothes). The sounds coming from the room made them think I was reenacting some of the action items in the paper. The room quieted down about an hour later, and we actually slept.

Morning came quickly as we packed up and drove to Milan and the vineyard. We unpacked, and the boys went into town (with their own credit cards) to shop. Tony took Stephan and me to the tasting room to test out some of his new blends. I asked if he had any Chianti with a sweet note like cinnamon. "Intriguing, I would never have thought to tweak that formula. I mean, it won't be this year, but I think I can work on it between this year and next." Stephan went over the books with Tony and realized that Tony was doing much better than when we first met, even though we (and the boys) were his only customers. The boys had him making all sorts of new tastes, and Tony admitted that he sold some bottles to the local restaurant we liked to frequent (so we could have our wine when we ate there).

The morning that the fashion week started, seven of us (Tony Jr. joined us in town) sat in the front row, taking notes of the brands we liked and deciding which stores to visit after the shows. The boys asked Tony Jr. if he'd like some new togs (I'm thinking they just wanted to see more of his body). He agreed, and they whisked him out before he could rethink his decision. "He's a big boy and can handle himself, Carl," I smirked, and we strolled out into the street and headed to the restaurant. The owner sat us down, asked which wine we wanted, and we said to surprise us (knowing he was going to get our wine for us). The food started pouring out of the kitchen even before we ordered. We decided to just let him feed us, so that's what we did, as we placed the menus on the table. Never disappointing, we feasted on all his best dishes. Antipasto (of course), Sopa Tuscana, calamari salad, eggplant Parmesan, fettuccine Al pepe, meatballs in sauce, grilled garlic rubbed bread, chicken cacciatore (I think Stephan whispered that we were good and to stop cleaning out the pantry). He sat with us over wine, and we said that we knew about the wine, as we were staying with Tony. He laughed nervously until we burst out laughing, letting him know it was all right. He didn't want us to pay, but Stephan insisted and dropped two grand on the table. We also told him that we would speak to Tony and tell him that selling to the restaurant would be okay, and Tony would give it to him wholesale. His eyes lit up, and he went to split up the money with the staff. We returned to the vineyard and discussed the deal we made with the restaurant. Tony seemed happy with the news. He asked about Tony Jr., and we said he went shopping with the boys.

"Hopefully, he doesn't spend too much," said Tony, and we assured him that the boys were paying for the trip. The boys returned late into the night, well after we had all tucked in, and we figured that we'd talk in the morning. Breakfast was simple, fried leftover polenta with fruit and caffe' ristretto or espresso for us. The boys came down smelling the espresso. Tony Jr. looked inhibited as he took his seat near his father. We broke the tension and asked about their shopping. "Did it all go well, and are we getting a view of the new clothes?" The boys smiled like the cats that ate the canary. Tony Jr. blushed, and Tony Sr., Stephan, and I roared out loud. Hunter told Tony Jr. to start the show and shooed him through the archway toward the bedrooms. We went to the living room and waited. He started out with the casual clothes (and if I weren't married, oh boy) and went to more formal clothing. Tony Sr. asked him where he was going to wear these clothes, and Jr. said to the clubs. Just then, a worker came in, and we went silent. Then he said, "Boss, I need you in the fields, the new vines aren't doing well." We were silent because this guy was Adonis in the flesh. Raven black curly hair, Mediterranean blue eyes, light black hair on arms and legs, and a washboard stomach (I think I'll need to do some laundry). The curls falling around his head, and a couple hanging down to his thick eyebrows. He was sweaty, but no one was complaining. Tony Sr. followed him to the fields with Stephan in tow. We watched that butt move until he left our field of sight.

Later, Stephan and Tony Sr. returned and said the new vines just needed some other nutrients to succeed and ordered them. We settled in and relaxed for the night. Stephan and I went to more shows in the morning, and the boys went to get a tour of the new vines with worker Giovanni. They stayed out for a long time, and Giovanni seemed more than relieved when they came back. I wanted to question the boys about their antics, but thought better of it in the present company. The boys accompanied us to the last few shows, and we went back to 'our' restaurant. The owner gave us the entire back room for the upcoming feast. Stephan asked for the usual, and the food started popping up from thin air. The boys, Tony Jr., Stephan, and I munched to our hearts' content until we couldn't pack any more in. The owner allowed Stephan to pay for it, and he smiled widely (I think he made his monthly profit today). We ushered our new ingenue home so his father wouldn't worry. Tony Sr. knew then that he would probably need to hire someone else to tend the fields (as his son had acquired a taste for the delights of the city).

Come to find out, Giovanni had a younger brother looking for employment (so it all worked out). We waited with bated breath to see the younger brother and were not disappointed, although he hadn't developed his brother's muscles yet. I thought to myself, 'they sure do make them beautiful in Italy'. The time came for us to bid farewell to Tony Sr. and take our leave. Hunter and Stephan headed back to Calcata, Anthony and Eddie got dropped off in London, and we returned to Baltimore. We found the house abuzz with activity and went in search of Judy. Jeff told us that Ellen was in labor and was preparing to take her and Harold to the hospital. We assisted in getting our ride ready. We found Judy in the kitchen with the fill-in chef, making our dinner. Dahlia was with her to help out and, surprisingly, had it well in hand. I reminded Stephan that I could have made my 'world famous' sandwich and was rewarded with a punch to the shoulder. "Don't even suggest that," said Stephan as Judy looked on quizzically. He told her the story, and she fell into a chair laughing until tears formed. Dahlia asked why everyone was laughing, and I was forced to recount the stories from my early days. "And if it hadn't been for your grandmother, we'd still be eating them," Stephan added. The memories bubbled to the surface, and we had a moment of silence for our beloved Trudy, mother, grandmother, and house mother to us.

Later that evening, the phone call came announcing the birth of a bouncing baby boy named Harold Victor Garibo Jr., 21 inches, 7.5 pounds, and with a mound of brunette hair. Pictures to follow, and what a nice way to end the year 2050. I just nodded to Stephan and gave Harold a brief raise as I knew Stephan would be offering it. The house settled back into routine, and we relaxed into a few months of quiet living. I can't believe that Thanksgiving and Christmas were upon us again so soon, and as usual, that put the house in motion for another blitz of activities. The decorating alone took a week. The boys decided to stay home, but our 'brood' was large enough to fill that gap. I selfishly wanted to get to New Year's Eve so that Stephan and I could be alone. But when the parties started, I was glad to be involved. The week between Christmas and New Year's gave us a scare, though, as Harold Jr. developed pneumonia and had to be rushed to the hospital. It took about three days, but he rallied and was home on December 30. We finished the year as quietly (and grateful) as it came in. Bring on 2051, we found a letter soon after the new year from Tony Jr. asking to visit America, and could he possibly stay with us? I was hesitant at first, so Stephan made a private call to Tony Sr. Sr. said that if we agreed to host, he would let Jr. come.

So much for a quiet year, but new blood in town might be a good thing, and Tony Sr. would be at ease knowing his son was in good hands. What I found out was that Hunter and Stephan had prompted the request, and they invited themselves to Baltimore at the same time (Stephan spawned little devils to be kind). The troops were due the following week, so we rented them a house for the duration, close by. At least they wouldn't be disrupting our house, and goodness knows that I didn't want to think what would be happening there. Heck, Tony Jr. might be straight (that would teach the boys). I could envision Tony Jr. bringing home a girl after hitting the clubs, and then I giggled. Stephan looked in my direction, and I just shrugged it off. The boys arrived on the 'bus,' and we sent Aaron to get them and deliver them to their digs for the week or however long. They settled in as Aaron arrived back at the house. Dahlia received word that Jeffrey had started his fourth semester in mandatory classes but was going to matriculate into political science (politics to us laymen). Great, a politician in the horde. I was hoping for a lawyer and Stephan for a scientist, but whatever. Isn't it funny that the family we wanted was the family that found us and evolved into such a grand masterpiece of patchwork tapestry? It seems that we found out that Tony Jr. liked the attention and the clubs the boys took him to. He let his looks get him dates and phone numbers from both guys and girls. The boy was letting his freak flag fly. I had to appreciate that he was at least discreet when dating. What I didn't realize was that both Hunter and Stephan had the pleasure of his company. Oh well, to each their own. I preferred monogamy and couldn't imagine needing more than my Stephan.

The next few months followed the last few, and things were just floating along, and I, for one, was grateful. Stephan got that wanderlust in his eyes and set his sights on Holland, Netherlands, of all places. I didn't question him but asked for the conversational version of the Danish language through Bumble. I at least wanted to tell them what I wanted to eat. Stephan took the lessons as well, but mastered the language before we left. It was to be a short one-week visit, but as with all things involving Stephan, we winged it, and I rolled with the punches. We rented a villa in Amsterdam, and I have to say I was impressed by its simplistic charm and beauty. I reserved final judgment until I had tried the menu items. We were sent to the Jordan neighborhood restaurant to try Stamppot (mashed potatoes and vegetables topped with sausage). Then a stop for supper in the Indonesian restaurant in town for

Rijsttafel (rice table with curries, flavorful satays, sambals, and pickles). We were told not to miss the Stroopwafels (waffles with caramel filling, usually heated over a cup of coffee or tea to soften up the waffles). The food was more appealing than I first thought. We toured the city on a sightseeing cruise through the canals. Then turned our attention to Dam Square for the shopping and restaurants. We waited until the next day to see the Van Gogh Museum with its masterpieces (I asked Stephan if he had any, and to my surprise, only a couple of early works). We left Leidseplein (the nightlife center) for later in the week. We spent a sunny afternoon in Vondelpark (and sat by the lake just relaxing and eating sandwiches). We finished our unofficial tour at the Heineken Experience (yes, that Heineken Brewery). I was glad that Stephan had sated his wanderlust for a time, and we returned to the villa. I did ask him why he chose a city he had never been to in the last 539 years. Stephan corrected me by saying that he had heard of Vincent Van Gogh (1853 – 1890) and visited his studio in Arles, Bouches-du-Rhône, France (where he lived). He let me know that he had stayed in Gauguin's room during his visit. Van Gogh was straight, so no hanky panky went on (for which I was glad). That's why he had a couple of works. He just wanted to visit his friend's original country, the Netherlands. I left it alone as I already had my answer, plus I got a taste of Europe besides Italy. I suggested that since we were already in Europe, maybe a stop in France or Spain would be a good idea. Stephan opted for Spain as he had connections with the heiress apparent Leonor, princess of Asturias, daughter of King Felipe VI of Spain and Queen Letizia. I didn't question him anymore and let him have at it. We were invited to stay at their country house (a 30,000-square-foot home), which we kindly accepted. Leonor greeted us along with her staff when we arrived. I felt uneasy because I didn't know how to act with royalty (this being my first occurrence). Stephan took the lead, as always, and showed me how to act. He bowed and did not reach out, as that was frowned upon. I just ape his actions and got through the introductions. She left us to the staff and took her leave (after kissing both of Stephan's cheeks). What a house, and this was their home away from home. I wondered what the castle looked like. We were taken to the best guest suite facing the mountains and slopes. To say the view was awe-inspiring was to be simple; it was breathtaking. Snow-capped mountains reaching the azure blue skies, the tree line filled with pines, and the slopes with wildflowers in full bloom. I asked Stephan to go for a walk in the back gardens, and the gardener was summoned to attend to us in case of any questions about the flora. The tour was magical, and the information coming from the gardener was intense (although he was speaking in Spanish and only Stephan understood and conversed with him). The chef prepared Paella (the national dish of Spain), which contained shrimp, clams, sausage, peppers, rice, onions, saffron spice, and anything else they could think of. We ate until stuffed, and there was a lot left over. We stayed the week and then sent word we were leaving, giving the staff gifts for their kindness and generosity.

The next stop was home (after shopping for mementos for our 'family' back home). I will say traveling was much better in the 'bus' than flying any other way. We put on jammies, spread out in the seats, and slept most of the way home (you couldn't do that flying coach). We were given a five-minute warning as the states appeared on the horizon. We dressed and prepared to deplane, heading for customs. That done (after an hour), it was the drive home. The staff grabbed the bags, took the gifts inside, and we collapsed in the den to get our bearings. Dahlia called us to eat, and we barely picked at the meal (the jet lag came early). We went upstairs and just slept.

The next few years were quiet (as we were accustomed), and we watched as our 'family' grew and matured. Judy and Jeff finally retired (without fanfare), and Dahlia and Aaron just morphed into the position. Jeffrey was due to graduate in May 2053, so we prepared the house for another party. I asked Stephan about a possible gift, and he asked me how old our cars were. "Time for shopping, I think," was all Stephan said. We went to see Tony but were told that he had retired (had it been that long?). The dealer's son said he could recommend a salesperson, and we expected someone like our Tony. The salesman was quite the opposite, looking down his nose at Stephan (bad move, kid) as though he couldn't afford a Maserati, let alone a Bentley. Stephan called the dealer over, requested that he look up our purchase history, and said he'd wait. The dealer came back, ashen-faced, and told the salesman to go polish a car, then asked us what car we wanted. Stephan began with, "I believe the quality of sales people you've hired has diminished of late. I think we'd be better suited with one of your competitors" (knowing the dealer now knew of our history and possible loss of business, groveled before him). My dear Stephan made immediate demands before reconsidering going elsewhere. He required that the salesman watch as his commission slipped away. Then Stephan made them take us for test drives and detail the cars (although they were pristine already). Only then did he give in and buy our matching Bentleys. The salesman nearly vomited seeing his multi-thousand-dollar commission walk away. Stephan did shake Dan's hand (the dealer), but did not say he'd be back.

Jeffrey's graduation party was adequate but not like we were accustomed to. We did gift Jeffrey a Bentley, mine to be exact, as Stephan's had been given to Aaron and Dahlia. Then we settled into a pattern of relaxation at the beach house on good days. I kept up my journals (but didn't realize Stephan was doing the same). Dahlia did my transcribing when she wasn't running the house. She delegated most of the tedious duties to the staff and kept our business private to herself alone. I don't think Aaron knew what I wrote. We received a thank-you note from Jeffrey, and it said that he decided to enter local politics as an ombudsman to start. That way, he could pay his dues without much difficulty (the kid had a head on his shoulders).

Our beach days came to an end as our September visit to the vineyard drew near. We packed up and headed east to Italy and Rome. Hunter and Stephan were expecting us, but we were not expecting to see Tony Jr. there at the villa. It seemed that the boys were having their fun, and so was Tony Jr. The villa had become an orgy palace (something Stephan frowned upon – discretion was always a must with him). He admonished Junior in private for disrespecting his ancestors. Hunter could do as he wanted, but the Orions had class. I tried to lighten the mood and redirect Stephan, but to no avail. He was adamant about his convictions. We left the next day for Milan, and Stephan told Junior to fix this mess. I had never seen Stephan this upset and again tried to appease him. He looked at me, his eyes returning to that enduring blue, and he told me he was okay and not to worry. I held his hand the rest of the way to the vineyard. I saw Tony Sr. and gave him greetings from Rome and let him know that Jr. was fine. Tony took us to the main house, and we got situated. We were taken to the testing room later and were introduced to 'Chianti Canella' or cinnamon Chianti. It was exactly what we were looking for. He said that the restaurant sold out every time it was served. I was beyond pleased, and Stephan was amused.

The new clothing shows were becoming stale to me, and I began to get jaded about the new designs. I think Stephan felt the same way as he outright yawned during the catwalk presentation (note to self – talk to the designers or simply put away the checkbook). We decided to skip the rest of the shows and stayed at the vineyard for a few days before returning to Rome (Calcata actually). It seems Junior purged the crass from the villa, and Tony Jr. was sent home. Hunter asked about our purchases, and we told him that we bought nothing. He was disappointed but not shocked, as he had seen the coming attractions as it were.

We decided to visit Anthony and Eddie before returning home and called ahead. They were ecstatic about our arrival. Eddie hugged us tight and led the way to the den. Dear Anthony was hard at work making deals and selling stocks just as fast. He waved as he yelled into the phone. He held up his hand as if to say five more minutes, and he'd be with us. We left him to his chaos. Eddie escorted us to the patio, and we enjoyed the quiet beauty of the manse and gardens. We were drinking cocktails when Anthony joined us. "Greetings, grandfather and Carl. You know, that doesn't sound quite right, Carl. What would you like to be called?" I shrugged, and Stephan (ever the snarky one) said, "Call him Pawpaw Robin." I whipped around, red-faced as Anthony said, " Okay. "Stephan, could I please see you for a moment?" and led him off to complain. He shushed me and kissed the red out of my face. "Everyone knows about us, so why bother yourself. Why do you think we have a dog named Alfred?" I had to laugh at that, and my mood changed. We rejoined the boys and enjoyed the rest of the evening. Sleep came after I teased 'The Batman' for an hour (I edged him for all it was worth).

A VERY sleepy but satiated Stephan arose as I came from the shower. "Morning, I hope you slept well", he answered, "Quite well, pawpaw, it seems you can still rise to the occasion." I hugged him and then poked him in the ribs. He disrobed me and slid his hands down my sides. He returned my teasing and left me in a state of arousal as he went to the shower. Since I was dressed appropriately for the bath, I decided to take the plunge again and 'assist' my hubby with his shower. The boys must have thought we died as they sent staff to check if we were indeed alive. Surviving the embarrassment, we left the shower and dressed for the day. We stayed the better part of the week before returning to the nest. It was Aaron who was waiting at the airport for us, and Dahlia greeted us at the door. It's amazing to have lived through 3 generations of staff. We got a visit from Jeffrey Allen (now a local politician), and he explained his aspirations over dinner with us. His campaign needed money, and he thought we might be able to assist in this. The questioning came like a Senate confirmation hearing, hypothetical situations, stated assertions, and plans for the future. Stephan literally grilled the kid until exhaustion (he figured if his money was going to help, the kid better be extra sharp and on point). Jeffrey exceeded expectations and Stephan shook his hand and said, "You're ready kid. I hope you realize I did that for you're own good. No one will grill you that hard and you will dazzle them with you're expertise. I will back your candidacy." Jeffrey, Dahlia and Aaron smiled knowing he was a shoe in for the position.

The years went forward, and in 2058, we welcomed our new state senator, Jeffrey Allen Halstead, to the Maryland state legislature. Meanwhile, Eric's grandson, Nathan Jr., turned 21 years old, and his granddaughter, Rita, turned 15. I was turning 91 (how was it possible). I laughed inwardly as I realized that my husband was 546 (not much of a difference if you consider us both old and ancient). Stephan and I were going to celebrate our 39th wedding anniversary. I wanted to commemorate the occasion early, but surprisingly, Stephan was almost impossible to reach. I pondered it while I took Alfred for a walk. An idea struck me, so I planned my surprise. The day came, and I asked Stephan to retrieve our suits from the cleaners, so we could celebrate in our special way. I told him it would be a quiet day for us both (hopefully he believed me). I flew in the boys from both England and Rome, called the troops in from everywhere, every generation, and put them up in the nearby hotels. Our Anniversary arrived, the suits came back, and I had Stephan dress up with me. I had the staff let in the entire group (dressed as their favorite Batman villain), and we descended the stairs to the event (it was cosplay on steroids). I noticed that Stephan couldn't stop smiling as he recognized everyone. My ruse had worked, and we partied late into the night. I will never forget the moment Stephan stepped forward, stopped the band, and said, "Family, guests, staff, and especially my husband, I thank you all for this; you will never know how much I love the outpouring of your love. Pawpaw, may I have this dance?" With that, Stephan took my hand, led me to the dance floor, and played 'our song' (Living on Love by Allan Jackson). We danced to the thundering applause of our guests. I teared up as we shared the moment and moistened the shoulder of his cloak. We cut the cake as we did on our wedding day and then let the staff serve the guests.

I didn't know that 'Batman' had ideas of his own. When the party died down, he took me to the balcony and held me tight and whispered sweet nothings in my ear until it was nearly dawn. We watched the sun rise on 'our empire'. The guests who were left started leaving, and we simply showered, dressed, and went to breakfast. The four boys joined us for breakfast, and Harold made eggs Benedict for us all. Dahlia came in later and wanted to discuss matters of the house, so I excused myself and kissed Stephan before leaving. It seemed I had gone way over budget for the party (about $20,000), and she wanted to know how we were going to overcome it. Seems I'm getting pretty good at juggling the books to make it out of financial troubles. Dahlia worked her magic, and together we solved the problem. "Don't make me spank you, Carl.

Please don't let it happen again, as it raises my blood pressure." I almost promised her, but knew better, as it would be a lie.

Stephan asked me to come into the den and asked me to have a seat. "I have to tell you something, but I don't want to upset you. This morning, as I was showering, I found something, and it's been bothering me all day. Could you give it a look?" By now, I was shaking and trying to keep it together as he sounded so serious, and never before had I seen him so concerned. "Whatever it is, Stephan, we'll get through this together. What is it you want me to see?" With that, he bowed his head and showed me his hair. When I asked what I was looking for, he said, "I found a gray hair today. That means I'm starting to age." I almost hit him. "Really, Stephan, that's what's bothering you, a single gray hair. I thought you were going to show me a tumor, a wound, or something worse. But a single gray hair, at 546 years old, I'm surprised you have any at all." I guess Stephan realized my discontent and leaned into me and tried to lighten the mood. I finally settled down and said, "Stephan, I was really concerned and was preparing for the worst. Please don't do that again." Stephan twirled my hair and said, "Sorry, hun, but I never had any before. At this rate, I'll look your age by the time I'm 700." I resisted the urge to punch him, but the thought was there. I told him that we could call Chuck to see if he had anything in his bag of tricks to help him out (it seems I could be catty if pushed). Stephan pushed my head away and, smirking, left the room. I went to the kitchen for a snack.

Another couple of quiet years, and then finally, my writings were to be published. I got my royalty check for the first 100k printings and a box with a dozen copies. I called Stephan to show him the check before depositing it. "Stephan, see, now we have two writers in the family." The check was for $500,000. What a good way to start 2060. I started using hair color to mask my true age, and Stephan was the first to notice.

"I may have to cheat on my husband, cutie", and with that, swatted my butt. I told him I didn't date married men, but if he decided to divorce, then call me. We both fell over laughing when we realized that Dahlia was listening. She just shook her head and walked away. That started another fit of laughter. After lunch, Stephan asked if I wanted to visit the warehouse, and I eagerly agreed. We told the staff we'd be gone most of the day and maybe overnight, as the camp was closer to the warehouse. I threw together an overnight bag, got in the Bentley, and Stephan drove away. We arrived at the warehouse gate and saw that Bob was there checking on things. He waved us in and came to the car. "Any problems we should know about Bob?" Bob shook his head and said that things were tight under his direction. We waved him off and left the car near the door. I liked the car gallery, but my love was the art gallery. I went on ahead as Stephan spent some time with his cars. From the second floor, I could hear cars roaring to life and then quieting down. I myself pulled paintings from the collection to view, as we had an empty wall just for that. I had to Google some of the artists, but those I knew or had come to know were the ones I preferred. Stephan had a Da Vinci sketch, a couple of Raphael, several Botticelli, and a couple of Donatello. My favorite by far was still Narcissus by Caravaggio, as it was actually Stephan on canvas. When Stephan joined me, I asked if we could take that painting back to the house and put it in the bedroom. Stephan nodded, and I showed him my appreciation by kissing his cheek. We stayed too long and headed to the camp for the night. I was first to the door and unlocked our love nest for the night. The lights came on, and I headed to the kitchen to make us something to eat. Stephan brought in his bag, took it upstairs to the bedroom, and came down for supper. I handed him a bologna sandwich and tried to hold back a laugh, but couldn't. Stephan took a big bite and then tried to feed it to me. It got messy from there, but we were laughing too hard to do much more than that. I finally moved over and showed him the real meal, and he said sarcastically, "I'm too full after that sandwich." I gave him pouty lips and puppy eyes, and the laughter started again. We settled down and ate. The only problem was that we were the staff tonight and had to clean up after ourselves. The evening ended with a good glass of our wine, followed by a joint shower. I finished drying off before Stephan and went to the dresser and put on my nightwear. Stephan ducked his head into the room and hurried to finish as he had a suit on the bed to wear. All alone as Batman and Robin, with the entire house to ourselves. Holy capers, Batman, what a night (tomorrow could wait).

We arose (still wearing some of our outfits) and headed to the showers. We decided to get breakfast on the road (we really didn't want to mess up the camp kitchen again) and loaded up the Bentley. We got home to a flurry of action. We immediately went in search of Dahlia to see what was happening. She said quickly that Harold Jr. got too close to the stove and dumped a pot of scalding hot water on himself, and the ambulance was on its way. We removed ourselves so they could handle it, but stayed nearby if needed. Jr. was 10 now and Harold's only child. He was frantic, Ellen was on the phone with 911, and the boy had been placed at the door with cool wraps so the attendants could whisk him away to the burn unit more quickly. The ambulance arrived, and we sent the parents with Aaron driving behind the ambulance to the hospital. We yelled to Aaron to keep us apprised of the situation. Stephan took the responsibility of getting a temporary chef in to keep the house running smoothly. We waited along with the other staff to hear about Jr. Aaron, who finally called, assuring us that the burns were mostly first degree and that he suffered less because of our quick thinking. I told Aaron that we were sending food to the hospital for Harold, Ellen, and him. He told me thanks and gave us the room number and floor so we could deliver the food more easily. I turned to everyone and gave them the good news, and the mood lifted.

Stephan retreated to the den, and I followed him in. Our sanctuary was always comforting. I poured us both a stiff bourbon, and we settled near the fire in our favorite Louis the fourteenth chairs (I have to say the luxuriousness of the velvet was a delicious feeling). After what seemed like an hour, Stephan spoke and started an unexpected conversation. "I found a new book titled "Outlive" by Peter Attia and Bill Gifford. It was published in 2024 and suggests ideas about longevity. It was an interesting read if you'd like to peruse it. I left it on the mantel." I wondered why he was reading such stuff, as we probably knew more than anyone else about the subject. "Stephan, why are you so interested in it, as you actually lived it?" He shrugged me off, but I knew he was worried about something. I didn't push but told him I'd give it a look. He reached out and placed the book in my hands. I decided to leave him with his thoughts and left the den.

The climate had calmed down as I entered the kitchen and saw the temp chef. I requested a sandwich and wasn't prepared for his answer, "Sorry, but I only cook for the owners. The fridge is over there. By the way, who are you anyway?" I told him Carl or pawpaw, and he just turned his back to me as if dismissing me (I couldn't wait until he saw Stephan and treated him like that). Dahlia saw the interaction and nodded to me as she approached the arrogant snob and set him straight. "Chef, I suggest you treat the entire household as if they are the owners." The chef, not knowing that Dahlia had hired him, asked, "And who do you think you are? I only report to the house manager, and I don't see him around." I almost spit out my sandwich as she exploded all over him. She yelled for Bob, had Bob grab the chef before telling him that SHE was the house manager, and that I was the homeowner. He started to apologize as Bob ended his tenure with a stiff walk to the door. "Oh well, he wasn't that good a chef anyway. I'll get another one for dinner, boss." I nodded as I took my sandwich (followed by Alfred) to the patio. I told her over my shoulder that Stephan and I could eat out tonight. She acknowledged that and told me thanks. Stephan joined me on the patio, and Alfred ran to him as I didn't share my sandwich. I told him that we'd be eating out tonight to give Dahlia a little longer to replace Harold temporarily. He grabbed me and headed for the pool. After the surprise wore off, I turned the tables and held on as he tried to dunk me in. Together we entered the pool at the deep end, and we both came up laughing (I think we needed the moment as decompression from the earlier events). I kissed my man and then told him that he was paying for dinner as penance. He said okay and then dunked me again as if to say it was already paid for. I grabbed a towel from the chair and dried myself off as best as I could, and then threw the semi-wet towel at Stephan and went to change. He followed me upstairs to exact his revenge, and I shrieked as though he was scaring me. Dahlia shook her head, giggled privately, and left the scene quietly.

Harold, Ellen, and Jr. came back late that night as we were out dining. Jr. looked a little worse for wear, but okay, and Harold and Ellen were exhausted from the stress they went through. Harold asked Dahlia where we were, and she told him that we had gone out for the night and not to sweat it. The look of relief on his face said it all. He and the family retired, and I happened to spot their car as we were returning. Morning would give us any answers we needed, so we continued without delay. That night, the Bat Signal was shown on the ceiling of the bedroom (it seemed that the dip in the pool only delayed someone's libido). Time to be the dutiful sidekick, lights out.

Morning arrived, the sun was shining bright, and the smell of fresh coffee was drifting up to us as we descended the stairs. I could almost taste it as we entered the dining room, and the cups were filled with that nectar of the gods. Harold brought out eggs Benedict on toast points as I sipped the first sip. He asked if we wanted bacon also, and we both shook our heads no (pity, as Alfred followed him into the kitchen, assuming that he was going to eat well today). I ate well due to hunger from all the 'exercise' from the night before. Even Stephan finished his meal, conceding that he was famished. I asked if he was up for a shopping trip and asked him to go to Barnes and Noble Bookstore with me. He looked at me quizzically but nodded and told me he would drive. We took our leave and headed down the highway. We almost got swiped by a guy with what amounted to road rage. It seems he was gunning for us as he stayed near us on the highway. Stephan decided to evade this 'person' and took the next off-ramp. The guy crossed two lanes just to get off behind us. I noticed and told Stephan about it. He looked back, not recognizing him but noting that he was indeed tailing us. He told me to contact Bob, give him the license number and make, model and color of the car. I did as told and Stephan decided the guy needed a lesson in courtesy so he drove into a parking lot that had security cameras. The guy pulled into the lot and Stephan simply pointed to the cameras and flipped him off as he sped away. When he had left and we couldn't find him anywhere, Stephan put the car in motion and went home. He needed answers and knew Bob would have them. We sought out Bob as we parked the car in the driveway. Bob took us aside and told us, "That car belongs to the 'chef' we hired as a temp for Harold. It seems he got mad after I unceremoniously gave him the boot for disrespecting the household. What would you like me to do, as in teaching him his place?" Stephan requested that he be brought to heel (using an old expression, Stephan, you're showing your age, lol). Bob grinned ear to ear and said, "Got it boss, I know just what to do. (for some reason, Eric came to mind)." I decided not to inquire as I needed plausible deniability. My thoughts were that New Jersey was about to increase their population by one (pre-canned and delivered fresh). I asked about the shopping trip and Aaron said that he'd drive us in his car and we accepted. We got to the store and Stephan wanted a coffee as I browsed. I actually wanted to know if the authors of "Outlive' had other thoughts and books about longevity. He also wrote 'Spring Chicken' and 'Ledyard' by Bill Gifford and 'The outlive cookbook' by Peter Attia. I was now wondering if they knew something and purchased the lot. I found Stephan in the cafe and he asked if I was done shopping, I nodded and we left the store. I spent hours pouring over the books to see if I needed to talk with Stephan. It seems that the guys were advising about how to improve the quality of your mortal life, not to overcome death. I gave the cookbook to Harold and placed the other books in the den library. I didn't mention it to Stephan again.

The next day, I passed the den and noticed Stephan going over a journal from his past. It piqued my curiosity, so I stuck my head in the door and winked at him. He waved me in, and I asked what he was re-reading. "I'm going back over some of my exploits from 1714 in France, before Louis 'The Sun King' died, and I went to visit. Those were the golden days, especially if you were in favor. Louis always made a show of dressing, eating, and the social graces. I was looking at the meals, the formal dances, the wardrobe, and the materials used. I kind of miss that time. That's when they first started producing the real champagne. My dalliances with the artists, singers, and courtiers. I'm sorry if that makes you jealous, but it was 253 years before you were born, so there's that." I was wondering about the interest in the nostalgia (as I went into overthinking mode yet again). I said nothing and let him continue. "Do you think we'll be reminiscing about our beginnings in another hundred years?" I told him yes (although I didn't think I'd be there to remember). "I think we should live in the now and leave the future to itself.

Stephan nodded and came in for a little canoodling. We sat on the rug in front of the fire, and I poured two bourbons for us. We clinked our glasses and sipped the nectar and simply felt the peace of the moment spread over us. Bob came in a few minutes later, stating that our 'situation' was over and that we'd never hear from our temp again. We never asked another question about it, and Bob, smiling, left us to wonder in silence. I decided to take Stephan on a trip back to Paris so he could fully enjoy the days gone by and remember the good times. Also, I could use the time to enjoy the food and culture. I set the trip up and asked England and Italy if they were interested. England accepted, and Italy declined, stating that they would love a visit after our gathering. I extended our plans, and soon the day for departure arrived. I made sure that we had enough clothing for the whole time and any other 'essentials' we might need. The 'bus' left the ground and we relaxed until Paris came into view. An hour later, we were at the hotel Chateau Des Fleurs on 19 rue Vernet 75008, Paris, near the Champs Élys ées. I had booked the suite with a balcony overlooking the best view Paris had to offer. I figured that Stephan deserved the best, and I wanted all his dreams to come true. The boys arrived later and took the suite one floor down. Eddie and Anthony joined us for dinner in the pub, and we feasted on the pub fare. A basic 3-course affair starting with salade cretoise (fresh greens salad), merlu braise (braised hake with virgin sauce and basmati rice), and finishing with croissant au chocolat, crème vanille, and framboises (chocolate croissant with vanilla cream and strawberries). We purchased a couple of bottles of champagne to go with the hake and dessert. The waiter saw that we weren't French, and I heard him say something in French and nod towards us. Stephan, my dear champion and fluent French interpreter, stood and spoke to the waiter in French. I don't know what he said, but the waiter took on a whole new demeanor. Knowing better, I let it slide as I knew Stephan had just handled it. Not only did the waiter snap to, but the maitre'd attended to us as well. The bill came, and as I was prepared to pay it, the maitre'd took it away, saying it was on the house. Stephan thanked him and went to the waiter and tipped him heavily. We left knowing we'd be better received next time.

The boys went barhopping, and Stephan and I strolled the main streets. I window shopped as we strolled, and Stephan took in the view around us. He stopped in front of a patisserie. I came up alongside him as he glanced through the glass and turned to me and said, "This shop has been here about four hundred years. I remember the proprietor being brought to the King to present his creations. Louis loved them and bestowed a medal upon the owner. Would you like to try some?" I nodded, and we entered the shop. It smelled delicious, and Stephan stepped forward as the clerk approached. The clerk talked in broken English (or tried to) until Stephan told him that he spoke fluent French. The clerk relaxed, Stephan told him what he wanted, and the clerk was gone and back in a flash. I assumed the regular retail stuff, but these creations looked specially made. I asked Stephan what they were, and he said Creme Brulee. It was Louis' favorite back in 1700. I cracked the shell (as I had seen Stephan do) and tasted it, true pleasure. The vanilla custard was perfectly velvety on the tongue, and the flavors melded wonderfully. My guy knew his stuff. We ordered more goodies to be shipped back home for the troops and left the shop. Stephan got us coffees to drink, and we just sat along the street watching the people. I was hoping Stephan was enjoying himself when, in a moment of passion, he leaned over and kissed me as the sun set (can you say magic was in the air). We walked hand in hand back to the hotel.

We were greeted by two slightly inebriated relatives, and we guided them into the elevator. We dropped them off at their door, ensuring that they got in, and then walked up the remaining floor to our suite. I undressed to take a shower and tested the water for heat. However, the water was tepid at best, so I decided to take it in the morning. Coming back into the bedroom, I saw a dark figure lurking in the corner. It seems Batman found his outfit before I had the chance to dress up. I noticed the suit on the bed, and he pointed to it, saying, "Hurry Robin, there's danger afoot, put on your outfit so you can slide down the bat pole." I told you there was magic in the air.

The morning came late as we had slept in, showers were taken together to conserve water, and then we dressed for the day. I called the concierge service to see if I could get the suits cleaned (knowing if they turned on a black light, we'd be busted). They were wonderful about it, and we set out. I asked Stephan where he wanted to go, and he said Versailles. Having never seen it, I was eager to go, and we hired a guide and left. I have to say that opulence beyond Baroque style was still an understatement for this place. The hall of mirrors was extravagant. The ballroom and throne room are unbelievable. It would take days to fully expose yourself to the grandeur. Stephan pointed to the writing desk that had samples of letters to Louis XIV, noting that one of his letters was there, and the two of us laughed to ourselves about it. Next, we went through the clothing exhibits, where I was shown the outfits that Stephan wore during that time. I quietly took a lot of photos (I think you know why) and we went to have lunch. The castle was serving a menu from the golden era. We dined on delicacies and then drank some more champagne. I was glad to have given Stephan his dream of reminiscence.

Our trip was quickly coming to an end, and we prepared for Italy. Anthony and Eddie told us to give the other boys their good tidings, and we departed for Italy. The boot appeared soon, and we landed. A car was waiting, and we were spirited away to the villa. Junior greeted us at the door and said that Hunter had gone to the vineyard to get a shipment before we arrived. Hunter arrived shortly after us. He had the staff unload the bottles, and I noticed our Christmas wine among the crates. I inquired as to Tony Sr. and Jr. Hunter said that they were all well and sent their greetings, as well as an invitation to visit if possible. I told Stephan that we should, and he agreed. Today was for the boys, tomorrow was for the visit to the cemetery, and then we could arrange our time for a visit. I loved Stephan for his eternal remembrance of his relatives, gone but never forgotten. The boys had a surprise for us; it seems that Hunter had a few of his long-time relatives visiting as well. Borgias and Garibos together gathered to celebrate Pope Alexander VI's ascension to the papacy on August 11, 1492. His birth name was Rodrigo Borgia from Spain. I looked him up and found out he fathered a host of kids and died in 1503. He was poisoned once and was thought of as substandard as a pope. Who was I to judge, he died 9 years before my husband was born. The festivities went on and we joined in as in-laws. The wine flowed without end and the food just kept coming. We decided to hold back and see what happens. We were not disappointed as the relatives drank and loosened up. Stephan listened to them speaking Italian and Spanish with a little French thrown in. They thought we didn't know their conversation and Stephan whispered the translation in my ear as we listened. It turns out they were pretty impressed with Hunter and Stephan and we were being honored as special guests. Finally, something nice for a change. I got up to leave as the dancing started and Stephan arose to say his good nights. They were totally unprepared and surprised when they heard Stephan address them in all three languages. That was my high point for the evening. We walked away and Stephan smiled his million dollar smile. I just placed my hand in his, placed my head on his shoulder and let him lead me away to bed.

Morning found Stephan and me drinking espresso with the staff when Junior and Hunter graced the scene. We decided on a light breakfast of Gruyere cheese, bread, and apple slices. We got ready for the cemetery by going wreath shopping in town before heading to the graves. Wreaths placed, prayers said, and quiet contemplation taken, we headed out to the vineyard. Tony greeted us and took us to the vineyard tasting room. He was allowing Jr. to mix his own Merlot. He wanted Tony Jr. to invest in the business as Sr. was getting on in years and wanted the legacy winemaking to endure. Jr. had us taste his creation, and to my surprise, he had a winner. He told us, though, that he would need more money to expand his fields for the grapes. Stephan told him that it would not be an issue. Tony called at the house and had his wife make a big lunch for us all. Jr. brought a couple of bottles of his wine, and we sat under olive trees, eating simple but tasty home cooking. We told Tony to ship another season to our house in Baltimore and then thanked them for their hospitality. We returned to the villa as the new party started. I sat on the side and just let it happen without me. Stephan got into a few conversations with the Borgias, now that they knew he could understand their native language. Ever the pro, Stephan controlled the situation and left them happy and agreeable. He came to me and asked me to go swimming in the pool. We donned our swim suits and plunged in. Some of the guests were surprised, and others asked if Hunter had more suits, as they would also enjoy some time in the pool. Soon, the pool was half full of nearly naked people, and Stephan and I swam to the edge and watched the mayhem. What fun, and then Hunter and Junior dove in, joining us at the edge. Hunter loved the scene, and Junior just took it all in. The party started to get intense with the drinking and such, so we left the pool and went to our room to change. By the time we reached the patio door, things had settled down, and people were drying themselves and sitting around the pit fire Hunter had started. We took a glass of wine and joined the folks around the fire. Our day was complete. Sleep came as the sky welcomed the moon's return. Two days later, we said our goodbyes and headed to the airport. The bus was ready, and so were we. Next stop, Baltimore, and our beloved home. Somehow it seems that coming home evokes two emotions, that of fear that there's a problem needing attention, and that feeling of being welcomed back in the nest and home ground.

Aaron picked us up at the hangar and drove us home. So far, so good. We found Harold and Dahlia in the kitchen having coffee and discussing tonight's dinner menu. Hugs, instructions as to what's going to be delivered and gifts handed out, we inquired as to Harold Jr. "He's one tough kid, but there will be a little scarring from the second degree burns. But all in all, he's fine." I was still waiting for the other shoe to drop. Bob told us nothing was happening on his front, and we had stayed on budget for the trip. Even Dahlia was impressed with me. Okay, now I felt weird because nothing was wrong. I went upstairs to unpack when the call came in that Eric had been taken to the hospital (after all, he was 75 now) and not expected to make it. Stephan reached out to Nathan, and I reached out to Nancy to find where he was taken, and Nancy told me John Hopkins, so I asked if we could visit, and she said of course. It took about fifteen minutes to get there, and we explained that we were family so as to attain admittance. Eric looked pale and very frail, but rallied when he caught a glimpse of us standing there. I approached him, and he tried to sit up. I reached out and assisted him into an upright position. His eyes cleared and teared slightly. Nancy was on his other side holding his hand as Nathan walked in dressed in his scrubs and white coat. He went straight to the chart and read the vitals. I forgot that he might be on duty today. We all looked at him for any signs of problems. Nathan began, "It says here that Dad tried cleaning the gutters but only succeeded in overexerting himself. He'll recover, but it will be slow. Now, Dad, please call someone to take care of it. Try to stick around, we'd like some more time with you. Besides, Nathan Jr. is 23 now and in pre-med. I'd like you to be there when he graduates." Eric nodded his head, and we all sighed in relief. We stayed to support Nancy, and Jr. ducked his head in after classes. We ordered food in and stayed until we were thrown out. Nancy hugged us both, and we said to keep us informed, and she nodded.

Well, it wasn't a horrible problem, and I could relax, having the other shoe finally on the floor. Stephan and I went to the den for some quiet and bourbon. The fire crackled and hypnotized me into a serene stupor. I followed Stephan to bed, and I slept being spooned and enveloped in my husband's strong arms (now I knew tomorrow would be okay). Morning came with its usual barrage of questions about Eric. I answered them one at a time and then asked for breakfast. Coffee with eggs Benedict and Mimosas were placed in front of us, and we devoured them just as quickly. I went to the patio to write (something I had been remiss in doing and needed to memorialize in my journal). My trip to France and then Italy, the sights, the sounds, the food, and the experiences. I remembered how exciting it was to read Stephan's private thoughts, and that set me to delving in deep. I didn't get into the weeds, but I didn't leave much out either.

The new year came, and then another, and soon it was 2062, my 95th birthday. Stephan was going to be 550. Nathan Jr. was in medical school now. Dahlia and Aaron were empty nesters. Time kept marching on. I was still on my pills and hadn't noticed much of a change, which was good. Stephan now had salt and pepper hair, finally. He looked to be about forty-five and dashing. His looks had matured enough to be stately. We started looking more appropriate as a couple. Jeffrey Allen Halstead was re-elected to the state senate (much to Dahlia's delight, so much to brag about). I asked if he had a love interest, and Dahlia took out her phone and showed him. "Here she is, her name is Christine. Her family name is Calvert. They are an old family going back to George Calvert, a founding father of Baltimore. I think there may be a wedding announcement soon." I looked at the photos and smiled. When I left her, I called Bob for a little more information on the family. Can't be too careful. Bob grinned and went about his 'business'.

I stopped in the doorway of the den when I noticed Stephan banging away on his laptop. I stood saying nothing as he typed. He spotted me and waved me in. It seems that he had some journaling to do, also. I stood beside him as he pointed to his screen. I read the excerpt and smiled at him. "Should I blush or edit it out later, big boy?" He stood and grabbed me by the waist. "Close and lock the door, and I'll really make you blush." I rose to the challenge and hurriedly locked the door before returning to my guy (yes, blush was the color of the night).

Bob returned to me the next day with the information I requested. It seems that Christine was pristine (pun intended). However, the family had enough skeletons in their combined closets to fill a novel. I asked for the notes in case I needed to use them as leverage and filed them in my desk (no need to leave them out for wandering eyes). I thanked Bob, and he looked disappointed that I didn't want him to use his exceptional skill set yet. Stephan came prancing into the den after Bob left, so I didn't mention my conversation with Bob. "Why are you in such a good mood, not that I mind?" Stephan almost sang his response, "It's because I feel especially happy today." By the look in his eyes, I

knew he was up to something, probably a surprise for me (or somebody was being relocated to New Jersey). I let it go, hoping it was my surprise. He popped a bottle of our special cinnamon wine, and I got out our wine glasses. "A toast to us and our future", we clinked glasses and took a swig. Just as tasty as I remembered. "Now tell me, what's this all about, Stephan?" He smiled and then showed me his latest check from the publisher. I saw the check, kissed my guy, and then he asked where I wanted to go. "We've been to England, France, Denmark, Italy, and Greece, but I've never been to Hawaii. What say we troop up and invade the islands?" Stephan rubbed his chin, thought for a moment and said, "How many you thinking?" I rounded it up to 30 people and said that the bus could handle that. He returned my smile and said, "Round em' up, cowboy, and I'll make the arrangements."

I called Judy and Jeff, then Harold and Ellen, then Dahlia and Aaron, Nathan and Anita, Anthony and Eddie, Hunter and Stephan, and the kids of the above. It came out to 28, so I invited Bob along as well. The logistics were daunting, but we made it work. We decided on two weeks and literally rented out a hotel wing for our group. Stephan and I rented a BNB for us, and I made sure to find a local dry cleaner near the rental. The boys arrived the day before departure and stayed at the house. We assembled at the hangar, and it took about an hour before we were in the air. I think Stephan had the most luggage. Hawaii came into view, and the pilot showed us the island where we would be staying as we passed by. When I questioned him, he said that the island was too small and we would have to ferry to the island (oops on my part). I searched out transportation while the plane was unloaded. I found one local, but he said it would take two trips to get us all there. Stephan and I took the second group to lunch as we waited for the ferry to return. An hour and twenty minutes later, we were all on the island, and the troops got settled in the hotel. Stephan and I took longer to get settled as the owners were nit-picky about the rules (note to self, buy a property here if we ever come back).

Stephan, ever the diplomat, calmed their fears, and they left us to it. I was out at the in-ground pool when he came out flashing the keys. It was about this time that Hunter and Junior descended upon us. Soon after, Anthony and Eddie showed up. Oh well, quiet time could wait. They said that the troops were spending the day at the hotel pool with the kids, so they bowed out and came our way. As the boys changed into their swimwear, I mentioned to Stephan about hosting a Luau, and he agreed. I called around and found a site that held them weekly. I booked the entire event for our troops, and they were happy to have a private party (meaning they could let loose more, and we encouraged it). I returned to the pool party and the boys, and Stephan was in the pool. I made the mistake of getting close to the pool and got dragged in fully clothed (thank god I left my wallet in the house). They ganged up on me, and Stephan stayed back, enjoying the show as they stripped me to my shorts. Thankfully, I had lost my dad's body before the trip. Harold showed up in time to make us lunch and left right after setting it out for us. The affair was simple: deli sandwiches and drinks (which we used as mixers except for Anthony). Refreshed, we went into the villa and dried off and dressed for the event tonight.

We informed Harold that the troops were to join us at the Luau site and sent him the address. When we finally got there, the 'family' was indulging in appetizers. We joined the festivities and settled in just as the dancers took the stage. Torches lit, and the batons set on fire, the dancers whirled around and beat their chests (I don't know which of us was enjoying the guys more). We rewarded the dancers with free drinks and got to know them individually. We had them join us at the feast, and they eagerly took places near us. The night came slowly as the sun ran away beyond the waves. The stars shone bright in the night sky (not having to compete with city lights). The event came to an end, and the troops left for the hotel. Stephan asked me to walk the beach in the dark serenity under the stars. I took his hand, and we strolled for about half an hour before turning back. We arrived back at the villa, and Stephan got frisky. As we were finally alone, he decided clothing was optional, and seeing him relaxed, I followed suit. The rest of the night was 'magical'.

The rest of the first week went lazily along as we got everyone together for more merriment. We had Tony Sr. send a large shipment of wine to Hawaii, and it arrived on the first Friday of our vacation. Stephan surprised me with a glass-bottom boat tour and invited the entire entourage along. I was astonished at the delights of the reef wildlife, and the kids were mesmerized. The other adults looked on with varied levels of interest (did I mention the wine went with us?). All in all, it was a good day. The hotel put on a buffet, and Stephan and I invited ourselves to the feast (after all, we were the ones paying the bill). The second week went the same way as the first, and by the end, the troops were happy to pack up and return to Baltimore, England, and Italy. We got home late Sunday night and let everyone else tend to their own needs. I took the suitcases upstairs, and we just plopped into bed, exhausted from the trip. Tomorrow could wait.

Monday arrived, and we went downstairs following the scent of fresh coffee. We found it in the hands of Dahlia and joined her at the counter. It took me several cups to rev my engine enough to handle the affairs of the day. Dahlia seemed to get going on one. Stephan took his and disappeared into the den. Alfred was beside himself, going from one person to the next, getting his love from each one of us. He settled down after about an hour, then went to the den and slept in his bed by Stephan's desk. I went to the patio and took in more sun (I just couldn't get going; I needed a vacation from my vacation). This went on for the next few days until the jet lag left us.

Stephan got a letter from the BNB guy and seemed less than pleased. He called for Bob, and then I knew something bad had been written in the letter. I asked Stephan to let me read it, but he insisted that the less I knew, the better. Now my 'spidey' senses kicked in, and I dreaded what Stephan had read. I quietly went to Bob later and asked about what Stephan had told him. "He just wants me to clarify to the BNB guy that Stephan is dissatisfied and disappointed with him and why." Another dead end. I would have to wait and see. I guess I didn't have to wait long. Signs started showing themselves, like Bob being missing for a few days. I looked up the BNB in Hawaii that we rented and saw it was for sale, price negotiable. Two days later, I overheard Stephan talking to someone on the phone, and Stephan said to purchase something now that it was reasonably priced. Again, later that week, I viewed the BNB and saw it was off the market, purchased at a sale price. I feared the worst, but Bob reappeared the next day smiling like Eric after a fight. I knew then that the owner had really crossed swords with Stephan. Thankfully, I told myself that the sharks were feasting and nobody would be found. All I said to Stephan was that I noticed that the BNB in Hawaii had been sold to a new owner. He smiled and said that the owner had agreed to sell it to us. I blew him a kiss and left him and the subject alone.

Later that night, I cornered Bob and told him that Stephan told me all about the owner, and then Bob said, "Well, at least you'll have a new vacation home and the owner won't be caught videoing you two again. I removed all the recording equipment and destroyed the evidence. Aha, now the story came out. I was fuming inside, but didn't let on to Bob. He had done his job (albeit with a little too much fervor and joy). Bob turned to me just before leaving, "By the way, boss, you two look cute in your suits." I blushed and wondered what else he watched before destroying the tapes. I was glad that Bob was on our side and not a disgruntled employee.

The next couple of months were boring, and I dedicated my time to writing. My journals were getting as juicy as Stephan's. I guess that's what happens when you live this long. So 95 hit, and I got my physical. Our doctor knew our secret and said that Chuck did a good job because I still had the physiology of a 50-year-old. I took that as a compliment and set out to ask Stephan how he fared. He looked concerned and finally said, "Looks like I'm mortal after all. Doc says I've probably got less than 2 hundred years left before old age sets in." I slapped his butt and told him not to scare me like that. "But it's fun watching you react when I do." I grabbed him and pushed him upstairs, saying, "Better get my licks in before that happens." He beat me upstairs, and that meant my turn to visit the cleaners tomorrow.

The rest of the year passed, and Christmas was once again upon us. The troops were coming, and this time Tony and family said they could make it. Dahlia and I got the logistics worked out and the reservations secured. We sent the 'bus' to Italy to help with the accommodations for travel. Harold was teaching Jr. (now 12 y/o) how to cook, and Jr. was catching on quickly. Dahlia's son, Jeffrey, was also able to make it. He brought his date, Christine Calvert, and we got to take a closer look at her. We wanted to make sure that 'our' state senator was marrying well (already knowing she was from a prominent family). She was worldly, kind, and most of all gorgeous. Dahlia led the couple around like trophies, and she beamed as the attendees agreed with her. The highlight was when Jeffrey called everyone into the main sitting room as he took to his knees and proposed to Christine. He had to ask her twice as she was stunned. She finally said yes, and for the next hour, all one could hear was corks popping on champagne. I took Dahlia aside and asked what the kids needed, and she said a location wedding place. I told her I could think of a place in Hawaii, and she kissed my cheek. "Can I tell the kids, or would you and Stephan want to?" I shooed her in the direction of the kids and told her that I'd tell Stephan of the present we were gifting to the kids. She came back to me grinning, saying that the kids were euphoric by the gesture. I corralled Stephan before the kids could thank him and told him what 'we' had done. He thanked me as the kids came up to us. I went to Dahlia a little later and told her that she'd have to work a little harder on my manuscript if she wanted me to fund the wedding, also. She said, "No problem, they'll be thrilled and so will her parents." Finally, something I could personally do for the family.

The date was set for the following year, but in May, before the real heat conquered the Pacific. Dahlia did the work, and the editor was astonished that the book needed so little in the way of editing. I received my first royalty check in time for the nuptials. I handed the check to Dahlia and asked if she needed more, to which she said no. I had to go to the bank so they would accept the deposit, and I left the rest to Dahlia. Stephan asked if I wanted to go to England for Easter, and I decided that it would be nice to go as a couple and said yes. He called the boys and asked if the coachman's house was available for a visit, and Eddie screamed over Anthony, "Tell them yes, I just finished the restoration. They'll love it." We both laughed as Anthony waved Eddie away from the phone. "I guess you heard that, seeing as the whole county here heard it. Let me know the details and I'll have this side covered."

Stephan took over the conversation and shooed me away as he got the details from Anthony. Later in the evening, Stephan discussed the details with me and said to pack as we were leaving in 2 days. Departure day, and we were taken to the hangar. Something seemed off as the regular pilot wasn't near the plane. Stephan inquired, and they said that our regular pilot was ill and this was his replacement. Stephan called the regular guy, and he was in fact sick, and Stephan asked when he would be ready to fly again. It wasn't like Stephan to act like this, so I whispered in his ear, "What's up?" Stephan whispered back, "I think it's a setup to ship drugs using our plane." Stephan made another call to the security and had them come check out the plane with a drug dog before we put anything on the jet. Sure enough, they found a couple of kilos of Cocaine in the storage area. They took the pilot into custody and led him away. Security asked Stephan how he knew, and he shrugged it off and simply said it was a hunch. They recommended a new pilot with good credentials, and we loaded our luggage and lifted off.

We arrived in merry old England about two hours late and saw Anthony pacing back and forth as we deplaned. "What took you guys so long? I was worried, and Eddie is tied in knots with worry." Stephan told him about the incident in detail, and then we left for the estate. Eddie was waiting at the door as we went past to the coach house. He followed us there (and with hands on his hips) demanded to be told the reason for the delay. "I've been toiling away for three days, and then you spoil the surprise by being late." "Sorry, Mom, for the delay, but we had to detox the plane before take off." I saw Eddie's face ease, and then he worried about the surprise. He shifted into hyperdrive and literally pushed us inside, not wanting to wait any longer. There, we saw some of our paintings from the English warehouse. I saw a pastoral one that touched my soul, and I stood in front of it. I found out it was a painting by John Constable and was painted in the 1800's. Stephan liked the one by J.M.W. Turner. Eddie was righteously happy that we loved his restorations. He then invited us to the main house for dinner, and we went gladly.

Over dinner, we discussed the details about the tardiness and the uncovering of the drugs on board. The dinner was basic (aka – not worth writing home about) but satiating. After dinner, I went for a walk with Eddie as Stephan and Anthony talked business in the den. I told Eddie about the wardrobe that I had seen in France from the Louis XIV era. "I've got this idea running around my head about recreating those costumes for Stephan." Eddie burst out, "I just happen to know a costume designer who can do that for you. He creates all my fashion stuff. Very high-end and unique. I'm sure that he'd be more than happy to do it, although it will be somewhat expensive. "I'll send the pictures I took, and you can hire him. I'll also need the shoes to match. This is going to make our next Halloween event magical. I'll need quite a few other outfits as well." Eddie was already on the phone with his clothier. He turned to me and said, "It'll cost close to $500,000 for everything, and he can start tomorrow." I told Eddie to assure his friend that the money would be dropped off the next day. "Oh, Eddie, I can't wait until Stephan descends the stairs and sees everyone dressed. But you must keep this to yourself." Eddie nodded and smirked, "You can bet you'll see us there in October. Have you told Italy yet?" "No, but I'll let them know later."

Stephan and Anthony (looking like bookend Adonis') nodded to us as we went into the library to join them. I almost had to pinch Eddie to get that smirk off his face, but I settled on a subtle elbow to the ribs. He calmed down before they noticed, and I felt a little relief. I was handed a Bourbon and a cigar, but opted for just the liquid. Eddie made himself a light mixed drink and sat by Anthony. Stephan was pontificating about his newest project, and Anthony went on about his newest trades. We dutiful partners sat and listened, then nodded our approval (even though we were probably the most uninterested people in the entire estate). I listened to Stephan as he stated that he was in the process of writing a fiction novel about time travel. My ears pricked up. Now he had my attention. Stephan went on about the framework and a few ideas he had (then I began to wonder where that came from). Eddie was busy getting Anthony a mineral water and making himself another drink. Anthony started on again about his latest conquests in the stock market, and Stephan mentioned that he might want to look into the stocks of a particular publisher. He told Anthony, "I hear they need an influx of funds, and I could use the leverage when my book is done." Anthony took notes and said, "I'll get right on it, Grandfather." I had to remember that they were actually generations apart.

Days later, we headed home and said our goodbyes. We got to the airport and boarded. Tired and a sense of relief as I was getting uneasy about my trips to the airport (having had 2 incidents now). Baltimore welcomed us as we landed and pulled into the hangar. Aaron pulled up, took our luggage, and readied himself for the drive home. Home seemed to open its arms to us, and now the jet lag set in. Tonight was going to be just sleep. A hot shower and the comfort of Stephan's strong arms around me in bed were all I needed as I drifted into my private heaven. Morning interrupted my slumber and robbed me of the warmth of Stephan's body as I arose to start the day. Coffee aroma filled my olfactory senses, and I followed the trail. It led me to a filled cup on the counter (Dahlia must have heard me and prepared it). Two sips later, Dahlia appeared and brought her cup and set it next to mine. "Well, how was your trip? How are the boys? How much do I need to rewrite into the budget for this trip?" I nearly spilled my coffee as I said, "How about $600,000?" She threw up her hands, and the look was priceless. I calmed her down and said that the trip and the budget were only $100,000 and that the rest would come from my personal account. She slapped me upside my head and said, "That's for grandma, as I know that's what she would have done." I rubbed my temple, but started laughing, knowing that Trudy would have been worse.

Along came 2063, 44 years together with Stephan and me turning 96. I could always feel better when I realized that Stephan was much older. I never thought in my mortal life that I would live this long, let alone in this lifestyle. A quick prayer and a long thanks to God or kismet or whatever was controlling my destiny (maybe the fates). Whatever it was that brought me this far on my journey, my gratitude. I couldn't wait for spring in Baltimore, as the flowers come early here. When the leaves appear, and the grass wakes up, I get excited. It's the best time of the year for me. I took my breakfast in the atrium with Alfred waiting for his share. Stephan joined me shortly, and Alfred was assured that he would have a good leftover. Stephan nibbled and picked at his scrambled eggs and toast while taking his time with his coffee. About four bites later, Alfred got his meal, and I added to his plate. I asked Stephan what was on his mind, and he just said he was trying to decide which way to take his book. I knew better than to offer advice, and after a peck on the cheek, turned and left him to it.

I went back to my journaling, having now completed my tenth volume. I started having fun with Dahlia by adding in a few mentions of the capers of Batman and Robin (with enough details to ensure she would blush as she transcribed). To inspire me further, I wandered through the house and communed with the true beauty of the structure. I take my time perusing the artwork and sometimes just sit and study the form and coloration, how the subject plays kinetically in the foreground, while the background seems static. Maybe I should try my hand at it, but then no, leave it to the professionals. Stephan appeared while I was in my revelry, then came to me and asked if I was alright. "I just needed to appreciate what we have, I needed to understand that I was given a gift most people will never have." Stephan hugged me and said, "And that's why I fell in love with you, because of this moment and every time you bring me back to my origins. I know it didn't start out that way, but I'm so glad it went there. You do complete me." He said no more, but leaned in for another kiss and left me to my thoughts. I continued my tour, and that infused my next entries for my journal (how do you tell the world what I have seen, experienced, and tasted). I took the time before dinner to do some introspection and came to the realization that I had changed (if even for the better). My taste had gone from bologna to bolognese, from beer to champagne, and from fast food to cultural cuisine. My clothing went from ratty t-shirts to silk and haute couture. I went from having art print posters to real, original masters from periods of history. I went from driving a Honda to driving a Bentley. I ate the best food, had staff to keep the house running, and could travel anywhere in the world on a private jet. I knew I had to keep reminding myself that this was a picture-perfect life, and it was all due to a young man who entered my life. Maybe it started because he wanted to see if I was getting close to outing him and his secrets, but it evolved into the love match I could never have seen coming.

Dahlia rescued me from my thoughts, and I went to dinner with a new appreciation for my life. I called for Alfred, and we sauntered into the dining room. I sat next to Stephan and asked that the kitchen staff, Dahlia, and Aaron join us. Stephan looked on quizzically but said nothing, as was his stoic way. I toasted us all and raised my glass to my husband (who had started it all). It may seem maudlin, but it was cathartic for me. My hope would always be to enjoy today as your last and treasure those in your life that made it so. Few people have that honor. Stephan departed for the den (with me in hot pursuit), and I poured us a long Bourbon. Stephan got the fire going, and we relaxed on the rug, gently touching each other and hugging as we felt the warmth envelop us.

Stephan finally asked, "What's got into you, Carl? I haven't seen you this cuddly since Europe." I looked into his gorgeous eyes and told him about my day. Stephan clinked my glass and simply said, "You're welcome, Robin." Well, tonight just got planned (now I couldn't wait till Halloween). Well, Halloween was coming soon, and I had Dahlia make the invitation list and the hotel reservations. The week leading up to the main event, people started showing up. First was Anthony and Eddie (with the entire set of attire for the party). Then Hunter and Junior appeared (and I hoped that Stephan hadn't caught on yet). I had Dahlia get the camp ready, and we stashed more people there. By the time October 31st arrived, we were all ready. Eddie dropped off our outfits, and I set them out for Stephan and me to wear. We showered, and then he saw the clothes. "Where on earth did you rent these?" I fibbed a little and said, "From an antique dealer, so better not ruin them."

I nodded to the band to start playing the music from the late 1600's and then we descended the stairs, Stephan dressed in a suit befitting King Louis XIV, all silk bow ties, ermine cape, purple velvet pantaloons and vest, heeled shoes, silk stockings, and embroidered with inset semi-precious jewels (it actually cost $53,000 just for his suit). Mine was a little less fine (so Stephan could stand out), and the crowd looked on as though they were courtiers from the period. I took my man's hand and continued to escort him down the stairs as people came up to touch his clothes. I let him move about the room as though he were back at Versailles before getting everyone's attention. "Raise your glass to our "King", may he live forever." The crowd hooted and hollered and whistled, then clinked their glasses, and the event was off to a glorious start. Stephan hunted me down and, slipping in next to me, took my hand and led me to the dance floor. He asked the orchestra to play a waltz and told me to just follow him. We danced in the middle of the room, and the lights were highlighting our moves (talk about strutting around like peacocks). Later that night, I sat next to Stephan, sipping wine, and said,

"Well, did I measure up to your fancy parties of yore?" I saw Stephan turn to answer, and no words came, just glassy eyes and a single tear running down his face. He nodded, and I had my answer, no words required. We finished the party late in the evening with fireworks lighting up the night sky. The partiers left for their sleeping quarters (I bet they got stares from the locals). Stephan led me to the patio and looked up at the stars. "I would give you the stars if I could, Carl. I never thought my life would be this fulfilling. After Svetlana was left behind to protect myself, I figured that I would need to go through the centuries alone, having only one-night stands and maybe a few dalliances. But you, a straight man, stole my heart and gave me a life filled with love. Yes, the family grew, but you are different; no words can tell you how much better it is living as your spouse." My tears flowed as I reached for Stephan, and he allowed them to stain his raiments.

We spent the rest of the night cuddling each other, letting our emotions out freely. The fire died before sleep took us, and I knew that I'd be dreaming sweet dreams, hoping Stephan would have the same. Morning came, and so did 'the morning after'. We finally dragged ourselves down to the kitchen (Alfred having already consumed our breakfast). I decided on coffee and toast while Stephan ate a bagel (hoping to absorb the remaining alcohol). Bob came around and, smiling, said, "Hey boss, how's the hangover? I noticed you drinking a lot last night." Stephan flipped him off, and I just covered my ears, and Bob sauntered out onto the patio and left us to our agony.

We sent the costumes to the cleaners with Eddie, and he gave explicit instructions on how to clean them. He also told the cleaner that he would personally inspect them after the cleaning to ensure that they were left intact. The cleaner knew Stephan and me well, so I knew Eddie would be satisfied. I called the cleaner myself and told him that he'd be well compensated and to try his best. Then I called the tailor to see if the 5th set of our 'special' suits was ready for pick up (yes, those suits, they wore out again). He said yes, and I told him that Bob would be by to get them (penance for those earlier comments).

We decided to go to camp for the weekend, and while we were near the warehouse and the weather was mild, Stephan asked me if I wanted to take a few spins from the car collection. I was surprised, stunned actually, that he offered that, but I immediately took him up on it. I decided on the 1932 dark green Duesenberg and then the silver Rolls-Royce Phaeton. I swear we drove nearly a dozen cars before Stephan called a break and we headed to camp for dinner. Harold packed our meals so we wouldn't be starving when we got home (also to keep the camp tidy, as we never cleaned the kitchen to his expectations). As evening drew near, I took out the new suits and presented them to Stephan (who disrobed on the spot). I followed suit, and soon the suits were tossed aside, and we frolicked like wood nymphs around the house. You could have heard a pin drop as we turned to find Bob standing in the archway. We grabbed for anything to cover our embarrassment as Bob stood still, taking in the scene. Soon, we were all laughing to mask the awkwardness of the situation. Bob finally said, "Hey, guys, it has come to my attention that someone has been nosing around the warehouse. How do you want to handle it?" I looked to Stephan for the answer, and he said, "First find out the intruder, then if he appears on the grounds, bring him to me unharmed so I can deal with him." "Good enough, boss," and with that, Bob left us.

Stephan made sure that we were alone and then dropped his shirt, ran to the pool, and jumped in. Not to be left behind, I followed and slipped into the water (I guess it was cooler than anticipated because we were out in seconds. I threw Stephan a towel and wrapped the other around me. We tore into the food and satiated our hunger (at least the nutritional hunger, the other hunger would have to wait). Still au naturel, we finished our meal, grabbed our suits, donned them quickly, and headed to the bedroom. Let the games begin.

We headed back home the next day and found Bob. "Well, fill us in, did he show up?" Bob said, "Yes and no, the person showed up again, but it's a she and she put up quite a fight, but I wrangled her and got her here, she's with Dahlia and Harold in the kitchen. Word to the wise, she's a wildcat." Oh great, another project. We entered the kitchen expecting the worst and found it calm and peaceful. Dahlia came over and said,

"These are the folks I was telling you about. Stephan, may I introduce you to Elizabeth? This is Stephan and his husband Carl. Now I know you have a lot to talk about, so we will leave you all to it." We got refreshments and headed to the den, but detoured to the atrium instead. I was about to mention it to Stephan, but thought better of it. He always knew best. Stephan started the conversation by asking Elizabeth about herself. She stated that she was a descendant of the Massimo family (that would be Aurelius Jr. and Olympia's line circa 1757). She had come seeking answers in Baltimore, as she had heard stories of long-lived relatives and wondered if by chance they were true or not. She followed the breadcrumbs to the warehouse and was about to gain entrance, but Bob had stopped her. I was about to re-direct her when Stephan said, "Well, you've come to the right place. Tell me, how far back can you trace your ancestry?" Elizabeth thought for a moment and continued, "I know that the Massimos weren't the original family name, but that name came from my however many great grandfathers back. But that's as far as I could find." Stephan asked why she wanted the information, and she replied, "Because I'm 64 and was born in 1999. Do I look that old? I then went through the family history and heard about the long-lived ancestors. Stephan motioned to Elizabeth and me to follow him into the den, and I knew that this was gonna blow her mind.

After we got settled, Stephan went to the mantle, leaned an arm on it, and started, "Elizabeth, what would you say if I told you that I was your many times great-grandfather and I'm 551 years old. Would that freak you out? How about my husband Carl, who is 96 as of this year?" Elizabeth sucked down the rest of her drink and asked for another. I poured us all another round of Bourbon and got ready for her reaction. Elizabeth stood, approached Stephan, hugged him tight, and sighed, "I knew it, I knew I was on the right path. Mom and Dad told me to let it go, but I knew in my heart there was more to it." We settled in for the duration as Stephan showed his granddaughter many of the journals and keepsakes of the past millennium. She was over the moon as she heard some of the stories that Stephan retold. Then we went through the house, pointing out the paintings and their stories. She got to see the ivory mannequin that Stephan had gotten some 400 years ago. We went into the dining room, where Elizabeth found Bob, and when he saw that Stephan was okay with her, he quietly left out the side door to the kitchen. Elizabeth asked about the warehouse, and Stephan said that he would take her on a private tour. I figured that meant I was to stay behind, but Stephan quickly corrected his statement to include me.

We put Elizabeth up in the guest room for the night. Stephan asked where she was staying, and she said the Comfort Inn. Stephan got the information and sent Aaron to collect her things and settle up with the hotel. When Elizabeth was taken upstairs for the night, I went to Stephan to ask how he really felt about her. He said, "This is more than I had hoped for, now I have three more like me. I wonder if she's straight or gay. Time will tell." The next morning, we found Elizabeth in the kitchen with Dahlia, Harold, and Bob. It seems that the tussle between Bob and Elizabeth created some sexual tension, and they were trying to take it to the next level. "Well, that answers one question," I said to Stephan. He nudged me and laughed. "Maybe another generation on the way soon."

We ate breakfast: scrambled eggs, breakfast sausages, toast, and orange juice. Elizabeth and Bob went on a formal tour of the grounds as Stephan and I discussed how to go forward with this new relative. Stephan contacted his genealogist to make the family tree to ensure that Elizabeth was really related. Bob would not be much of a help as he was smitten with her. Stephan decided to wait on the tour of the warehouse until he was sure about her. We did, however, afford her all the civil amenities of a guest in our house. Stephan went in search of the pair to inform Elizabeth that some business had come up and that the warehouse would have to wait. She seemed disappointed but accepted Stephan's ruse (did she have a choice?). I decided to engage her in a different way, by plying her with alcohol with lunch to loosen her up. Maybe she would let something slip during her inebriation to paint a more accurate picture of her intentions.

Elizabeth, having the opportunity to indulge, took my bait and soon wound up sloppy drunk. The conversation turned to her past, and I found that she was susceptible, like Anthony, to addiction, though her drug of choice was alcohol. We kept talking, or rather she kept talking, and I listened. She had heard stories of a possible family connection and figured that if they had any truth, then it served to reason that they must have accumulated vast wealth. She was down on her luck and was looking for some financial assistance (the aha moment I had waited to hear). I let her go to sleep off the effects of her liquid lunch and went in search of Stephan. It seemed that he came looking for me also, so we adjourned to the den to compare notes. It turned out that she was indeed a relative, and I explained about my conversation with her. "That answers a lot of questions about Elizabeth. Poor child needs an intervention. Hopefully, she accepts some help. Only then will she reap any rewards from me."

So far, Stephan had helped Anthony, then Dahlia, and now we turned our attention to help Elizabeth. We took Bob into our confidence and asked for his assistance in 'cleaning up' his special friend. He agreed as he didn't want to date a project; he wanted a partner. We waited until dinner and had Bob join us under the guise of escorting his date. We started the conversation calmly by serving only non alcoholic beverages.

She asked about something stronger, and we stated that we had noticed her affinity for drinking. She got defensive and almost left the table until Bob intervened. "Hey Liz, wait, they are only trying to help you. Please take a moment and listen to what they have to say." She took her seat, and we explained that she wasn't the only one who had needed our help. We brought up Anthony, but decided to let Dahlia come forward only if she wanted to. "If you intend to live a long and prosperous life, you need to get to it soon before it's too late. Remember, longevity is not forever if you don't protect and nourish it. Other relatives have died 'young' because they took chances with their health." This unsettled Elizabeth to the extent that she sat deflated in the chair. "What do I need to do?" is all she said. We told her that we would take care of all the arrangements for the rehab and then welcome her back after her completion of the program. Dahlia told us she would help Elizabeth pack, and we knew what was up. She was going to come clean and show Elizabeth a path to a better life. When we said our so-longs, she hugged us both, and Bob drove her to the facility.

Stephan was left feeling both happy for her and sad to have to watch her leave. "I've been in this place before when I had to leave behind my loved ones for my safety. The problem comes when you learn that they die before you reconnect." I didn't have that type of event in my life, having always been there when needed. Then I remembered that I wasn't in Rome when Lucius Sr. died after he lost his wife. Maybe I could empathize. We entered the den and just enjoyed a fire quietly, alone with our thoughts.

The primary report from the rehab stated that Elizabeth should go through a 30-day detox, then another 3 months of therapy. We showed Bob the report and told him that we'd keep him in the loop as we heard back from rehab. Bob thanked us again and, as usual, slipped out the door. Dahlia let it slip that she imparted a little wisdom as she talked to Elizabeth, and we nodded, knowing that all along. Stephan got started on an inheritance for Elizabeth. We rented a house nearby, furnished it, and called Eddie for the interior decoration (should have called Eddie first, as he basically donated everything we bought and redid the entire interior). Note to self, never start a project without first consulting the decorator.

We found ourselves in 2064 now, and I certainly started feeling old as I neared the hundred-year mark. We prepared for the return of Elizabeth. The reports were glowing, and the counselors commented that she ended up being a model to the others, so much so that she was offered a peer counseling position. I could only wonder what made the switch flip for her. No matter, as long as it happened for her. Bob went to retrieve her, and we put up the decorations at her new home. It was not supposed to be anything fancy, but as everyone already knew (and so did my bank account), Eddie made it exquisite. It rivaled his estate in England. Oh well, she should like it. Note to self, buy the home before making the alterations (as it costs Stephan 3 times the original cost now). Bob and Elizabeth showed up, the confetti flew, and the party started. Elizabeth looked healthier than when she first came to us, and Bob was ecstatic about that. Bob walked her around the house, asked if she liked it, and she nodded her assent. We let Bob tell her it was hers by handing her the deed. After the party, Elizabeth told us that she had accepted the job offer and that Bob would be moving in with her.

Elizabeth asked for a small favor until her funds started, a loan to get her by until payday. Stephan took her to the bank and showed her the account he had set up for her. He introduced the bank manager to her, and the CSR took her into a room to go over the details of the account. Elizabeth paled a bit when the CSR told her the beginning balance was

$1,000,000. She peered out the glass wall and looked back at the CSR. She got up, shaking slightly, and came out to see Stephan smiling at her. She didn't exactly know how to take it and simply hugged him. Then she hugged me also, to my amazement. What a way to start a new life. Her steadfastness in believing got her to this place, and now she could fully appreciate it (welcome to my world, girl). We left the house and headed home. I didn't want to imagine those two alone after so much time apart.

Two days later, Bob inquired about getting staff for their abode, and I deferred to Dahlia to handle it, knowing two things – she had the inside track on hiring and that we wouldn't be paying for it. Then Stephan showed up and asked if we could visit Elizabeth. That meant he would be taking her shopping for clothes and a new car befitting her new status (and that we'd be paying for this). So went the rest of the day and up to and including dinner. Eddie joined us and ended the meal with an invitation to the estate in England (now that she was related to him also). He told her of the manse that Stephan originally purchased around 1650 – ish. He also mentioned how he restored the manse. Anthony (the actual relative) got an honorable mention later.

I sequestered Stephan away from everything so as to have some quiet time. I needed the downtime. It seems that sometimes you just need to decompress. We let the rest of the year pass as peacefully as we could, only writing as a pastime and letting the world turn without us. We spent the summer at the camp, only allowing intrusions for the summer get-together. Fall came, and so did my birthday, October tenth (meaning 97 years old). Stephan realized that I was not happy about the number, and he said, "Most people don't have that gift of long life" (that changed my perspective sharply). Bring on the party. Stephan made it an intimate affair for just the two of us. When I saw the birthday cake in our bedroom, I knew tomorrow would be a messy morning (note – wear washable clothing tonight).

Morning came, and I just showered with clothes on, making a mess everywhere. Stephan came into the bathroom, more disheveled than I, and I could only laugh as he got in the shower with me. It took half an hour to clean up (and I pity the staff cleaning up our mess). We went to breakfast, having left a note with apologies and a couple of hundred-dollar bills as a thank you. Dahlia looked at us as we smirked at each other off and on. She shook her head and said, "Do you think I didn't hear you guys last night? That's why I had Alfred stay in the kitchen. I didn't want to have to get him groomed today." More laughter, and that made Dahlia smile as she waved us off. The weekend came around, and Elizabeth came to call. She talked about her new job, her time with Bob, and a host of other things. We had her stay for lunch, and she asked Harold for a simple "bologna and cheese sandwich'. I almost spat my soda in Stephan's face as she said that. Thankfully, it detoured through my nose first and dribbled down my cheek. Stephan told her that we usually don't keep it on hand, but Harold came up with some (to Stephan's grimace). I chanted, "Finally, a girl with my taste!" as I received an elbow to the ribs. "Don't encourage her, or that's all I'll have in this house." Okay, I went too far and knew it was time to make up with hubby. He tried to stay upset, but I did my best puppy dog eyes, and that got to him. "Butt hole, come here so I can make up." I sidled up to Stephan, and he tickled me intensely until I begged for forgiveness. "That's what you get", then he kissed me and sent me to my writing with a solid smack on the butt. Tonight was going to be long and exhausting.

Dahlia came to me asking for a little assistance with the transcribing, and Elizabeth overheard. "I can help out Carl, I took typing and secretary skills classes in school. Graduated top of my class. I can take dictation, I know shorthand, and can type 60 words a minute." I looked at Dahlia, and she at me, and we decided okay. "But what about your day job?" she simply said, "If you can match my salary, I'll give my notice and work here. Everyone who's here says they would need a bomb to go off before they'd think of leaving you two. Must be good, heck, even Dahlia is the third-generation lifer. I've never seen a happier crew; it's as if they're family and not staff. "Okay, Dahlia can interview you, and if you pass muster, she can put a package together with benefits and salary." Dahlia looked at Elizabeth and whispered in her ear, "I told you he'd roll over. Screw the 2-week notice, start tomorrow."

Elizabeth went to find Bob and give him the good news. Dahlia told me that she had it all set before asking me and just needed my consent to proceed. "That's why you're in control of the house." I gave her a peck on the cheek and sauntered out of the kitchen toward the den. My laptop got a workout for over three hours, as I recounted some of the events of the past few months. Stephan entered, heard the clacking of the keyboard, and slipped back out after pouring two bourbons, leaving one for me within reach but away from the computer. Elizabeth came back the next day, a little late, as she had to inform the facility that she needed to care for a family member long term (which was a stretch but accurate, seeing as she would be tending to me). "They even gave me a severance package to boot." Stephan's luck ran down through the generations like no other family. Note to self – never leave this family, EVER!

We were prepping for Christmas when Bob came to us and said that a bad part of Elizabeth's past was trying to re-enter her life, and wanted to know if Stephan would mind if he took care of it. "As long as we don't need to order more barrels marked, 'for New Jersey'." He laughed and said he'd pop for the barrel if need be. We shrugged and told him to just be careful. He left quickly with a smile on his face (shades of Eric, more deja vu). We waited to hear if the news had any stories about missing people, but saw articles about hit squads being seen around town. I started to get concerned and voiced it to Stephan. He reassured me and asked to have Bob see him. They went to the drawing room and talked softly. Bob took off, and Stephan said it was all right and that Bob had it all in hand. I feel that Stephan was pulling some strings and was strategizing with Bob. I had to ask, "What was that all about? Is Elizabeth in danger, are we?" Stephan sat me down and said, "If you want to know, I'll tell you, but know it's complicated and could get sticky if not played right."

My spidey senses were off the chart, and I started shaking (as per usual). "Okay, tell me. I want to know as I'm part of this family." Stephan took me to the den, closed the door, and locked it. Now I was shaking like I had parkinsons and poured two Bourbons for us. Stephan took a strong draw on his and started. "I'm only telling you because you asked. I need to preface this with a tale from the war between Russia and the Vatican. Yes, I was only the interpreter, but I was on the front lines and had to deal with generals, fighters, and spies. I had to know who to trust and who to keep secrets from. I was actually a double spy for Tsar Mikhail and had his implicit trust. This is what it's like now. I wanted to keep you out of this, but here we are. I owe you the truth and know that I can trust you with my life. The people we're dealing with are really evil, and they think Elizabeth knows too much, as she dated some consigliere of a crime boss. Now they want to tie up loose ends, and that includes Elizabeth. Bob needs help this time as it's just too large for one guy. I authorized a mercenary squad to assist him with protecting her and us. They will be blending in with the staff, so if you see new people, don't worry, they're on our side. Do you want to know more?"

I shook my head no and went in for a comforting hug. Stephan gave me a quick one and then unlocked the door and left.

This was going to get ugly, I just knew it. For the first time, I felt real fear, and I couldn't shake it. I wasn't feeling good and went in search of comfort. Alfred came to the rescue and cuddled me until we fell asleep in each other's arms. Sleep was fitful at best, and I think I dreamed different scenarios of how I was going to die. Worse yet, some included Stephan. How would I ever go on if he died? I tried to disregard those thoughts, but they kept coming. Poor Alfred had to get off the couch as I was twisting like a pretzel (to sleep, perchance to dream). I was ready for dreamless nights ahead.

Stephan was right about 'new staff'. I started staying away from windows, hated going out in my own garden, and actually refused to leave the property just in case. He was being aloof, and I started feeling disenfranchised. I couldn't write, couldn't sleep, and had hardly any appetite. When Stephan noticed my clothes hanging off me, he became concerned and returned his attention to me. He tried to assuage my fears and comfort me but until whatever this was ended, I'd be nervous. "That's it, I'm making my move. I can't stand seeing you like this. It ends tonight." Stephan called for Bob and the 'new staff'. They went into the den, closed the door and got to work. Two hours later, they came out and headed into the city. Bob took the lead, Stephan was on intelligence and the 'staff' were armed to the teeth. My nightmares were coming true (all because I couldn't handle the wait).

I watched the news for any notices. Around 10:30 pm, breaking news came on, and they started with the headline – "Many people injured, a shootout with mafia members, and people dead and dying in the street." I strained my eyes looking for anyone I recognized. My heart stopped when the phone rang. It was Bob saying that the people after Elizabeth had been eliminated, but that Stephan had been wounded and was on his way to the hospital. I got the information, dressed in seconds, and was out the door, tears in my eyes, and tried to drive as quickly as possible without speeding. I arrived at the hospital at the same time as the ambulance. They had Stephan under a blanket that was soaked with his blood. I ran over but was stopped feet away from Stephan. They rushed him into the ER and straight to the operating room. I felt faint and proceeded to fall to the floor before I could tell them that I was his husband. Awakening to smelling salts, I showed them my ID, and they ushered me into a private room. The Internist came over and told me the ambulance guys had called ahead, and the operating room was all set upon arrival. It was going to be tough going for the night, and I should go home. Bob got to me right after and said he'd tend to me so they would let me stay at the hospital. He tried to calm me down, but I was inconsolable. "How could you have let this happen, Bob? You know how much I love that man, and now he may not make it." Bob spoke softly, "Carl, I got flanked and one of 'our guys' got a shot off in Stephan's direction. I didn't realize he was a double agent until the shot got off. Don't worry, he got his. We need to concentrate on Stephan now." I knew what I had to do, so I got on the phone to Italy and England, and Bob got the bus ready for two quick stops and a return to base. I got in touch with Chuck, and he said he was on his way. I called Dahlia and told her to set up the atrium as a hospital setting. I told her that Stephan had been shot and was being operated on at the moment. The surgeon came in after 4 hours and said, "There was a lot of blood, but the shooter missed all the vital organs. He should pull through." I told him to get him past the intensive care needs and that we had a private physician and a hospital set up in our house. He looked shocked at that assertion, but nodded okay. I asked if Stephan needed a transfusion, and I believed that I could donate. He thanked me but said that it was all handled. I prayed like an Atheist in the foxholes. "Please spare Stephan, and you can have my final years. That's the dearest thing I have, and I offer it to you." Bob heard that and sat beside me, hugging me to comfort me, but all it did was start my tears falling in rivulets.

Bob got coffee through the night, and we waited for any change. They let me see him at 8 am. I entered the ICU and saw him, unlike any other time in my life. He was fragile and pale. The paleness of his skin, the lackluster eyes, and the blank expression on his face. Hooked to several bags and electronics, breathing with assistance. This was not my husband; my guy was always the strong one, my hero. Now I had to be Batman, and it scared me. What if that was going to be the way forward? Stephan motioned for me, and I placed my ear to his lips. "Carl, don't worry, I'd take a bullet for you." He tried to laugh, but it hurt, and he smiled. My husband was in there, and all would be well. Now I knew it. "Rest, babe, I've got you covered, and we'll have you home before you know it."

It took three days and a note from Chuck, but they allowed him to come home. He arrived by ambulance, and when they pulled him from the back, he was greeted by the entire family, Anthony, Eddie, Junior, Hunter, Dahlia, Aaron, Elizabeth, Bob, Nathan, and family, Harold and family, Senator Jeffrey and family, and the rest, too many to mention. Jeff took me aside and said he'd make sure we'd be fine, and that he would use all his clout to make it go away. Stephan was taken to the atrium and settled in as Alfred jumped on the bed to greet him. I tried to shoo him off, but Stephan let him stay, so I backed off. Dahlia had set up the visiting schedule after consulting with Chuck. She stated, "This is to be adhered to, and anyone disregarding it will be shown the door."

The house was abuzz with activity for the next few weeks as Stephan recuperated. Visitors (including me) were given specific times, and if you missed your time, you lost out.

The day I came for my time slot and saw him sitting, I went to him and knelt down, caressing his cheeks and with glassy eyes said, "I love you so much, and if you ever do something that foolish again, I'll shoot you myself." He reached out, grabbed me, and we kissed. "You just wait, Robin, you'd better get your sleep now. That signal will be lit all night." Finally, I got my husband back. I could wait for the whole story. I spent the next few days writing in my journal, in between the tears and screams of frustration, powerless to change the circumstances or the outcome. I had become a watcher and witness to history. Now it was memorialized in words for posterity. Elizabeth was going to feel odd transcribing these notes.

I'd like to say that the years 2065 and 2066 were calm, but that would be wrong. We ended by having a recession, a stock market drop, and a supply chain kerfuffle. Thank goodness we had a slush fund that got us through this period without a problem. Anthony needed a loan to cover the shorts in the stock market, but he came through it without a drink. Elizabeth was now talking about marriage, and Bob was happy with it. Jeffrey had made it to the US Senate, and as good as his word, our 'problem' had disappeared. Stephan and I had weathered the storm in pretty good shape, and the family was still together. Stephan kept a log of the loans in his ledger, and Dahlia kept track of the payments back. We ended 2066 with a great Christmas. Stephan gifted the balances of the loans back to our family so they could return to their lives (seeing as how we had more than enough financially). Bring on 2067. Stephan and I had our traditional New Year's Eve party in our room, and this one was special. Batman rose to the challenge, and Robin, the ever faithful sidekick, was there to 'support' him.

January 2067, and in ten months, I'd turn 100 years old. I wonder what Stephan had in mind, and if I wanted to know. After all, he was 555 years old himself, and we had been married since 12/25/2019, or 48 years. Stephan's hair had aged from the 'incident'. He was now sporting a couple of silver streaks in between the beautiful blonde hairs. At this rate, he could be a white-haired old man by the time he was 600. I was not far behind, so I surprised him by coloring my hair back to its original color. Stephan noticed right away, and let's just say it 'moved' him.

February saw me with a sadness I thought I wouldn't feel. Our beloved Alfred went to sleep for the last time, cradled in my arms as the rest of his family members looked on. As he fell asleep and the once strong heart stopped, I covered him over, and Bob took the body to the waiting grave in the garden. We had a portrait done, and it was placed over the mantel in the den. Faithful to the end, forever free in eternity. It took a while to get over that, and my writing reflected it. It became maudlin and dark. Stephan talked to me about it, but I couldn't move on. He had entered our lives as a joke and left a gaping hole where his love was missing in the end. Stephan, always the strong one, took matters into his hands and said for me to get in the car. He was taking me for a ride. He asked Elizabeth to join us, and we drove into the country. He pulled into a farm, and Elizabeth looked at me while I shrugged my shoulders. I guess it was a wait-and-see time. Stephan pulled up to the house, shut off the motor, and got out. "Come on, we've got things to do." I followed him up the steps to the door, and he rang the doorbell. A pleasant woman answered the door, asked us in, and then I found out why we were here. Barking, nothing but barking going on in the next room. She opened the door, and five fluff balls bounded out and into the room. It seems that Stephan had gotten hold of the breeder where Alfred came from and had reserved one for me. "I couldn't stand seeing you miserable, so I picked out Alfred's sibling. Yes, they are all younger siblings to Alfred." I sat on the floor and let them attack me. Three of them turned away after a sniff, but one curled into my lap. When I reached down to pet her, she licked my face, and I knew who was coming with us. "I'm going to call her Winnie." Number five was in Elizabeth's lap, and she said," Well, I guess Sarah's coming with me." Stephan went to settle up with the breeder, but he had a shadow. He turned to see big brown puppy eyes asking for a pet and reached down. "I guess Mary's coming also. So now we have the complete set of the three Sanderson sisters." We loaded them in the car and headed home. I called ahead and had Aaron go to the pet store and buy provisions for three dogs. They were to grow to the same size as Alfred, so manageable.

By the time we got home, the dogs had settled down and fallen asleep. We carried the pups in and were a sensation when the staff saw them. "They're gonna be so spoiled. I just know it." They went outside, pottied, and were brought back inside. Elizabeth took her leave, and the other pups barked as if to say goodbye to Sarah. Little did they know that they were going to grow up together. Winnie never left my side as we navigated through the house. Mary was more adventurous but stayed somewhat close to Stephan. Bedtime got crazy as the pups wanted to snuggle with us. They finally found a place at the bottom of the bed and settled in. I guess people with kids feel the same way.

Morning was complete chaos as the pups pottied in the bedroom before we could get them downstairs. Note to self – get puppy pads today. After the clean-up and our showers, the pups ran ahead of us, Mary in the lead, down the stairs and into the kitchen. Their breakfast was waiting for them, but Dahlia sent them outside to potty. Since they had already done their business upstairs, they just ran around sniffing everywhere. Dahlia called them back, waited until they figured out what this lady wanted, and then she showed them their food bowls. More chaos as they destroyed their breakfast, launching it across the kitchen. Stephan laughed, but was alone at this moment. Then he stepped into the water on the floor in his stocking feet. Now we all laughed, except Stephan (oh, sweet instant karma).

Stephan left (with Mary in tow) and headed back upstairs to change socks. Winnie came to me after vacuuming up her food (score one for team Winnie). Dahlia casually informed me that there was a dog training class nearby and starting soon (she read my mind). I said, "Well, get on the phone. Tell them they will have three new candidates." Dahlia laughed as she dialed. All I heard was, "Incoming," as Sarah crashed the party. More chaos as the pups regroup in play in the kitchen. Elizabeth came around the corner with a "I'm sorry," and the look on her face said it all. "How was your first night with Sarah?" She stared at me as though I already knew (and I did). "Do you really want to know? Okay, well, first she barked until I took her out of the crate and let her sleep with me. Then I woke up and put my feet into my poop-filled slippers. I took them off only to step in her pee. It went downhill from there. Happy." I feigned sympathy as she went to freshen up. Sarah settled down when we let the pups back out to play in the yard. I snuck a peek into the garden and saw Aaron playing with the pups, really getting their energy out. Hopefully, they would come back in and sleep. Dahlia returned, saying that the pups were registered and that they would start Monday of the following week. Elizabeth asked if Sarah could enroll, and Dahlia said, "I should have asked you first, but I also enrolled Sarah."

Elizabeth mouthed a thank you to Dahlia and turned to her business (typing my sordid ramblings).

So life was a happy chaos until the pups graduated from obedience class (Winnie got the highest honors, go team Winnie). Poor Sarah came in the bottom ten percent, having a mind of her own (I think she thinks she's a cat). The house settled again as it was time for a trip (to anywhere at this point). We decided that since we had the dogs, camp was our best option if we wanted them with us, so off to the beach we went (with the troops in tow). I have to say, the kids were great with the dogs, and the 'sisters' had a wonderful time running on the beach. We took long walks along the beach, Winnie at my side and Mary walking behind Stephan (those classes really worked). Back at the camp, the dogs ate and slept most of the time. Even the kids got worn out. Two weeks later, we packed up and went home. Winnie and Mary rode in the car well, but Elizabeth told us that Sarah almost jumped out of the car on the drive (thank God that we didn't pick her). We wanted to go to Italy, England, and maybe even Greece, but the thought of leaving the girls put us in a tough spot. We decided to limit ourselves to Italy and only stay a week. We called Tony, who said, "Please, by all means, come and stay at the vineyard."

At that, we kissed the dogs, said our goodbyes, and left for the airport. At first, I couldn't see the 'bus,' but Stephan said it had been in the hangar for repairs and inspection. They brought it out, but it looked very different. "Surprise, Carl, I upgraded the old girl. Do you like?" I looked at her with a sense of awe but also a small bit of sadness as our 'old faithful' had been replaced (how much history did I have with that 'old girl'). I took steps toward the new girl, and the stairs beckoned me to my next adventure. Stephan walked up behind me as I entered the cabin. "Sit anywhere, I'll call for the steward and get us cocktails." Wheels up, fifteen minutes later, we headed to the vineyard. Italy came into view through the clouds, and we set down at a local airport (customs was much faster here, so Stephan decided to use this one going forward). A limousine was waiting for us, and we traveled to the estate. The Tonys were there to greet us, and we went to the tasting room as the staff took care of the luggage.

Tony Jr. had come a long way from the wild child that we first came to know. "Tony, you've done a good job raising Jr. He seems a natural in the vineyard, and his new wines are delectable." Sr. blushed slightly and nodded, saying, "The honors go to his mother; she was always there to keep him on the straight and narrow." Now it was Mrs.'s turn to blush. She gave Sr. a peck on the cheek and left us to the matters of the day. We talked business until it was time for dinner. Tony told us that we had to stay as the Mrs. had been cooking for 2 days before our arrival. We dined on the finest antipasto, including prosciutto, salami, Calamata olives, 4 different cheeses, toast points, olive oil, and balsamic vinegar for dipping. Then came the gnocchi with vodka sauce, meatballs, and the pasta with oil, bread crumbs, and Parmesan Reggiano sauce. Then came the ripe figs and Muscat wine. She brought out the cannoli, but we were stuffed. We begged her to allow us to box them up and eat them later, and she gave in (but had a pouty look on her face as though we might discard them – I would never pass up dessert).

We took the dessert to our little bungalow. Stephan crashed until I joined (having finished off my cannolies). He rallied, and we christened our Italian bed. Sleep was full and lengthy. Jr. came to wake us as the clock said nearly noon. We got up, made a call to Rome, and invited the boys to join us at the vineyard. Jr. became excited as he hadn't had their visit this year. Soon we were all together sampling more wine. Jr. asked if we were interested in acquiring a new vineyard (it seems the neighboring property was up for sale and was adjacent to his father's. I just asked how much and knew that the check would be forthcoming. To my surprise, Junior spoke up and offered the funds (to my great relief). Stephan assured that he would toss in what Junior couldn't cover, not knowing that Anthony had given Junior some inside tips on stocks, and now Junior had his own wealth. I almost forgot that.

Hunter was also flush with cash after selling his boutiques in the States (it seems that the Orions and Borgias were lucky in more ways than one).

But as we spent the week, I started missing the sisters back home (who knew having dogs would affect me this much). We said our goodbyes, got to the airport, and took the new 'bus' home. Flying home seemed to ease my mind, and I fell asleep until Stephan said we were about to land. I looked out the window as the wheels appeared below us. Customs done and headed to the house, I started getting anxious (as I always do). Things were fine, and Winnie and Mary came to us tails wagging and happy to see us. Treats were being handed out as the infamous Sarah came around the corner. Barks and jumping (the wild child to the end). When the sisters calmed down, we sent them out to the garden to expend the remaining energy. Then we turned to the matters at hand and got the details from Dahlia on how the house had managed in our absence. The accounts and bills were fine, but she said that Bob wanted to see us (and as usual, my senses went on high alert). We found Elizabeth, and she said Bob was at the warehouse but would be home soon (can you say acid reflux and heartburn). Now I was getting worried as no one would tell us anything about what we were facing. Stephan said it was probably nothing and not to worry. Bob finally got home and asked us to go to the den. "Bosses, I don't know how it happened, but I need your help. It seems that Elizabeth and I are expecting a baby later this year." You could have blown me over with a feather. I was stunned, Stephan was amused, and Bob looked terrified. "She told me she was past baby-rearing years, so we didn't use protection. She thinks it's fine, but what am I supposed to do now?" Stephan sat him down, and I gave him a stiff Bourbon (which he downed in a single swig). "First, we get her a good pediatrician, then set up a nursery in your house. Then we watch him/her grow up with the finest teachers and send him/her to college." It only calmed Bob a little, but he was 65 now, and I could see the fear in his eyes. "That means I'll be 87 by that time." We laughed, he shook his head, and we told him it would be alright.

"Go get Elizabeth, and we'll go over the strategy." With that, we pushed Bob out the door and toward the atrium. I poured two more Bourbons, handed one to Stephan, and said, "She'll be 65, and he'll be 66. We both know she'll be around, but I do pity Bob. Can you imagine bouncing a baby on his knee?" Stephan actually chortled at that. Elizabeth appeared with Bob in tow. "First of all, you kids need to be more careful in the future. However, since this is your first time, we'll help. Elizabeth, have Dahlia assist with the doctor. You, Bob, need to get a good-paying job. Carl might be able to help in that area" (we really tried to keep a straight face while saying this, but it ended up in a laugh fest). Bob was the least enthusiastic but came around as we called him bad grandpa.

We let them go, and then I looked at Stephan. He was bemused, and I was finally relieved (having thought the worst). We'd better get Bob a protege, seeing as how he won't want to get into a situation with a wife and kid. Stephan agreed, and I went in search of Bob to ask for recommendations. Winnie followed me out of the den as Mary curled up next to the hearth. I found Bob and explained what Stephan and I had discussed. He said he had the perfect candidate and said he would contact him immediately. He then turned and said, "And what was that smart ass remark about me getting a real job?" I doubled over laughing until he punched my shoulder. "If that bruises you, you'll be in big trouble, young man." Even he had to laugh at that. "I'm outta here. I'll make the call now." I went to the kitchen (with my shadow Winnie) as she knew she was about to get another treat.

Miss Sarah must have heard the bag open as she came bouncing in looking hungry. Winnie sat politely, and Sarah nearly stole it away from her. She ripped the bag, and treats went flying around the kitchen. Harold came in and nearly fell to the floor after crushing a biscuit. More chaos before Elizabeth got control of her and put her outside. "How far along are you?" Elizabeth said 4 months, and then I said, "That doesn't give us long to get the nursery done. Should I get Eddie, or did you want to tackle it yourself?" Elizabeth said, "Well, if you're paying, I'd love to have Eddie. If not, then I'll manage." I went to make the call to see if Eddie was available. Eddie asked what the budget was, and I told him, "The budget is whatever it takes to get it done, and I EXPECT a family discount." Eddie said, "Send the 'bus' in a week, and I'll be ready" (of course, he wanted a private jet). I went in search of Dahlia to re-write the budget in anticipation of the deficit to come.

We sent Aaron to collect the decorator at the hangar. It took more than an hour, and he asked to have a rental truck for the 'items he bought' (Dahlia, double that deficit and add a few hundred thousand more for incidentals). Eddie showed, but more importantly, Anthony came with him. I was shocked and impressed. We set them up in the guest wing of the house. I sent Anthony to the den to see his grandfather while I got the receipts from Eddie to refund. My fears were calmed somewhat when I added up the bills. It seemed that Eddie was going easy on me (he had only spent $53,852.39). I shipped the 'items' to Elizabeth's house (the one Eddie designed) for installation. I joined Stephan and Anthony in the den. Upon entering, it looked like a gentleman's club. The guys were standing, both drinking (Anthony was having sparkling water and Stephan Bourbon). I decided on wine (Jr.'s blend). I heard them talking about stocks and decided to listen, as I knew nearly nothing about the stock market.

They were talking about a new start-up company investing in a new technology. It was a fourth-generation AI. It could not only think but also had analytical powers that were much better than the previous iterations. The technology would be able to be used in robotics. This could correct any mistakes in its own programming. I was confounded, but Anthony was ecstatic about it. Stephan was intrigued. I kissed Stephan, hugged Anthony, and walked back out. I'll leave it to them. I overheard Stephan say to count us in as I left. I just hoped that it would be as good as they said. By now, Eddie was coming back from Elizabeth's house and found me in the atrium. The news took my breath away, "I believe I can keep it under one million for the renovations and decorating." I thought better than to say anything, but then blurted out, "It's a nursery, not a castle. And what about the family discount?" Eddie said, "That is with the family discount. You liked the other decorating I did, didn't you? After all, you asked for me again." Resigned to my fate, I nodded and went for another glass of wine.

Bob showed up right as I was pouring the wine. "How bad is it? I could hear you two down the hall." When I informed him that the nursery was going to be more expensive than the rest of the house, he paled and looked concerned. "Do you think Stephan will even help pay for it?" I looked straight into his eyes and said, "You'd better hope that he does well in the market. It's going to cost about $1,000,000." Bob left me to find Stephan (probably hoping to brown-nose a lot more). I went to play with Winnie. I couldn't think anymore today. Dinner was in the formal dining room, and the subject of the stocks came up. Stephan said, "I want to invest $10,000,000 in the new company. I think I can get Anthony to pay about $10.00 per share. If it does well in the IPO, we'll be wealthy." I didn't understand the last statement. We were worth about 1.5 trillion in US dollars. Stephan clinked glasses with the boys as I looked on in confusion. "Stephan, can I see you for a moment in the pantry?" We entered the pantry, then I turned to Stephan and decried, "What's going on? I thought we were all set. Do I need to do something with the budget? Just tell me the truth so I can prepare. I don't care if we need to economize; I've lived like that before. But please be honest with me." He took my hands in his, looked at me with those perfect eyes, and said, "We're beyond wealthy. What I meant back there was that our play money would be almost limitless. How would you like to buy an island in the Pacific?" I fell forward into my guy's arms and nearly fainted. "You're playing with my emotions again. You know how sensitive I am about you and your assets." Stephan kissed me and smiled those pearly whites. "That's why I fell for you. You never cared about my wealth to sustain you, only me."

We went back to the dining room as the plates were being collected. Hand in hand and smiles all around. The mood of the room changed to frivolity. Music was piped in, Anthony started dancing with Eddie, and Stephan grabbed my hand to try his hand at it. I looked like a novice as the other three danced around the room. Thankfully, I had Stephan to lead me, so I looked less foolish. The music stopped, and we all left for a drink in the den. Stephan lit a fire, and we relaxed with the warmth filling the room. The boys left us after an hour, and Stephan called me to the rug. We reclined and watched the glowing embers as the flames licked the logs. What a day, now for a quiet night and a better tomorrow.

Anthony found out that the IPO was scheduled for the next day and was able to get us in for a dollar a stock before the opening bell. That meant that we would have 10,000,000 shares. I waited with bated breath as the day went on. Both Anthony and Stephan went about their business as though we had nothing going on (I was crapping egg rolls). The closing bell rang, and then the guys came to find out how we fared. It seems that the company had a really good IPO, and it soared to $150.00 per share. I advised Stephan to sell, but I knew I should not have bet against the house, as by the end of the week, the stock had climbed to $542.00 per share. Anthony brokered the stock, and we added about $5,000,000,000 to our account (now about that island in the Pacific). Stephan asked if I wanted to take a short trip to our new vacation home before the baby came. I said yes, and we packed up and got in the 'bus'. We arrived in Fiji and chartered a boat to Wakaya Island. As we landed, Stephan handed me the keys and said, "This is our private island, Carl, as promised." I just looked, dumbfounded as usual. "Yep, this entire island is ours. I got it for a steal, only $1,500,000,000. It came with the house, dock, pool, and everything inside. If you want, I can hire Eddie to decorate." "Don't you dare call Eddie, he'll charge us the rest of the money you made. I think we can make do with a coat of paint." The house, the guest house, and the boat house were perfect as is. I guess you can get a lot for 1.5 billion dollars (move-in condition). We had staff showing up the next day, so we ate cold food (which was better as it was 90 degrees out during the day and we had fire pit fires for the evening). That was the night we pranced around the fire in our suits. Batman and

Robin were half-lit and really free to engage in cosplay (the only thing we left behind was the bat signal).

The morning started with a bowl of cereal and a trip to the dock to greet the new staff. All male staff departed the schooner, and I knew Dahlia had a part in this somehow. Stephan smiled and turned to me, "Do you approve? I had Dahlia work with the locals to make sure they were vetted and bonded. And maybe because they are all gay. I wanted you to have everything, eye candy and all. May I introduce the Gardner Tom, 25 y/o, he'll be responsible for planting anything you want to see (6'3" and solid muscle, I'm guessing around 220 lbs). Next is the cook, Dale, 22 y/o, fresh out of cooking school (a twink with a 26" waist, looking like dessert). We have to share the butler, Allen, 35 y/o (auburn hair and polite). Our handyman is Bruce, 40 y/o, and willing to build anything you need (except the hammock for the bedroom and looking like a brick outhouse). Finally, Jim, 30 y/o, will serve as our personal security (Bob approved and probably my favorite).

They stowed their clothes, personal effects, and gear before tending to their duties. Mostly, they toured the island to get their bearings and figure out what they were going to need to do their best job. They ended up having dinner with us and putting their requests in for improvements. We noted all their improvements, and Stephan explained that some would happen immediately, and some would be project work over the next few months. They asked if we were moving there, and we said no, just using it as a vacation destination. However, they would be full-time with time off for vacation and personal time. Allen called me aside and asked if he could bring his husband to the island. I said that as long as he could be vetted and bonded, then yes. If not, then Allen could turn down the position. He left to make a phone call and get the matter resolved to our mutual satisfaction. Dale, effervescent and cute as a button, asked what we would like for dinner. I gave him Harold's e-mail address and told him to get recipes from Harold. Dale was told to use his discretion for meals. Jim had a laundry list of things he needed to secure the island, and I told him to call Bob, and it would be sent over. Bruce was more aloof than the others, preferring to be alone most of the time. I sought him out to ask about a pergola for the fire pit area. "Sure thing, boss man. It'll take about a week to get the lumber and stuff. Then about 2 weeks after that." I tried to engage him further, but he turned to get to work. I accidentally called Tom Jim and received a small rebuke. "Sorry Tom, too many names to remember all at once. Could you and I talk about the gardens. I'll need your expertise on local flora so I don't look asinine." He looked at me and said, "Sure Stephan, what would you like to know?" (payback was a bitch, and now I knew he was too).

The following week was busy as the materials for the pergola, the flowers and plants, Allen's husband and the new security equipment all arrived at once. The guys got to work and the island turned into the paradise we wanted. Allen introduced us to his husband, Darren 33 y/o and very handsome (which made me wonder how they got together until I thought about Stephan and I). We stayed until we got a call from Baltimore. We said so long to the troops and took our leave. I have to say that I hated leaving just when it was getting done but duty called. The trip was a long flight and we got home around midnight. The dogs were about the only ones up when we arrived. Winnie wet the floor she was so excited and Mary went to Stephan hesitantly as though she had done something wrong. He coaxed her to him and then as if a light switch flipped, she was all over him. A young man turned on more lights and asked if he could help us. "My name is Albert, I'm the new security person (26,6'3" and everything and a bag of chips in a tight uniform, black curly hair, blue eyes, and a 30 inch waist going about 190 lbs if I were to guess). I was the first to speak (being polite of course), saying, "I'm Carl and this is my husband Stephan. As you can see, we own the house and by extension, your bosses." He excused himself and apologized for not knowing. "We've been through this many times, just relax and tell Bob we're home. He wanted to talk to us when we got here." "Sure thing boss man, again, sorry the inconvenience." As he left, I could only stay where I was and stare at that pant crease as it formed a perfect bubble butt.

Stephan just smirked and said, "I'd have thought you got enough of that on the island." I shrugged my shoulders and followed him upstairs, watching my guy knowing where I would be tonight.

The next day Bob appeared at the breakfast table as we ate our favorite breakfast, eggs Benedict on toast points. The girls were waiting patiently for their share and did not go away disappointed. Bob started by saying that he didn't have to send anyone to New Jersey. That made me feel better. He did say that there had been a break-in at the ware house though. I asked what they got and he said nothing. He was on premises when he heard the alarms. "They broke through back door and when the alarms sounded, they split. I assume from the footprints that it was at least three guys. Options guys?" I said, "If you can track them, find them. If not, then return and fortify the back door and put cameras there to ensure more security." I wondered who would try Stephan yet again. One week to the day, Bob and Albert arrived and produced three young 'hoodlums'. I felt sorry for the youngsters as they were shaking in their boots. "What have we here? Three would be thieves thinking I wouldn't mind if they raided my warehouse. What do you have to say for yourselves?" Two of them put their heads down and let the third guy speak, "We have seen the car collection when the doors were open and actually just wanted to see them up close. We didn't mean any harm mister." Stephan went over to them, walked around them and asked Bob and Albert what did they think we should do. Albert took the lead and asked the boys if they had jobs. In unison, they said no. "How old are you boys?" at first, the boys didn't speak, then they spoke up, "We're only 18 sir. This would ruin our future and like I said before, we're sorry for the incident." Stephan stepped forward again and said, "How would you like to work for me by protecting those cars. That would mean you would have a constant cash flow and my guys would have more hands to help keep them clean and polished. They could keep the place more protected as you fulfill other duties and you could fill in as needed for their vacations." The boys looked at each other as though they had hit the lottery (and in actuality, they had). "Here's $100 apiece. Get uniforms and clean up. You start Monday and will report to Albert." They left and got a ride home.

"I love what you just did Stephan. This just makes me love you more you old softy." Albert nicknamed the guys Huey, Dewey and Louie. I laughed until I cried and Stephan had name tags made to reflect their new monikers. I had to think they wouldn't even know what that meant. We welcomed the new year (2068) as well as baby Robert Stephan Randolf (Stephan's eight times great grandson). I couldn't wait until we could get back to the island. I was curious about the improvements. Before we left, I asked Albert about Huey, Dewey and Louie. "They're doing better than I could have hoped. I think they just needed a mentor to get straight, no pun intended Carl." I smiled and thanked him for his patience with them.

We loaded up, left the ground, and headed back to Fiji. We made it back to the island late and just took the luggage to our room and slept. Morning found me in the middle of a staffing dispute. I went to the kitchen of the main house to look for some coffee and found Jim excoriating Allen and Darren about not informing him about visitors to the island, even though we were the owners and their boss. Allen kept saying it was at our request, but Jim was having none of it. "I want to be informed of every person that comes to this island, period. How do you two expect me to keep the peace if you keep breaking the rules? Wait until I talk to the boss, you'll find yourselves on a boat back to Fiji." I let him get it out and then entered to show him I was there. "Morning, boss, sorry you had to hear that, but rules are rules. "Jim, I really appreciate that, but I expressly told him not to say anything as we were late incoming and didn't want to bother you all." Jim felt betrayed (I saw it in his eyes) but said nothing. He glared at the duo and left the kitchen. Dale came prancing in, saw me, and settled down. "Welcome back, Carl. Can I make you something for breakfast? Is Stephan joining you? How about some eggs Benedict? I know you two enjoy them." I told him that I'd love some coffee and that he could make the eggs as I knew hubby would be down directly.

Allen quietly thanked me for taking the blame, although we hadn't talked last night. He and Darren went to see about Stephan as I watched the coffee maker (Dale) making coffee. He over-accented every move as though dancing for my delight (little did he know that I had no sexual interest in him, and his efforts were for naught). Tom showed up when he smelled the coffee brewing. Seeing me, he greeted me and asked when I wanted to see his efforts and the results. I told him that afternoon, after I had acclimated myself to the time change. He nodded and left to tend to the garden. Bruce was the next to appear and simply said, "S'up?" I shrugged and filled his cup, and he left without another word. Stephan, yawning and stretching, entered as the coffee finished. Dale poured the coffee and returned to the stove as though he was the dutiful wife (good luck with that, young-in'. He's spoken for). I talked to

Stephan about Jim, and he told me he'd handle it (my man, making my life easy).

Dale finished the plating, served the breakfast, and went to start the menu for dinner. Jim appeared as we were finishing and asked to speak to Stephan (unaware that I had prepared him). Stephan said, "Whatever you need to say, you can say in front of Carl. We speak as one." Jim started to protest, but Stephan stood stoically and crossed his arms. "Boss, how do you expect me to keep everyone safe if they keep breaking the rules?" Then he made the mistake of taking a similar stance and crossing his arms. "When we got here, we didn't want to make a fuss as it was very late. I know the system Bob sent and know that you were aware of us. If you really wanted to run security, you could have left the hut and found out that we were here." That took the wind out of his sails. Deflated, Jim backed down from Stephan and apologized. "I didn't mean any harm, boss. I was just looking out for you in your absence." Stephan went to him, stood face to face, and said, "Then you failed us. Maybe you want to take that boat trip to Fiji. Now go apologize to Allen and Darren and come back and see me. We'll discuss your future." Jim tucked his tail between his legs and snuck away like a guilty child caught with his hand in the cookie jar (how Stephan controls the situations like this is stunning to watch).

I thought Dale was going to climax seeing Stephan at his best. That's the trouble when you hire all gay men. The intricacies of running a house under these conditions can be hilarious to your health. Bruce came in and saw Stephan; they grunted at each other, and I think I saw Bruce grin. Stephan had broken through (he must know the unspoken bro code). I went to the garden to find Tom and inspect the results of his efforts. Stephan called Jim to the office to discuss his actions. Poor Dale was left alone in the kitchen to attend to the dishes. I heard Stephan ask

Allen to get Bruce and bring him to the office (piquing my interest). Five minutes later, I saw Bruce and Jim leave the office, Jim infuriated and Bruce as stoic as Stephan. I caught Stephan's eye, and he motioned me into the office. "I let Jim go and offered the job to Bruce, seeing as he installed the entire security equipment and knows how to use it." I said it was too bad that Jim had such a bad attitude, and maybe we should watch for any retribution on Jim's part. "Good idea, I'll take it up with Bruce." We left the office and watched as Jim gathered his personal items and got on the supply boat escorted by Bruce to ensure that he didn't cause trouble for us in Fiji.

Dale looked despondent as he saw Jim leave (he was handsome), and I thought maybe they were an item. Allen came to us and thanked us for that decision. "He was ordering everyone around as though he was our boss, and only Bruce was left alone." I figured that Bruce would have laughed in Jim's face if they crossed swords. We decided to take our personal boat to Fiji to do some sightseeing and shopping. Allen, Darren, and Bruce tagged along. We got about halfway to Fiji when the motor quit. Bruce took a look and saw that it had been messed with. "Boss, the gas line has been slit. It allowed us to get into open waters and then empty out," Stephan asked if, by chance, there was fuel in the gas can to at least get us to Fiji. Bruce lifted the can, and it was about half full. "It should work if I can Jerry rig the hose." Allen worked with Bruce to make it happen, and Darren set out some sandwiches for lunch. We ate as we watched the handyman (tee shirt off and sweating in the morning sun) work. Allen kept getting things and handing them to Bruce. "I think we can try now, thanks, Al." The engine roared to life, and we were on our way. We made it to the dock as the gas sputtered out.

Bruce went to the hardware store as we ventured into town and the souvenir shops. Allen and Darren left us to it, and they went in search of specialty foods to dine on (date night gay style). I happened to spy a shadow figure near us, but hanging back. I motioned to Stephan and said that I thought we were being followed. That's the time that Bruce showed up. Stephan whispered to Bruce something, and he left us. Allen and Darren came up to us and were about to ask about our shopping as the shadow was thrust into the main street with Bruce behind him. "Got him, boss. He was trying to load his pistol when I arrived. I let him finish and then disarmed him. Say hi, Jim. You're about to be handed off to the marshal, and we should see you in about ten years if you're lucky. Fiji has strict laws about killing and guns," Jim stammered as he tried to feign innocence, "It's not what it looks like. It's just a coincidence that you and I were in the same area. "With a loaded gun and a chip on your shoulder. I think you'd better come up with a better story than that. I'm ready to press charges, and I can afford a much better lawyer than you." Stephan pressed his advantage, and Jim folded. Stephan stepped into Jim's personal space and whispered in his ear, "If I ever hear about or see your person around us or the island again, I'll make you disappear forever, Kabbish Jim?" Jim backed down again and promised that he would move back to the States. "Good boy, now go and don't turn back" (I wish I had the mettle of Stephan. Always the hero).

We returned to our paradise with our new protector and the boys. Allen and Darren hurried to their chores as we went to the kitchen with our new security guy. Bruce nodded toward Stephan, and with mutual grunts, they separated, and Bruce disappeared (another Bob). I so wanted to ask how that was communication, but thought better of it (as usual). Time drew near as we needed to get back to our beloved Baltimore. We gave our farewells and headed back. Fiji was becoming our favorite getaway, but Europe would always have our heart. We landed in Baltimore and arrived home to find the house abuzz as usual with chaos. The dogs found us, and the love fest began in earnest. Winnie and Mary were at our feet and ecstatic. Sarah got the zoomies, and that got the other girls going, so they were ushered to the garden to release their energy. Dahlia and Elizabeth asked about the island (I think they were more interested in it as a vacation spot than our exploits). We painted pictures of paradise to tease them and added that if they needed a vacation, they could 'rent' the island (knowing full well that it would be us paying the bill).

Aaron came around the corner and asked about the dogs (I think he loved the dogs more than Dahlia). Bob and Elizabeth came to the kitchen with Bobby Jr. I couldn't help myself as I looked into his face and saw Stephan in those eyes and the smile as I took him into my arms to show him my love. I couldn't emote it, but it felt like my family (even though there was no blood tie. I was actually the interloper, but I had been involved so long that it just felt right. I was accepted as the paternal grandfather for the next 8 generations. What a gift Stephan had bestowed on me. So many generations of descendants to watch grow. When I started this journey into the study of longevity, I could have never dreamed of this happening to me. How can you thank a person for this? My love seemed insufficient and shallow. My sensitivity showed, and tears of gratitude sprang from my eyes. Stephan looked at me quizzically as I let the tears flow. I would include him in my prayers for the rest of my mortal life. I started on a trajectory of my life one way, took a major detour, and now am living the fairy tale life of a princess.

Albert met us the following day to give us an update on the duck triplets. It seemed that they were on duty cleaning and polishing the Rolls-Royce when their friends came around. They were taunted and laughed at until the boys decided to exact revenge. They cornered the others and told them that they were now upstanding citizens, and the others should be so lucky as to find such bosses. "So, how much do you guys make? Our boss pays enough for us to have our own apartments and cars. You guys are still asking for allowances from your moms. Maybe we can get you jobs from our boss. We hear they need dog walkers." The friends wanted to start a fight, but Albert appeared and threw water on that. They left quickly but promised to return. Albert snorted at them and turned around. "Hey, Louie, stop antagonizing the natives." The boys got back to work on the Rolls-Royce as Albert checked the monitors for any funny business.

The following week, two of the other guys came over and asked if the triplets could get them a job, too. Huey looked at them and asked if they were serious. "Yeah, it looks like you guys got a cushy job, and maybe you could put a good word in for us." Dewey nodded at Huey, got a nod from Louie, and said, "Okay, but you better be ready to be loyal to them as they caught us breaking in and took us under their wing. If you 'f' this up for us, we'll end you." The other boys were brought before Albert, and he referred them to us. I went to do the interview and took them all at the same time. I had Albert do the background check beforehand and hit them with the hard questions. They wondered how I knew so much about their background, and I simply said, "We always know the answer before asking the question. That way, we can weed out the liars."

I asked Huey, Dewey, and Louie about them, and they spoke for them, so I hired them on a provisional period. They turned into good workers (as I assumed they would). Now we had a group of young guys to assist Albert in looking after the warehouse. As Bob got more involved with marital affairs and being daddy, Albert took on the role of security guy. He got wind of a reporter sniffing around and asked

Stephan how he wanted to handle it. Stephan asked that he get the scoop on him, and was corrected by saying it was a female reporter. "Well, see what you find out about her and who she works for." It took two weeks (it seems that Albert wasn't as good as Bob, but sufficient), Albert came back to Stephan with the report and said, "She works for the AP. She works for the arts and entertainment section." Stephan looked at Albert and said, "She must be looking into some of the reports that some original paintings have surfaced and is trying to find the possessor of the masterpieces." Albert wondered how Stephan knew already. Stephan always had a finger on the pulse of his world. "Just make sure that if she gets too close to me, she gets detoured." Stephan liked his anonymity. I liked, no, loved his ability to remain out of the limelight.

I wanted to know her name so I could research her on my own. Most reporters can be treacherous if necessary, and I wanted to protect Stephan at all costs. I found out her name was Julia Baker. Now to find out everything about her and her reporting skills. It looked like she was a Rhodes scholar and studied at Cambridge. She held a PHD. In classic art and a master's in journalism, she knew a good story when she saw it. How to cut her off from my husband and to make her take a different tack. I appreciated her effort (as a scholar myself), but loyalty to my Stephan was more important. I put a PI on her and found out that she had a boyfriend, but dabbled around on both sides of the fence. This could be her weakness (or strength). I got her schedule, went to her class under the guise of monitoring the class. She spoke eloquently, giving great content (heck, I would have married her in the old days). She ended her class by saying, "I have an automatic 'A' for the person who can find the provenance for the following paintings. Find the owner of "Narcissus" by Caravaggio and "The Night Watch" by Rembrandt. To the victor goes the 'A'. I knew that Narcissus was Stephan and that it hung in my bedroom. The Night watch was in the Baltimore warehouse on the second floor. I went home to discuss it with Stephan.

"How did you find all this out?" I told him that I went to the class as a monitor and she discussed it in class. "What do you want to do about this, Stephan?" He looked at me and said, "You've done enough, sweetie. I'll take it from here." I told him she was knowledgeable and that I thought she could be swayed under the right conditions. He nodded his assent and went to find Albert. Albert appeared soon after, and they talked for about half an hour. He returned to me and over dinner told me, "I've instructed Albert to set up a meeting with me. I'll determine what to do then." I asked to spare her any harm as I thought she needed to be around for future generations. "What makes you think I would do that, Carl? I want her around almost as much as you. We need more of her type." That calmed my fears, and we went to bed knowing that tomorrow would be better.

The day of the meeting came, and we showed up early to scope out the room. I sat apart from them with Albert. She showed up on time and sat with Stephan. Lunch was long, and I think I drank a bit too much, happy in the knowledge that Albert would be driving me home. She stood, thanked Stephan for his time, turned, and saw us and acknowledged us as well (she was more prepared than I thought). She took her leave, and Stephan came to us saying, "She said she would keep us out of it if she could see some of the collection. I told her they were in a warehouse in Rome. I offered her a rare glimpse of them up close for her silence, and she agreed. It seems that she wants the experience more than the exposure." It affirmed what I thought about her: integrity above infamy. Stephan and I discussed how we would make her dream come true without having her infringe on our privacy, and a plan was formed to make everyone content.

We got the 'bus' ready, she took some PTO, found the hangar, and prepared to have her mind blown. Albert joined us, and I asked that Dale (yes, that Dale from Fiji) be flown in as our personal chef for the trip. We all met at the airport and went to the villa of Hunter and Junior (they knew we were coming with guests). I called Tony Jr. and asked him to bring wine for the weekend. We arrived at the Villa, and Junior appeared at the door. Dale barely contained himself until Hunter came to the door and hugged Junior. What a picture, Me and Stephan, Albert and Julia (who by now were getting close), Hunter and Junior, leaving poor Dale frustrated to the nth degree. We sent Dale to the kitchen to help with dinner and set about allowing Julia to get the tour of the villa. During this time, we unloaded the paintings and sent them to the warehouse for her to 'discover'. Within the next hour, Tony Jr. arrived with the wine. We sent him to the kitchen to torture Dale even more. We all took turns sneaking a peek to see how Dale was faring with Jr. Sparks were flying, and soon the boys were flirting big time.

Dinner was late but tasty. Jr. joined us at the table, but poor Dale had to serve and kept brushing against Jr. (talk about sexual tension). We finished with a glass of dessert wine, and then Albert took Julia to the gardens for a walk. Dale quietly asked about Jr., and we said to go for it as he was a vintner and a good one (did we mention that he swung both ways?) The guys were having at it, and we thought about how we were going to replace Dale on Wakaya. Julia returned with Albert on her arm (who knew, except us). We discussed the visit, and Julia perked up. Albert knew we had set it up earlier. He went along with it for us and planned the tour. We decided that tomorrow would be okay and sent the warehouse a notice of our visit and the people to expect.

Julia got excited and was up early, and met us in the kitchen over breakfast. Jr. unexpectedly appeared at the table and said that he had stayed the night at Dale's request (knowing that the half-hour drive was too much for Jr).. We smirked, knowing that Dale was smiling a bit too much and winked at Jr. every few seconds. Our twink chef was a hussy, and Jr. had found his soulmate. We got in the limousine and arrived at the warehouse about twenty minutes later. Inside, we let Julia open the door (as I had done decades ago), and I watched for her reaction. I loved reliving the time I first entered Stephan's world. She entered, stood still, and looked around as though to get her bearings. She didn't see the paintings and asked about them. I told her that we stored them on the second-floor gallery. We walked up the flight of stairs and let her lead the way into the gallery. She took about three steps forward and then stopped as though frozen in place. Her eyes widened, and she quipped, "Am I

dreaming, or are these actually real?" Stephan reassured her that they were real and that she could inspect them up close if she wanted.

Julia took her time and really got close. I thought she was going to notice something weird, but she confirmed that they were authentic. She looked at Stephan and asked, "How? How could you have all these original paintings? And why does this one look like a self-portrait? That would make you in excess of 550 years old." "Good question, do you really want the answer?" She paused, thought about it for a moment, and then said, "Yes, lay it on me. "The answer is yes, that is my portrait, originally painted in the Renaissance. She freaked out, reason leaving her, and rational thought checking out. "You asked, and I replied. Truthfully, I might add." She looked at the painting and back at Stephan. He simply said, "Welcome down the rabbit hole, Alice." She took a minute longer and asked for more. Stephan showed her some more of the gallery, and she nearly fainted as she gazed upon original works for the first time in her life. She affirmed them by the brushstrokes and the content. "Why have they never been shared with the world?" Stephan told her that it would have meant sharing his age, and that would lead to more questioning. "That's why I kept it secret. That's why you need to keep it secret, my dear."

She continued her perusal and asked more about Stephan and how he stumbled upon these unknown masterpieces. Stephan regaled her with intimate stories associated with the paintings (a truer acolyte was not to be found). She thanked Stephan genuinely as we headed to the roof for lunch. She had so many more questions, and Stephan gave her the true answers without redaction. Albert interjected with a question of his own, "Should I be afraid and maybe wear garlic and a cross?" We all laughed as Stephan again took to recalling why we were so 'good looking' for our age. "I have kept out of the limelight so that I could enjoy my life with Carl. It wasn't always that easy, as when I had to leave Svetlana, my wife, around 1646 after about 32 years of marriage. She died before I returned, and all I had were descendants who did not know me. I have dabbled with both sides of the coin, as it were, and then I heard about Carl in 2005. I became his intern, and things led to us finding that we really were meant to be together, and we married in 2019." Albert looked like he had been hit with a board. Julia was almost off her chair because she was so engrossed. I smiled as Albert asked my age. I said, "Well, I was born in 1967, so that would make me 101 now. That also means that next year, at Christmas, we'll be married 50 years," Albert asked how I was managing staying younger if I hadn't been born with Stephan's genes. "Well, if I tell you, then you have to die." Albert gulped, Julia giggled, and Stephan and I smiled. "It's a trade secret, but if you want to know, you have to play bottom for a decade." Albert sat straight up and said, "Hard pass on that, boss." We all laughed again, and the subject got dropped (although I could see Julia's eyes concentrating and taking mental notes for later).

Back at the villa, Dale and Jr. were preparing a feast for us all, using the house chef as a sous chef (bet that ticked the chef off). We dined on the best food that could be garnered from the market. Dale allowed the chef to put together the antipasto, and it melted in my mouth, of course, toasted bread, then prosciutto, salami, and pepperoni, provolone, Gouda, and Parmesan cheese, Calamata olives, both black and green, endive, radicchio, and leafy lettuce, and peppers, both hot and mild. Then the wine poured, a hearty Chianti, manicotti stuffed with ricotta cheese filling and red gravy sprinkled with reggiano parmigiano. Next came the meatballs simmered in red gravy all day, served with vermicelli noodles. Dale decided on Italian gelato for dessert with Prosecco. I chirped, "What, no cannolies for bedtime? What a disappointment." Dale looked shattered, but said he could get some and not to worry. Stephan waved him off and said that I really didn't need the extra calories (at least until tomorrow).

Morning coffee was interesting, Dale and Jr. were having coffee (and Dale had cannolies displayed predominantly on the center of the table). Albert was serving Julia her coffee. We opted to have the house chef make us espresso (to soothe his ego). Hunter and Junior came along shortly with wreaths in their arms (I knew what this meant). Stephan requested Julia's presence on our trip to the cemetery. She quickly gathered her stuff up and followed us to the waiting cars. We got in the first car with Hunter and Lucius, then Albert and Julia in the second car. We arrived at the tombs and removed the old wreaths. Stephan took Julia's hand and introduced her to his parents' graves, then Fausta's, then the others. She noted the dates, and Stephan said that she could take photos here. She grabbed her phone, took about one hundred photos, and, being polite, left us out of the pictures (this lady has got class). We whispered to Albert, "This one's a keeper. Don't mess it up." She asked permission to look around and take other photos of the nearby stones and tombs, to which Stephan said yes. We ate lunch, prayed over the graves, collected our guests, and headed back to the villa. I told her how I had gotten the villa way back when, and she couldn't believe she had lucked out this much. Again, she requested to take photos, and Junior guided her around the villa and showed her the restored gardens (meanwhile, we had the paintings reloaded onto the plane and ready for their journey home).

The day after, we finally packed up for the trip home. Julia had fresh flowers delivered with a gift basket for the staff and a special memento for the hosts, a copy of her book about the arts of the Renaissance. They received it with grace, and we parted. We got to the airport and saw police in the hangar (never a good sign). Stephan went over, talked to them for a few minutes, and they left. Stephan returned to us, cool as a cucumber, and told us to board. I had my heart in my throat, but said nothing, and Julia and Albert looked at each other quizzically but got on the plane. Wheels up ten minutes later and on our way home. I leaned into Stephan, and he said, "I'm tired, we'll talk when we get home" (code for let's not talk now). I leaned on Stephan's stoic shoulder and fell asleep. Our beloved Baltimore came into view, and we landed around noon. Luggage was sent to customs, and we followed. It took about half an hour to clear customs, and we left for the house. Aaron picked us up, and we arrived about one. The girls had just woken up from their nap and were on us in a flash. Winnie and Mary came with us, and I inquired about the infamous Sarah. "She hasn't left Bobbie's side since his birth. I think she believes that he's her kid the way she acts. If he cries, she goes ape until Bob or I do something." Finally found a job for her.

We went to the den to be calm and allow the jet lag to take us. The girls curled up in their beds, and I finally had the chance to ask Stephan about the police. "The customs people saw the paintings being loaded and wanted the lowdown on it. I simply told them they were reproductions and showed them the receipts." Looking amazed, "And just how did you get receipts for old masterpieces?" Stephan took them out of his jacket pocket and handed them to me. "This isn't my first rodeo, Robin. I had them made up, suspecting they might get antsy seeing works of art leaving the country." My hubby is always a step ahead of everybody. By the time I headed upstairs, the painting was replaced on the wall. Stephan showered as we prepared for sleep. The girls waited until Stephan was in, and then they joined us on the bed.

The next week, I sent Elizabeth to monitor Julia's class, and she reported back that she gave a report to the class about her trip to Italy. She showed photos and talked about the history and the culture, and recommended that everyone should go at least once in their life. That satisfied me, and that was good because she and Albert were getting serious. By Christmas, they were an item, and he asked about proposing to her and what he should do about a ring. I knew what was coming, so I told him to wait a couple of days and say nothing. I talked to Dahlia and Stephan, and we coordinated the Christmas event to have enough witnesses around. We whispered to Julia's parents to join us that night, and they were pleased. I took Albert to the jeweler's and 'we' got Julia a 2-carat blue brilliant cut round diamond surrounded by her birthstone, sapphires. The Christmas was Bobbie's first, and kids and adults of all ages went to the atrium for a toast. We maneuvered Julia's parents near the front and had Julia in front of the fountain. I went to her (the distraction) and proposed a toast to all assembled as we raised our glasses. Albert took his place by her, and as she sipped the champagne, he took a knee and presented the ring. He proposed, she accepted the ring, said yes, and her parents came forward. A perfect end to 2068. Stephan handed the kids an envelope, and in it was a check for $1,000,000 and a note saying that they could be flown to Wakaya Island for their honeymoon. They hugged us and graciously accepted.

Stephan clanked his glass, raised his goblet, and said, "Welcome to the family, Julia and Albert. As you know, we tend to adopt families here." Elizabeth handed me a letter from the island. I had no doubt what it said, but opened it to find that our dear twink Dale was planning on moving to Italy (surprise, surprise). It said that Tony Jr. was in need of a chef for his vineyard, and so this was his two-week notice. I showed the letter to Stephan, and he laughed, "Surprise, surprise. I wondered how long it would take those two to move in together. What say we take a trip over the new year and personally deliver the package to the vineyard?" I agreed, and we made the arrangements. A week later, we were in Fiji and headed to the island. Wakaya welcomed us, although they were a little unprepared. Dale saw us and figured that we would be mad. "Welcome, bosses. I'm glad and sort of sad to see you. I'm sorry about the notice, but Tony says he needs someone there as soon as possible, so that's why I sent you a letter." Stephan stood before him stoically, stroked his chin, looked down, and finally said, "Took you long enough, kiddo. We knew when you were in Italy that you two kids would be together, and besides, Tony can't run that 'big' vineyard by himself." Dale ran to me and hugged me, and then Stephan cleared his throat and said, "And to see that you get there, we're taking you there personally on the family bus." Dale ran back to Stephan and hugged him harder. "I've interviewed a few replacements and sent them to Bruce for final selection. I think he's in the kitchen with them now."

When we got to the kitchen, only Bruce and one other person were there. They were having samples of the dishes. "Hey, boss men, this is Jaime, he is the one that I'd like to recommend to replace old Dale there. He's 24, right out of Culinary arts school." We looked as Jaime came over to greet us. He was easy on the eyes, with auburn hair, another one with a tiny 28-inch waist, dimples, and a smile he must have inherited from Stephan. "Very glad to meet you. I have my credentials here if you'd like to read them. I have presented Bruce with some of my better samples, or would you like to try my abilities for yourself? Just ask and prepare to be amazed." Stephan looked at him for a moment before saying, "I'd like eggs Benedict on toast points, please." True to his word, he sprinted to the fridge, got the ingredients, and started moving around the kitchen as though he had lived there for years. Ten minutes later, he presented three plates with what looked like heaven on a plate. Bruce, Stephan, and I took our places and chowed down. It was devoured in minutes, and Stephan looked at him and said, "I'd like to offer you a contract, open-ended. I like your style, kid, you have the sass and the talent to back it up." Jaime shook Stephan's hand, said he could start today if we wanted, and Stephan said that he could start. "Good enough, I'll go store my luggage." As he left, I looked at Stephan and said, "How did you know he had luggage with him?" Stephan grinned, "I told you, he has the stuff to make a good chef, and he just proved it to us." I turned to Dale and said, "Time to pack up, Dale, we leave after breakfast tomorrow."

True to my word, the wheels were up by ten a.m. We were on our way to Italy. The boat appeared below us, and Dale began to get nervous.

"What happens if it's only a fling? I'll be left in a strange country all alone." I told him to go see Hunter and Stephan Jr., and they would send news to us, and we would get him back to the States. "You guys are the best." Stephan told him to change his clothes and prepare to land. "That should calm him down a bit." We deplaned and headed to the customs department. It took a little longer as Dale had crazy papers, and we had American ones. The limousine was waiting, and we set off to the vineyard. Tony was there waiting for us. He had his staff bring in Dale's luggage. "You can put them in my room for now." We snickered, knowing that they'd never leave there until Dale wore them. We were ushered into the dining room, where a chef was prepping the table for a meal. Stephan couldn't help himself, "Good of you to hire an interim chef while waiting for Dale." Tony blushed at that, knowing that we knew. "That's why we decided to get him here quickly. I know how much you missed those hot buttered buns that he makes especially to your liking." Even I blushed at that. Only Stephan hadn't blushed. The food came, and we settled down to a fine meal and good wine.

We decided to stay in the guest house overnight, and I brought in my suitcase so we would have clothes for the night. Stephan looks so good in black, and I look so good in red and green. Morning came, and breakfast was light (as usual on flight days). We gave our goodbyes to the new couple. I leaned over and whispered, "Let us know when the nuptials are, boys." They were blushing again but waved us away, and we headed home. 2069 came with a flash. Summer was set for the wedding of Albert and Julia. We made it home just in time for Bobbie's christening. The girls were happy to see us, and they were getting their muscles now. Everyone smiled at us as though we were the butt of a joke or they had a big secret, and we weren't allowed to know it. I decided to ignore them and went to write in my journal. Stephan went to the den to write (I suppose). During spring break, we decided to rally the troops and go to camp. A couple of weeks of pure chaos, but it was fun to have everyone there. We were up to about 60 people, so we had Harold hire a staff to help feed us. I took my guy by the hand, and we walked around the compound seeing what we had developed in ways of family. We enjoyed wine, a stroll, and the quiet times and talks with little groups of family (the best times were then, we got to be so engaged).

Those two weeks passed in a flash, and we were back to the grind (if you can call it that). Elizabeth was telling me that I had more than enough to send to the publisher, and I went over it with her. "I think it's got too much personal material in it to publish, don't you think?" She nodded and said, "Well, what do you want me to do with it? I can toss it in the trash if you want. I only took the better part of a year to construct a readable book from your hen scratching and random thoughts." "Point taken. I'll let Stephan read and decide what to do next, okay?" She nodded and left me to drink away my doubts.

Summer arrived, and the wedding was getting close. I knew because people were gathering at the appointed places we assigned them for their stay. Julia took Elizabeth and Dahlia to wedding dress shopping. I called Julia's mom and gave her the address and time so she could be there. She didn't have a ride, so I sent Aaron to get her. She nearly fainted when the limousine appeared, and Aaron knocked on her door. She arrived and was there when the other girls arrived. The dress was picked (after 4 hours), and they all took the limousine home (go figure, I think it was because it had champagne and snacks). Bobbie was fidgeting all day until Elizabeth got home, and Dahlia went straight to the kitchen to get ready for dinner. Aaron left to clean the car up and polish it. Stephan came out of the den, having read the book, and said, "I think it's okay to publish. Besides, we can use the money. We're down to our last trillion."

Only my man can joke like that. He was right, though. We had been spending around $10,000,000 every few months. Heck, I checked my account, and it only had $15,000,000 left in it.

"Okay, I'll send it in tomorrow. How about dinner?" Stephan said nothing but grabbed my hand and led me into the dining room. We got our tuxedos ready and bought one for Albert. I loved the fitting; he was so awkward and uncomfortable, reminding me of my first trip to the clothier. I whispered to Stephan to get him the silk underwear, too. He snickered and motioned for the clerk to add it to the bill. The day was near, and we got the venue ready, acting like doting parents. The morning of the wedding, we got the groom ready, readied ourselves, and went to the site in the limousine. Stephan acted as the best man, and I acted as the usher. We had hired an orchestra, and they played throughout the day. Doves were released as they kissed to seal the deal, and everyone headed to the reception. We had to have it at the event center as there were about four hundred people at the reception. We had it buffet style so we could get more people served quickly. The music was muted while dining, and then the traditions occurred. I was glad to be married, therefore not having to try to catch the garter. The kids left the hall later in the night as we kept the party going for the guests.

I was glad to be home after the wedding; it was a great time, but it wore me out. Stephan cuddled for most of the night, and the girls just curled up at the bottom of the bed. Morning came and went as we slept until 11:30 am. Showers taken and finally dressed, we presented ourselves for lunch. Sandwiches and a drink for lunch. I went to write some more.

Fall came, and so did my 102nd birthday. Stephan planned a small get together (and by small I mean about 30 people, you know, just family).

I saw the cake, and gratefully it had three candles, a 1, a 0, and a 2. I blew them out and hoped I would get my wish. Stephan gave me a card and asked that I wait to open it. I slipped it into my jacket pocket and kept opening the other ones. What do you give a guy who can have anything his heart desires? For me, it was Stephan's continued love (which he made clear I had). I waited until we were in the bedroom to open his card and was actually surprised by the contents. It had a beautiful handwritten card, and opening it, I saw a document. I read it, and it said that it was the last will and testament of Stephan Orion naming me the sole heir. In the event of my demise, it would be divided by all legal heirs and made provisions for all of our staff (family, actually).

I hugged my guy and told him that I really didn't need it and that it should go to his heirs and staff. "I can't tell you what it means to me to be able to give you my estate, Carl. I realize that I may live longer, but I want it airtight just in case." Tonight was going to be special; tonight was going to be just Stephan and Carl, no games, no playing, just plain love for two people. I sent the will to our lawyer for safekeeping and walked into my future feeling secure and safe.

Halloween came, and Stephan requested another trip to the past by holding another costume party like the one that had happened a few years ago. I called the players and noted to them that Stephan wanted another "Grand Soiree" in full dress. They agreed, but I didn't tell Stephan until he saw his outfit laid out on the bed. "You really want me to wear that old thing again?" "Why not, after all, I paid $53,000 for it, and it cost another grand to get it cleaned and stored." He smiled as though anticipating the night. I dressed in my outfit and led him to the staircase. "May I introduce the host for the evening, his 'majesty' Louis XIV, the 'Sun King'. The crowd looked up, cheering him on, and he took on the persona easily and waved at the guests as he descended the stairs. We were greeted with toasting flutes and toasted with the others as we mingled. I to this day don't know who enjoyed the party more, Stephan or me (although I'd bet on Stephan). The look in his eyes, as though he was there in 1714 in Versailles, actually brought palpitations to my heart and a smile to my face. He called the dance, and I let him lead me to the floor (praying I still remembered the steps). It must have gone okay because we received an ovation after finishing. The evening ended around three in the morning, so Dahlia called the dogs to the kitchen for the night as she figured they'd be up far sooner than us (and she was right). Stephan stayed in character the rest of the night as we bedded down. Good thing we've been monogamous over the years (as he didn't use protection as was the custom back then).

With Halloween over, that meant Thanksgiving, Christmas, and our official fiftieth wedding anniversary. Thanksgiving was held at the camp (for about 70 people). Harold asked Dale to come assist (so that he and Tony could escape the daily routine of the vineyard). They arrived around four days before the affair (taking full advantage of the pool when not cooking or receiving wine from the airport). Dale wore tight hot pink Speedos so he could tease Tony, but Tony wore an electric blue Speedo to accentuate his physique and hairy chest. I couldn't help but look and laugh when Dale saw his partner prancing around like the 'cock of the walk'. He hurried over and tried to say that he would have preferred him in board shorts. "Babe, if you can flaunt your body, then why can't I?" Dale motioned downward and said, "But you're slightly excited, and people are staring." Tony smiled and said, "Well, that's why you wore the hot pink speedo, isn't it? You know they're my favorite. I'm just letting you know I agree." Needless to say, Dale led Tony to the guest room for a 'nap'.

Stephan came out, asked where the boys were, and I said, "I guess wearing Speedos makes them 'sleepy'." He laughed, and we sat to enjoy the sun. Later, as the sun set, we took a stroll along the beach as the horizon swallowed the sun and the sky turned crimson. Returning to the camp, we found the lovebirds at work in the kitchen (fully dressed). We tasted a few samples of the wines that came and then turned in for the night. Thanksgiving came, so Stephan and I ate light for breakfast and took the dogs for a walk. We walked in to sheer chaos, everyone running around, lots of loud talk, and not much getting done. Dahlia came to us and said, "Don't worry, just a little bustle before the calm of dinner." We decided to leave the main house and take the three girls to the beach. They ran in and out of the waves, getting totally wet. It was okay until they shook off by our sides. We wiped them down (after we dried off). That lasted a minute or two, and then they ran back out to enjoy the fall in Baltimore. I chased them into the waves, having an intimate moment with them and remembering their brother Alfred (I missed that boy a lot). We came up to Stephan, and I joined the girls as they shed the water off, and I shook my head, getting Stephan wet. He was faster than I thought as he grabbed me and pulled me onto his lap. A quick slap and then he said, "That'll teach ya kiddo." He released me, helped me stand, and then he stood in front of me, and we kissed as the girls did their worst. We dried everyone off and headed to the house. The girls were almost dry as we entered. The house, as suspected, had quieted down, so we went to our bedroom and dressed for dinner. We were served a glass of wine and were told dinner would be in half an hour.

The dinner menu was simple, the first round was Sopa Tuscano with grilled bread, and next came a small side salad with creamy Italian dressing. The main event entered on platters and set in the middle of the table. We had suckling pig roasted to perfection, several turkeys looking like they came from a caterer, garlic mashed potatoes with turkey gravy, cranberry sauce, both smooth and chunky, stuffing with apple bits, acorn squash hot with brown sugar and butter, relish trays with assortment of goodies, red and white wines (water or soda for the kids). Like I said, simple for our house. We toasted the kids for their effort and chowed down. Dinner took around two hours and then the guys went to the atrium (where we had a 75 inch screen set up with football on it. Cigars and Bourbon were set out and the doors were closed so as not to affect the kids. The rest of the troops dispersed around the camp. Stephan and I took some time to congratulate Harold, the staff, Dale and Tony for their efforts and handed them all envelopes with a small token of our esteem ($10,000 cash each). Dale was over the moon, Tony and Harold were appreciative but non plussed, and the staff joined Dale in their joy.

We joined the boys in the atrium and watched football into the night. The house got quiet and so Stephan and I went to the den for a night in front of the fireplace (somehow fur on naked flesh is a turn on). One more Bourbon and then a cuddle on the fur rug and under a fur coverlet on the warm hearth about 5 feet from the glowing embers. I said, "Today was a success, who could ask for more?" Stephan whispered in my ear, "I can." We pulled the coverlet over us and giggled like school girls.

The joy of everyday life. Morning found us looking like we had just had a workout at the gym. We threw on some baggy sweats and tried to sneak upstairs without being noticed, and only got as far as the bottom step when I heard Dahlia laughing out loud. She set the girls on us, and we scurried up the steps as the dogs chased behind. Newly showered and dressed more appropriately, we came downstairs behind three four-legged vacuums. "I was wondering when you two would be gracing us with your presence. People are getting ready to leave, and they wanted to say their goodbyes." We took our roles slightly more seriously and tended to the civilities. Dale and Tony said they would wait for the 'bus' to be available (I think they just wanted a little more time away). "No problem," was all Stephan said.

Christmas was next on the list, but we opted for a 'small' affair, family only (which meant about 60 people). We went shopping and had packages set for delivery almost every day. We even babysat for Bobbie one afternoon (basically making sure that he stayed asleep) while his parents shopped for him. I started getting suspicious when people stopped talking whenever Stephan and I walked into a room. Stephan told me I was overthinking stuff again, and he would know if anything weird was going on. I let it go, but my gut wasn't having it. I kept my thoughts to myself and started listening more intently and being more observant. Maybe this time, I could be the one to discover something to bring to Stephan. The week before Christmas, the tree went up, and the hustle and bustle of the season took full concentration. Stephan and I decided not to spend on each other (and we both knew we'd be out shopping for the other 'unofficially'). We decided on new tuxedos for Christmas and had our fittings. Aaron picked them up Christmas Eve, and we tried them on (mistake number one, as they turned us both on, and one thing led to another). Thankfully, we were able to extricate ourselves before much damage was done, and we would still be able to wear them tomorrow. Needless to say, we were late to dinner and had sandwiches (or some of them, as we had to share with the girls, even though they had our dinners).

I asked our personal staffer to repress and steam our tuxedos for the next day, and he took them away. An hour later, a knock came at the door to our room, and our tuxedos looked good as new. I knew better than to let Stephan see them and hurriedly put them in the closet until tomorrow. Morning, and we dressed for breakfast in our formal pajamas.

Arriving in the kitchen, we got our coffee and headed to the dining room. Dahlia ran in front of us and said it was off limits as they were still working on the last-minute adjustments for the day. We returned to the table and had our Eggs Benedict with the staff. It was as though Dahlia was trying to hide something. Around ten a.m., we were told that the dining room was ready. We walked through the door and froze. Banners were everywhere, people all around us, Mimosas in hand, and they started chanting, "Happy 50th anniversary to you." Stephan, ever stoic, turned to me and kissed me (garnering a cheer from the crowd). I had to hug him because I broke into tears of joy, and I needed time to recover. I think I saw a tear form in the corner of his eye (which meant he was surprised, also). Dahlia and Elizabeth came over first and kissed us, followed by the guys shaking our hands. Dale and Tony hugged us, and Harold brought in our cake, a four-tier cake, surrounded by cupcakes for the kids. We replayed our wedding day and fed each other cake from the bottom layer. We were very careful about the Pajamas (as they were silk. Thankfully, we didn't put on our tuxedos. Christmas continued after that small celebration, and we went to the atrium for presents. We had 'Santa' disperse the gifts to the tots, and then we sent them off to play in the sitting room (yes, we had a sitter in the room after all, we're not animals). The time came for presenting our gifts to the staff, and the others assembled. Let's just say they were not disappointed. I mentally added up the amount we spent and figured that the book better be a best seller. Stephan reached for a small gift and handed it to me. I said, "I thought we agreed no gifts this year." Stephan smiled as though he was the cat that caught the canary. "Just open it, Carl." I opened it and found a velvet box inside. I carefully opened the box (it looked antique) and saw a bejeweled necklace. "This must have cost you an outrageous fortune, Stephan." He took it and placed it on me. It was the most stunning piece I had ever seen, let alone worn. "It's called the 'Hortensia' as it was named after the Queen of Holland and sold to Louis XIV. Now it's known as the 'Hope'. It was stolen after his demise, and I had purchased it for my collection. I had it set with fifteen more smaller diamonds and added a diamond necklace. The blue diamond in the center is 45.52 carats." I cradled the stone in my hand, saying, "This is too much, Stephan." He told me this was in his collection and he wanted it for his love. "Just enjoy it, Carl. To another fifty years" (as he whispered in my ear, it's worth about $350 million now). Everyone raised their glasses and toasted us again. I knew that I'd only wear the necklace in the bedroom.

It was my turn to surprise Stephan with a present. He looked at me, and I just shrugged, saying, "Something about a goose and a gander. Now open it." He set down his drink and opened the gift. It wasn't the Hope diamond necklace, but it was a matching set of cuff links, shirt studs, and a tie pin inset with chocolate diamonds. He held it up as though I had given him the keys to the kingdom and then kissed me. We left the frivolity to get dressed for the rest of the day. Stephan took time dressing, fawning over the accessories for his tuxedo. I got dressed and placed the necklace below the bow tie. We stood together in front of the mirror, and Stephan said that we needed a painting done to commemorate this day. I told him we could get a snapshot, but he insisted on a portrait painting. "We can take a lot of photos, but I want a life-size portrait of us together, Carl." I nodded, and we left the room knowing that these tuxedos wouldn't make it past the photos. I had Stephan add the cape from his costume before we had the official portrait photos taken (for the best effect). I researched for the most respected portrait artist (as I wanted to have a portrait likened to the Queen of England on her seventieth anniversary on the throne).

Reflective and somber yet entirely regal. This was to be our legacy portrait. I found a woman and had her interviewed. She jumped at the contract, no questions asked, and took the photos we supplied. She told us that it would take about six months and maybe a little more, depending on the weather. I handed over the photos and left her to it. She was given half of the commission down to start (I asked to have the original coat of arms and the original lettering in Greek added to the bottom, a surprise for Stephan).

We started New Year's Day 2070 on Wakaya Island and were met by the team. Tom, Allen, Darren, Bruce, and the new cook, Jaime. It seemed as though there had been some bonding while we were away, as stoic Bruce had Jaime by his side and Jaime kept looking up at him with a sparkle in his eye. Allen took the luggage, and Tom took me to the garden. True to his word, he had transformed it into a paradise fit for us. I doted on his expertise as he led me through the labyrinth, telling me all about the new plantings. It took about an hour, and then I went in search of my guy. I found him and Bruce grunting away and having a smoke as well. Jaime asked us what we wanted to eat, and we told him a salad and a sandwich would do us fine. He winked at Bruce, then flitted away to the kitchen. I really couldn't help myself and asked Bruce, "How's it feel to have an admirer? Should we be planning nuptials soon?" He grunted and left us alone. Stephan shook his head and said that we should just leave him to it and let things take their course.

Lunch arrived moments later, and we had a nice antipasto with a rare roast beef sandwich with horseradish sauce on the side for dipping. I dove in, and Stephan picked his way through. Lunch ended, and Jaime came to remove the plates. "What's wrong, boss? Didn't you like it? You haven't even finished half of it." Stephan assured him that it was fine and pointed to my plate. "He'd have licked the plate if I'd let him. He loves food, me not so much. I just eat to live." "Noted, boss, I'll downsize your portions for now on." Stephan thanked him and handed the plate to me. He didn't have to ask me twice. We stayed, and I watched as the guys tried to hide their feelings when we were around. "That's just plain cute watching them." A few days later, I happened to catch Jaime leaving Bruce's room early in the morning. I let him get to the kitchen before letting him know I was there. "Morning, Jaime, got any coffee?" Jaime was taken aback and said, "Just got here, can you give me a couple of minutes?" "No problem, I have issues getting started after lovemaking too." Jaime blushed, knowing he was busted. "Sorry about that boss but things just happened. I'll let Bruce know not to let that happen again." I laughed, whispering to him, "I think you two make a great couple. Don't you dare let him get away."

Jaime almost cried because he was so happy. He hugged me and got me coffee. "Eggs Benedict for two?" "Is there any other breakfast?" Jaime didn't know how to take it so I said, "Yes, eggs for two. Give me about an hour and I'll go wake the hubby." I left to awaken my guy and found him in need of some 'relief'. Who am I to deny him assistance. I slipped in next to him and let nature take its course. We returned to the kitchen as the eggs were served. Jaime almost laughed as he saw me in the same shape as him earlier. I looked at him and shrugged, "Well now we're even." He giggled and left for the kitchen. I think he found a mentor in me now. Note to self, if this is the feeling you get from being human, I needed to do it more frequently.

As we were eating, the almighty Bruce graced us with his presence, and the look on his face was priceless. He looked refreshed and eager to face the day. I saw Jaime out of the corner of my eye, and I winked at him like a sorority sister, and he winked back (our own chapter of the Beta Omicron Iota or BOI club). Personally, knowing that they (Jaime and Bruce) were only given this short time on Earth, I envied them for having more passion due to the need to 'hurry' before the end. It almost made me rethink about lasting this long. Then I thought about the gift I was given and the years with my everything man and reconsidered my position. I wouldn't trade it for the world. Stephan roused me from my meditations and asked what I wanted to do today. I responded, "I just want to breathe you in, memorize your touch, and feel your emotions as we walk in our garden." Yeah, it was Maudlin, but at least I was honest. I wanted to always feel this way, grateful and humble and protected. Stephan said, " Okay, " and led me away.

We weaved our way through the garden, stopping along the way to enjoy the flora and steal kisses when we thought no one could see us. I acted like the kid in Spring, hormones raging and trying to sate them. For his part, Stephan was seducing me to the point where we almost lost it. "If you don't stop teasing me, I'm going to have to do something about it." Stephan removed his shirt and said, "Take me, I'm yours." Well, I tried to be nice, but nature called and I answered. We returned to the house in our briefs and got ready for a hearty lunch. Jaime prepared a rice dish with coconut milk and exotic spices. I think he used goat meat and tons of local vegetables. It was delicious, and Stephan actually ate two servings. Jaime said nothing as he dished up the second serving, and I simply said, "He worked up an appetite in the garden. If Tom asks about some ripped clothes out there, just tell him it was us."

Jaime almost doubled over in laughter when I said it. "Will do, boss. Do you want more?" I said no and told him that he should share it with the staff, as it was delicious. "Especially share it with Bruce. As they say, 'the way to a man's heart is through his stomach'." Jaime smiled at me and went to call the others (after he plated a dish for Bruce). I left with Stephan, and we settled near the fireplace with our Bourbon and a couple of cigars. Tom came to us a little later to report that he had found clothes, ripped apart, in the garden, and wanted us to know. I really wanted to toy with him and 'clutch my pearls in despair,' but Stephan spoke up and told him that we got frisky and thanked him for his concern. "Just trash them, Tom. Sorry for the inconvenience. I'll try to be more careful in the future." Tom replied, "No problem, boss." Then he whispered into Stephan's ear, "Hope it was all you wanted it to be." Stephan nodded, and Tom left with a big smirk on his face. Maybe hiring a full staff of gays was a good thing. I felt sorry for Tom, being the only one alone. Feeling guilty, I let Tom know that if he needed help with the landscaping, we could afford to hire another guy to assist him. I also said that he could interview and hire whomever he thought was best. He opened up and said that he knew someone who needed a job, but wasn't the best. "What's his name and story, Tom?"

Tom started out with his name, Tory. "I saw him when I went for a pint in Fiji. He's a native guy, aged 19. He was getting some heat from the barflies, and I intervened because I hate seeing someone like him getting bullied. Can I be brutally honest? (I nodded) I was him when I was young, and it kills me to see it now that I have matured. He came and sat with me, and it kind of went too far, and we hooked up. I'm really into him now, and we see each other when I get back to Fiji. I'd love to have him here, but he wouldn't be much of a help in the garden," I asked, "Is he trainable?" Tom said, "I believe so if given a chance, but I wanted you to have all the information up front. After all, you'd be paying him." I told Tom to interview him and if all went well, to bring him on board. "I believe we have enough space to give him his own room. If not, have him bunk in with you until accommodations can be made." Tom grinned as he said, "Not a problem, boss. I'll 'interview' him tomorrow when I go to town for supplies."

I left him to it and felt better about solving his 'problem'. I went in search of Stephan and bumped into Bruce. He grunted, and I returned it. He smiled and continued on. I was actually getting this bro stuff (well, it was a beginning). Stephan was on the phone with Baltimore. He waved me in, and I paled as he looked serious. He ended the call and said we were needed home. I hated it when he talked like that. It made me feel helpless because I was too far from handling it. I wanted to ask him what the situation was, but went and found Allen to assist in packing. We went with Tom to Fiji and headed to the airport. The plane was waiting, and we left shortly after. The trip home seemed to take days instead of hours. Then customs took longer, and the ride home made me nauseous. Stephan stepped out onto the driveway, and Mary greeted him by wiggling around. I wondered why Winnie wasn't there and then got sick thinking she was hurt or missing or dead (please not dead, I couldn't take it). She rounded the corner, and my fears calmed down, but not before I cuddled and coddled my dog. Stephan walked straight to the kitchen to see Dahlia. I followed behind by only a step and saw the problem: Dahlia was in a cast and was sitting in a chair. "Sorry for calling you boys home, but this 63-year-old body let me down a few days ago. I turned too quickly and broke my femur. The doc says it's osteoporosis and I need to be off it and take Calcium pills going forward."

Elizabeth and Bob came into the kitchen, not knowing we were home, and looked surprised as we weren't due back until next week. "We just came to see if the 'lady in charge' needed anything. We told her not to call you two, not that you wouldn't be concerned, but we wanted you to have a quiet time in Wakaya." I calmed myself, seeing that nothing horrendous had happened. I finally spoke, saying, "I'm just glad that everyone was around to handle it. Thank you, Elizabeth and Bob. By the way, how's Bobbie?" Elizabeth let me know he was in the atrium with the nanny. I left the kitchen in search of my little buddy (with Winnie on my heels). Stephan asked Aaron about Dahlia's real condition and if she would need to step down, and he answered no. "She's a fighter like her mom and grandmother. She'll be good as new in a few weeks. I'm helping out until then, and Elizabeth has taken on many duties as well. You would be proud of how much she does." Stephan nodded and then sat with Dahlia to catch up, as it were.

Bobbie saw me and crawled over wanting to be picked up, and I lifted him into the air. I caught him on the downturn. He cackled and wanted more. I gave him raspberries on his exposed belly, and he laughed all the more. Winnie started jumping up, so I put Bobbie on the floor so Winnie could have her turn to kiss and slobber all over his face. He wiped it off and kept laughing. You could say that he was in heaven at that moment. The nanny said it was time for a nap and proceeded to take him away. He fussed a bit but was asleep within seconds. I went back to the kitchen as Stephan was winding up his conversation with Dahlia. He nodded toward the den and, taking his cue, followed behind. Once the door was closed, he turned and said that he thought that Dahlia was ready to retire, but didn't want to break the chain. I asked if we should reach out to Nathan Jr., 32, and his sister Rita, 27 (Eric and Nancy's grandkids). They weren't related to Trudy, but they were family (so to speak). Stephan told me to go ahead and make the call. Nathan Jr. wasn't really interested, but Rita was over the moon at the prospect. It seemed that her husband was not making much money and they were expecting in the fall. I asked her to meet me at the restaurant a couple of miles from the house. She brought her husband, Bill Markette (whom she married in 2065). We talked about the duties and told Bill that we could hire him as well. They were interested but not sold on the idea until I told them the salaries they'd be receiving. Bill made their decision on the spot, "When do we start?" I told him that once we talked to Dahlia and set her mind at ease, they would be officially put on the payroll. Bill felt crushed at the delay, but sensing his dismay, told them that the salary would start immediately. He cheered up quickly, and his appetite improved.

After the meeting, I returned and told Stephan we were set for the torch pass. He said that he would handle Dahlia as he wanted to do it in such a way as though it was her idea. I agreed spontaneously and wondered if Bobbie was up from his nap yet. I took the dogs out for a romp in the garden and to expend their energy. Stephan headed in the direction of the kitchen, and I silently wished him good luck. It was near dinner time, and I was cautiously optimistic about seeing everyone at the table. Dahlia came in on crutches and sat near me while Elizabeth and Bob arrived with Bobbie. Aaron showed up soon after and sat near Stephan. Dahlia spoke up and said, "I've talked with Stephan, and he's offered me a new position in the household, and I've decided to accept it. It would mean that Elizabeth would assume my old position, and I would become Stephan's private secretary. He wants to write a new recollection of his life and needs someone full-time as he has a lot to coordinate. I can't handle both types of work anymore, so if Elizabeth would, could you please man the ship from now on?" Elizabeth agreed, and the deal was done (my guy could charm birds from the treetops).

Elizabeth and I worked with Dahlia to handle the budget and the bills. Aaron said he would continue to drive us as long as he could. Bob worked with the triplets and found that 'Louie' had risen to the top of the group as far as responsibility went. Bob asked Stephan if it was all right to promote Louie to a higher position, and was told to invite him to the house for a talk about it. Bob sent for Louie, and he arrived shaking in his boots. He was escorted to the atrium and told to wait as Stephan wanted him to sweat a little. Stephan and I stepped into the room, and poor Louie looked like a deer in the headlights. Stephan motioned toward the chairs at the table. Louie sat (I think I heard him fart as he sat). Stephan spoke, "I hear good things about you at the warehouse. I was wondering if you could handle more responsibilities?" Louie calmed himself and asked, "What did you have in mind?" Stephan pushed a paper in front of him, and Louie read it. His eyes kept getting larger as he read further. "Are you serious? When can I start? I mean, thank you for the opportunity to prove myself to you. By the way, sirs, my real name is Declan Meyers, and I'm 20 years old, but you can call me Louie if you want, everyone else does, although I don't know why." Stephan and I chuckled at that and said, "Louie it is then. So, we take it you accept the new position?" "Absolutely, sir." Stephan rose, shook Declan's hand, and said, "Call me Stephan, and that's Carl. I'll let Bob know that the warehouse is your responsibility now. Keep up the good work. You're family now." Declan smiled as he left, and we knew he'd be cock of the walk for a while back at the warehouse. I told Bob to check in for a while until he was sure things were running smoothly. "Sure thing, boss."

I suggested to Stephan that the warehouse boys join us at camp for a weekend, and he thought that it was a great idea. "I'll have Bob rent some guards for the weekend and have him take the reins for that time." I told Bob to ask the boys about it, and he said okay. We set the date for the end of July and went a few days ahead to prepare for the drink fest. I was hoping for a swimsuit fashion show (I'm married, not dead). The boys showed up en masse and proceeded to check out the place. Declan oversaw them to keep them in line (he wanted to make a good impression and was hoping that his fortune would encourage the others to respond in kind). They opted for the food and beer and hit the sand for volleyball. They wore board shorts on the beach (bummer). Stephan and I wore our Speedos. Dale and Jaime would have been in heaven, but I was disappointed. Nothing to see here. Then the captain of the guards (Declan) decided to join us in only wearing his Speedo, neon orange (things were looking up). The boys started cat-calling and whistling at him until Stephan stepped onto the sand in his neon blue. The boys quieted down, and a few even asked if we had more. I asked for sizes and called the store for a rush delivery. They were being distributed to the willing lads about an hour later (getting better). I joined Stephan on the beach, and we joined the kids for some volleyball.

Harold brought food to the tables near the sand, and a cooler was laid open full of beers. The boys feasted on sandwiches (not bologna, though) of roast beef, Capicola, egg salad, turkey, and tuna salad. As for the beers, there was Budweiser, Coors, Michelob, Corona, Labatts, and Dos Equis. Harold brought out sliced lime wedges for the Mexican beers. Stephan and I opted for our wines from Tony Sr. and Jr's vineyards. Declan limited his consumption so he could show us his best side, while the boys had a drinking contest to see who could drink more (after all, how many times do you get to drink your fill on someone else's dime?). When Declan saw us drinking from footed glasses, he asked what we had. I told him, "We own two vineyards in Italy near Rome. This is especially made for us and our grand-kids in Italy and England. We travel there, to our home in Hawaii, and to our private island of Wakaya near Fiji." Declan said nothing, but you could see the expression on his face saying, Who are these two guys, and how much money do they have? I wanted to explain it to him, but decided to wait a while. Declan helped get our lightweight drinkers into the camp (after they had vomited up their beers and lunch). I almost pitied them, but thought that it was a good lesson to learn early. I suggested some dinner, but they said as one, "No thanks, we're turning in early." Declan joined us at the table and tried a glass of our wine. "This is delicious, do you guys drink much?" Stephan simply replied, "We keep it on hand for entertaining and some for dinners such as this." I looked at Stephan for a cue, and he nodded, so I said, "We are men of means. Yes, that means we have stuff, actually a lot of stuff. We own properties and even have our own plane that we call our 'family bus' as it moves our family and friends around more quickly. I believe that you like what you've witnessed and have seen so far. Let me tell you a short story of a security guard named Eric. He started the way that you did. He worked up to security chief of staff and even lived with us, traveled with us, and went all over the world. Bob took his place, and it looks like you will be filling his shoes, although they're pretty big. A word of advice, keep doing what you're doing and create a depth of personnel, which means help the others you believe could fill your shoes when the time comes, and your promotions will get you where you want to be. This life can be yours if you want it." Declan Louie Meyer floated on air to his room and dreamed of his future. I yawned, and Stephan took his cue to lead me to bed.

Morning, coffee, and Harold's Eggs Benedict, and waiting for the hungover group to appear. They appeared, one or two at a time, and asked for pain relievers. We dosed them, and they took dry toast to start. Declan came down, clapping them on the back and asking how their night was. Groans from the gallery were all he heard. He had scrambled eggs for breakfast with buttered toast. "Anyone for volleyball today?"

More groans and shaking heads. I had an idea, and Stephan said that since the other boys were out of commission, why not? We took Declan for a ride and took him clothes shopping as befitted his new position. We took him to Hunter's old shop. We inquired as to the new owner and were told that Hunter had basically given it to his cousin, Edward Garibo. He greeted us and said that Hunter gave him the store under the agreement that Hunter would continue to get 20 percent of the gross profits.

We presented Declan to him and said that he needed new clothes from the inside out (meaning he was going to endure the same embarrassment as I did all those years ago). He followed Edward to the back and was rewarded with silk boxer briefs and socks (and had to show us for fit, or so we told him). Then the pants and shirts, blazers and suits. Tees and swimwear. Fully humbled, he showed us the entire collection, and we picked our favorites. He nearly fainted as Stephan handed the black card to Edward. The total was a year's wages. "I really can't accept such an expensive gift…" Stephan cut him off and said, "And that's why we're doing this, because you've shown yourself as loyal, humble, and not entitled." He thanked us again and went to pick up his packages before I stopped him. "Edward, please have them delivered to the house tomorrow, thanks." Edward took the parcels to the back of the store for delivery. "One should not have to carry packages when delivery is an option." Declan nodded and followed us out of the store. The next stop was the auto dealer. "Pick a car as befits your new position. It's a little thing we do to welcome new members of the family." Declan looked around and said, "But these are all high-end luxury cars, how about a nice Camry or Civic?" Stephan took Declan by the hand and pushed him into the driver's seat of a light gray Maserati. "How's that feel? No words, good, we'll take it. Register it in his name, and we'll pick it up tomorrow." The dealer hurried to his office to process the paperwork as Declan fainted away. He came to, still behind the wheel of the Maserati. Stephan said, "I have standards for my inner staff, and driving a good car is one of the rules." Declan regained his composure and finally spoke, "Thanks, but what did I do to deserve this?" I spoke up and said, "This is for handling yourself well yesterday and today. It makes me proud that you stepped up and stayed much more sober than the others, even when presented with the chance to overimbibe." I've never been much of a drinker, as my father is an unofficial alcoholic. Mom and I agreed when I got this job to apply myself as it would take me places." He placed his hands at ten and two and seductively fondled the steering wheel. He then got out and followed us to the door. We got back to the camp as the other guys had rallied and were on the beach tossing a ball around. The dogs had picked their new buddies and were chasing them to and fro. Declan acted as though nothing had occurred and went to play. Stephan mentioned, "He's going to make a good replacement for Bob. That kid has a level head on his shoulders." I replied, "I believe you're right on that count."

The weekend ended, and the boys left to go back to work the next day. Bob reported that the warehouse was fine and the rented squad had been paid after signing their NDA's. I called Declan on Tuesday and asked him to come over and collect his new wardrobe and the car. Needless to say, he fairly flew to our house. We invited him in and had Bob join us in the atrium. "I've asked Bob here to be your mentor as there are more things to being our head security than guarding the warehouse. We need security here also, and Albert will not be enough. I know that you can't be in two places at once, so I'm going to ask you who you'd like to nominate to replace your warehouse duties." Declan thought long and hard about his replacement. "If I had no other choice but to choose from the cast of guys at the warehouse, I'd have to go with Dewey, I mean Leonard Sardone. I usually have to call him to handle stuff, as he's the best at getting results. He's 22 now and shaping up nicely." Stephan looked at Bob and said, "Well, Bob, what do you think? Should we give the kid a shot?" Bob took a moment and then, smiling, said, "Dewey takes after me a lot. I'd say go for it." Stephan nodded and then answered, "Have him come here for an interview, and I'll see if he has the chops." Now it was Leonard's time 'in the barrel'. Declan smirked as he remembered his interview. I had Declan go fetch him in his new Maserati. Declan hopped to it and soon returned with the next 'victim'. Declan led Dewey into the atrium and had him sit at the table. Stephan entered, and Dewey rose to shake his hand. "I was told to come see you, sir. Is everything alright?" Stephan said, "Actually, no, Leonard. You see, Declan has been promoted to be my house security, and that leaves a gaping hole at the warehouse. He spoke for you, saying that you could handle the warehouse. Is this true?" Leonard looked at Declan and back at me. His body relaxed, knowing now that he wasn't in trouble. "Sir, yes, sir. I believe I can. I tried to emulate what Declan and Bob did, and I think I'm ready."

Stephan walked to the boy and said, "Congratulations, son, you're promoted starting today. Carl and Elizabeth will fill you in and get the papers for you to sign." With that, he shook Leonard's hand and left for the den. Leonard followed me to the office, where Elizabeth was placing papers on the desk. Leonard looked at the papers and saw that they had been made out with his name before the interview. "Did you intend to hire me anyway?" I told him that we had spoken to both Declan and Bob, and actually, this was just a formality that Stephan insisted on. "Boy, he really knows how to intimidate people, doesn't he?" "You have no idea. He still gets the better of me, and we've been together fifty years." Leonard signed the papers, and then Declan returned him to the warehouse.

Stephan called me into the den and closed the door. "Could you light a fire while I pour the Bourbon and grab the cigars?" I knelt at the hearth and had it roaring in minutes. I turned to see my guy bare-chested and removing his trousers. I went to him, took the trousers and folded them, placing them on the chair. "You're a little overdressed for the occasion, don't you think?" I smiled, disrobed, and followed him to the fur rug. Thankfully, the fire warmed the room quickly, and we settled in for a while. I got up and dressed as the embers lost their glow. Stephan reluctantly did the same, and we went to dinner.

Declan was asked if he wanted to move into the house, and he said that he would have to consult his parents, as they had started depending on his room and board payments. I took Declan aside and asked about their finances. "They are doing okay, but their debt load is climbing as they're trying to save for my younger brother's college." I asked if there was anything else that he knew that they needed. "I don't want to bother you with their problems, boss," I told him that Stephan and I always liked to help out people in our orbit. Declan opened up a bit more, "To tell the truth, they're barely getting by. Dad needs a newer car because he's keeping it going by duct tape and rubber bands. Mom hasn't bought clothes in years and…, I hope you don't mind but I gave half of my clothes to my brother so he'd look good for high school." I listened intently and then said I would talk to Stephan about a small gift for his parents if he wanted to move. "Thanks for anything you can do and thanks in case you can't." Declan couldn't help himself, he came to me starting to shake my hand and then bear hugged me to show his gratitude. "This money will set my family up for life, thank you." He left and went home and I went in to see Stephan. I started to talk and

Stephan said, "Just let me know how much they need. I was eavesdropping, sorry." A kiss and a hug, and I was off to the office to call the bank about Declan's account.

I called Declan and told him that we had auto-deposited money into his account so that his parents wouldn't know it was us that had donated to them. I told him the amount ($500,000), he muffled a scream, and whispered into the phone Thanks. "Tell them you saved this up or that it was a bonus, yeah, that's better, and that you want to share it with them. Let me know if that's not enough. By the way, where is your brother intending to go to school?" He told me that he wanted to go to Colombia as he knew he couldn't dare dream of Harvard or Yale. "Does he have the grades for the Ivy League?" Declan replied, "Actually, yes, he's going to be the salutatorian of his class." I said, "Well then, let's set up an account for him and for his college so that he goes where he wants."

We set up the accounts, and I let Declan know so that he could tell his brother to dream bigger. Stephan appeared as I hung up and grabbed me from behind, hugging me tight and kissing my neck over and over again. We finished the night with a walk in the garden along with the dogs and then retired for the evening. I guess that doing good deeds makes one sleep deeply and soundly. We were awakened by the sound of Elizabeth calling the girls to breakfast (probably ours). We got to the kitchen as Bobbie was finishing his cereal. Harold made us omelets and sausage with hot buttered toast. Albert showed up and asked, "Am I being replaced, boss? Why is Declan taking my place?" Stephan coolly said, "You're not going anywhere, we just thought you could use some help with security. Declan can travel with us, and you can keep the home fires burning." Albert calmed down and asked for a toasted everything bagel with cream cheese. Harmony reigned again in the Orion-Omega household.

Albert left to make a phone call (presumably to Julia to allay her fears). Declan showed up on time, properly dressed, and sought out Albert to see what he could do to assist him. Albert smiled at that and took him on a tour of the security features and then to the security hut where the monitors were. I stood back and wondered how big this 'family' had become. We called a house meeting so that the troops knew who the others were and what duties we expected from them. I took Elizabeth as my private secretary, Dahlia was Stephan's, Aaron was replaced by Bill Markette (Rita's husband) to drive, and Aaron was given the task of washing, polishing, and maintaining the dogs (a job he did with relish). Albert was home security, Declan was our personal security (for home and travel), Rita took over bills and budget under my command, and the staff began reporting to Rita, although Elizabeth and Dahlia still held authority in her absence. I told everyone that Bob was to be consulted on legal and security matters as he was a licensed private eye and could assist if needed (note to self, ask if Leonard wanted to be a private eye also). That sorted, calm restored, we took a trip to the warehouse with Declan. I had him drive the gold Bentley for effect, and we appeared at the gate. Leonard snapped to and let us in, looking envious of Declan. Declan took the car to the workers to wash and polish as we talked to Leonard. "How's the new job working out, Leonard?" Leonard said, "My folks call me Leo, in case you wanted to also. It's going great, I think the crew is looking forward to getting promoted as well, so they are working harder by the day." Stephan asked Leo to walk with him, and I left him to it. I went to the gallery with Declan and had him order lunch for everyone as he knew what they liked. He ordered fast food, and I chuckled because it would be like Stephan had been stabbed in the eye. I asked if Leo had a candidate in mind as his replacement. "I feel as though I should recommend Huey, I mean Johnny Jones, but Arnie Schwartz is a better choice." I told him, "Good choice, and so you can keep Johnny's loyalty, tell him that you want him to do special duty in the gallery, and it comes with a raise of 10 percent." I chimed in, "Lunch is set up on the roof. Call the troops to eat." I walked up with Stephan, wanting to see the look on his face as he saw the food laid out. This was going to be priceless. Stephan prepared for a tasting of culinary delights and got Burger King Whoppers and fries. He looked at me and frowned, but said nothing. I served him (almost like a dare), and he unwrapped the burger and fries. He almost bit into it, but since one of the boys was late and he didn't get any, Stephan kindly shared (all of it) with the lad. He stared me down, and I had to laugh (I knew that Robin was gonna be walking bow-legged in the morning).

Morning came too soon, and my prediction came to fruition. It seems Batman doesn't like fast food either (note to self, place the order myself from now on). Breakfast was light, Stephan had his eggs scrambled, two slices of toast, and a rasher of bacon. Mary couldn't wait, so she got the lion's share. Winnie got mine so she wouldn't steal Mary's portion. We loaded up the Bentley, got Declan to drive (Poor Bill probably thinks we don't trust him). We arrived at the warehouse, collected Leo, and off we went to the clothier. We got to park in front of the store (I think they reserved the spot for us) and took Declan and Leo inside. Declan knew what was in store, but Leo was nervous. Edward almost fell over a patron as he ran to us (He wasn't missing this commission). We showed him his next victim, and Leo was shooed into the changing rooms. The best part of the day came next, yes, the silk boxer briefs. Leo was shy and awkward at first until we applauded his fitted attire (he had NOTHING to be ashamed of; that boy was built like a brick house). Did

I mention he carried a sack of family jewelry that was barely contained? Leo started getting into it when the shirts and trousers arrived, and by the time the suits appeared, he was modeling as though he was being paid for it. We paid the bill, Edward just took the clothes away as he knew to deliver them, but Leo seemed let down. Stephan let Declan give him the news, "One should never carry parcels when delivery is an option." I laughed, and Stephan smiled as he nodded at Leo (mind blown). Declan asked where we were going next, and Stephan smiled at him. "Yes, boss," and Declan drove to the dealership. Leo entered the showroom with us behind him, and he asked if he should retrieve something for us, like parts for the Bentley. "What do you drive Leo?' Leo looked at Declan, then us and sheepishly said, "A used Camry, why?" Stephan called over the salesman (who was waiting for his cue) and took Leo to see the Mercedes and Maserati. I placed him in a nice Mercedes and he sat frozen, afraid to speak. "Well, another one with no words. Wrap it up for Leo," Leo asked why, and again Declan answered, "It would not serve the bosses to show up in lesser vehicles given your new position." He animated at that and went over every gizmo in the car. "Do you mean it, boss?" I nodded, and Stephan went to sign the papers.

Back to the warehouse, dropped off Leo and Declan, took us home. "How was the drive, Declan?" Declan declared that it was the best car he had ever driven. "Good, I want a new one as the mats got dirty." I wondered who was to get mine, as Stephan always got a matching set for us. I asked Stephan about my Bentley, and he said, "What makes you think I'm buying you one?" I looked straight into those blue eyes and retorted, "Never mind then," and turned to leave. Stephan grabbed my butt and said, "I was thinking about Rita for the other one. Did you really think I'd let you be seen in an old used car?" I had to hug and kiss my guy then (I hope Rita likes silver).

I asked Declan when we got home if he had a passport, and he said no. "Well, we have to cure that. How will we get you to England, Italy, Fiji, and wherever else we go?" Declan stared, amazed at that statement. "Yes, Declan, we want security wherever we go, and you're it. Tomorrow we'll go to the post office and get it situated. Ask your mom for your birth certificate, and don't forget your license." Declan answered, "Yes,, boss, I mean Carl. I'll call her right now." About five minutes later, the doorbell rang. Since I was passing through, I answered the door and found a handsome young man there. I asked his name, and he said, "I'm Davin Meyers, Declan's brother. Mom wanted me to deliver the paperwork he requested. Is he here?" I smiled; this kid didn't know me. "One moment, sir, let me get him. You can wait in the atrium through those doors to your left." I turned to get him and saw Declan entering from the kitchen. I motioned him over to me and whispered in his ear what had just transpired. He smiled, and I told him to just play along. He was all in. We entered the atrium,, and I announced him, "Master Declan, this is Davin Meyers for you." Davin came over,, and Declan had a hard time keeping in character. "That will be all, Carl." I turned and left. I wish I had been a fly on the wall when he disclosed the identity of the 'door man'. Davin saw me again in the portico and tried to apologize for his behavior. I laughed and told Davin that I had planned it and that Declan had just played along. "I had to kid, it was too good not to." Davin spoke up, "Do I thank you or your husband for the college money?" I said, "It was both of us and it is our pleasure to do some good in the world. Have you decided on Harvard or Yale?" Davin shrugged and said, "To conserve the money, I've decided on taking the transferable credits at a two year college and then going to Harvard for the last two years." I returned with, "smart and handsome, a great combination. If you find yourself in need of more funds, let me know and don't worry your parents, okay?" Davin smiled meekly and said, "Thanks, as you can tell, I don't take compliments well." The kid was blushing fire engine red. I let him go (knowing where Declan's old car was going).

I decided I had to rag on Declan about how handsome his brother was,, and maybe that was why he hadn't introduced him to us earlier. Now it was Declan's turn to blush. Stephan appeared,, and I had to stop my chiding. Stephan asked who was at the door. I replied, "It was Davin Meyer, Declan's brother and the recipient of our new college grant. You should see the kid, he makes Leo look like a rag doll." Declan asked to be excused,, and we waved him off and went to the den to compare notes.

I told Stephan that I was going to get Declan his passport and asked if we should get Davin one as well. "Why not? I can tell you're sweet on the kid." I responded by saying, "I just want the kid to be able to travel like the other kids at Harvard. I know what it's like to feel out of place in a situation where money is concerned. Yeah, that kid was me before you." Stephan told Declan to make sure to get Davin's paperwork in order and have him come along with us. "Tell him we'll pick him up at his parents' house" (Stephan really wanted to meet them to see how they were living). They seemed to be raising good kids. The Bentley, loaded with three bodies, we left for Declan's parents' house. We pulled up in front of a small Cape Cod, painted white, and Stephan noticed that the roof and exterior needed some work. Stephan had Declan announce us and we we were invited in. Davin ran into the kitchen, circa 1950 styling, and sat as we were asked to sit. "I'm David, and that's Jennifer, my wife, and we're the parents of these two scalawags." Stephan stood and shook David's hand. "You have quite the grip. Glad to finally meet you both", said Stephan. He introduced me by simply saying, This is my husband, Carl." David continued the conversation, "We would like to thank you for the finances you provided. With the money you provided, we can add on a room so that Jennifer's mom can move in now that she's retired and getting more frail, to be polite. It's very kind of you to be helping the boys out. I really was wondering how we were going to get it all done, so thank you again." Stephan allowed Jennifer to get a hug in before I stated, "We'd better get along, as the boys have appointments for their passports, and I don't recommend being late." The guys got into the Bentley,, and Stephan decided to drive, so I claimed shotgun and off we went.

"Sirs, thank you so much,, but why would I need a passport?" asked Davin. Declan gave Davin the stare of death as if saying, "Don't look a gift horse in the mouth. Don't jinx it. Just roll with it. Don't question your benefactor." I turned sideways and said, "Because you'll probably be traveling in the future, and as Declan will be traveling, why not set you up also?" Davin let it drop quickly and said no more. About an hour later, the task was done, and we asked if the boys wanted something to eat. "Sure, there's an Arby's around the corner." Stephan stared at me, and I gave my counteroffer, "How about Italian? You like Italian food, don't you? Stephan knows this darling restaurant, and they cater to your every wish." The boys agreed, and Stephan smirked as he drove past Arby's. We got a booth near the kitchen, and Stephan said to the Maitre'd, "I'd like the chef special, the boys look hungry, so we'll start with the antipasto and rolls, thank you." Our waiter appeared and filled the glasses with wine and set the bottle on the table, no questions asked. Declan saw the label and asked, "Isn't this a bottle from your vineyard boss?" Stephan nodded, and Davin whipped his head around to his brother to see what to do next. Declan raised his glass to toast us, and Davin followed suit. We clanked the glasses and took a strong sip. The food started with antipasto with all the meats, cheeses, and relish items and hot rolls fresh from the oven. Davin dug in, Declan waited to see how we approached it, and was soon knee deep in delicacies. The boys decimated the tray before the actual food arrived and felt bloated, but gave their plates a good old college try at finishing them. We had plenty to take home for later, as we knew that the overstuffed feeling would hurt later. Davin finished his, and Declan came in a close second. We got doggie bags, and Mary and Winnie would probably get it all.

We got Davin home and later talked to Declan about his parents' home. "Dad wants to add the room in the back for grandma because she has a hard time getting around. I know he actually wanted to save for a vacation, but that's out now because the priorities have changed." I asked where they had wanted to go, and he said, "They had wanted to go to see some equatorial island, Fiji, I believe. It was to be their twenty-fifth wedding anniversary gift to each other." Stephan looked at me, and I nodded quietly. "When is your grandmother due to move in?" "Well, not until after the room is built. So, six months or so. That's if they can finish on time." Stephan said, "Can you assist me in a covert plan to help your parents?" Declan nodded and started, "First, Carl, call our contractor and get him over there after they leave on vacation. Declan, motivate them to accept a free trip to Wakaya Island, yes, our island, and they can go by the family bus. Do they have passports?" Declan shook his head no. "Well, we'll get them their passports as well. I'll set up the appointments. Now, as for the house, a new roof, new siding, new windows, and an open concept, so if your grandmother needs a wheelchair, she will be able to get around easier. A new bathroom. Anything else that you can think of?" Declan tried not to look shocked and asked, "Can you afford all this? It would be wonderful and I'm sure that they'd appreciate it very much but that's a lot to do on their budget." Stephan looked at him and said, "Just believe when I tell you, I or we (looking at me) can and will afford it." Declan ended the conversation with, "When do we start?"

September rolled around, Davin left for college, and Leo started his college course for PI school. We shipped off David and Jennifer to Wakaya (yes, we informed the staff that they were coming). We went to our new project and watched the renovation weekly. They started by packing up the interior, removing and replacing the roof with solar power-gathering tiles. The siding went next, but it had to wait until the permits were attained to get the addition done. The entire project took about six weeks (I hope the folks were enjoying themselves on the island). We let them come home and sent the limousine to get them from the airport. They arrived and stepped out onto their new driveway. "What happened? Is this even our house? How, why?" I went with Stephan to our newest 'family additions,' and Declan led the way to the house. Jennifer entered first and stopped in her tracks. David joined her and looked around. For a moment, everyone held their breath, waiting for someone to talk. Jennifer teared up and used David's shoulder as a towel. David let her tears flow as he said, "There's no amount of thanks to show our appreciation. Why is there a door where the window was?" Declan led his father to it and said, "Open the door and find out." David grabbed Jennifer's hand, and they entered together. Inside, they found a bedroom, a sitting area, and a sliding glass door to a newly installed patio with a bathroom attached. "Declan said that he had wanted to work with us to get everything ready for Jen's mom. I hope this is enough." David started to say something, but Jen said, "It's more than I could have dreamed of. She's going to love it."

David asked how much the bill was and that he would sign over the money to cover it. "This is our gift to you, just enjoy it." Declan hugged his parents and let them settle in. We took our leave and David and Jen stood at the door waving goodbye. Declan drove home and I could see tears of joy in his eyes that he had made this possible for them. I asked Declan about his brother. "How's college going so far for Davin?" Declan said great and dropped the subject. "What's the matter, Declan? Usually you're talkative, but now nothing. What's up?" "I really don't want to say anything to ruin the moment. Okay, Davin thinks you're being nice to my parents and him so you can seduce him. There, I said it. It's out in the open. He likes what you're doing for him but he's waiting for the other shoe to drop." I realized that my harmless flirting was being taken wrong. "Oh my god, I'm so sorry. I thought he might like being appreciated. I have no other intentions, I love only Stephan. I do like to gist and kid around but I NEVER meant any harm. Please bring him around next time he's home so I can clear it up." Declan said ok but I knew that I had to fix it quick. That poor kid thought I was a predator. I went to Stephan for advice and he said, "That's what you get when you don't know your audience. Do you want me to intercede on your behalf. You know I'm pretty good at that, remember when I had to make the king of France and the Pope come to terms? That was much tougher than this little misunderstanding."

Stephan asked Declan to drive him into town and said nothing to me about it. They were gone most of the morning, and when they returned, I saw them talking, joking, and Declan looked happy again. I waited until Stephan came in the house and Declan was parking the car in the garage. "What's up?" Stephan looked at me and said, "It's all fixed. Davin is happier now and Declan has his sense of humor back. That's what you wanted, isn't it?" I hung my head and said, "Yeah, but I wanted him to know I felt that way." Stephan said that I could make it up to him with a massage so he led the way and I followed, knowing my guy had my back.

Thanksgiving came and went. The house got ready for Christmas, and we all joined in. Bobbie had started walking (with help). The three sisters were filling out and looked more like Alfred now. (Don't know why, but I still miss the old guy. Albert and Julia told us over Thanksgiving that next Christmas, there would be an addition to the house, a girl if the results were right. I asked Bob when he was gonna get a playmate for Bobbie, and he said, "Never, I got snipped. I don't need another at my age." We both laughed loudly, and that brought the dogs in, and then Bobbie was looking for Daddy. Life was never going to be boring around the house. Christmas invitations went out, and the 'bus' got called into action. Davin got home from college and came to visit Declan. I saw them together and told Declan to take the Bentley and take his brother to lunch on me. They asked if I wanted to join them, but knowing their taste, I politely declined. I think Davin took that as a sign that I was stand-offish now. Declan elbowed his brother, and they took my silver Bentley and off they went. Anthony and Eddie arrived the week before Christmas, and Hunter and Junior came in a few days later. I invited Declan's family to join our celebration, hoping that it would bridge the divide that I had created and that Stephan had fixed. Christmas day came, the kids got their presents, and I made sure that 'Santa' had presents for the staff, friends, family, and the Meyers (Yes, grandma came also). The dinner was over and above the usual fantastic affair. The kids ate first, then the parents ate (We sent the kids to the atrium to play, and we had a sitter to keep everything on an even keel). Feast of the seven fishes, Italian cookies, red, white, and Holiday wine flowed. Harold, Jaime, and Dale cooked specialties from their regions. Tony Jr.'s wines were a hit.

We thanked our new 'family' and handed out around 100 envelopes. Jen brought us a gift as well. She had Stephan, and I opened it after dinner. It was a specialty afghan with our names stitched in.

Stephan accepted it for us, and I hugged it out with Jen. David got a handshake from Stephan, and the boys each said thanks for their presents. I was introduced formally to grandma, "This is my mother, Violet Thomas." "Nice to finally meet you, I or we hope you like your room." Violet simply said, "Thank you, son. I was wondering how it got done so fast." She called me son, although I was 104 and she was 63. I let out a small chuckle and returned to Stephan.

Christmas was in the rear view mirror and onto New Year's. We decided to stay home this year and do our usual quiet dinner and night in front of the fireplace, toasting each other and bringing in 2072 with a tender kiss (wrapped only in fur, wink, wink, fade to black). I hoped that it would be a quiet year, and I think God took that as a challenge. It started as I had hoped, quiet and calm. It took a nasty detour around Easter when, out of the blue, Aaron had a stroke, and Dahlia officially retired so she could tend to him. Rita added Dahlia's duties to her duties and took on the secretary role as well as the house manager. Then flea season hit, and it was all we could do to keep it at bay. Spring in Baltimore was warm, so we decided to make a tradition of taking the warehouse staff to the camp. The guys had a great time, and we got all the eye candy we could ask for. Sun, sand, and lots of bare flesh (winner, winner, chicken dinner). One of the boys got a jellyfish sting that we had to get fixed at the hospital. He had no insurance, so Stephan paid the bill.

Summer arrived, and the plane needed repairs, so flying to Italy was postponed. I suggested flying first class, and you would have thought that I had stabbed Stephan. He gave me dagger eyes and said, "I'm not lowering my standards at my age. You can go, but I'll wait for the private plane." This was a new thing for Stephan, as I had never known him to be this unreasonable. I wanted to ask why, but thought better of it. He would let me know in his good time, and I was okay with that. It turned out that a new virus was taking over Europe, like the Spanish flu in the early 1900's and the COVID in 2020 (had it been that long since America shut down, wow).

I silently prayed that things would get better, and I guess my prayers were answered as the plane got fixed, Aaron regained about half of his functioning (Dahlia was happy at that), and everyone had their passports. I asked Stephan if Fiji was okay, and he said yes. I told Declan to prepare for a trip, and he asked where. "Fiji, my boy. Is this your first trip away?" Declan nodded yes and then asked if Davin could accompany us. "If he wants, there's plenty of room on the plane." Declan took out his cell phone and texted for all he was worth. I heard a ping, and Declan said, "Davin would be happy to join us. It sure will be a blessing for mom and dad. They have their hands filled with grandma." I thought for a second and asked if they would like a caregiver to spot them and give them some respite. "Thanks, but that gets expensive, and you've already given them so much." I calmly said, "Put them on the phone, I'll talk to them and let them decide." Declan dialed and handed me the phone, "Hi David, Carl here. Declan and Davin are coming with us to Fiji. I had an idea and wanted to run it past you and Jen. If money wasn't an issue, could you use a care giver for Violet?" "That would be perfect, but it is an issue so…" I interrupted him at that point and said, "I'll call a good reputable agency and get her started. How about four hours a day to start and see how it goes." David replied that it was going to make their lives a lot easier. "Consider it done, now here's your son." I returned the phone to Declan and went to find Stephan and Rita.

The following week, Violet was sorted (to everyone's satisfaction), and we were airborne. Davin and Declan were excited and looking all over as we soared to the island of Fiji. Stephan and I slept because we knew how long it was going to take. We landed, took the car to the pier, and boarded the boat to our island. Tom and Tory (yes, he took Tom up on his offer) steered to the island. Tory, not knowing about the boys, said, "New meat for the island?" I quickly dispelled that idea and championed for the boys. Tom whispered to Tory and Tory apologized, saying, "Sorry, bosses, I thought that since they were with you, well, that they were gay too." Declan and Davin shook their heads no, and we all had a good laugh. Thank god that went well, I was nervous there for a moment. Wakaya came into view, and I said, "There she is, our island." Davin said, "You mean you own a home on the island, right?" Declan shook his head as I replied, "No, we actually own the entire island. It came complete with a house, but it's all ours." Davin was taken aback, shocked, and wondering how we managed to have so much wealth. Declan gave a stare that meant 'let it go, bro, and just enjoy'. The dock appeared, and the staff was on hand to assist us. Allen and Darren took the luggage and took the boys to their rooms. Bruce and Jaime took us to the house to confer about issues and budgets. Tom and Tory tended to the boat. The boys got settled and found us in the kitchen. Jaime asked if they wanted sandwiches or something more filling. The boys opted for sandwiches so they could investigate the island. We told them to have Tom and Tory show them around, as they'd get lost. "The island may not seem big, but it is." They dashed off to find Tom as we concluded the meeting. Jaime asked us what we wanted to eat, "Something light, after all, we just landed after 19 hours on the road, so to speak." Jaime suggested pasta primavera. "Sounds good, how about you, Stephan?" He turned and said that the pasta would be sufficient. Jaime hopped to it and said that dinner would be in about thirty minutes. Stephan grabbed a couple of glasses and a bottle of wine and popped the cork.

"Carl, what are your feelings about Tory? I just have this inkling that something's off with him." I looked at Stephan and said, "So it isn't just me. I think you're right. Should I have Bob and Albert check him out?" Stephan nodded and said, "Just keep it between us. If I'm wrong, then no one will be the wiser." I took out my phone and made the call. The return call came after we got into bed. "Boss, the information you want is being sent to your messaging app as we speak. It ain't good, and you can thank Albert for the new technology search." Again, Stephan hit the nail on the head. Poor Tom, I really was hoping for good news as I didn't want to lose Tom, but Tory had to go. It seemed that Tory was dealing drugs and using our boat now to procure and sell.

Stephan called Tom and Tory to the office the next day, with Bruce there and me as witnesses and muscle (on Bruce's part). "Tom, it has come to my attention that Tory has been dealing drugs, and we can't have that. Tory, you are being terminated effective immediately, and Tom, I'm sorry, but he is leaving now. You can bring him his things later." Tom looked at Stephan and then Tory, "Tory, you said you gave that crap up. Are you still dealing?" Tory started to say something and just flipped us the finger. "I don't need this job anyway, and Tom, you were just my patsy. You're not even good in bed." At that, Tom wasted no time in decking Tory (out of hurt more than anger). Tory mentioned suing, and Stephan stepped in, "Think twice, little man, before you take me on. I've never been bested, and I can make you disappear. Now move that sorry ass, and Bruce will take you to shore. Boys, would you mind accompanying Bruce so that Tory will behave?" Declan and Davin said in unison, "Sure thing, boss." I snapped around and looked quizzically at Davin, thinking When did we hire him'. Tory left, and I went to Tom so that he could let it out. "I thought he loved me. What a fool I was, thinking he would change for me," I said nothing, just letting him vent. It took time, but he said, "I'm really sorry that I brought that trouble to your island. Does this mean that I'm fired too?" I shook my head and said, "Tom, you weren't doing anything wrong. You've only been loyal and great with the landscaping. So no, you can stay if you want, but it's up to you." Tom thanked me and left me in the garden with my thoughts (Tom Taking time to patch that hole in his heart).

My thoughts turned to Stephan and how he handled the situation. I guess I could look all eternity and wouldn't find another like him. He was truly unique among men. I prayed silently to my God, thanking him for my life. The moon came out around the cloud, and the garden took on an ethereal pale glow (I guess he heard me). I turned in and wrapped Stephan around me. A bear hug to spoon in. Sleep enveloped my thoughts, and I bathed in Stephan's warmth. Tonight eased away as the moon meandered through the night sky.

Morning and the boys were at the table with Jaime as we walked in, wearing only boxer briefs. The boys were a little amazed as this was the first time they had seen us like that. Coffee was handed to Stephan, and we said, "Here we dress very casually. Feel free if you want, everyone else does." Declan didn't bother, but Davin took it as permission and dropped his pants. "This is great, wow, you guys really know how to live." Jaime smiled and plated the Eggs Benedict. Davin kept at Declan until he gave in and 'freed' himself on the island. Tom took an interest in the boys and asked about their leanings so as not to cross any lines. "I don't know, we never asked." Tom asked if I minded if he indeed asked them, and I said, "As long as you accept the answers, then no, I don't mind." Tom grinned and went to the garden. He found Davin first and tried to get into a conversation, hoping to get a feeling about his sexuality. Davin came on very straight, so Tom excused himself and started the pruning of the trees. About an hour later, Declan crossed his path and asked about the flora on the island. "I can give you a private tour and explain the plants and their fruits." Declan smiled at Tom and accepted the private tour offer.

Tom asked when Declan would have time so they could take their time, and he said, "Well, I think that tomorrow the guys are going into town, so that would be the best time." Tom agreed and said, "Tomorrow at ten. See you then." They turned away, and both smiled as they left one another. Lunch was announced, and Jaime set out an island affair, fresh fruit courtesy of the island, mango, papaya, bananas, along with produce from the garden and smoked meats from the smokehouse. Sandwiches were made with abandon, and drinks were served. The boys opted for soda and Stephan, and I opted for private stock wine, a nice fruity white Muscato. Discussions became plans for the following day in Fiji, and Bruce was given the itinerary so he could determine our best route. Davin was all in, but Tom and Declan opted to stay behind. Allen and Darren opted in, so the day was locked in. We decided to have a beach day and spent the afternoon in the sand. The boys collected shells and driftwood while we soaked in the sun. Evening crept up on Allen and us, and we made a fire in the fire pit. Music drifted in on the waves from Fiji, and the crackles coming from the fire were the only sounds being heard. Even the boys were quiet, having had a long day. We left the beach as the fire became a bed of embers and the boys turned in soon after. Allen extinguished the embers and walked back to the house.

Morning arrived, and we ate light, then went to dress for the island. By nine thirty, we were on the dock waiting for the staff. The boat left the dock at nine forty-five, and we set out for Fiji. Meanwhile, on the island, Tom waited for his guest to begin the tour. Declan showed up in a tank top and briefs with flip-flops. Tom wore board shorts and a golf shirt with socks and hiker boots. Declan blushed, realizing he was underdressed. Tom said, "You're fine, it's all preference here. Heck, you could run barefoot and naked and no one would care. Let's get started." They took the winding path through the garden and into the timbered area. Tom described the trees and bushes and pointed to a particular spot, "And here's where I found the bosses' clothes after one of their interludes. Yep, they got it on right against this tree." Tom looked at Declan for a response, but Declan's body had already given up the goods. Tom smiled and said, "Looks like there's more wood in the forest than the trees." Declan tried to hide the fact that his 'wood' looked like English Oak. Tom just smiled and continued the tour. Declan finally spoke, "Are you trying to embarrass me or just ribbing me because you think I can take a little joke or two?" Tom said, "I'll let you decide, Woody." Declan replied, "Oh good, now I have another nickname, when does it stop?" Tom asked, "What's your other nickname?" Declan said, "They call me Louie, and I have two friends back home that they call…" "Let me guess, Huey and Dewey, right?" Declan countered, "How did you know? I don't even know what that means." Tom leaned back against a tree and laughed full-hearted. Declan studied Tom's body as he sweated in the sun spot. "See anything you like, kid?" Declan quickly looked away, ashamed that he got caught staring. Tom led the way to a spring-fed pond. Declan watched as Tom disrobed and jumped, nude, into the pond. "Come on in, the water's warm, and you've been sweating a lot lately." Declan hemmed and hawed for a few seconds and then said, "I don't have my swimsuit with me." Tom laughed and said, "Don't let that stop you." Declan decided to join Tom in the water, dropped his clothes near Tom's, and backed into the water for modesty's sake. The problem was that Tom enjoyed that more but said nothing (as things were going well up to then). Declan relaxed in the water, and Tom soon joined him near the shore. "Just take in the sun, it's really rejuvenating." Declan had to admit that it felt fantastic, and he melted into the rippled water. He let his guard down and asked how Tom felt about having gay bosses. "I'm okay with it. You see, I'm gay also." Declan then said, "What's it like with other men? I mean, like kissing, is it different? And how do gay men have sex? Do they actually get together or do they just help the other guy get off?" Tom asked gently, "Do you really want to know? I will answer all your questions, but you have to promise to not take offense to what I'm about to say." Declan said, "Okay, I promise. It's just that Stephan and Carl, Anthony and Eddie, and Hunter and Junior seem so happy together." Tom said, "Okay, as far as kissing goes, it's the same as with boys and girls, the more experienced you are, the better the kiss. Gay men have normal sex, but with different areas of the body. We have what's known as a top and a bottom. The top is more assertive and penetrates his partner. The bottom is more passive and gets penetrated. You have to remember that we have an erogenous zone in our butt that women don't. When it's engaged, both guys get beyond excited and climax. That's the story."

Declan was listening intently as Tom spoke. "Can I ask a personal question?" Tom nodded and said, "If you want to know, I'm a top and an experienced kisser." Declan said, "What if I asked you to kiss me so I'd know the difference?" Tom leaned over and cupped Declan's head in his hands and went in for a deep and elongated kiss. When the two broke, Declan had stars in his eyes and said, "I've never felt that way with a girl, wow, just wow." The two lone islanders took the rest of the afternoon to answer the rest of Declan's questions.

"We'd better get back as the last boat to the island is due in half an hour." Declan and Tom dressed, and they returned to the house, hand in hand. The boat arrived on schedule, and the lovebirds helped in taking the supplies to the house. I asked Tom how his day was, and he smiled at me, and that smile said everything. I joined Stephan, and we went to the house. Davin was all talk at the dinner table, describing his adventures in Fiji. "I really need to thank you, guys, for this. My classmates only got to go to Miami. Boy, are they going to be jealous." Declan tried to shut him down, but I just told him to let Davin go as I felt the same way on my first trip with Stephan. "If I remember right, it was England and Anthony was there at Stephan's estate. It was overwhelming to me, but nothing to Stephan." Davin continued his saga until dinner was over.

Stephan and I took our usual Bourbon and cigars to the patio and sat looking out over the trees, watching the waves come in and listening to the sounds of the island. Note to self, memorialize this in my journal. I asked if Bruce had seen Tory anywhere, and Stephan simply said, "I think he went to New Jersey, but I could be wrong."

Our time in Wakaya came to an end, and we prepared for the return trip. Goodbyes were said, and I caught a kiss out of the corner of my eye. It seems Tom was going to be lonely again, but this time it could be rectified by travel. Declan was quiet on the return to Fiji and only took orders as needed, and boarded the plane with a final look towards the island (oh great, now I had two lonely guys pining for each other when they just started a relationship). While waiting for the plane to lift off, I called back to the island and talked to Tom. I asked if he could find time to come to Baltimore and redo our gardens. He agreed on the spot, and I felt a little better. I ended the call and turned to Declan and said, "I wonder if you could help Tom with our gardens in your spare time when he comes this month." Declan's reaction was more pronounced than I anticipated. He smiled widely and said that he was looking forward to it (another issue sorted).

Baltimore never looked so good, and I couldn't wait to see the girls and Bobbie. I walked into the house, and chaos ensued. Greetings and gifts all over. I let the boys go see their parents and gave them a gift for their grandmother, Violet. It was a flower vase and a journal with a card that said, "A place to keep your flowers, and memories, all our best, Stephan and Carl." In the tradition of the early 2000's, Violet sent us a thank you card with a quick note, "Thanks from your favorite lady." Calm returned after an hour or two. We had a small, intimate dinner with the house people and turned in. With the girls at our feet, we cuddled and fell deep into sleep.

Morning in Baltimore, I went to the balcony and stretched in the morning light. Stephan woke when the girls stirred. He went to shower, and I unleashed the girls upon the world, and they bounded down to their breakfast. I joined Stephan, and we washed each other's backs. Shower finished, we dried off and dressed rather quickly as we had eggs to save from the dogs. The hollandaise sauce was just finished as we arrived in the kitchen, and Harold plated the eggs and set them in front of us. Rita mentioned that we got there rather quickly, and we just looked at each other and laughed, remembering our time from Trudy to Judy and then Dahlia (almost one hundred years of continuous threats).

Declan and Albert appeared and got coffee to start their day. Bob and Elizabeth came in next, carrying Bobbie (who wanted me to hold him). He fussed until I reached out, and he fell into my arms. Raspberries to the belly, and he was all better. The kitchen was filling up fast.

Our dishes were set on the floor for the dogs, and we left the area. Declan called me aside and asked about when Tom might be arriving. I gave him Tom's number (knowing all along he had it) and said to call and find out if he was so interested (meaning I knew his secret). Declan took the paper and left. I already knew he'd be flying in a couple of days, as the fall was upon us, and that was planting season here in Baltimore. I watched to see if he was calling Tom and caught a bit of the opening conversation. "Hi Tom, Carl gave me your number to see when you're coming." Tom was heard to say, "In 2 days, Woody." I had to leave as I heard those words. So he had a new nickname. I almost revealed myself by laughing, but held it in just long enough to get a bit away.

It had to be the longest two days in Declan's life, knowing that his secret lover was coming. He offered to go to the airport and collect our landscaper. I nodded, and he left like Hermes to Olympus. It was weird that it took ten minutes to get to the airport and an hour to return, hmm, oh well. The unkempt duo arrived as I had the dogs out. Declan's demeanor seemed lighter and more enthusiastic than before. Tom was upbeat, also. I wonder why. I went to Tom and asked if he had found a person to tend the island in his absence, and he reported, "I got my brother, Matthew, to do it. He needed a job and is almost as good as me." I asked if that meant he could stay longer, and he added with a smile,

"As long as you want me, boss." Declan saw Tom with me and came over and Tom said, "Hey Woody, I mean Louie, I mean Declan, how's it going?" Declan knew he was busted, and I said, "Just kiss the man.

He's traveled half way around the world and we all know you have the hot's for him." Declan shrugged and went for it. "Fine, now get to work, you two. And by the way, Woody, Tom says he can stay for a while." I left the guys, smirking all the way.

Stephan saw it all play out and asked if I was finally satisfied, and I grinned and nodded. "You know that we'll have to get a new gardener for Wakaya." I said, "Way ahead of you. Matthew's already there taking care of it." Stephan snorted, "And just who is this Matthew?" I told him that it was Tom's younger brother and that he needed a job, and since Tom recommended him, I took the chance. "Just remember what you just said because I'm holding you responsible for any problems ahead." I sidled up to Stephan and said he could 'punish me' if it didn't work out. "Just remember what you said." A quick kiss and we went for a nap, seeing them together was so 'tiring'.

Anthony and Eddie dropped us a line and said that they wouldn't be available for Christmas. Stephan came to me and asked if I wanted a quick trip to England. I jumped at the chance. I went to Declan and asked if he was ready for a trip to England, and he balked a little. I asked if maybe Davin could go with us, and he texted him immediately. Davin must have had speed texting because the response came back instantly, "Ask them when they need me and I'll work it out with the professors." Declan relaxed, knowing that we were willing to substitute. He wanted as much time with Tom as possible. I had Declan text Davin the agenda, and he got the permissions and work required for the missing time. He said he would have to do a couple of Zoom sessions with the lecture teacher, but that would be minimal. We left on Friday and arrived at Heathrow hours later. Davin helped with our luggage and anything else that was not taken care of. The limousine was waiting at the private hangar, and he was impressed with the 'over the top' accommodations we received. He opened the limousine door and let us get in. He followed behind and marveled at the inside. Stephan was kinda 'meh' about it, and I was about the same, but Davin wanted to inspect everything and asked to open the moon roof. Stephan acquiesced, and the world appeared to Davin. He stood up, stuck his head and torso out of the car, and took in the surroundings. As we got close to the estate, I tugged his pant leg, and he returned to his seat. "Bosses, this is unreal. Thank you so much for letting me take Declan's place. Call me anytime." We nodded as the limousine turned into the long drive. Trees bordered the road up to the main entrance, and Davin noticed someone at the door.

Stephan said, "That would be Eddie, the Lady of the house. Try to be nice, Davin." Davin noted the label, 'lady' of the house. The limousine stopped, and Eddie opened the door, and Davin almost tumbled out. Eddie took an extra look as we got out, and it was hugs all around. Davin was respectful but careful in this situation. "Where's Anthony?" Eddie said, "In the office, making more money, where else?" We left the staff to get the luggage and told Davin to come with us. Eddie stood by the open door as Davin entered the portico. He stopped, looked around, and said, "Do all your relatives live like this?" I nodded to Davin and let Eddie do his usual tour with Davin. We opted to go find Anthony and said that he was in good hands. We found Anthony, and he waved us in. "Hold that stock, they just made an acquisition, and that's why their money on hand is so low. Give it a month and watch it explode once the dust settles." Anthony ended the call and came over, "Welcome, grandfathers. You look well. Was Eddie there to greet you?" I told him that we had brought a new kid with us and that Lady Eddie was giving him the tour. "I guess that means that we have time then," He led us to the patio and gave us both a cigar. We smoked as we awaited the duo and saw them coming from the formal gardens. Eddie looked happy, Davin looked impressed, and Anthony asked if we wanted supper, as it was around 9:30 pm. I said I could eat, Davin said he was starving, and Stephan said he could pick a little.

Supper in England, Davin was about to be surprised by the blandness of England's cuisine. I had bubble and squeak and blood sausages. Stephan had a mince pie, and Davin tried everything. After supper, he whispered to me, "Is this the norm here in England, because the food in Fiji was much better?" I whispered back, "Wait till you taste the food in Italy and France, it'll knock your socks off." As we left the dining room and entered the den, Eddie pointed out the artworks. "These are the original masterpieces, by the way." Davin looked at me for guidance, and I nodded yes that these were indeed original and not replicas. "They must be worth a fortune. I've never seen art like this before. I've seen your paintings in the Baltimore house, but didn't think they were real, are they?" I nodded yes, and the kid fell silent (his internal mind was trying to calculate our worth and came up empty).

Davin had just let our world into his, and he shook at the extremeness of examples of wealth. Anthony asked Davin his name, and Davin said, "I'm Davin Meyers, and I'm here to assist your folks with any needs they might have while abroad." Anthony blew his mind by saying, "Stephan is my great-great-grandfather." Davin looked at Stephan and then at Anthony and asked, "How? He looks the same age as you. Am I crazy, or did I just hear you wrong?" Anthony was about to explain that he was 375 years old when Stephan said, "I'm older than I look." Hopefully, Anthony took the hint and dropped the subject. Davin was shown to his bedroom, and I told Anthony that the kid wasn't aware of our stats. "Hell, Carl is 105, I'm 560, and you're 375. Do you think he can wrap his head around that at 19?" Anthony answered, "I guess you're right. Some things are better left unsaid."

The next day we went to London for some shopping. Davin was in heaven as we let him go on a spending spree with the black card. He felt great, and we took him to a real Italian restaurant in London. He was allowed to drink legally here, so we went bar hopping also. Getting him back to the estate was a joy ride as he started getting queasy, and we thought he might lose it in the limousine. He rallied and made it back, but left his mark in the driveway. He ate little for the rest of the night and turned in early. Morning came, and so did Davin's hangover. We suggested that it could have been worse, but Davin couldn't fathom it, so we asked for Bacon, buttered toast, eggs sunny side up, and that was enough to send poor Davin to the restroom again.

Davin shaped up after getting the hangover drink and taking a walk in the garden. He came back about the time his color did, and he apologized for his error in judgment. We patted his back and said, "We've all been there, kid. It's been a while, though." He attended to us for the afternoon, and we let him have the evening off. Davin found me on the way to the restroom and asked if he could have a minute of my time. "Sure, kid, what's up?" Davin asked me about what Anthony had said yesterday. "Is it true that Stephan is Anthony's great, great-grandfather?" Do I lie or come clean? I decided to let Stephan handle it as he was more prepared. "I suggest if you want to know more about Stephan and Anthony's relationship, you should ask Stephan." I thought that was a pretty good answer, but the look on Davin's face spoke volumes. He wasn't going to leave it alone. I got to Stephan before Davin did and voiced my concerns. "What if he finds out the truth about us?" Stephan looked at me with those baby blues and said, "I'll take it from here. Thanks for the heads up." I left, but didn't like the look in his eyes.

We finished the week and said our goodbyes, Eddie seeing us off at the door. Davin ensured that we had everything and got in the limousine. "All set, bosses." Stephan grinned, and we went to Heathrow. Wheels up an hour later, and we were off to Baltimore. During the flight, I tried to get some sleep and ended up resting with my eyes closed. I heard Stephan bring up the subject with Davin. I listened intently as the conversation got started. "Davin, you asked a question back at the estate, and I believe that you didn't like the answer. I have nothing to hide, so ask what you really want to know. Just be ready for the answer." Davin hesitated and then said, "If what Anthony said is true, then you'd be over a hundred years old. Your wealth confirms that. I only know that vampires survive that long, but I've seen you eat garlic, food, and drink wine for days. You move around like a human, so what's really the truth?" Stephan simply replied, "First, I'm not a vampire, so let's put that to bed. Next, I, or should I say that Carl and I are wealthy because we invested well and have written many highly successful books. Next, I am 560 years old, and Carl is 105. Anthony is 375 years old. I'm telling you this because you asked and I don't lie. I have no need to." Davin looked at Stephan as though he was joking, but Stephan's eyes told a different tale. "You wanted to know, so there it is out on the table." Davin looked dazed but finally said, "Why would you tell me this. I'm freaking out now. I don't know whether to believe you or not." Stephan called Davin to sit by him and then produced one of the many journals from the 1700's.

"Let me interpret this for you, as it's written in French. 'In the court of King Louie XIV, I received a traveling scroll to present to the Pope. He allowed me to travel through the countryside and to his border under his protection. Rome was to receive me, and I was to have an audience with Pope Clement XI concerning the bull Unigenitus (in response to the Jansenist heresy). Davin looked with enlarged eyes as he listened to Stephan continue. After finishing a few pages, he handed the journal to Davin. Davin kept looking at the journal, then at Stephan. Stephan shrugged and said, "Always be careful what you ask for, you may get it." I was unsure where to go with Davin knowing our deepest secret. Stephan asked how Davin felt knowing our truth. "I should be happy, but now that I know, I feel sorry, privileged, unsure, and several other feelings I can't put words to yet." Stephan said he would only share that knowledge with trusted people, "Heck, your brother doesn't know, and I think that it should stay that way, don't you?" Davin nodded and stood. "Thank you, sirs, for the trust you've shown to me. I won't let you down." He left for his chores, and I said to Stephan, "You know he won't keep it a secret, don't you?" Stephan reassured me that he was in control and that telling Davin that not even his own brother knew would be enough. "He is now in the inner circle, and knowing him and his brother, they will surprise you." "As long as you know what you're doing (as always and ever), I'm okay with it."

With the school year coming to an end, we decided to take the boys back to Europe with us. Stephan asked them if their parents were okay with it, and they had their father call us with the response, "It's alright as long as it won't cost us too much." Stephan assured that it would be on us, and David then said, "Just keep us informed on their whereabouts, as we would like to keep tabs on the boys." That situation dealt with, we prepared for the trip. Phone calls were made, destinations finalized, and the 'bus' readied; we took our leave of Baltimore. The boat came into view, and the boys inquired as to where the first destination was. "I thought you might like a tour of our winery. Then onto Rome and our usual get together with one of my other grandchildren, Stephan Jr., and his partner, Hunter. Then, to the cemetery to place wreaths on my parents' tombs. Then maybe onto Greece, my birthplace." I thought about Russia but thought better of it and said nothing. The bus landed, and we cleared customs as a limousine headed our way. Declan was the first to speak, "You guys sure do know how to live it up. Have you always had money, or did you earn it? I don't mean to pry, but I'm just not used to this kind of treatment." Stephan assured him that we had earned it after 'years of effort'. This got a chuckle out of Davin and a strange look from Declan.

We arrived at the vineyard, and Tony Sr. came to receive us. "Ciao, guys, glad to see you again. It's been too long." I told the boys to expect a feast, and they were still overwhelmed at the amount of food Tony's wife had laid out. Tony Jr. and Dale showed up just as Maria (Tony Sr.'s wife) placed the beginning course on the very large outdoor table. Homemade crusty bread, antipasto with all the frills, and wine, a lot of wine. Conversations continued as the wine poured and two more guests showed, Junior and Hunter. "I asked them to join us, and when I told them you were bringing the boys, they jumped at the chance. Besides, who can resist my Maria's cooking, eh?" Tony Sr. said with a smirk. We all laughed at the flirting going on between these two seniors. Declan took it all in and then started a conversation with Dale about his time in Fiji and how he managed to end up in Italy living on a vineyard. "It's all thanks to these two guys. They're like the pied pipers of romance. Look at Junior and Hunter. Hunter used to be Stephan's personal shopper, and look at him now. Don't forget about Eddie, same thing, and fell for Anthony. You know most of Stephan and Carl's story. It seems that they always find the right people for others. Besides, now that you're family, get ready for the experience of a lifetime," Declan said, "Davin and I are not family to anyone here. I was just a kid making bad decisions when Bob caught us at Stephan's warehouse. "And look where you are now. Eating in a vineyard in Rome with world travelers, being driven around in limousines, and flying in private jets. Enjoy the moment, and you'll probably end up with someone special. "But I'm not gay, not even interested in that sort of thing. "Look at Bob and Elizabeth, Dahlia and Aaron, Albert and Julia, and the list goes on. Being around these guys gives opportunities that you would never have. Just mind your business and follow their lead. No one that I've ever met has been worse off after meeting them." Declan nodded his ascent (not knowing of all the new occupants in New Jersey).

Dinner done, the guys got a personal tour of the winery and the samples of existing and new flavors. Declan and Davin were highly impressed and looked puzzled at the others as they just took it in stride. Tony Jr. and Dale invited them all to their winery the following day, and after looking at Stephan for a cue, accepted. Returning to the guest rooms, Stephan started getting frisky as I readied myself for bed. "I will need a shower if you're thinking what I believe you're thinking." Stephan smiled that gorgeous smile and said, "The shower water is already heated." Who was I to turn down a deal like that, it would be a good sedative.

The farm's resident rooster heralded the break of day, and I watched as my husband arose from bed looking like a mature Adonis, still beautiful after all our years together. To think that he found me as a straight middle-aged man, poor as a church mouse, eating bologna sandwiches, and then to be gifted this surreal life that most people could only dream about. I knew internally that he would outlive me, and since I was being introspective and maudlin, it gave me pause and made me think about my own will and estate. I called our lawyer quietly and had a will prepared. Most was left to Stephan, but I left some royalties to Bobbie and a few others. I decided to keep it to myself as I didn't want THAT conversation with Stephan. I knew he would understand and follow my requests, but then he would try to ensure that I lived on forever. I knew my body was slowing, albeit at a snail's pace, but it was indeed aging. Here I was, 105, now that it was 2072, with a body and mind of a fifty-year-old. I took a long, hot shower and dressed to start the day, hopefully keeping my mind too busy to think deep thoughts.

We had breakfast, and Declan and Davin were amazed at the simplicity of breakfast compared to dinner and supper. We had espresso coffee, cheese slices, and grilled artisan bread. Fruit to finish, and off we went to Jr. and Dale's vineyard. We waved goodbye to Tony and Maria and sped off. The boys met us at the gate and ushered us into the winery tasting room. The boys were over the top impressed, and Dale kept them engaged. Tony told us that his vineyard began getting notoriety due to his new creations. He didn't ask for money but hinted that it could fast-track his success. I took Dale aside and asked how much they needed to get moving. "I hate to say anything without Tony here, but between us, we would need about $100,000.00." "Easier said than done, kiddo. I'll have Elizabeth cut a check, or better yet, I'll have you get with her to have it sent electronically." Dale blushed a little but nodded and then came in for a big bear hug.

That settled, we rejoined the group and toured the vineyard. We returned to the main house only to find Junior and Hunter there, enjoying a new flavor of wine. "We thought they kidnapped you all. Junior had the staff prepare a lunch for us all," said Hunter. The boys sat near us, and the others sat across the table. Lunch was as good as dinner was the previous evening. The next few days were spent shopping, and then the main event, going to lay the wreaths. I mentioned to Stephan quietly that Declan was still unaware that our age was beyond his comprehension. "I never lie, and if it comes up, then so be it." As we laid the wreaths in front of the names, Declan looked intently at the dates and looked quizzically back at Stephan. "I don't mean to be rude, but you said that they were your parents, and they died in 1580 and were from Greece, but were interred here. Nothing is making sense, and I'm really confused."

Ever reliable, Stephan replied, "Well, the secret is out with you. I am 560 years old. These were indeed my beloved parents, and they traveled around the known world, but I was born in Greece; they loved Italy the best, so I had them return and, in turn, buried here. Does that answer your question? If you need more time to process that, fine. By the way, Davin already knew." Declan turned to his brother, who simply shrugged his shoulders and continued placing wreaths. Declan asked another question, "So you mean that's why you have amassed such wealth, because you've been alive for centuries?" Stephan smiled that devilish smile and just stated, "Exactly." Declan's mind raced, and I could see Stephan was having fun with this kid. Stephan finally eased the kid's mind by saying, "No, I'm not a vampire (which elicited a giggle from Davin), and yes, I'm mortal as you or Carl. I've been around kings, queens, royalty of every level, and known many prominent people. The paintings you protected and have seen around the compound are real; heck, I even sat for a few myself. I've invested well, leveraged my money to work for me, and that's why I can be so generous to others. This needs to be between us due to security reasons, and I presume that you'll keep these truths private now that you've been allowed into our inner circle." All Declan could do was nod and say, "Your words are safe with me, but I'm not so sure about Davin here." That earned him an elbow to the side and laughs all around from us.

Baltimore beckoned us home, and we returned to the real world. Declan and Davin went home to report in and hand out the gifts they bought (with Stephan's black card). The girls were waiting, and even better, Bobbie came teetering upright towards me. I lifted my little buddy high up and raspberried his tummy. His laughter raised everyone's spirits for a moment. We went in search of Dahlia to inquire about Aaron. "It happened while you were in Italy. He suffered another heart attack, and this time it's bad. He's bedridden and non-verbal now. You can see him if you'd like." We nodded and entered the room. It looked like we were entering a hospital room, and he was hooked up to many wires. At least he knew us and could wave us in. We sat with him and told him of our adventures in Italy. We also told him that he would receive the best care that Baltimore had. He seemed to relax hearing that, so we said our goodbyes and went in search of Elizabeth. She was in the study with mountains of paperwork and receipts. I went to assist her, and Stephan eased out of the room. I found him later in the atrium. I had two cigars and two snifters of brandy for the decompression period. We just sat and held each other's hands. I felt sad and could only imagine how many times Stephan had been here. Words seemed empty and useless, so we kept vigil in silence, glad we had each other.

The following day, Stephan was on the phone getting things sorted, and I was busy paying bills when we were interrupted by the sounds of sobbing. I went to the door of the study and found Dahlia weeping. "He's gone" was all she could get out before breaking down completely. I went to her and held her shaking body as she released a torrent of tears. The house went into mourning. Stephan took the lead and made all the arrangements. I was on guest duty, and Elizabeth was in charge of house duties during this time. The day of the funeral was somber; all of their relatives were in attendance, along with the household. The liturgy was meant to be uplifting, but it consoled no one. People arose to acknowledge his accomplishments and his worth within the family. We were asked to speak, but begged off as we thought the family should control the day. As bad as it was, I could not help but look at Stephan with loving eyes as he stood stoic and handsome above the group.

The following reception was less somber, and people shared intimate moments and funny instances as a celebration of Aaron's life. Stephan took a moment and, in a rare instance, shared a time when we adopted the three sister dogs, and Aaron basically took over the reins, looking out for them and training them (after he had to clean up their housebreaking fiasco). Laughter erupted, and we then knew we'd be alright going forward (laughter has a way of doing that). Leave it to Stephan to lead the way out of darkness. I got up to get a drink and felt an unfamiliar stiffness in my legs, but I didn't let on. Maybe old age had raised its ugly head to let me know I was not gifted the Methuselah gene.

Days went by, and 2073 came into view. The house readied itself for the holidays, and Elizabeth took on most of the duties. Dahlia tended to ascribe Stephan's newest book. I went shopping and had another episode, so I cut my trip short. Declan noticed and asked about it. "It's nothing, probably slept wrong," I said, but thought, " Note to self, see a doctor. By this time, Chuck Tidwell (the doctor) had succumbed to old age. Ironically, he had made the magic pills that Eddie and I used. I needed a new doctor and reached out to Hunter and asked which one he had used while in the States. Hunter didn't quite remember if they were still alive, but gave me the name of Oswald Tucker. I looked him up through the registry and found him. The profile stated that he was in his late seventies but still practicing part-time. I made the call, and he actually answered his phone. "Hello, my name is Carl Omega, and Hunter Borgia gave me your name. I am looking for a new doctor as mine is deceased." The doc laughed and asked if maybe I'd like a younger doctor, as he was alone in his practice and only worked two to three days a week. I told him that was okay, and he said, "Then come in on Thursday, and I'll sort you out."

Thursday came, and I told Stephan I had to run an errand and set off. "Let Declan drive you so he can get out for a while." I think he wanted to pump the kid later to see why the secrecy. My guy always steps ahead of me. I replied, "I can drive myself, I'm looking for gifts, and I don't want his prying eyes seeing in case some are for him." Stephan waved me off with a peck on the cheek. I hurried to the appointment to see what was going on. I rang the bell, and an old man greeted me at the door. "Hello, I'm Doc Oswald, but everyone just calls me Doc." "Hi, I'm Carl, nice to meet you." He led me to the examining room. "Strip off and get on the table. I'll be back in a few." He didn't offer a gown, so I undressed to shorts and socks and got on the table. A knock on the door, and he re-entered the room. He looked like a Norman Rockwell picture. He had a stethoscope around his neck and a long white coat. "So what brings you in today?" "Well, lately I've noticed stiffness in my joints, and it's getting harder when I sit too long to get right up." He looked at me quizzically as though I should have been able to figure this out on my own. "You do know that you're old, don't you?" I laughed and said, "Better than most, Doc." He told me that he knew my 'condition' because he had treated Hunter, and he was 'afflicted' with the same ailment. "So, now's the time to come clean with me, how old are you actually?" "Okay, I'm 105, is that what you wanted to hear?" The doc didn't even flinch. "That's exactly what I needed to hear. I can't assist in your health without us both being honest." "Well then, Doc, I need to give you more information." I reached into my pocket, retrieved my pills, and handed them to him. "These are longevity pills developed by my last doctor, Chuck Tidwell. You see, I'm not exactly like Hunter; I don't carry the recessive gene, and these are the only way I'm able to stave off old age."

The Doc nodded and said, "I knew Chuck. Great guy, and he consulted with me while developing these pills. Now I can see what you need. These are sunsetting in their effectiveness. I can help in adjusting to a new regimen and dosage." The relief on my face was noticeable, and I shook the doc's hand with both of mine. The doc stated, 'Give me a week and I should have this sorted. I could really use Chuck's notes, though. Do you think I could see them?" "Not a problem, I'll have them for you tomorrow, thanks again, Doc." He handed me back the bottle minus three pills. I went home with hope in my pocket, but no way to secure the notebooks of Chuck's without raising suspicions from Stephan.

I needed a distraction or to just tell Stephan the truth. I decided on the truth because Stephan always knew, and this time I wanted to be on the right side of the argument.

"Stephan, got a minute?" Stephan waved me into the den. He sat at his desk, and I pulled a chair close. "I went to see a doctor today. I saw Doctor Tucker, one of Hunter's old physicians. I need to be totally honest, I'm afraid that the pills aren't helping much anymore. He knew about Hunter, Chuck, and the pills. I believe we can trust him, and it will help Eddie also. What do you think?" Stephan waited a few seconds for that 'Stephan effect' before he responded, "I'm glad you were finally honest with me. I noticed more than I let on and wanted to see if you'd come clean, and now I'm happy." I sat on his lap and hugged my man.

"He'd like to see Chuck's notebooks to try and fix the formula. Can I have them, please?" "Of course, but I would like to meet him. I could probably use him too, that's IF I really need to." I led Stephan to the fireplace and set out the fur rug.

We received a call the following week that Doc had some good and bad news. He asked us to visit him the next day. I hate when it's said that way, and the waiting made it worse as I, the eternal overthinker, couldn't sleep much that night. Stephan bore the brunt of my tossing and turning but managed a few hours' sleep. Morning came, and I had no appetite, but Stephan did, and he actually ate more than I did, and it didn't go unnoticed. "Relax, how bad could the bad news be, Babe?" I couldn't sleep last night, just overthinking how bad it could be. You know that. Do you know how many scenarios raced through my mind as you slept?" Stephan took my hand and said, "I would wager about a thousand. Am I close?" He always knew how to get to me, and I couldn't hold back a laugh. "For your information, Mr. Orion, it was more than two thousand!" and I fell into his arms, happy again.

Doc met us at the door, and I introduced him to Stephan. "I figured I'd meet the infamous Stephan soon. Please come in. He locked the door behind us, and I took note. We were led into his study instead of the office, again noted. "Which news do you want first, good or bad?" Stephan interceded and said, "The bad first, you see my husband, the worrywart, can't stand the suspense." The doc said, "Okay, I can't improve on these pills even with Chuck's notes." My heart sank. "But the good news is he was working on a different, more permanent solution. That's why the secrecy, I don't want anybody, even by chance, to hear this but you guys. I took up where he left off, and well, here, try this…" as he handed me a vile of light blue liquid. Stephan grabbed the beaker, looked it over, and handed it to me. I asked how much to drink, and the doc said to take it all, about six ounces. "Bottom's up" as the beaker was emptied. It didn't taste bad, but it didn't taste great either.

I was wondering if it was going to be a Jekyll and Hyde moment, but all I did was get a little dizzy. Sitting down, the room spun, and then nothing. The spinning was over, and I felt the same. "I don't think it worked, Doc." The doc said to give it a few hours, and then I'd see results if it worked. I asked to go home, but the doc asked us to stay in case of any side effects. Stephan said okay for both of us and asked the doc what he'd like for lunch. "I usually have a bologna sandwich on white bread with Miracle Whip." I stared at Stephan just as I doubled in half at the expression on his face. Stephan quipped back, "How about a little French cuisine for lunch today, my treat?" Doc said, "Sure," and Stephan speed dialed the restaurant before Doc could change his mind.

Lunch arrived, much to Stephan's relief, and we munched out (or at least I did, having starved myself over breakfast). I think about an hour after I took the solution, I started to feel funny again, but this time, no spinning or dizziness. I went to the mirror over the mantel and saw that my face looked different. Subtle but different, definitely different. I looked younger than before, and I noticed that my hair had much less gray in it. Stephan came to me and nodded that it was happening. The doc nodded and said that he believed that he had cracked the code to renew oneself. He asked if we would allow him to take it also, but Stephan warned him that I had been injected with blood from a recessive gene individual, and the results could vary or even kill him. "I'm 77 years old, I'm willing to risk it. If it works, great. If not, I had a good run." Stephan said, "Sure, it's your solution and so therefore your option. I'm glad you asked, though. It makes me happy that we can count on you as we did with Chuck. How long between doses, though? What will you need in the form of money to reproduce it in quantities for Carl and

Eddie?" Doc simply said, "Actually not much at all and I can just bill you monthly. It would come to about five hundred a month, including visits. If I can use it, then the cost will go down, of course."

Stephan looked at me and then at the doc and said, "You have a deal. Here's a check for ten thousand as a token of our goodwill and to get you started correctly." Doc led us into the lab and showed us the serum being produced. "It will probably need to be taken one dose monthly until the effects are where you want them, and then twice a year to keep it there." We left, and Stephan asked me to call and let Eddie know about the good news. I was fairly floating on air as we entered. I could feel the youthfulness return more than I could see it, and for that, I was happy. I would be able to extend my life and thereby my marriage to my fantastical husband.

I called Eddie, and we talked the better part of the morning. He let me know (in minutia) everything happening in England. The call ended as Stephan announced lunch. "Please just summarize that three-hour call," said Stephan. I laughed and told him it was basically an okay from Eddie. "And that took three hours?" "I can always give you a complete report, Mister Nosy Rosy, if you'd like." Stephan chortled, "That's alright." We lunched and talked about any trips this year. "Definitely England this year and maybe even Greece. The boys haven't seen them yet." We agreed and set to making arrangements when the phone rang. It was Fiji calling, Bruce was on the phone, so I handed it to Stephan. I listened intently to our side of the conversation, and it was serious. "How bad is it? How much damage? Has it been reported, and what did the insurance people say? That's ridiculous, of course, I'll call them. That's highway robbery. How soon can you get a crew out there for restoration? Great, we'll be there in the next few days to assess the problems and deal with them. Thanks, Bruce." Stephan hung up the phone and said, "Plans have changed. Call the boys, we're off to Fiji, and let Tom and Declan know they'll have to go also." I did as asked without knowing the full reason, but cornered Stephan later in the den. Stephan made it short and sweet, "That kid Tory nearly burned down the entire compound. Bruce and the staff made them back off, but our bedroom and half the kitchen were lost. Poor Tom, his gardens were trashed as they beat feet away from the island. I talked to Bob and Leonard, and they will be joining us on this trip. Between Bruce and Bob, a team will be assembled, and Leonard (newly graduated from P.I. school) will be the lead on information gathering. That kid just sealed his fate, trust me." I had never seen Stephan like this, and once was enough.

The trip planned, the plane readied, and the flight went wheels up in a matter of hours. Fiji came into view, and the car took us to the dock where a boat was waiting to take us all to the island. The boys were nervous as Stephan was barking like a dog protecting his bone. The island, our precious haven, lay partially ruined before our eyes. The staff of Allen and Darren were there to greet us, but woefully unprepared for the crew we brought. I asked the boys, Declan and Davin, to assist Allen with the luggage as it was exceptionally heavy (God only knows what Bob and Leonard brought along). Bruce met us at the main house and led the tour through the damaged areas. Jaime made a makeshift kitchen to keep everyone fed. Bruce and Bob went into the living room (turned war room) to make plans and then motioned Leonard to join them. Stephan told me to help Tom and Declan with the gardening and leave the 'details' to him and the others. "The less you know, the better, Babe." I wanted to object, but as usual, thought better than to question Stephan and sauntered off.

Stephan joined the group in the living room. Leonard left first and called for a boat to Fiji. Bob unpacked one of the suitcases and asked Bruce what his choices would be. Bruce pointed to a few items and said he had to make a few more calls for additional 'supplies'. Crap was getting real, and detailed plans were finalized before dinner. Leonard returned the next day and convened the group in the war room. Places, times, and events were discussed. I stayed in the kitchen with Jaime, and he looked at me with fear in his eyes for Bruce. "They'll be fine. Trust me, Stephan will see to that. He helped wage a war between the Vatican army and Russia back when Mikhail Romanov was on the throne, a personal friend of Stephan's (oops, maybe should not have shared that). Jaime was too upset to think about that last statement, and we concentrated on the matters at hand. Stephan came out of the room and simply said, "It's set, tomorrow, the team will head into Fiji to end the terrorism of Tory." I tried to sleep, but I remembered when Stephan got shot before, and I almost lost him. I held him close, tried to memorialize everything about him, and then asked for loving one last time, just in case. Stephan laughed it off and said not to be afraid, but acquiesced. I think he needed it too.

Morning light and the troops on the island converged at the dock, loaded for bear. You'd have thought they were going to invade Fiji instead of handling one man. We, the couples, kissed our men and sent them into battle, praying they all came back and were uninjured. Tom, Declan, Davin, and I were assigned to guard the island and look out for boats (meaning to stay away from the fray). Tense hours lapsed without any sign of a boat or news from Fiji. Tom spotted our boat in the distance, and we tried fervently to see individuals and count bodies aboard. Tom had a spyglass and shouted out any details he could glean. The count going away was 4, and he said he saw five men coming back (so far, a good sign). They got closer, and Tom assured us that all were accounted for but said nothing about the fifth man. It seemed like an eternity for the boat to navigate the last half mile, but the boat docked.

We greeted our conquering heroes, but all eyes were set on the unknown guy tied up and hooded. Stephan had Bob and Bruce take the hostage to the garden behind the main house. I looked at Stephan for a clue, but his face was poker straight. I looked at Tom next, and that gave the game away. I said nothing but knew who was there, none other than the infamous Tory. Tom and Declan ushered Leonard into the house, and that left me with Davin and Stephan. Stephan was the first to speak, "Take Davin in the house, I'll be along in a minute." Davin wanted to ask something, but I mouthed no to him and told him to let it go. Thank God the kid picked up on it and stayed silent as we left. Once inside, he quietly asked, "What's going on, and who is that guy? Is he the one who did this?" I just nodded as I thought about cracking a joke about New Jersey and smirked to myself.

I knew Stephan would tell me the outcome during cuddling. Jaime served us sandwiches, and as we were finishing, I thought I heard a muffled scream from that direction. The guys came in soon afterwards. Stephan asked about a local architect nearby, and Bruce asked why. "I think a bigger patio out back would be nice. The view would be great" (oh well, New Jersey lost out to Fiji). Davin, always curious, asked me in a whisper, "What happened to the guy?" I said, "Stephan probably punished him and set up terms for restitution, then sent him away." I knew, but why traumatize the kid?

Plans for the restoration were formalized, and we made plans to return to Baltimore. Tom needed to remain behind, so I concocted a need for Declan to stay behind and return on the next flight. He thanked me quietly.

Our beloved Baltimore came into view, and we landed and headed to the hangar. There seemed to be some action going on, and as always, I prepared for the worst. Stephan looked nonplussed as usual, and we taxied in. As we deplaned, a couple of officers greeted us at the tarmac. "Mr.

Orion and Mr. Omega, may we have a word with you?" Stephan stepped forward and asked, "What is this concerning, gentlemen?" The officer in charge spoke up, "Sirs, it has come to our attention that your plane has been logging excessive miles lately and we'd like to know why." I got nervous but Stephan, stoic as ever, simply said, "We own many properties around the world and this time we had to make an emergency trip to Fiji as an arson nearly destroyed the estate home. I also have homes in Italy, Greece, and England. Please feel free to investigate, and you'll find I have relatives there that I visit on a regular basis. We have investments in Italy and warehouses around the world. It will probably take your office about 6 years and around 5 million dollars to find out what I'm telling you is accurate. So please, go traveling, and I'll see you in about six years. Good day, gentlemen." I stood trying to look calm as the officers were waved away by my husband (did I say I was beaming with pride at the way my guy handled them so easily).

Home sweet home, and the vignette was one of serenity and calm (at least until the girls heard our voices). Winnie and Mary came bounding out and drooled on us until we were soaked. Rita followed the girls and greeted us. I inquired as to how Dahlia was coping with the loss of Aaron, and she said, "Dahlia immersed herself in typing out your thoughts and then scratching and even got us involved trying to decipher some. (Note to self: print or record into a recorder going forward. Stephan and I headed to the den for some downtime, so I got the cigars and wine as Stephan started the fire. Lying across the fur rug, smoking, sipping wine, and cuddling certainly recharged Stephan's batteries. I lay my head on his bare stomach and turned to see his eyes and said, "You really should try to write a book on how to handle sticky situations like you did today." I received a tousle of my hair as Stephan quipped, "It's not a thing you can learn, you have to live it to learn it."

Nighttime brought us a full moon on a warm night, so we snuck out to the patio sans clothes to completely ground ourselves to the earth. We would have gotten away with it if Sarah hadn't started barking. Embarrassed and reaching for a blanket, we saw lights coming on and bells and whistles going off in the compound. Soon, we were surrounded and heard screams of laughter, and we joined in. Stephan shrugged his shoulders and offered, "Busted, would you believe it if we told you we were patrolling the yard and tripped a sensor?" More laughter, and we excused ourselves for the evening.

We literally flew up the stairs before they could follow us in and closed the door behind us. "That was a close one, Batman. What happens next?" "To the closet," was all he said, and the laughter continued into the night. Morning came, the dogs got our breakfast, and we finally rallied around 11 am. Rita smirked as we sheepishly entered the kitchen. "Dahlia asked me to tell you when you finally came down that she sent the rug to the cleaners this morning and it won't be back until Wednesday." Stephan smiled that million-dollar smile and simply nodded. I asked if there was anything easy to make for lunch, and Rita said, "I left two bologna sandwiches in the fridge if you're really hungry." Stephan grabbed the cell phone and called up the restaurant for lunch. I tried to go to the fridge for a sandwich, but Stephan glared at me, and I immediately changed my mind. We went upstairs to shower and dress for lunch and ended up getting the lunch delivered as Stephan WAS hungry but not for bologna.

Lunch arrived, and we ate in the atrium. The three dogs circled us like a pack of wolves lest we drop anything to the floor. Their patience was rewarded when Stephan finished his plate (which looked untouched) and set it on the floor. My plate looked like a starving man was in the room (actually, I was starving after the night and morning exercising). I put it on the floor, and poor Mary licked it clean in seconds. I mentioned to Stephan that we had wanted to go to Greece and take the boys with us. He nodded, and I set out to ensure everything got handled. I made sure that the plane was inspected and ready for takeoff. I checked all the passports and made the appointments for vaccination shots where necessary. We decided to do the shopping in Athens (for the boys, of course, wink, wink). All that was left was to contact the boys' father and mother and to reassure them that they would be fine.

I called Fiji and told Tom and Declan to fly to Greece and meet us there. They hesitated, and I said that the private plane I had hired would meet them in Fiji, and not to worry about the arrangements. The mood lightened quickly, and they acknowledged the plans. We hit the airport, looking for officers who were friendly and kind, but they were nowhere to be found (surprise, surprise). Wheels up at 5 pm EST and onto Greece. Davin was interested in asking Stephan all the questions I had asked, and I noticed Stephan's smile as he answered them all (I think he really liked talking about his unique life). The trip took 8 hours flying east, and the only thing I recognized was the boot of Italy as we flew over. Greece came into view as the sun rose in the east. The time difference would normally give me jet lag, but I slept most of the way. We landed in

Greece and went through customs. Thank God we had nothing to declare, and the passports were up to date.

We spent time near the airport until Tom and Declan cleared customs and joined us in the limousine. Stephan told the driver to take us to the best restaurant in Athens. Instead of taking us to Karamanlidiko's for the specialty, Pastirmas (meat and flat bread), he drove past the restaurant and straight to the suburbs and deposited us at the door of a private home. "You like better, sirs," was all he said. Stephan was elected (due to knowing the language) to knock on the door. The door opened, and Stephan smiled as he said," Pardon me, but our driver was asked to take us to the best restaurant in Athens, and he brought us here." The woman (talking in Greek) said, "Please come in and tell my son to park the car in the back." Stephan translated to us what she said, and we entered the home. We stood in the entrance way (that would make Eddie jealous) and then led us to the dining room. Stephan asked something in Greek and then told us to sit around the giant table. Declan and Davin sat across from us, and Tom sat next to Declan. Our driver appeared from the kitchen and said, "Mother will serve soon. Wine for anyone?" Stephan scanned the room and saw hands and nods from us all. He went to the cupboard and retrieved a bottle. Popping the cork, he served us all a white wine called Assyrtiko (a wine with an ancient history). The mother produces a large plate of Tzatziki and Saganaki. Small plates were already on the table, and the food was served family style. I could have filled up on that alone, but the food had just started. Soon, moussaka and souvlaki arrived (along with bread and salad). The boys pigged out, as did I, and Stephan picked through it all. I asked the boys how they liked it, and they said it was great. The son grinned from ear to ear as they said that and said something to his mother.

When the boys conceded defeat and tried to thank our hosts, Stephan translated it back to her while her son went to the cupboard and produced a clear bottle and a small bag of beans. Mom brought over small glasses with an ice cube in them and placed them on the table. Sonny poured the liquid into the glasses (which turned the liquid white), and then he placed a coffee bean on top. "We call this Ouzo, and it's a dessert liquor to cleanse the palate." The boys were wary about imbibing, but Stephan graciously accepted his and raised his glass, saying, "Yamas" (which meant 'to our health!'). Glasses clinked, and our hosts joined in the toast.

The son came over to Stephan and whispered in his ear. Stephan nodded and followed him out of the room. Soon laughter was booming from the kitchen, and Stephan, the son, and the mother entered but had changed their outfits into authentic Greek wear. Stephan happily announced, "Please thank my relatives Andreas and Vasiliki Orion for this banquet. They are my kin from my dad's side. Vasiliki is my first cousin." The questions started coming fast and furiously. Stephan fielded all the questions simply, and when satiated with the answers, the tribe was informed that we were to stay there for the night. Tom and Declan bunked together, Davin alone, and Stephan and I got a deluxe room with a fireplace, couch, and king-size bed. I asked if Stephan knew ahead of time, and he said no, but said that Andreas had suspected that they were related when he heard the name of his pick-up. His mom confirmed it, and they had set up the 'ambush'. I asked how old Vasiliki was and if her son Andreas was also a long timer. Stephan said that he knew Vasi was but didn't have a clue about Andreas. Then I asked why Vasi had a son but carried the Orion name. "That's easy, Vasi knew around 1600 that she was different so she decided to stay single." A quick cuddle, and we joined the household in an easy and deep slumber.

Morning in Greece seemed different than in other places, being laid back and simple. Stephan let me know that this was the house in which he was born. I rolled into him and let his warmth spread over me before he removed himself to ready himself for the day. Sadly, I arose and left the comfort of our bed. I tried to memorialize this place, in 1512 when my Stephan entered the world. A plain room in simple eloquence looking out at the Saronic gulf waters, serene with wisps of clouds interrupting the sun's warmth. Nestled in the city of Piraeus (the port visible from our balcony). We were called to breakfast and went to the table where we were greeted by the others in our party. "What took you so long bosses? We were looking for the family dogs to give your breakfast to." Stephan bent down near the boys and whispered, "Maybe you should save the food until you can find a new job here in Greece." The boys weren't quite sure how to interpret Stephan's response so they quickly changed the subject (and their attitudes). I leaned over to the boys and said that Stephan was joking but not to push their luck. "Only Trudy, Judy, Dahlia and Rita could get away with it. Now, what's on the agenda for today boys?" Stephan talked to Andreas and said, "Andreas knows where to get a new wardrobe and some souvenirs, anyone interested in going with us?" (holding up the cherished black card and waving it around).

They answered in unison, "Yes boss, when are we leaving?" Stephan motioned to the plates on the table, "As soon as you boys help clean the table for Vasi." I never saw the boys move so fast. Tom assisted Andreas with readying the limousine and we all bundled into the back and were soon on our way to the town center. It seemed like a step back in time when we left the limousine and started our pilgrimage into the sales district. The streets were cobblestone and the shops had open doors and outside displays of wares. I stopped to watch a lace maker work and was overwhelmed with the ease and expertise of their work. The clicking noise coming from the wooden shuttles as they were shifted around entranced me and Stephan had to nudge me to break the trance. "The clothing store is this way lover." I followed mindlessly as I took in the aromas of the street. The food smelled delicious, then onto a Zaharoplasteio or pastry shop. The clothier shop was a quaint little place and so our expectations were lessened until we found out that the guy was a tailor and all the clothes were handmade. Stephan went over to the man with Andreas and they talked as we looked at the fabrics and sample clothes that adorned the walls.

They joined us, and the man motioned for each of us to stand before the mirrors as he took our measurements. After the awkward moments of getting our inseams measured, we stood as he brought samples of cloth and held them up to us, one after the other, until he seemed satisfied. He never consulted Stephan, and we just let it happen. The boys looked to me for a hint as to what was happening, but I just shrugged and looked as surprised. The man left us, and Stephan, Andreas, and I left the shop behind them. I championed for the boys so as not to get them in any hot water. "Stephan, I thought we were going to buy some clothes?" Stephan quipped, "We just did." I looked back at the boys and shook my head.

The next stop was the pastry shop. Entering into the aroma of fresh-baked phyllo dough products, Baklava, buttered phyllo dough filled with chopped nuts and cinnamon, Kataifi, shredded phyllo with chopped almonds soaked in syrup, and Loukoumades, light, fluffy doughnuts deep fried and then soaked in syrup. There were many other delicacies to try, and we did. We left with bags of treats and some for Vasi. We had to pass by the lace maker's shop on the way back, and I made a pit stop. Stephan followed me in and was at the ready to present his card for my purchases. I bought most of the pre-made lace doilies and edgings. Stephan shook his head as I spent nearly a month's commission on the items. "You should be glad that I love you, but they will make lovely gifts." Stephan asked for their business card and asked if they shipped to the United States (knowing this was not the end of my buying spree).

Back in the car but not back to the house yet, Andreas said something to Stephan, and was answered in Greek. We ventured out of town and to a large cemetery. Andreas acted as our guide and pulled near a group of mausoleums. We disembarked, and Andreas led us to the Orion family plot. Andreas and Stephan translated for us and said it was Stephan's relatives. I asked Andreas if he knew any of them, and he smiled (knowing I was phishing for clues as to his age). "Since everyone knows about mom, yes, this is grandpa, Acacius Orion, and next to him is Uncle Adamantios Orion, mom's brother." "That doesn't actually answer my question Andreas, so I'll be blunt, how old are you?" Andreas' smile widened and he finally said, "Mom had me in her early hundred's, so this year I turned 411 years old. Are you satisfied now Carl?" I blushed and tried to hide my embarrassment, but then, everyone wanted to know. "Yes, thank you. Stephan's 561 and I'm 106." Andreas looked directly at Stephan and said, "Robbed the cradle, did ya?" That broke the awkwardness, and everyone started laughing. I knew better, but I giggled like a schoolgirl and got a 'wait till later' look from lover boy.

The boys took rubbings from the headstones and decided that they were going to need to take foreign languages if they were going to stick around us, if only remedial. The troops rallied, and we returned to the house. The boys asked to be dismissed so they could go to the beach, and we nodded. Andreas asked his mother for her diaries so Stephan could catch up on family history in Greece, and went with Vasi to retrieve them. Andreas asked me, "Are you a long timer? 106 and looking 50 is quite a trick." I confided that Stephan, Charles, and Oswald created a solution to assist me with longevity. "Well, it worked. I'm glad Stephan has someone. I lost my love Eleni and my two children Nikolis and Anastasia in 1750 due to Typhoid fever brought on by infection from head lice and poor hygiene. I married her when she was 15, and I was 74. They were the best 15 years of my life." Andreas tried hiding his glassy eyes as he reminisced about his lost love.

I left it there and just placed my hand on his shoulder to try and console him, if only a bit. Stephan re-joined us and held the diaries. "This will make for some good reading later. How are you two getting along?" I suggested a glass of Ouzo and that gave Andreas an excuse to leave us and regroup. Stephan looked at me and said, "I can't wait to see how my family faired during all those years after we left." I gave Stephan the low down on Andreas and finished as he re-entered the room. The mood shifted slightly as we tried to down play our affection in front of Andreas. The boys joined us before dinner and we made a fire in the pit. Vasi called us to the table as the last of the food landed. The center piece was roasted lamb accompanied by hearty side dishes of lemon-roasted potatoes, stuffed cabbage rolls, and appetizers of Spanakopita (spinach pie) and Dolmades (stuffed grape leaves). Dessert was melomakarona cookies, drenched with honey. Wine and Ouzo flowed and bellies filled quickly.

The boys dispatched the dishes to the kitchen without comment and Tom left with Andreas to walk the garden. Declan returned from the kitchen in time to see the guys leaving and ran after them. Davin saw the diaries and asked if Stephan had found anything interesting. "Would you like me to translate some of them for you?" Davin jumped at the chance saying, "I never really liked history before, but now I can't get enough of it. Especially things about you and your family." They left for the sitting room and I followed behind. Stephan began recanting the chronicles of Vasiliki. "It says here that Vasiliki was born to Acacius Orion in the year of our lord 1552. Her mother Anastasia (Andreas' grandmother) then had Adamantios two years later (1554). The family decided to stay behind when my family took me to Rome, Italy." Stephan read ahead in silence and Davin looked at me for a clue and I silently shook my head to let him know that if Stephan wanted it shared, he would in his time. "I think that's it for tonight guys. I need to digest some of the private thoughts of Vasi. I hope you understand." Davin feigned a yawn and said goodnight to us and left.

I knew I'd get to know the details later so I suggested retiring for the evening also. We went to our room and settled for the night. Nothing else was said. Stephan left our bed around midnight and went to the balcony and stared into space. The night was warm, the sea breeze was salty and pleasant and the moon was illuminating his front and putting him in shadow to me. I left him with his thoughts and turned away to sleep. I woke when Stephan returned to bed. He slipped in behind me and held me tight. Now I started to fear that the diary held some information that was really shaking my guy and there was nothing I could do but let him process it.

Morning came, we showered for the day, and got to the breakfast table before the others. Stephan engaged Vasi in Greek, and she spoke slowly and with intent. Stephan showed actual emotion as Vasi continued talking. I heard names Sebastian and Penelope, but couldn't make out anything else. Vasi teared up as she told a story. Stephan got glassy-eyed (something I wasn't accustomed to). I had to remember to ask about them. The troops came bounding in, and the conversation ended. I quietly asked Stephan if he was ok and if I could do anything to help. He wiped the tears from his eyes and simply said, "Later, babe, okay?" I nodded and let it go.

Stephan scanned the diaries to Rita, then gave them back to Vasi with a thanks and a hug. Time was coming to an end in Greece, and we had a farewell dinner fit for kings. I asked about our clothes from the clothier, and Stephan said they would be delivered to Baltimore. "The clothes took longer than expected to sew, and so I told him to send them to our house in America with his business card." We spent one last night in Greece and headed to the airport. Our bus was waiting faithfully at the hangar, and we were grateful. Everyone stretched out for the flight home.

The boys fell asleep three hours into the flight, so I took the time to question Stephan about his conversation with Vasi. He said that Sebastian and Penelope were his parents, born in 1478 and 1488, respectively. "Vasi's diary describes the reason why my parents left Greece, and it wasn't kind. You see, Sebastian and Acacius were brothers, and in order for them to keep the family home, Acacius started to talk about things that we were warned not to. Father was the elder, so by birthright, he should have gotten the home and lands, but Acacius made it very uncomfortable for our life in Greece. Father decided to let Acacius have the property to save our family, and so we moved." He continued his story recounting the events that Acacius created that caused the departure. It was not a good parting, and there was some bad blood between them. "Vasi and I reconciled, and I'm hoping the future is better."

I was glad that he confided in me, and I couldn't help but hug him tight and kiss his cheek. He returned the affection, and we fell asleep in each other's arms.

The pilot announced our arrival, and we touched down as the sun broke the horizon. Baltimore, home sweet home. The boys were delivered to the Meyer residence, and we got home just after breakfast. Harold asked if we wanted something quick or maybe a light brunch set out. We opted for the brunch, and Harold left us with Dahlia and Rita. The girls were running in circles until we let them out into the garden to play. Thankfully, everything was running smoothly, and Bobbie ran into my arms. He started asking me if I brought him anything from Greece, and I handed him a package wrapped in cloth. He made short work of it, opened the box, took out the handmade toy, and kissed my cheek before running out again. Bobbie was getting old before my eyes, five, and getting ready for kindergarten.

Elizabeth shook her head, saying that I was spoiling him, just before Stephan called Bobbie back to get his other gift. "You two are setting him up to expect this sort of thing." Stephan nodded and handed her a roll of handmade lace from the lace maker. She quietly took it and turned her frown into a big smile. "That's what I thought. You're just as eager as Bobbie." We all started laughing as Bob entered the kitchen. "Hey, boss, got a second?" Stephan strolled off with Bob (a hint that something was up). I tried to glean the topic of the hushed conversation, but they left too quickly. I turned back to the table as Harold had the meal laid out.

Stephan came back alone, took a seat, and asked if I minded if he left for a while. I told him no, but my 'spidey senses' were jolting me from all directions. He and Bob left and went off in the Bentley. I asked Elizabeth if she knew what was going on, and she just shrugged. "I'm as in the dark as you." I started to worry and went out to play with the dogs and take my mind off the guys. Davin arrived and sought me out. "Did you hear? Declan is thinking of quitting and moving to Fiji.

Something about moving there to be with Tom. What's going to happen if he goes? Is Stephan here? Can I talk to him?" I calmed the youth down and asked him to sit. "Declan and Tom are an item, although they have been keeping it on the down low. Sorry, Davin, I thought he would have told you. I can tell you from my view that love is love, even if the rest of the world isn't okay with it. You see, I am or was a straight guy before Stephan came along. We had so much in common, and it evolved into a deep friendship, and I actually fell in love with him, although I couldn't explain why, it just went there."

I think Davin relaxed a little after I said that. He shrugged and finally said, "What's going to happen to me then?" "First, Davin, you're not going anywhere. You are as much a part of this 'family' as Dahlia, Harold, Bob, Elizabeth, or Bobbie. We built this collection of individuals from every type of background as our 'family'. I guess you're stuck with us until you decide to leave. Consider that point moot. Now, as for Stephan, he's out with Bob and don't ask because I don't even know where they went. Now help me wrangle the girls back inside and stop fretting."

Stephan appeared from nowhere and asked me to join him in the den (the plot thickens). He poured us a goodly amount of bourbon and handed me mine. "Let's sit" (another bad omen). I sat on the edge of my chair as I waited for the shoe to drop. Stephan started, "Bob let me know that there was a problem, and so I left to see for myself how bad it was." I started to talk, but Stephan hushed me. "Let me finish. First, Oswald is dead. Someone broke into his lab and took his life. Then they stole his notes, even the ones only we knew about." I put down my drink as I was shaking violently. "Stephan, those were the formulas that were made for Eddie and me. What happened next?" Stephan calmed me. "I contacted Leonard, and he came immediately. He and Bob are working the case.

They will get the person responsible and hopefully recover the notes. I don't think he or they know what they have yet."

My sorry butt couldn't stop shaking so Stephan took me into a tight embrace until the shaking stopped. "Let's wait for Leonard until we decide what to do." It wasn't long before Bob called us out of the den. "Leonard's back and has some information for us." We followed Bob to the atrium where we found Leonard. "Bosses, first let me say that I'm sorry about Oswald. He looked as though he was a gentle man. I scoured the room for clues and found that it was a single bullet to the head so thankfully he didn't suffer. I had to dig the bullet out of the wall and saw that the trajectory was from the building across from his, meaning that Oswald was shot dead before the intruders entered. There were papers on the floor so I believe they just took what they could find and left in a hurry. I went to the building and found a casing that matched the bullet. My forensics guy got a print off it and I'm waiting for a classmate to search the databases for an identity. We should know something soon." Stephan patted Leonard on the shoulder and thanked him for his expediency. "Keep us informed." Bob said, "What do you think boss? Should we call the police or handle it ourselves?" Stephan simply stated, "Let's go to the lab and look to see if they got our notes. Carl, would you come with us? You know that stuff better than any of us." I nodded and went to get a hoodie. We all met in the car and headed to Oswald's lab. "If we don't find the notes there, let's try his home, behind the lab/office."

We arrived and split up. Bob and I went to the lab, and Stephan and Leonard went home. I scooped up the notes and papers from the floor as Bob looked around. Observant as usual, Bob saw more than I and pointed out a footprint in the dust. "Oswald had small feet, and this print is large, size 12 if I'm not mistaken. It's a work boot, not a shoe." Bob took out his phone and took photos of the room. The photos seemed insignificant to me, but what did I know? I scanned the papers and saw nothing like what we wanted. We left the lab and went to the back and found Leonard and Stephan standing in front of a painting. "Hey Bob, how are your safe-cracking skills?" Bob went over, swung the painting out of the way, and allowed the safe to be seen. "If y'all can be silent, it shouldn't take long. This is a 4-tumbler combo lock." He bent his ear to the safe and started twisting the dial. To his word, the safe opened in less than a minute, and we saw papers inside. Apparently, the robbers had missed it. I removed the papers and notes, along with the rest of the contents of the safe. I was about to start perusing them when Stephan motioned for the door and said, "Let's take them and look at them at home."

We loaded into the car and left. We got about 2 blocks down the street as police cars arrived at the doctor's home (Stephan must be psychic or blessed, and for once, I was entirely glad to not have questioned him). Home again and right to the den we all went. Leonard was a little rattled going into our private den (I don't believe he'd ever been in this room). I set out the papers and notes from the lab and the safe. "Stephan, come here. I think these are the notes you and Oswald made." Stephan came over and verified that these were the notes for the formula. "At least those thugs didn't get their hands on these." My reaction was one of relief. Now, if Stephan and I could recreate the serum, I would be fine.

While securing the papers in the desk, Leonard got a call. He said it was his buddy so Stephan asked to have it on speaker so they all could hear. "Alex, I'm here with my bosses and Bob, my mentor. Everybody, this is Alexander Harding, my friend. Whatcha got for me?" Alex spoke clearly saying, "The casing came back with a name and a home location. The shooter is Johnny 'Eagle Eye' Thompson. His last known address is located outside of Baltimore in Ellicott City, 13 miles southeast. The street address is 143 Lockwood. He has a rap sheet the length of my arm. He is 5ft 6in and weighs about 141 lbs. Brown hair and tattooed heavily. Most identifiable tattoo is on his left shoulder of an eagle carrying a heart with the word mom across it." Leonard spoke up and said, "Got it, thanks bro." "Any time, hope you catch him." Leonard ended the call and sat back, waiting for the new instructions. Bob spoke, "Well, that means there was at least two in on it as the footprints I saw were too big for that rat." Stephan sat and thought for a minute before speaking. Rubbing his chin, Stephan spoke, "Bob, you up for a visit with little Johnny?" Bob grinned and said, "You have to ask? I've been wanting to exercise a few demons for a while and this is just what I need." Stephan rose, "It's settled then, Bob, take a few friends and have fun but call me when the demons are gone as I want to talk with him myself." Bob, smiling, nodded and headed to the kitchen to tell Elizabeth to keep his dinner warm.

Leonard was still waiting until Stephan said, "Leonard, you did great, now go home and get some rest. I'll call you with any further instructions." Leonard left us alone and shut the door behind him. I went to Stephan and asked what he had in mind for Johnny. "Just some questions, why?" I was never quick on my feet so I had no retort for him. He slapped my butt as he passed and winked at me as he opened the door and departed the room. I took that as a sign and followed him to the foyer. No words came but he stopped on the second step of the stairs, turned seductively and undid his belt. Turning back he continued up the stairs (I beat him to the top, meaning he had a date with the cleaner).

It was after lunch the following day that Bob called, Stephan excused himself and left me saying he'd be right back. I knew he was on his way to talk to this johnny kid. I told Stephan to be careful and that I loved him. He slipped away quietly and headed out. Stephan pulled up near the house indicated. Bob came to the door and said the kid was inside but not very cooperative. "Don't worry, I have my ways of getting what I want." Stephan entered and saw the kid in a chair and tied down. I think Bob's friends ruffed him up a bit and he had a black eye. "I want to ask you some questions and I expect you to answer them." The kid told him to piss off just before being returned to unconsciousness. Water splashed his face and he awoke. "Who worked with you? What were you looking for? Why did you kill Oswald?" The kid was about to spit at Stephan but thought better of it. "Wouldn't you like to know." Stephan produced a knife, quite sharp and slightly large. He split the kid's jeans open and pointed at his genitals, "And I suppose you'd like to keep those to use in your future endeavors." Stephan placed the knife on the insertion point as the kid rethought his previous statement. "Wait man, I was hired by a man on the phone but not to take him out. I did supply the ammo and no, I didn't get his name, he told us to get him paperwork and then drop them where our pay was to be. I worked with my friend. Now will you let me go?" Stephan left the knife there as he pushed for more information. "Where was the drop spot and when were you supposed to be there?" The kid didn't want to give that location away but with a nudge of the knife, reconsidered. "Down at the bus stop on Collins street. Man, I told ya everything, please don't cut me." "Now Johnny, who was with you?" This time johnny needed no prompting and answered, "Jerry, Jerry Miner, he lives 3 doors down with his mother." Stephan said, "Good boy, now call him and ask him to come over." Bob undid his hands and handed him back his phone. Johnny hit the number and it rang twice. "Hey Jerry, come over. I need to talk to you. Thanks, see ya in a couple." Bob lead Johnny into an adjoining bedroom and returned as the door opened. "Hey Jo…" was all Jerry got out as Bob grabbed him and put him in the chair where Johnny was. Hands tied as Jerry squirmed and legs flailing, Bob hog tied him to the chair.

Stephan sauntered over and said, "Hello Jerry, I need to ask you a few questions, okay." Jerry spat at Stephan and missed. "I really don't want to hurt you but I will if you insist." Jerry wanted to put up a macho resistance until he saw the knife. He quieted down quickly. "That's better, now who hired you to ransack Oswald's lab?" Jerry shrugged and said that Johnny handled all that stuff. "I just helped with the gathering of the papers (and by the look of his shoes, he was saying the truth about being there). Johnny was brought out of the bedroom and Jerry was asked about the drop location. Johnny tried to answer but Bob covered his mouth, "Let Jerry answer." Jerry started sweating as now he had to come up with the same answer or face the fact that they were both lying. "I believe it was a couple blocks from here, down near the bus stop." Stephan performed the same action on Jerry and left his now soiled shorts in the open. "I need a street name Jerry and since you live around here, that should be relatively easy for you. I suggest if you want to keep those jewels intact, you'll answer me." Jerry mumbled a street and the knife settled closer to the mark. "I said Cooper Ave, now back off with that knife, please" Bob brought the boys together and now Johnny was sweating. "Johnny, you said Collins street, which one of you are lying? Or are both of you lying? I can make you both disappear and no one will look for you." Johnny spoke first, "I'll take you to the exact spot, please don't hurt us." "First, which spot is it, Cooper or Collins?" "Jerry wasn't in on it, he gets confused sometimes. Believe me, it was Collins" Stephan and Bob noticed the side eye from Johnny to Jerry and Jerry said, "He's right, it was Collins. I was mistaken." Bob said, well, we'll soon see, won't we boys." The boys were placed in Johnny's sedan and told to give us directions. First destination, Collins Street. It took 3 minutes and it had a bus stop. Then we turned onto Cooper Ave, again it had a bus stop. The singular difference was that there was bushes near the Collins street bus stop. We opted to stop near the Collins Street bus stop and look around. Bob found foot prints and took more photos. They went back to our car, Stephan drove behind Bob in their car and we deposited the boys, tied and gagged in the police parking lot with a note about them and the murder of Oswald tucker. Bob got in the car with Stephan and they left, sure that the cops could take it from there.

Now that the immediate actors were rendered neutral, Stephan and Bob returned to the house and assigned Leonard another task. I saw them return (and in one piece thankfully) and followed Stephan to the den with Bob. Door closed and Bourbon poured for three, Stephan started the conversation. "Carl, we found the two bad actors and neutralized them." I thought I knew what had happened but then Stephan quickly added, "We left them in their car, tied up with a note saying what they had done." I awkwardly seemed proud of my husband for not having dispatched them and sent their carcasses to New Jersey. "We have a boss man to find and discover his motives and we need to before the cops get there. Any ideas guys?" Again, Stephan wanted me in on the decisions (something new for me and I beamed with pride for my guy). Bob showed the photos he took at the bus stop. We perused them looking for clues. Bob pointed out the foot prints and Stephan noticed that the tracks led further into the bushes. I enlarged the photos and saw that the dirt was multi colored in the foot prints. Three pretty sparse clues to go by but it was something. Bob called Leonard (who was at the bus stop) and told him what we saw. Leonard reported that the dirt in the foot prints was dirt from the beaches near our house. The foot print itself was a shoe from a high end store, gauging from the emblem depression. Finally, the tracks ended at the next street over and a couple blocks down (Cooper Ave). So the boys had actually both told the truth but for different parts of the tale.

Bob asked Leonard to send a photo of the emblem in case Stephan might know the maker and maybe where they were sold. "I know that emblem, it comes from Dan Brothers Shoe store, over on South Charles street near Federal Hill." Leonard acknowledged that he thought the same and had gone to the store, looking around, and found a sample shoe on the wall (at least the money spent to send this kid to P.I. school wasn't a waste). Our clues, although thin, were starting to come together to paint a picture of a well-to-do person, with enough money to pay underlings to do the dirty work, who was a sharpshooter, who knew Oswald's movements. Now we needed a motive and a name. Stephan and I went to the shoe store and presented ourselves. The Bentley parked at the front door would cover any doubt about why we were there. An attendant came over, all smiles, and asked what he could do for us. Stephan flashed his pearly whites and inquired about the shoe on the wall. The clerk took the shoe off the wall and said that it was one of the best made there, and few people purchased them. Stephan gave him our sizes, and the attendant left the front of the store for the back room. He returned quickly, but not before Stephan noticed the ledger book on the counter. Stephan told me to sit and mentioned that I had terrible taste in shoes and wanted me to wear more elegant shoes when out with him. I should have been hurt, but knowing the game that was afoot, I just sat and played my part.

The clerk knelt in front of me and gave me his entire attention (bad move on his part). That allowed Stephan to lean on the counter and peruse the client list unbothered. The clerk was asked to see if they came in black and light brown (sending him to the back again). Stephan read the names and looked at the dates of purchase, knowing that the emblem image was too defining to make the shoes too old. Three names came up as purchasing them. The clerk returned, we finished the fitting, and Stephan even bought a pair for himself. The clerk rang up the purchases and almost fainted when Stephan presented his black card. "Please come back any time and ask for me, Henry Allman." Stephan nodded and said, "I'll do just that, Henry, thank you." We left the store, and Henry had a lucrative morning. Stephan asked me to write down the names he saw. "First, Ludwig Hardt, second, Adolphus Winger, and third, Geoffrey Baird."

We got home, took our packages upstairs, and came down to the kitchen. I handed the paper to Bob and said, "Set Leonard loose on these names." Bob nodded and left. We ate lunch and decided we 'desperately' needed a nap (note to self, get new outfits, maybe two). Later that afternoon, Leonard popped in to give an update on the names. We took him to the den and then let him educate us. "You can take Ludwig Hardt off the list; he's an out-of-towner in a wheelchair and is about 90 years old. Adolphus Winger is a long shot, as he was out of town for the last six months on business. That leaves Geoffrey Baird. He lives in town, has been around, and has a house near your camp. He has money, and he is a part-owner of Dan's Shoes. Curiously, I have noticed that he has been to many doctor appointments recently." Stephan told Leonard to concentrate on Geoffrey.

"Do you think Geoffrey knew about Oswald and wanted his serum for himself?" "That's exactly what I'm thinking, Carl." Stephan went on to say that we should wait until Leonard came back with more accurate information. I sat back, looked at Stephan, and said, "Well, our money was well spent on that kid. If what we suspect proves out, I suggest a visit to our camp and check out this guy ourselves." "That won't be necessary, Carl. If it's true, then we'll visit him in person. Money has its advantages, and I'm one who knows how to leverage it well." I left it there, knowing he meant it and having read his exploits, knew full well he had it all in hand.

It took about a week for Leonard to update us, and all the suspicions were right. "It seems Geoffrey is also an expert shooter. He is suffering from multiple sclerosis, and it is deteriorating his health." Stephan thanked Leonard and sent him on his way (with a big bonus check in hand). Stephan planned his next several moves as any good chess player would. I watched in awe as my genius of a husband set his plans in action. "He must belong to one of the clubs I have a membership in. I can get his number from there. We know his address, and I can get any other residence addresses from Leonard. We can get his schedule and routine from Leonard or Bob. I think Leonard already has the attending doctors' names and business addresses. This will be fun. Bob can scan the residence for guards and electronic detectors." I just nodded my head at the thoroughness of his mind in creating his 'battle plans' (no wonder Mikhail Romanoff won the war against Rome).

Two days and a meeting later, Stephan made a call to Geoffrey Baird. "Geoffrey, Stephan

Orion here, I'd like to come talk to you. It seems we have a lot in common and a sit down sounds about right at this time." Geoffrey exploded into the phone, "How did you get this number and what do you want? Do you know who I am? I'm highly connected, and I can bury you. Now leave me alone and don't ever call again!" Stephan was nonplussed and calmly said, "Now now, Geoffrey, you've been a bad boy, and Johnny and Jerry have already named you (what a bluff) as the shooter in Oswald Tucker's murder. Shall we talk, or do you think you're so highly connected that they'll help you out? I think not. They'll cut you loose after I present the proof to the new D.A. Remember, he needs a good win right now, and he'll jump on this case." Geoffrey calmed a bit and asked when and where to meet. Stephan said the next day at noon at Geoffrey's home for lunch. "And have it catered, I prefer Italian, thank you."

I stared at Stephan and finally said, "That's adding insult to injury, demanding lunch on top of talking." Stephan smiled and said, "That's showing him that I'm in control and it cuckold him. He'll have henchmen there and will try a show of force, but it will be fruitless as I tell him I have hit men aimed at his men. I may have to prove it, so don't be surprised if his house goes up for sale, if you know what I mean." I told Stephan to be careful, "this man thinks he's as dangerous as you" (well, no sleep tonight for me).

Morning came, and I tried to keep Stephan in bed as long as possible. He arose, took a shower, and came into the bedroom looking as much an Adonis as always. I whistled at him, and he dropped his towel. Damn that man, he was hot and knew it. Thankfully, I put a ring on it, and he's loyal (not to mention, mine, mine, mine). I took my shower and noticed that Stephan stepped in behind me and washed my back. That's all it took to seduce me, and we cut my shower short. Breakfast could go to the girls for all I cared. I think that was so Stephan could decompress before his showdown with Geoffrey.

Bob accompanied Stephan to the meeting, and I don't know who else he had hired for the event, but I knew he was bringing an army with him just in case. Stephan arrived at the agreed-upon time, and Geoffrey answered the door himself (although his thugs were all over the house). Stephan stepped in with Bob behind him, simple and confident.

Geoffrey led them through the home to the dining room, where the food was already laid out. Stephan complimented Geoffrey on his home as a good guest would. If you hadn't heard the prior conversation, the scene would have been proper. Geoffrey offered Stephan a seat, and Stephan chose the one away from the window. Geoffrey stared but said nothing. "Shall we eat first, or would you like to talk first?" Stephan, always the gentleman, said, "Let's eat, the conversation can wait a bit." Geoffrey was starting to get irritated at the nonchalance of Stephan's presence. "Fine" was all he said and sat with his back to the window.

Lunch was okay, and they stared at each other all during the meal. Finally, Geoffrey couldn't handle the civility anymore and stammered, "Get on with it. What do you want?" Stephan wiped his mouth with his napkin, looked directly into Geoffrey's eyes, and said, "Answers, Geoffrey, and I expect you to be open and honest." Geoffrey went off like a sky rocket, "You're getting on my nerves. I could have you shot dead right now with a simple gesture." Stephan said calmly, "The same could be said for you, dear Geoffrey, so sit your butt down and calm down before you regret your words. You see, I neutralized all three of your sharpshooters before knocking on your door, and the seven guards you have are in my guys' sights. Shall I go on?" Geoffrey felt like he was in the presence of a godfather and quickly sat down. "Good, let's start. I know you pulled the trigger; the question is why. I know why, but I want to hear you say it, Geoffrey."

Geoffrey started slowly, knowing he was out of his league with Stephan, "Okay, I'm dying, and I heard that Oswald had something that would really help me, but he wouldn't share the information with me." "Go on." "I wanted to get the formula and have it synthesized for me. So I took him out and had the boys get the papers for me. By the way, how did you find out it was me? I covered all my tracks." "Apparently, not good enough. Besides, I ask the questions, you answer them, continue." "As you well know, the papers weren't there, so it was all for nothing. There, is that what you wanted to know?" Stephan rose, put his hand on Geoffrey's shoulder and said, "I have what you want but I can tell you, it won't help you. That serum doesn't cure anything but aging. If you are sick or injured, you die, simple." Geoffrey sank into his chair as Stephan said, "I'm going to let you live, but if I even sniff that you're being a bad boy again, I'll make you disappear, Kabbish?" Geoffrey nodded as Stephan and Bob left the manse and proceeded to drive away.

Stephan returned to my arms, and we spent the late afternoon in the den as Stephan recanted the tale of the day. "I knew you had it handled, but I didn't think you had it THAT covered." Stephan looked at me and finally smiled his disarming smile. "You're so cute when you've underestimated me, and after all this time," and booped me on my nose. We left for dinner with the 'family'.

2073 came to an end quietly, and we looked forward to another year of adventures ahead. Midnight arrived, and we clinked glasses of champagne in our room, kissed long and deep, then slipped into bed for a well-earned sleep. We went downstairs to greet 2074 with everyone when Bobbie handed me a note. "I wrote this for you, and I drew the picture. It's you and Uncle Stephan under the tree. See, there's Winnie and Mary too." I thanked my little buddy for the picture and asked Elizabeth to put it on the fridge in a place of honor. He grinned widely and took his mother over to show her his work. Hopefully, 2074 would be our year. Davin took Declan's place, and we placed Declan on the

Fiji payroll. Word came back that the extended patio was finished and all the restorations were complete.

"Hey Stephan, what are the plans for our trip this year?" Stephan just shrugged, but I sensed he already knew what he wanted to do. "Maybe a trip to Italy and then to Fiji, or maybe England and Greece. I haven't been back to Russia in a while, but then Spain is always nice. Have you ever been to Rio for Festivale?" "Well, you decide and let me know, crazy man" (this should be an exciting year). We retired to the den for some quiet time. I played the voicemail from Davin's father, David, and heard, "Could you please let Declan know that his grandmother is failing, and if he wants some time with her, he will need to come home." I called back and let him know that I'd take care of all that and provide transportation to get him home. I called Declan and Tom and explained the situation and told them to be ready as I was sending the 'bus' for them. I called David back and informed him that Declan would be arriving in a couple of days. He thanked me for the expediency. I asked if there was anything else we could do for Violet, a 24-hour nurse or whatever. He said he'd talk it over with Jen and would let me know. I called Davin to the den, told him the news, and sent him home. "It seems like we'll be on our own for the near future. I suggest you choose wisely where we go." Stephan looked at me and said, "Then it's decided, Russia it is." I looked like a deer in the headlights. I knew no Russian, and I knew nothing about Russia aside from the stories Stephan recited to me about his time with Mikhail Romanoff way back when. I'd be entirely dependent on my guy (Thank goodness Putin had died and they became a democratic society).

True to my word, Declan and Tom arrived a couple of days later, and I sent Declan home and had Tom stay with us. "Why shouldn't I stay with Declan?" Tom asked. "I don't know if Declan's parents want to deal with your relationship at this time" (not knowing if they knew or not). "We've talked to them and told them everything. They'll be upset if I don't go." "Sorry, I just wanted everything to be easy on them. Okay, go be with Declan then." I threw my car keys to Tom, and he sped away (well, there's a funny side note to my biography). Funny how time changes attitudes (and living too long carries old biases). Stephan asked about Tom, and I explained that he would be staying with David and Jen. He nodded as though it was not a big thing. "How are the plans going? When do you want to leave?" I said, "Well, the plans are pretty well set, and we can travel whenever, but do you want to leave with Violet in a frail condition? I think we should make a house call and see how things are going before we leave. I really don't want to be in Russia, and then she dies. "Point made, let's make a visit. Do you want to drive or shall I?" I told him that Tom had my car, and we headed to the garage.

We pulled up near the house, there had to be about seven cars there, and walked up to the house. David answered the door and invited us in. They had a crew of people in the living room, and we were told that Jen was only letting three to four people in at a time. "I want to keep things low-key so Mom doesn't get overwhelmed." Our time came, and we saw Violet lying in bed, looking pale but in good spirits. Stephan handed her the bouquet of fresh flowers we brought, let her smell and peruse them before handing them off to Jen to place in a vase. Jen left to handle that while we sat by her bed. Stephan asked her how she actually felt, and she replied, "I feel like I'm near the end of my journey. It's been one hell of a ride, and you two made my last chapter the best with all you've done for my family and me. I can go to my rest knowing they're in good hands. Thank you for everything." Stephan, through glassy eyes said, "It has been my pleasure to know you and your wonderful family.

Indeed, I will take care of them as long as they want. Rest sweet angel, your wings await." I thought the last sentence was a little premature and hopefully would be taken as a token of hope. Violet thanked us for our visit and bade us farewell. I thought that odd also, as we usually heard 'I'll see you later'.

We took our leave, and Stephan said to move our plans out by one month. I wanted to ask why, but I think I already knew the answer. True to her word, we received word that Violet entered eternity during the night quietly, calmly, and with a light spirit. We went back to check on the family, and I watched as Stephan opened her bedroom window. A warm breeze blew in, and we were serenaded by a cardinal. A butterfly landed on the sill and stayed for a few minutes before continuing its journey. I caught a glimpse of a neon blue dragonfly fly by and flutter outside the window. If we needed a sign, they were there in abundance. The only thing missing was music (as the indigenous people do) to sing her way to heaven. Stephan offered to pay for the funeral, and David shook his head no as Jen thanked him for the offer. Stephan was determined, and they finally acquiesced and let him (that's my guy, bull-headed, but in a good way).

The funeral took place about one week before the move-out date (how did Stephan know?). Stephan told them to plan on visiting Fiji once we got back and ensured that all was up to Stephan's standards. We opted for a mausoleum for Violet and went to the blessing the day after the funeral. Stephan insisted on gold-flecked marble for the structure. The door was flanked by a Corinthian column on each side. Stephan insisted on urns at the corners of the tomb so that we could place plants every year in memory.

We decided to fly out the following day and let Fiji know we'd be a day early. Wheels up at 10 am, and we were on our way to Fiji with Davin and the others in tow. We all slept for most of the flight. Deli sandwiches were packed, so hunger wasn't a problem. Davin ate two, I ate one, and Stephan picked his apart and ate some of his as though it was a charcuterie board. Finally, Fiji came into view, and we readied ourselves for landing. Into the airport, customs cleared, and into the limousine to the harbor where our boat was waiting. Bruce was waiting at the pier with Allen and Darren to take us to the island. Not much was said until Wakaya came into view. Davin spoke, saying, "It looks so serene and inviting, no wonder you bought it." Stephan nodded to him and whispered in his ear, "Blame it on the 'wife'." Davin chuckled at that, but I "AHEM'd" my guy and crossed my arms, turned to shun him. Arms wrapped around me, and Stephan kissed my neck. "I surrender already, mister man." The kissing continued, and I felt like the most appreciated person on the boat, or should I say the world.

We approached the dock, Bruce jumped out and secured the boat. Allen and Darren took the supplies and foodstuffs to the house. Tom and Declan appeared together, hand in hand, and Davin ran to join them. The 'family' reunited, we all went inside. I was asked if I wanted the tour, and I said okay, and Stephan nodded. Allen guided our steps, and we saw all the renovations along with the improvements. If you didn't know it, you would never know there had been a fire. The architects excelled and matched the original structure perfectly. They upgraded the materials used and added extensive solar panels and wind turbines to reduce the electrical and heating/cooling costs. We heard "dinner is served," and we headed in the direction of the aromas, all the while drooling, savoring the upcoming feast by Jamie. 'Island' salsa (with mango and Sriracha hot sauce). Toasted flat bread, ham slices cured in the island's smokehouse, and salami from the main island. The main course was roasted piglet, surrounded by Polynesian root vegetables. Dessert was a simple sorbet made with papaya. We ate as though it was our first meal in a week, and even Stephan ate heartily (totally out of character for him).

I nodded to the others and then side-eyed towards Stephan so as to have them take note. Stephan caught on and then casually mentioned, "I need to keep my strength up for tonight and leered in my direction. The group erupted in laughter and started making jokes about how to relax, how to limber up, and more NSFW, sordid, good-humored joking, and pointed to me. I guess I stepped in it as I knew how my night would end (I hope the costumes were packed).

We awoke very early in the morning, went to lunch, and then Tom and Declan took us on the tour of the 'new and enlarged' patio. Tom made sure that the trees were moved out and replanted so that the view became even more exquisite, with lower plants and bushes framing the entrance to a private beach, facing the open seas and magnificent sky above. Tom had placed a fire pit with seats on the beach and on the corner of the patio. "I know where we'll be tonight." Stephan grinned, and so I casually mentioned that everyone was invited to join us (as parts of me needed more rest than just sleep). Stephan looked disappointed but said nothing (as usual).

The week went fast, and we headed home, making room for the Meyers. I asked if Davin wanted to stay behind and come home with his parents. "I didn't know that it was an option. I'd love to take you up on it, but how will you two get along without an entourage?" Stephan retorted, "I think I've gotten along pretty well in the 550 years before you came along." Davin felt foolish now, and I whispered to him,

"There is only one winning move when taking on Stephan, don't play." Davin nodded, apologized to Stephan, and went to tell Declan the news.

We boarded the bus and left Fiji behind. We stopped in Sacramento due to a sensor issue and had to stay for a couple of days. I rented a limousine for us as Stephan booked us a rental home for the stay. The limousine came with a driver. I inquired about a restaurant, and he suggested fast food. Stephan heard that and grabbed his phone, googling up proper restaurants. Stephan called out to the driver, "1112 2nd st, The Firehouse Restaurant, if you please." He nodded and headed in that direction. We arrived, he parked, and got the doors for us. Stephan asked if he would like to join us, and at first, he declined, saying, "That's too ritzy for me, I live on a driver's salary." Stephan reached into his pocket, produced his black card, and said, "What if I pay? Now, how's your appetite?" The kid looked at the card, knowing its value, and just nodded as Stephan led the way inside.

Stephan and I weren't exactly dressed for the place (not to mention the driver), but Stephan was undeterred. He marched up to the maitre d ' and asked for a table. The guy looked at us and was about to say something when Stephan waved the 'magic card'. We were seated at a private dining area and were asked what we'd like to drink. "I'll have your best chardonnay, please." He disappeared, and the driver just looked at my guy and said, "Can I ask you a question, sir?" Stephan nodded, and then the driver continued, "Who are you and where are you from?" Stephan cleared his throat and said, "My name is Stephan. This is Carl, my husband. I am originally from Greece, then Italy, then France, Spain, Portugal, England, Russia, and finally the United States. Why?" "I was just wondering cause I never saw anyone take control like that before." Stephan calmly said, "Well, now you have. What would you like to eat?" pointing to the menu. "I don't rightly know, I never saw these kinds of foods before." "Would you like me to order for us?" The kid nodded sheepishly. "No problem. Let's start with an appetizer, the Firehouse trio, smoked crab and risotto cake, braised local pork belly, and Carpaccio Crostini. Then, butternut squash soup with pumpkin seed brittle, crème fraiche, and micro herbs. Now for the entree, oven roasted maple duck consisting of central valley farro, cipollini onions, golden raisins, frisee fines herbes, peach demi-glaze, spiced marcona almond crumble, herbed beurre monte. For dessert, I think a simple Grand Marnier Soufflé, raspberry puree, vanilla bean, and Grand Marnier Anglaise. That will be all, thanks."

The maitre'd took the order (expecting a large tip, no doubt) and left us to our wine and rolls. I broke the silence by asking the kid his name. "My name is Miguel, Miguel Esteban sir. I was born in Puerto Rico, but my parents moved here when I was 4, so I guess you can say I'm from here." I asked him why he was driving limousines for a living. "I lost both my parents in a car accident when I was 19 and had to fend for myself. I don't make much money as I don't get many demands for a limousine. You are actually the first this month, so money is actually really tight" (again, probably playing Stephan for a big tip). I asked him his age, and he said, "I'm 27 but look much younger" (sounds like he wanted a happy ending for us and him. Sorry kid, but that guy's all mine). As he mentioned, the appetizers arrived. The kid chowed down, and we picked, knowing how much food was coming. I enjoyed watching him as I was remembering my first time with Stephan eating out and acting pretty much the same as this kid (it was good to remember these things and how far I've come).

After the meal, I asked Miguel if he wanted the leftovers for himself, and he readily agreed. The maitre'd boxed the food and brought the check. He left it in front of Miguel, and he nearly choked when he saw the total. Stephan took the check to the host station and talked to the Maitre'd. They left for the kitchen, and the kid started to squirm. "What's going on? I thought he could afford this place." I calmed him down and said, "Stephan likes to thank the chef and staff personally when he enjoys a meal. Watch when he leaves the kitchen and see the staff." The kid responded, "But he barely ate anything." I told him Stephan rarely eats a lot.

The Maitre'd led Stephan to the host station and took his card. Stephan signed, then handed the maitre d ' some money. The maitre'd smiled ear to ear and wished us a good night. We rose and headed for the door. Miguel thanked us profusely, hoping for the same kind of tip. We arrived at our stopover 'house', which looked like a mansion to the kid. He pulled up to the front door, and we got out. Stephan asked that Miguel be available at 10 am the next day, and he promised. Stephan handed him a couple of bills. Miguel seemed disappointed until he recognized the man on the bill. Ben Franklin, three to be exact. The smile returned quickly, and Miguel left us to ourselves. We went inside and got comfortable in the den. "It's not like home, I miss the rug." I laughed, and we sat on the floor enjoying the fire (electric is just not the same as a real fire). We made the best of a spontaneous moment.

We used the bed, showered, but didn't really utilize the whole house. We ordered in for breakfast and took the trash with us. Miguel arrived promptly, Stephan called the air crew and found that the bus was ready for flight, so we had Miguel take us there. He pulled in front of our plane and went to get our bags. He asked if it was ours, and Stephan said definitely. "It's the only way to fly." Miguel said to us it was a shame we were leaving, as we were so 'accommodating' to him (and the money was outrageous). Stephan gave him a small wad of bills and had him give us his number in case we were back in Sacramento. We told him that we would probably start laying over in Sacramento on the way to and from our private island near Fiji. He almost fainted as we ascended the stairs and got on the plane.

I asked Stephan how much he had given the kid, and he said, "Does it matter?" I shook my head, and Stephan said, "Actually, I gave him enough to pay his rent for the next six months." I started hoping that the Meyers would be as kind to him as I knew Stephan had been. What was I thinking? Stephan would take care of it himself. Home to our beloved Baltimore. We arrived and entered the hangar, but I didn't see the limousine waiting. "I purposely didn't tell them we were coming home today. I wanted to give them more quiet time. Call the warehouse and have someone drive a car to pick us up." I called the warehouse and had Johnny 'Dewey' Jones come get us. I figured he could be away from the gallery for a few hours.

Dewey arrived about a half hour later in a classic 57 Belair. I recognized the car because of its blue and white paint job with the fins and all. We got back to the house and quietly slipped in until the dogs heard us and came running. Barking and tails wagging, Winnie and Mary just about wet themselves as they kept rubbing themselves against us (they were starting to look old due to their whitening muzzles). The troops descended, and the questions started. I looked around for Bobbie, and Elizabeth said, "He's at school." Things were running smoothly, and for once, I was grateful. Bob asked about Davin, and I said, "He's staying in Fiji and will accompany his parents when they come back."

We departed for the den for a smoke and a nice glass of Bourbon (I can't believe I'm just so nonchalant about this lifestyle now. I need to remember where I started so I can appreciate this more. Most people would kill to have what I have now). Stephan grabbed his diary and started writing in it about our latest adventures. I couldn't bring myself to write anything, enjoying the crackling of a real fire, a good glass of Bourbon, a Cuban cigar, and my person in the room with me, and a rug that was hopefully missing us as much as we were missing it. After half an hour, I called Stephan to me, and we settled in, happy to be alone together.

2074 went by fast, and we were now in 2075. My age seemed to be catching up as I was now 108 and Stephan 563. Spring arrived, and we lost sweet Mary to diabetes. Winnie mourned her more than the rest of us and walked through the house, sniffing for her scent. I left Mary's blanket near Winnie's bed to comfort her, and it seemed to help. Not a good way to start the year. I now wish that I had spent more time with her. We had her interred in the garden where she loved to lie. Stephan had a small sculpture placed with a plaque that read, "Sweet Mary, Rest in Peace, thank you for all your years of loyalty and love." Winnie would lie on the grave daily, even in the rain. Stephan asked if I wanted another dog, and I said no.

The Meyers returned from Fiji, and we went to retrieve Davin. I asked how their trip was, and they both smiled and said, "It was like a dream vacation. The boys were both there, and the staff was on point and very accommodating. Tom took us on a tour of the gardens, and we were surprised when we stopped in Sacramento on the way home. The driver said he knew you two; his name was Miguel, I think, and he made sure we were spoiled. The restaurant served great food, although I couldn't pronounce half the ingredients. We tried to tip at the restaurant and the driver, but they said you had taken care of it. So thank you for everything. If there's anything we can do to help you in any way, let us know," Jen said. Stephan just said it as our way of thanking them for raising their boys to be good men and for allowing us to share their family.

By summer, the gardens were in full bloom, but I caught Stephan reading some of his old diaries in the atrium. I didn't know whether to broach the subject with him or not, but I decided I needed to know where his head was at. "Hey Stephan, reminiscing about the good old days?" Stephan looked up from his diary. "Just reminding myself of my glorious life before and with you. I think you understand now, seeing as you've probably outlived even your expectations of what a long life is. You were the one looking for longevity, as I remember." I pondered the idea and then returned with, "So where are you in your journey? Are you up to me yet, or still in the 17th or 1800's?" Stephan laid down the diary and said, "Wouldn't you like to know?" "Actually, I would, husband." Stephan handed me the diary, and it was in Italian. I could make out a few words and pieced together that he was in the 1800's. "So I'm still about 150 years away in the future," Stephan said, "Looks like it," and fell back laughing in his chair. I literally threw the book at him and pouted. He stood and reached out to me. I turned three-quarters away from him and crossed my arms to make a point. He hugged me tight and said I was the best part of his story. I got all gushy and let him turn me back around before falling into him (the guy knew how to push all the right buttons).

I asked Stephan if he'd like to travel to Italy, and he lit up. "Do you want to stay with Junior and Hunter or do you want to stay at Tony's, senior or junior, makes no difference?" I looked directly into those beautiful eyes and said, "How about renting a villa close to all of them but not with them? I'd like you all to myself for a change." Stephan shot back, "What about Davin, do we leave him here?" I looked back at him and softened my tone, "Okay, maybe Davin and I stay with everybody for a couple of days and then take day trips alone, okay?" Stephan said, "We'll talk about it," and left it there.

I made the arrangements, and we decided to leave in June. June turned out to be rainy and damp. We held off for a few days, and on the first sunny day, we took off for Italy. The flight was easy, and the weather held up. The boat appeared through the clouds, and I relaxed, knowing that Stephan wanted to come back. We pulled into the hangar, went through customs, and headed to the rented limousine. "Where are we headed now, sir?" Stephan whispered in the driver's ear to keep me in suspense. I guess I'd just have to wait. We were driven into the country, but not towards the family manse, so probably one of Tony's homes. Surprise, neither had he rented a villa near Tony junior's vineyard. "You're a real ass sometimes, you know that." Stephan smiled widely and nodded. "I wanted my guy to be happy, is that so bad?" I lightly punched his arm before planting a sloppy kiss on his mouth. "Yes, I'm happy. So happy in fact, that I'm going to change into something special, wink, wink."

I was rewarded with a smack on my backside as I passed Stephan. I took several steps and turned to find Stephan right behind me. His smile just kept growing, and I started flirting. We found the bedroom and headed for the suitcases. I believe we set records in changing clothes. I don't know why, because they were about to come off at about the same speed. The night recorded the moments as we united as one.

Morning found the bedroom in tatters as we laughed and realized we had to clean up after ourselves. I took care of our clothes as Stephan took care of the bedding. Stephan called Tony junior and Dale to see if they were up for a visit. "We were in the neighborhood and decided to stop by if you want." Tony junior jumped up and down saying, "Of course we want you to visit, is Carl with you?" Stephan said to ready themselves for an invasion. "Bring it on," said Dale. Davin asked how Tony junior met Dale. I said, "Well, they met through us, and Dale left Fiji for Italy, that's why Jaime is in Fiji with Bruce." The villa we rented came with a maid, thankfully, so we left and traveled to Tony Junior's vineyard. We arrived, and the boys came to greet us. "Welcome to our home, do you want to go to the tasting room or would you prefer lunch first?" I was about to say lunch, but Stephan beat me to it and said, "Lunch would be nice" (I said a quiet thank you to God for that). We were led to the table where we were greeted by a young lady. Tony did the introductions, "Gentlemen, this is Isabella, my younger sister, she's helping me out for the summer. Bella, this is Carl, Stephan, and Davin." She said, "Very nice to meet you, sirs, come sit, eat, and drink." So we did. I caught Davin giving the eye to Bella, and I clued in Stephan with a nod. Stephan looked around as if taking in the view and noticed what I saw. Nothing was said, but after lunch, Davin offered to assist in the clean-up. Tony asked Bella to bring Davin to the tasting room when they were done and led us to the barn. "These barrels are new, but the aged wine is over there. We've been having bumper crops since your investments. Would you like some shipped home?" Stephan said to let him taste them first, and he'd let Tony know later. Davin arrived about 15 minutes later with Bella in tow. They seemed very happy together. Stephan decided on several cases, and Tony had them set aside for shipment. The time came for us to leave, but I could tell that Davin wanted more time with Bella, so I asked Tony if Davin could stay the night so Stephan and I could have some alone time. He winked at me and said yes. I asked Davin to stay the night at the vineyard and gave him my excuse. He asked if we could handle being alone and then figured out what being alone meant. He agreed quickly before we could change our minds.

We said our goodbyes and took the ride back to the villa. The maid was waiting and asked what we'd like for supper. Stephan gave her the menu for the evening, and she left us. Soon after, we were treated to a grand antipasto, a simple gnocchi with olive oil, garlic, and butter sauce, and crusty bread grilled and rubbed with garlic. Chianti to drink and a lemon sorbet to finish. She removed the plates, cleaned the kitchen, and said goodnight. We were alone under the Italian night sky. Stephan played some music and danced with me under the stars. The fire was ablaze and crackling in the fire pit. Magic was in the air as my guy led my steps. He finished with a dip and a deep kiss. I hoped he'd continue this mood through the night (I wasn't disappointed lol).

Morning came, and we awoke to the aroma of coffee drifting up to our room. We cleaned up and descended toward the kitchen. The maid (Elena) asked why we were in the kitchen serving ourselves, as she was there to do that. Stephan explained in Italian that we usually did that and asked her to join us. "What about breakfast, sirs?" Again, Stephan assured her that some cheese and grilled bread with the espresso would be fine. She finally agreed and joined us at the table. They talked in Italian, and I could only grab a few words here and there. He got her laughing, and they looked at me. I could only shrug, and then they laughed harder. We finished our coffees, and Elena cleaned up. We told her we were leaving for the day and would probably not be back until supper again, but to expect three for supper. She nodded and giggled as she went about her tasks.

"What exactly were you talking about that got her laughing?" Stephan told me to learn Italian if I was that nosy. I said, "Spill hubby or I'll ship the suits back home." Stephan yelled, "Okay, I'll tell you, but you've got to swear the suits stay with us." I nodded, and he said, "Well, she was telling me that she was not used to having such easy guests at the villa. She wished that all her guests were like us. I told her that we had our moments, but usually we're easy. Then I asked her who actually owned the villa, and she said a relative. I asked if they'd be willing to sell, and she said immediately that if she signed off, but that was her only source of income. I told her I would be willing to buy the villa and hire her as the house manager. She asked what that would mean to her. I said she would live at the villa, and keep it up for when we visited. I would pay for all maintenance and taxes, and she would always have a salary. I think she wanted to kiss me and said that she would get in touch with her cousin and try to make it happen. Then she looked at you and asked if you were the wife, and I said yes. That's when she broke out laughing. Sorry, but it broke the ice. How would you like to own this villa as our home away from home?" I showed him my yes, and we got ready to leave for Tony's.

We arrived at the vineyard gate and saw Dale tending to the vines. A look down the rows found Bella and Davin trimming the vines back. I said to Stephan, "I guess Davin and Bella are going to be a pair. What do we do if he wants to stay in Italy, and what would we tell David and Jenny?" Stephan grinned and responded, "If he wants to stay, then he stays. If Bella wants to come home with him, then she comes. Let the kids make their minds up. As far as David and Jen are concerned, we tell them of the kid's decision and let the cards fall where they will.

Always the logical one, Stephan just shrugged it off and went in search of Tony junior. Dale had pointed to the house, so we ventured in that direction. We entered the house calling out, and a servant told us Tony was in bed and under the weather. "Sirs, he's coughing badly, and I've already called for the doctor." I advised Stephan to wait for the doctor, and he nodded and called Tony senior. Soon, the house was full of people waiting for the diagnosis from the doctor. Dale was pacing back and forth, almost panicking.

Everyone surrounded the doctor to hear as he spoke," Anthony has contracted the flu and needs to be isolated, as well as anyone who has been around him in the last three days. Has everybody been vaccinated this year?" Heads turned, and to my surprise, no one nodded. "Looks like everyone here needs to isolate also. I can call the office and have inoculation shots delivered. Once vaccinated, you should be clear after three days yourselves." I called Elena and asked if she had been vaccinated, and she replied yes. I then told her we would be back in three days.

The shots arrived, and we were dosed. Now the waiting game. Thankfully, none of us caught it, but poor Tony was in for it. That kid was on liquids, threw up everything but his memories, and lost about 13 pounds before coming around. I think Dale lost that much or more from the stress and running everywhere. The doctor released us all, and we left Dale to it. It seemed that Bella and Davin had talked about their options and decided to come back with us. We informed Tony senior, and Bella came back to 'our' villa. Elena greeted us with good news. The cousin had decided to sell it to us in order to retire. The papers were drawn up and signed, and the villa was ours. Elena chatted up Stephan for the better part of an hour before bedtime. Again, I insisted on a translation that Stephan provided. "It states that Elena has control of the residence and speaks for us in all matters with the exception of a sale of the property." We welcomed the kids to the villa and said they could visit any time they wished.

We got Bella's papers and her passport along with a visa to stay in Baltimore, and then said our goodbyes and left to return home. Bella was really impressed with the 'bus,' but Davin took it in stride as he was becoming more comfortable with the lifestyle. Baltimore opened her arms to us, and we embraced our arrival. We waited while they went over Bella's paperwork, and they released her into our custody as I called for a ride home. We dropped Bella and Davin off at his parents' house (I wish I were a fly on the wall when Davin presented Bella as his girlfriend). We continued on until we finally arrived at our portico. We entered the house with full jet lag, but it seemed the house was all in chaos, decorating for the holidays. "Looks like we should have stayed away about four days more," Stephan said. Bobbie ran into my arms, looking for his presents. I had to put him down for a minute while I got his suitcase of goodies. "Thanks, Uncle Carl, wuv you!" as he took the presents and tried playing with them all at once. Elizabeth stared me down and said, "One day you're gonna get a piece of my mind, Uncle Carl." For once, I was glad to be home and hoped the holidays would be quiet (my lips to God's ears). As usual, the festivities were over the top, and we invited nearly all the extended family's relatives.

We moved the feast to a hotel with a ballroom, as we had anticipated about three hundred attendees. Stephan called the hotel and booked the whole place, rooms included (I don't even want to know how much he spent on that and then brought in Jaime, Harold, and Elena to cook the meals. I can only say that it cost about 1.5 million but was worth every penny to see the faces of everyone there. The surprise (if you could call it that) was when Davin proposed to Bella. The kicker was when Tom proposed to Declan. The Meyers' kids were getting married. Stephan nodded to me, and I went to take notes so I could develop a budget for the nuptials. The night was magical, and everyone talked about how they knew us and stories from their relationship with us. The moment that brought tears to my eyes was when Stephan and I were called to the front of the ballroom by Bob and Elizabeth, made to sit as they all toasted their hosts, "Here's to our hosts, Carl and Stephan, they brought us all together and stitched this varied group into a 'family'. May their love for us be as strong as our love for them, CHEERS!." We raised our glasses, clinked, and drank. Stephan arose and simply said, "Thank you all for allowing us to share your lives and your progeny. To many more years, Yamas!" The night ended a little while later, and we headed for home. I slept that night in the arms of "The crown of heaven's light" (that's Stephan Orion in Greek).

New Year's came with our little tradition in our room, and we ushered in 2076 with a kiss and new suits. Tom and Declan decided to wait until the fall to marry, but Davin was in a hurry. He couldn't wait that long, so he decided on a June bride as his mate. The consensus was June in Italy and the fall in Fiji. Bella wondered if they would have enough time to plan the nuptials, and I assured her that Eddie could handle it. I made the call, and Eddie literally screamed when I asked him to handle it (I'll either have to work until I die or Stephan will have to sell off assets). He asked about the budget, and Stephan took the phone out of my hand and told Eddie to just use his best judgment. Stephan then handed me back the phone and chortled as Eddie droned on about details in minutia (I think Stephan wanted some alone time).

The call finally ended, and I went in search of my husband. He was in the den holding a cigar and a Bourbon. He pointed to the mantel, and I saw he had set out the same for me. I closed and locked the door, lightly punched Stephan in his arm as he continued to laugh, and lit my cigar. "You knew he was going to talk my ear off and you said that anyway." Stephan nodded and raised his glass. I guess I knew when I was beat, but I leered at him and said, "This means it's 'other night' tonight. Bottoms up" (literally). We drank, and Stephan roared out loud with laughter, "We'll see about that. I can still get upstairs faster than you, Carl. Besides, my suit doesn't fit you."

Spring arrived, and we decided to spend more time in Baltimore. The Meyers clan became daily visitors, and Davin left Bella in Elizabeth's capable hands. Davin went about his duties and thought back to his conversation he had back in Fiji, "It doesn't matter if you're straight or not, people get introduced to others and matches happen." Eddie was in communication with Bella's parents, Tony Sr. and Maria, making plans and telling them not to worry about the cost (I keep getting heartburn just listening to the plans). Maria insisted on a wedding at the vineyard, and Tony Sr. gave in. We prepared to fly to Italy, stopping in England to get Anthony and Eddie. A few days later, we arrived at the villa, and Elena was waiting for us. The time from our purchase until our visit must have been kind to her, as she looked vibrant for an older woman. Her clothes had been upgraded, and she stood more statuesque. She let us know that the villa was ready for an onslaught of guests. I walked inside and saw that she had been renovating the interior. She mentioned that Eddie had come over to visit while making preparations for the nuptials and had advised her as to our tastes (more likely, he used his tastes. I guess we shouldn't have fawned over his renovations of the manor).

The time had come for the wedding, and the guests were arriving. Davin, Bella, David, Jen, Tom, and Declan were the first to arrive. It seems that the family 'bus' was becoming a necessity more than a luxury. Anthony broke away from his business and joined Eddie at the villa. "Feels and looks a lot like the manor, Eddie. I wonder why?" Declan and Tom asked about a bachelor party as the womenfolk grimaced. Eddie said, "It's all taken care of, boys. I have a menu, the music, and the entertainment hired" (I prayed that he didn't hire a stripper, but if he did, I hoped it wasn't a guy). The next off the bus were Junior and Hunter. Followed shortly after by Bob, Elizabeth, and Bobbie. The Meyers clan was having more of a problem with the cost of the trip, so Stephan stepped in and gifted the tribe with round-trip tickets. David quietly thanked Stephan and asked sheepishly, "How can I ever thank you and Carl for everything you've done, straightening out Declan, putting Davin through college, making Violet's last years wonderful, and now this. I have no words to match your generosity," Stephan said, "You have allowed Carl and me to share your family. That's worth more than anything money could buy."

David turned away and went in search of Maria, Jen, and Elena. Stephan stepped away, and soon Tony Jr. and Dale arrived and whisked Stephan away. About an hour later, three limousines, two black and one white, followed by Tony Jr., showed up. Stephan stepped out of the white one and said, "How do they look? I bought them for the wedding and to keep at the villa. I don't think Elena will mind." I kept thinking about the price tag for this wedding and shuddered, thinking about Tom and Declan's wedding in Fiji. I mean, a straight wedding pales in comparison to a gay wedding. With Eddie at the helm, I figured around ten million dollars.

The rest of the guests arrived and were shuttled to their accommodations. Tony Sr. had the entire vineyard prepared for the nuptials. Bella was kept away from Davin for a couple of days before the wedding, as Eddie had planned, and he notified the gents of the bachelor party at Tony Jr. and Dale's vineyard. Davin was brought by Dale to the tasting barn and made to sit at the head table as the festivities began. I was nervous from the beginning, but it was very tasteful and the night flowed along much better than I had anticipated. Eddie hired a beautiful stripper, but she was actually an exotic dancer and was much classier and stayed partially clothed. Davin was red with embarrassment, and we all laughed. The straight men were happy, and the gay men were talking about her outfit material and shoe combination. All in all, a good night.

The day of the wedding came, and Davin stood at the makeshift altar waiting for the bridal march to begin. The ushers sat everyone, then the mother of the bride and the mother of the groom. The music started, the ushers and bridesmaids entered and walked to the altar, and the march began. The entire congregation stood, looked towards the door, and Isabella and Tony Sr. appeared. They walked to the front, and an emotional Davin got all glassy-eyed and choked up. He came down to receive his bride from her father and whispered that he would always honor and protect her. They walked up the last two steps, and the ceremony began. It took about 45 minutes to read the bands and exchange rings, but then came the moment when the pastor said, "You may now kiss the bride." Davin leaned in as countless doves were released into the sky. The kiss lasted a bit, then they turned to face the assembly as the pastor said, "Please greet the newlyweds, Davin and Isabella Meyers."

The guests were ushered to the reception hall as the bridal party was taken for pictures. I will say, upon entering the hall, Eddie had gone beyond grand (and for the cost, it should have been expected). It was tasteful, elegant, and sublime all at the same time. The service for the meal was buffet, but not the ordinary fare. Elena, Jaime, Harold, and staff pulled out all the stops. Crudité, charcuterie boards, relish trays with Calamata olives, prosciutto and cheeses, pepperoni, artisan breads, olive oil, and balsamic vinegar. Then onto the salads, mixed greens, potato, and pasta. Followed by pasta and sauces, meatballs, and sausages. Following that were meats, prime rib cut to order, roast beef, chicken roasted, ham cured by Tony Sr., wines by the case, and imported champagne. The wedding and groom's cakes were in the corner. The wedding cake was a five-tier yellow cake with white frosting, yellow frosting roses, edible pearls, and the top had Lladro porcelain figures of a groom and bride.

Davin and Bella cut the cake, served each other (nicely so as not to mess up her make-up), and sent the cake to the back for cutting and serving. The music played, and people danced and drank far into the night. The newlyweds headed out for their honeymoon in (where else) Fiji. We went back to the villa and got some well-deserved sleep. I think everyone slept in because I went to the cold kitchen and made coffee in an urn. It finished as a sleepy Elena entered and began apologizing for not tending to us. Stephan grabbed her and spun her around as I served the coffee. Stephan told her that we could take care of ourselves if need be and not to sweat it. She smiled and started breakfast. "Eggs Benedict on toast points, if I remember, boys." We nodded, and I handed Stephan his coffee as he grabbed the newspaper.

I asked Stephan if he wanted to return home quickly or maybe go to Greece for a quick getaway. He shot me a quizzical look and then smiled and nodded yes to Greece. "I'll make arrangements for the others to take chartered planes home so we can use the bus to continue on" (I figured that after the money we spent on this wedding, what was another couple hundred thousand). We left two days later, after saying all the goodbyes, and headed to Greece. Stephan called Andreas so that they would be expecting us, and they were thrilled. Andreas picked us up at the airport, and we arrived to see Vasiliki waving from the front door.

Vasi ushered us in as Andreas parked the limousine in the garage. I could smell the food as we were led to the dining room. Andreas joined us as we sat and prepared for the feast. Stephan took a bit of each plate as it was passed to him while Andreas and I chowed down. Vasi looked at Stephan and told him he needed to eat more, as he looked undernourished. Stephan laughed and responded that he would lose his modeling contract if he ate more. She poked him, and they laughed heartily. I really loved the interplay of those two, and I think we needed the downtime to reset ourselves. We spent about a week there before heading home to Baltimore.

We arrived home, and it seemed quieter than normal. The girls didn't come to greet us, so we called out for them. Elizabeth came into the room and told us that, unfortunately, Winnie and Sarah both passed during their stay at the kennel. Stephan took note and said nothing more. I teared up, and Bobbie came to me and asked why I was sad. "I wish I had spent more time with them, Bobbie." Bobbie said, "But Uncle Carl, they went over the rainbow bridge to play with Mary. Mommy told me so. She said that they went, so when we go, they will be waiting for us there." I tousled his hair, hugged him deeply, and said, "You're right, I guess I just forgot, thanks." Then I went to the den and bawled my eyes out. Stephan embraced me and served me a Bourbon and started a fire. We sat in silence for our lost pets.

About a week passed, and Leonard showed up, interesting. Stephan took him into the atrium, and they talked for about twenty minutes. Leonard left, saying, "I'll get right to it, boss." I sidled up to Stephan and asked what was going on. "I don't believe that the girls magically decided to shed their mortal coil at the same time. I asked Leonard to nose around and see if there is any truth to it." I looked at Stephan and said, "What's the use? They're gone now." Stephan let me stay with my emotions as he led me out of the atrium. We landed in the kitchen and had a sandwich (Roast beef, tomato, and lettuce with Russian dressing, as I think Stephan has banned bologna in the house). "Let's just wait until Leonard reports back and see what's up, ok?" I nodded and munched away on my sandwich.

It took about two weeks for Leonard to get back to us. He went to Stephan, and he asked me to join them in the atrium. "Okay, bosses, first of all, I found the kennels to be very clean and spacious. The staff was very accommodating, and the owners actually took me on a tour. When I mentioned your names, they took me to their office and put the files out of everything they did and did not do during Winnie and Sarah's stay. I was told that they perished by natural causes, and the veterinarian concurred that in the file. What I saw during the tour bothered me a little, as things seemed a bit too tidy for a kennel. I wasn't allowed to see the other animals there, and that raised some red flags. I was gracious and left, letting them think that would be the end of it, but I contacted Alex, my forensics buddy, and we developed a plan to get the real story. It seems that one of their staff had some legal issues, and we used it to leverage him into spilling the beans about Winnie and Sarah. The first words out of his mouth were an apology for your loss. He then went on to tell us that the girls had gotten into some staff person's leftover lunch that had onions in it, as well as some grapes and chocolate bars. They neglected to get the girls to an animal hospital, and they died from the poisoning in their systems. The vet was paid to write that they died naturally. Please don't tell them I told you."

Stephan grimaced at the words, thanked Leonard, and told him to have Alex bill us for his time, along with a thanks. I could have cut the air with a knife as I saw the consternation on Stephan's face and the chill in the room. He simply turned, told me he was fine, and to ask Bob to see him in the den (by which he meant 'the war room'). I went in search of Bob and knew things were about to take on a dark tone. Bob was in the courtyard, and I motioned for him. He came close, and I told him that Stephan was waiting in the den for him. He smiled as though he was going to get a chance to work out his kinks. I tried to go with him, but he said, "It's better if you don't know what's happening, Carl." I stayed in the yard and took in the sun, just imagining what was about to happen. First would be battle plans, then the assault, and the coup de gras or final victory.

It took another month to map out the plans, assemble the strike team, and ensure that the vet would also suffer for abetting the crime. Step one: Find out everything about the kennel and the owners. Then any mortgage or lien on the property. It seems that the owners were heavily mortgaged and had used their family home to secure the debt (bad move). Stephan quietly bought the mortgage and called the note through a shell LLC. The owners went into panic mode and tried to contact the new holder of the note, only to be told that the CEO was in Europe on business and couldn't be reached. They then tried to gather their assets to try to get a loan to pay the call, but were told they were too heavily in debt   (

probably because Stephan had made some phone calls to the lending institutions. Faced with eviction and being homeless, they thought maybe to burn the place down and collect the insurance, but Stephan had that covered, too. The insuring company had been advised to cancel its insurance before the eviction. The insurance cancellation letter arrived before the eviction notice. The owners then tried to come to the LLC office on file (Stephan had registered it in Fiji, one step ahead), but realized they couldn't afford the price to get there.

They next tried getting more kennel boarders, but they were being boycotted for some reason. The last resort was to pack up and just leave it all behind and start over somewhere else. Stephan started laughing as his plans were working so well. Next came the vet. Bob called dibs on him and sent Leonard on a mission to find out about his foibles. It seemed that he liked dogs, racing dogs that is, and he really was not good at betting the odds. Bob bought out his debt and then paid him a visit. Five days later, the vet had relocated, and his office was closed (did I mention he relocated to...wait for it, you guessed, New Jersey).

Stephan realized that he now owned a kennel and a home, and he offered it to Davin and Bella. "Consider it a present to get started in this world." Bella said she would love to start up the kennel as a business, and they thanked us for the 'new', fully furnished home. That took care of the properties we had acquired.

The year was only half over, and so much had happened. The time was running away, and autumn was on our doorstep as was Tom and Declan's wedding (I'm getting too old for this much activity). Lady Eddie took the reins (although he was now 90) and really went all out to get Fiji ready for both the wedding and the reception. We arrived early to assist (and hopefully keep the price down, which was useless). Eddie outdid the Tournament of Roses parade with flowers, and the ceremony could melt the toughest of hearts. The reception took place on the new patio (I didn't recall it being that big). Tom was handsome in his tuxedo. Declan was led to the front by David and Jen and handed off. The resplendent couple recited their vows as the sun set on the clear, warm autumn breeze. Lady Eddie timed everything down to the minute, and the evening sky even matched the colors of the bridal party outfits. We flew in the chefs from all over our properties, and Elena even came to be a part of it. Andreas and Vasiliki made the trip from Greece, and of course, England and Italy were there. With the entire extended family as witnesses, the boys exchanged vows, promised their hearts to each other, and kissed. They turned, raised joined hands as the minister said, "May I introduce Mr. Thomas and Declan Everson-Meyers?" The assembly cheered as the guys walked towards the reception tent. Cameras flashed, and pictures were being taken to commemorate the occasion. The food was laid out, and I thought Eddie had overdone it: lobster claws, giant shrimp, grilled steaks to order, baked potatoes with all the toppings, salads from around the world, specialties from Greece, Italy, England, and France. I will say it was everything I imagined it would be – expensive.

We stayed on after the wedding, not so much as to have a vacation but to allow for the guests to shuttle back to their homes on the 'bus'. Note to self, get a couple more planes if we were going to keep the tribe together. We tried to bid 2076 goodbye, but the holidays stood in our way, so bring on the merriment and chaos. Bobbie (now eight years old and in third grade) couldn't wait to help with the decorations and write his letter to Santa. We decided on a toned-down Christmas (for us) and intended on just 50 or 60 people (foolish us). We had the family tree decorated and in the atrium. Elizabeth took over the duties for booking the hotel for our guests and the ballroom for our celebration. The staff was sent to decorate the hotel banquet room, and the joint chefs arrived and commandeered the kitchen for the event. I kept my eyes on Bobbie to enjoy the event through his eyes. The wonder, the joy, and the excitement he felt were contagious, and the whole family joined in. The highlight of the night was when Davin and Bella called his parents to the center of the room and presented them with a picture, the ultrasound of their first grandchild. Champagne and wine flowed through the rest of the night. Stephan stepped forward after the commotion, and congratulations faded and said, "Looks like married life agrees with you two. Did you inform Tony Sr. and Maria?" to which Bella said, "Of course, and they're thrilled. I called them last night and Tony and Dale as well."

The celebration went on into the night, and Stephan and I left to get a well-deserved rest. Breakfast turned out to be brunch, and even that was pushing it. Our eggs Benedict on toast points tasted great with our coffee. We had to return to the hotel for the goodbyes and farewells, and some were heartfelt and touching as we knew it would be a while before seeing them again. New Year's Eve arrived quickly, and we kept our tradition in our room. A warm fire, snacks, wine, and a new set of costumes

(They wear out so fast. We toasted our 57th anniversary (a week late) and waited until midnight, kissed, repledged our love, and ran for the costumes. Needless to say, no breakfast tomorrow.

Welcome, 2077, and with it the anticipation of a new child. I thought about Declan and

Tom is out in Fiji, and they know about Davin becoming a father. I was okay not being a father, as it wasn't on my bingo card, but the boys were different. I made a call and tried to work it into the conversation.

Declan answered and said everything was great on the island, but that Tom and Matthew (his younger brother) were out gardening. I asked how he felt about becoming an uncle, and he said, "I can't wait to meet the tike. Tom and I discussed having one of our own, but the cost of a surrogate is out of our budget even with our salaries." I asked if they had the money, would they try, and he said, "Of course, Tom would provide the half for the first, and I would for the second." "How much would it cost? I would be happy to go in with Stephan if you'd like me to ask him." Declan stuttered his response, "It would cost about $100,000 for each one, and we couldn't and wouldn't ask you to do this for us." I left it there and decided I would do that for them and Declan's parents. We talked more about the gardens, and I think I got his mind off it after a while.

I went into the den later, poured the Bourbon and lit one cigar, handing the other to Stephan. He held his up, and I lit it also. "So, how much do the kids need to start their little family?

I think we could get it done for around $250,000." I looked at him, blinked twice, took a swig of the Bourbon (note to self, don't chug Bourbon), and asked how he knew before I asked. "I overheard your conversation, silly. Now go tomorrow and wire the money and tell them to get started." Stephan smirked and slapped my butt as I arranged the blanket on the bear rug in front of the roaring fire.

2077 was looking to be a spectacular year with some happy surprises. Bobbie asked his mom for a puppy, and she said that he had to get our approval before bringing another dog into the house. Bobbie came running to me as he thought I was easier than Stephan. "Uncle Carl, Mom said we could get a puppy if you and Uncle Stephan approve." I put on my poker face and stroked my chin as I pondered the question (knowing full well he was going to get it) and said that I would talk to Uncle Stephan, but not to get his hopes up. He hugged me and left a bit deflated. Stephan came around the corner and asked Bobbie why he looked so down, but Bobbie said, "Nothing, Uncle Stephan," and walked by.

Stephan asked me, "What's up with Bobbie? He looks like his best friend died." I told him, "He wants to know if he can have a puppy, and he was told he had to get our approvals first." Stephan replied, "Did you tell him no? Is that why he's down? That's kind of hurtful, don't you think?" I looked directly at Stephan and said, "I told him not to get his hopes up because I didn't have your approval. Are you saying to go ahead because I'll tell him right now if you say so." Stephan called out for Bobbie, and he ran into the room. "It seems, young man, that you want a puppy. Are you ready to care for another creature?" Bobbie nodded and looked my way for support. I nodded, and he replied, "Yes, sir, Uncle Stephan." Stephan tousled his hair and told him to tell his mom and dad that we approved. I think the kid got wings the way he literally flew out of the room and into the kitchen. We followed behind at a slower pace and arrived as he was going over the type he wanted. "I even know what I want to call her, Caran, after Uncle Carl and Uncle Stephan." He threw himself into my arms, and I almost fell over trying to catch him. It was hugs all around as he thanked us all. Elizabeth shooed him into the living room as she finished the menu for the week. I called the breeder where we got Alfred and the girls, and they said they had a third-generation pup from Alfred's line, but it was female. "Perfect, please hold the pup for us. We should be out to see her this week." The deal done, I told Elizabeth, and she said she would allow it to be a surprise.

About three days later, I asked Bobbie if he wanted to go get some ice cream with us. He jumped at the chance but said he had to ask his mom. "I cleared it with her first, I'm not that brave to offer without her consent, Bobbie." Bobbie laughed and got in the car. I told him that we were going to stop off first to get something. We pulled up to the breeders, and he heard all the yipping. He looked at me, and we all got out and went into the office. The owner happened to have the pup in the office with her (what a coincidence) and let us behind the Dutch door. When you say love at first sight, this is what they meant. Puppy raced to the boy, the boy hugged the puppy, and we all disappeared in their eyes.

Bobbie, overcome with emotion, asked if she was available, and I smiled and said, "Did you think you'd have to ask that question?" Bobbie let Caran down, and she followed him, like a puppy dog. We paid the breeder, she finished the paperwork, and handed Bobbie the lead and a collar for his new puppy. We got in the car, and Bobbie assisted Caran to get in the back. We stopped for the promised ice cream and got Caran a puppy cup. Home was an experience as Bobbie led Caran into the house, and she marked her new home. As agreed, he got paper towels and cleaned it up without question. Elizabeth shook her head and said, "You're going to make that kid spoiled as if he isn't enough already." We all laughed, and Bobbie took her outside to play (with all the toys we bought for her).

Back to life with a dog. Looks like breakfast time is re-established, or it will go to the dog. Spring came with a visit from Tom, Matt, and Declan. Tom and Matt got busy with the gardens as Declan went to visit with his parents and brother. Isabella looked very pregnant at six months, and Davin was in the middle of doing the baby's room. Declan entered and asked about all the furniture. "I guess you are going to be busy with the twins coming, Uncle Declan." They hugged and went out to have a cigar that had a blue band. "Boys Davin, does mom and dad know?" Davin said, "No, and I want to surprise them, so don't say a word. We're keeping it a secret, even from Bella's parents." "But they know you're expecting twins, right?" Davin smiled and replied, "Nope, when I said a surprise, I meant it." The guys bent to the task of finishing up the room and called Bella to put her seal of approval on the result. Bella broke down in tears (those nasty hormones) and grabbed both Declan and Davin in a group hug and kissed her husband.

The guys left around two weeks later, the puppy having dug up some of the plantings, and Bobbie dutifully replanted them while praying they stayed alive. Stephan called Davin to see how things were progressing and was told that Bella was having early contractions. Stephan asked if he wanted a visiting nurse, and Davin went into panic mode. "Put Bella on the phone, Davin, please." Davin handed the phone to Bella, and Stephan inquired as to the nurse, and Bella said, "Yes, please, poor Davin is going out of his mind with worry. I know about this from mom as she was a midwife in her youth. It'll pass, but I think Davin won't make it until the boys are born." Stephan quipped, "Boys, as in twins. How wonderful, I know it makes sense that Davin is going crazy." Bella, realizing she let the cat out of the bag, said, "Please don't mention it around, it's supposed to be a surprise for our parents." "Don't worry, Bella, your secret's safe with me. Let me get you that visiting nurse. I'll call you with the details. Davin needs a Bourbon by the way." Bella laughed and ended the call.

Stephan made the arrangements, called Bella back, and set out to see Bobbie and Caran playing in the garden. I joined him at the door, and we watched as Bobbie played fetch and tug of war with the puppy. I leaned into Stephan and said, "Well, even though we didn't have kids, we certainly have raised a few, eh, Stephan?" Stephan turned and responded, "I didn't think you wanted any. I would have moved mountains to make it happen if I for one second thought you wanted them, Carl." That made me feel sad to have made Stephan think he had disappointed me. "That's not what I meant at all, Stephan. You have given me a life that, before you, would have been impossible or highly improbable. I love everything you have done for me and with me. I can't believe that we've been married 57 years already. I've enjoyed every minute, more than I should have, mostly." Stephan smirked, motioned towards the stairs, and said, "Prove it, Carl." I came in second and knew I had a chore for the next day.

The last trimester ended abruptly 3 weeks early, and we received the call to get to the hospital. Bella was in full labor, Davin was in full panic mode, and David and Jen arrived about two minutes after us and handled Davin. Stephan called Declan and told them to charter a plane home (at our expense) because he had already sent the bus for Tony Sr., Maria, Tony Jr., and Dale to join in the chaos. It was hard labor, and it went on for what seemed like hours before the doctors decided on a C-section. When Davin heard that, he fainted. As the surgical team assembled, Declan appeared with Tom behind him. About an hour later, Italy showed up. Thirty minutes later, the doctor announced the arrival of Dominic Anthony and David Declan Meyers. David and Jen, Tony Sr., and Maria were stunned. We tried our best to look surprised, and Tom and Declan tried to feign surprise.

Stephan and I took the family to the viewing room to see the babies, as Tony Sr. said, "Dominic was my papa's name." David smiled, knowing how the other twin was named. We went to the cafeteria for a simple repast (Stephan's nightmare). The families ordered whatever, but

I made sure to order a bologna sandwich. I asked Stephan if he wanted a bite (just to be fascias) and he let me know he certainly wanted to bite, but not the sandwich. I rolled on the floor laughing while everyone else was wondering what the joke was.

After, we were allowed to visit Bella, and while we were in the room, the babies arrived. Chaos ensued as the grandmas passed the twins back and forth. Bella smiled as everyone cheered Davin and Bella. Maria quietly told Bella something in Italian. The Tonys and Stephan roared while the rest of us were trying to translate. Bella said, "It was a surprise, Mamma, not a secret. Well, maybe a secret to you, but we wanted to see the look on your faces, okay?" Maria nodded as she passed the twin over to Tony Sr. Jen let David touch his twin and made sure he still remembered how. Bella recalled the twins, and the pictures started. Bella with the twins, Davin, Bella, and the boys, etc. Stephan had a gift in mind and presented the proud parents with a sitting for a family portrait, painted, of course. We took formalized pictures of Tony Sr. and Maria, David and Jen, so they could be included in the painting.

We left the hospital late, and Stephan offered to pay for a meal at our favorite restaurant. David and Jen begged off, but the Tonys and their entourage agreed, so Stephan called, and they said they would have the back room ready for us. We arrived ten minutes later and were seated quickly. Wine arrived without a word (it was from Tony Jr.'s vineyard). Appetizers appeared, then more wine, then the salad, more wine, then the pasta dish. Even Maria was impressed, so I asked the chef to see us. He came out of the kitchen and presented himself to us. The chef asked if we had any questions, and Maria asked about the pasta (in Italian), and the chef responded in kind. She said more, and it must have been good because the chef asked if she wanted to see the kitchen. They left for a few minutes, and Tony Sr. asked us about the wine. "It tastes like

Italian grapes but slightly different from mine." Dale said, "That's because it's from our vineyard, sir." Tony Sr. raised the glass, really inspected and sniffed it. He finally said, "Of course it's my boy's wine. He learned from the best, me." We toasted as Maria returned, and we finished our meal. Stephan left about $1000 for the staff and paid the rest with the infamous black card.

We put the Tonys up in the guest house, and we crashed into bed. Morning came, and two very tired guys rallied for breakfast. We informed the house that we had two new members, and I sat with Bobbie and told him he was to take on a big brother role for the twins. "Don't worry, Uncle Carl, I'll teach them how to treat Caran and be gentle, just like you taught me." (Did I say that I loved that kid?) The house started to wake, and the folks started assembling in the kitchen. Coffee was served, and Elizabeth calmly directed the group into the dining room. Breakfast was served as the new grandparents sat together and viewed the photos of the twins. "The boys have my eyes and your hair," said David to Tony. Jen and Maria (despite the language barrier) seemed to agree on different points as they viewed the photos. Stephan let it go on as he slipped out to the kitchen. I followed to find out what my husband was up to. "Too much commotion for me, that's all," said Stephan as he fed Caran the rest of his breakfast. Bobbie came in search of the puppy and found her at Stephan's ankles. He took her out for a walk in the garden.

Tony Jr. and Dale arrived with Tom and Declan in tow. We sent them into the dining room to join the others. I asked Stephan who he had decided on to give the commission of the portrait, and he said, "I think Deirdre Hampton, I saw her work, and she reminds me of Caravaggio." I quipped, "is that because she wants your body, the same as Caravaggio did?" Stephan shushed me so I nodded (giggling at my own joke) and left it to him to make contact. At that moment, Bobbie came running into the atrium screaming that Caran broke away from him and ran out the gate. The house went into immediate action to recover poor Bobbie's puppy. Elizabeth took care of Bobbie as Bob and staff combed the streets near the manse (thank God we had her chipped) in case this happened.

They couldn't find her and returned to the house. Bobbie ran to his father, and he shook his head no, and Bobbie became inconsolable. He turned to us with reddened and puffy eyes and pleaded with us to find her. Stephan, ever stoic, looked at Bobbie and promised all would be well. There must have been magic in the air as the doorbell rang. Stephan answered the door and was presented with Caran in Leonard's arms. Stephan stepped out of the way so Bobbie could see his beloved puppy safe and sound. "Thank you, Uncle Stephan, I knew you could do it if anyone could." Leonard set the pup down, and she ran to Bobbie, licking and kissing his face. Leonard opened the conversation saying, "I saw her on the sidewalk looking around and thought that it was Caran, so I called her to me, and she walked over." Bobbie took her into the kitchen, saying, "Uncle Stephan told me it was alright, and here she is, mommy."

The house calmed down, Bob talked to me, asking about better fencing and improved gates, and I gave him the okay to get it done. Stephan returned to the kitchen to a relieved Bobbie and a perturbed Elizabeth. She motioned for Stephan to follow her into the pantry. She said, "Uncle Stephan, now Bobbie thinks you're a wizard or something, and he thinks you can fix everything. What happens when you can't? Please let him know that the return of Caran was simply a coincidence and not a spell you performed." Stephan chuckled and said that he would talk to Bobbie about it. They returned to the kitchen, watching Bobbie and Caran play.

I went to the den to calm down and regain my composure (and yes, to have a glass of Bourbon). Stephan joined me, and we toasted to Caran's return. I told Stephan about the fencing and the gates, and my approval to improve them. "Good idea, can't let that happen again." We finished our Bourbons and left to continue our day. We went to the hospital to visit Davin, Bella, and the twins. We could barely get into the room with all the guests there. Flowers from all over the world adorned the room, and finally, the nurse had to tell us to limit the number of people in the room to four at a time. Stephan and I took our cue, said our goodbyes, and left the troop behind to make that decision. "What a change from a kid brother to a dad of twins. His older brother, from a neighborhood mischief maker to a groundskeeper, married a man and is living on Wakaya Island near Fiji. Then there is Tony Jr. from Italy and Dale from Fiji, now co-owners of a vineyard in Italy, and don't forget Lady Eddie from a clothier in Baltimore to a married man living in a manor in England and married to your nephew." Stephan said, "And then there is Stephan and Hunter in Italy. A Borgia and an Orion together." I took note of the myriad couplings we helped to create and the world that we opened to these people. I hugged my guy and let him know that I was honored to have stood by his side for this trip through part of his history. "Do you regret marrying me when you could have returned to Europe and had more impressive pairings like from your past with the kings, queens, royalty of every rank and important people of today?" Stephan turned my face to his, held me in his hands and said, "I regret nothing, without you my last seventy-two years would have been hollow. You complete me, dear Carl. For the years we have left, I will cherish these moments more than the last 350 years altogether. We have a legacy most people never get to view. Never doubt my love. Now let's look forward and enjoy all that the world has given us, Robin." I leaned in, kissed my man, and we left the hospital hand in hand.

Stephan called Deirdre and inquired as to how the portrait was coming. She invited us to the studio to check out her work. We stopped by the warehouse and picked out a couple of paintings to give her ideas for foreground and background. We got to the studio around lunchtime, so Stephan ordered lunch to be delivered. Deidre ushered us in and took us up to the loft. "The lighting is great up here. I can see why you chose it. Are you renting or did you buy it?" Deidre said, "Renting, if I could buy it, I would have converted the downstairs as a studio and teach art to make a living." Stephan took note and said nothing, which meant her dreams were about to come true if he liked the portrait. We showed her the paintings we brought, and Stephan said, "Maybe these can help you with the foreground and background." She scanned the paintings, one by Nicolas Poussin and the other by John Constable. Then she took notice of the names and started by saying, "Poussin is a 17th-century artist, and Constable is a 19th-century artist. How did you get them, or are they replicas?" "Trust me, dear lady, they're real and original." Deidre seemed stunned (as I assumed Stephan wanted) and asked where we got them. "Let's just say I had inside information and got them at a much reduced price."

Deirdre collected herself and said, "If that's true, then you're sitting on a fortune. These two paintings alone are worth millions. You said they were stored in a warehouse. That's insane, I mean, they're beautiful···" Stephan cut her off and said, "I know, but let's look at the portrait you painted for us first." She led us to the easel and removed the cover cloth. It was magnificent in every way. "You've captured them in the best way. It's a masterpiece, Deirdre." Deirdre said, "It will take another month to varnish and dry. I'm so glad you like it." Stephan remarked, "Since you did such good work, I'd like to gift you these two paintings and pay for the portrait. This way, you can buy the building and make your dreams come true." She crossed to Stephan and kissed his cheek. I just stood back as witness to Stephan's generosity with a gratitude I had come to enjoy.

The month went by, and we collected the portrait. We presented it to Davin and Bella and played with the twins for a few minutes before they left for their feeding and nap. Davin showed us to the door and said, "I was told that you two were gay matchmakers, and I had my doubts, but here we are, and you've given me a life I couldn't dream of. You took care of grandma, mom, and dad, helped out Declan and me, and still keep giving. I want you to know you are forever in our hearts and we will never forget you two." He hugged me and shook Stephan's hand. Stephan reached into his coat and produced an envelope, handing it to Davin. He kind of knew what was in it but said nothing, accepting it graciously.

I had to wait until we reached the car and then asked, "How big was that check, lover boy?" Stephan smiled and simply replied, "You don't want to know." "That much, well, how much stuff from the warehouse did you sell?" Stephan smiled and ended the conversation with, "You'll be able to park your car inside from now on." I shook my head and decided it was a no-win conversation and let it go.

I picked up a paper from the kitchen table and read that Sotheby's had two exciting lots for sale in their next auction, newly discovered paintings from Poussin and Constable. I laughed it off until it was noted that the possible sale would net around $300,000,000 dollars. I showed it to Stephan, and he chortled, "That's the least they'll go for." I just looked and shrugged my shoulders.

I left Stephan and went for a tour of the garden to ground myself. Images started appearing and coalescing in my mind. Stephan was offloading material things to people and being indiscriminate about it. It made me wonder why. He also was keeping it to himself as to his decisions. This in itself wasn't unusual, but the extent to which he was doing it was. I called Leonard and asked him to contact Alex (his forensic specialist) to dig into it a bit. I was hoping to see if there was a root cause for Stephan's sudden actions or if it was just a phase. Alex didn't get back to Leonard for a month, and then the report was sparse at best. I decided to go to the source and ask Stephan directly what was up. "Stephan, this is hard for me, but I need to know what's going on in your mind. I try hard to give you a wide berth as to your business, but I'm feeling something's wrong, and I want to help you if I can, but that's not possible if you keep me out. I love you, and if there is anything I need to know, please tell me. I can take it."

"Okay, but you have to promise me that you'll let me continue with what I'm doing." I almost fainted at that statement, thinking the worst, hoping for a silver lining, and doing my best to hide my fears. Stephan started, "My love, I'm 565 years old. I don't know how many years I have left, and I want it to mean something. I have taken a lot from this world, and I want to give some back. My mortality is rearing its head, and maybe I'm a bit maudlin, but I don't believe I've returned the favor. Forgive me if I've kept you out; it was not my intent. Let's become the largest philanthropists in history, even more than Warren Buffett." I quietly thanked the gods that nothing was wrong and that Stephan had confided in me. "We'll start tomorrow, today I want you to myself as I thank you for everything you gave me, babe."

We started our 'downsizing' by awarding our warehouses around the world to our descendants in those countries. The gifts were received well, and they lifted our responsibilities and protection costs greatly. The best was when Lady Eddie got his hands on the English warehouse. He screamed with joy, and I could envision him flouncing around the manse in a moo moo (outrageously colorful but tasteful, of course), announcing how he would use the statuary and artifacts in the manse. We gifted Tony Jr. and Dale (the least wealthy in Italy) that warehouse. They shared it with Elena and Junior, which was kind. The Greek warehouse went to Andreas and Vasiliki, although they were simple people and just kept it in case. We kept the Russian warehouse but decided to bring it to America slowly as we downsized our warehouse here in Baltimore. Since we didn't really use the cars in our warehouse, they were gifted to our 'family' here. That left us room to stash our Russian stuff. It was a full circle moment for Declan and Leonard, as that's why they ended up working for us. Johnny Jones 'Huey' was most appreciative.

(the gallery guard).

We felt better giving than taking, amazing how that works. We ended up gifting around three trillion in 'stuff' to our descendants and 'family'. I did some ballpark accounting and figured that we were left with only about one or two trillion in assets. Oh well, we'll try to make do. The Russian assets were tough to get over here as they had rules and regulations for art and artifacts (however, greased palms worked wonders). Soon, we were receiving boxes (which meant more bribes as they were true works of art and statuary). All in all, it cost us around $10,000,000 to get it all here. The warehouse received the boxes, and

Stephan coordinated the sorting and storing of the items. Johnny got excited to see the new art pieces (he took college art courses to learn more about art). Russian art and artists were his top interest, which made it important to give them special treatment.

I made a trip to see how they were faring and was surprised to see that everything had found homes. Paintings by Andrei Rublev from the 15th century, Simon Ushakov from the 17th century, and artists such as Ivan Zarudny, who painted under the reign of Peter the Great. Johnny, or "Huey" as we affectionately referred to him, was in his glory. He was in his senior year and wanted to continue his studies at the university. He eventually asked to go to St. Bonaventure University in upstate New York (as they were ranked no.8 in Russian Arts study in the world and no. 1 in the U.S.A). Stephan asked him to name his successor before going off to study, and he said, "I don't have a person that I think is qualified for such a task, but if I can have my baby brother Joey apply, I assure you he will try his best. He has always looked up to me since I came to work here. I want to give him the opportunity you gave me." Stephan stated, "Have him apply in person at the manse. I'll give him a shot at the position. By the way, how do you intend to pay for this college?" Johnny replied, "I've been saving all this time, and I think I have enough saved to afford it." I nodded to Stephan, and he said, "Nonsense, Huey, we'll pay for your education, save the money for a wedding or house." Johnny's eyes glazed over, and he thanked us profusely.

I couldn't wait until poor Joey got his interview (knowing how Stephan likes to scare the poor kids

). As was usual, the kid was led to the atrium as Stephan waited to make his entrance. We entered together, and Joey was unusually calm.

Stephan sat and pointed for Joey to sit. "I hear you would like to apply for your brother's position. What makes you think that you are uniquely qualified for this job?" Joey took out a small notepad and perused it for a few seconds before answering (he came prepared). "Sirs, I have listened to Johnny, and he has given you glowing reviews. I have seen him mature under your guidance, and I'd like to undertake that tutelage as it has worked so well for him (this kid had to have been coached as he was so smooth). Stephan rose to his feet, went over to the boy, and waited as the kid stood also. They shook hands and Stephan said, "Welcome aboard, Joey. I hope you're as good as your words." He shook my hand as well and then turned to leave. Stephan spoke, "You haven't been dismissed yet. I have a couple more questions for you. Where are you living? Do you have proper clothing for the job? What car are you driving?" Johnny returned to face Stephan and said, "With all do respect, what does that have to do with the job sirs?" Stephan (with a serious look) said, "I have strict standards for my employees young man and these questions are relevant for those reasons." The kid backed down and answered Stephan, "Sir, I live with a roommate, I have appropriate clothing for the job, and I drive Johnny's old car as I haven't been able to afford a better one." Stephan took control of the conversation by saying, "Be here tomorrow at 9 am. I will personally assist with your wardrobe, living accommodations, and car situation."

Stephan then said, "Now you are dismissed." Joey left, not knowing what else to add to the conversation. Stephan turned to me with his signature grin and burst out laughing, "I really like that kid. He reminds me of me when I was his age." I shook my index finger at him and said, "You just want to put him through what you did to the others, you wicked man." Stephan shrugged his shoulders and continued to smile as he walked to the den, waving in my direction as if to say, 'follow me'.

The following morning, 9 am sharp, the kid appeared at the front door. The staff let him in, and he stood in the hallway waiting for us. We appeared, and Stephan said, "We'll take my car. Now, where do you live, Joey?" Joey said, "Gwynn Oaks Landing on Windsor Blvd." Stephan countered with, "How much is your share of the rent?" Joey, perturbed, huffed, "$800 a month and half the utilities, so about $1000 a month total." Stephan asserted his dominance by saying, "Lower your tone, boy, I'm trying to help you, but I have to know how. Listen, I have strict standards for my staff, and you will be no exception. We are going shopping for you to raise your standard of living, so work with us." Joey's attitude quickly changed, and he apologized for any misgivings he had. "It's just that no one has ever been this kind. I've had to handle everything since my brother left," Stephan said, "Leave it to me, and you'll live a much better life." We pulled up at the clothier's and went inside. The new clerk walked over, not knowing us, and Stephan said, "We'll need a new wardrobe for Joey here. Start with the underwear and work outward. And Joey, I expect you to allow me a view to ensure it suits you." The manager came around the counter when he heard Stephan's voice and told the clerk that he would handle the account himself (being the clerk when we came with the other boys). I said, "I remember you, you were the clerk the last time we were here. It looks like you've moved up a lot since last time." He said, "With all the sales you threw my way, I made an impression with the old boss. He moved to corporate, and I took his place."

Stephan whispered, "Start the show, guys, we have more shopping to get to." The show started alright, the underwear being the best part. Joey came out with a nylon tank top and nylon briefs. It seems the boy was hiding a man's body underneath, and it stirred thoughts with all in attendance. He began getting off on presenting himself in his new clothes. We went through quite a fashion show. Stephan nodded his approval to the wardrobe and asked to have it all delivered to the manse. The infamous black card appeared, and the manager smiled. We left without the clothes, and Joey looked a little despondent. I whispered in his ear, "He bought it all, and it always gets delivered. We never carry items if we don't have to" (when did I become so nouveau riche).

Stephan next drove us to the car dealership. It was the Mercedes lot. Joey's eyes grew larger as Stephan stopped, parked the Bentley, and we got out. "Now, Joey, pick out a better car. Joey looked at me for a cue, and I just pointed to the showroom and said quietly, "The better ones are in there." He walked in and saw a silver E350. I motioned for him to sit in the driver's seat and try it out. He sat down carefully, and I went over to boost his confidence. He said, "Are you kidding me? I couldn't afford the insurance, let alone the payments." I explained, "We pay for the car outright; there are no payments, and your salary is more than enough to pay for your new life. You realize that your wardrobe costs over $10,000, don't you? Stephan wants only the best for his staff. Has your brother not told you anything about us?" Joey quipped, "What about my apartment? I can't leave Arnie alone to pay the rent. He can't afford it." I calmed him by saying that I would personally set up Arnie for a year so that he could find another roommate.

Stephan asked Joey about possibly moving to Luxury Federal Hill apartments near the manse. He just shrugged, and Stephan made a phone call and got an appointment for the afternoon. He then called ahead and got reservations at our favorite Italian restaurant. We arrived, parked, and went inside. Joey was God-smacked at the attention that Stephan got as we entered. We were shown to a corner table, and wine arrived before Joey took his coat off. "Tell the chef to give us his special." The maitre d left us, and we poured three glasses of wine. Joey wondered why we hadn't asked for a menu, and I shushed him and just said, "Wait." He enjoyed the wine, so I said, "It's actually from one of our vineyards in Italy. This is from Tony Jr.'s collection. Tony Sr.'s wine we have in the wine cellar." About that time, the antipasto arrived along with the grilled artisan bread rubbed with garlic. Joey perked up at the buffet before him. I told him to go easy, as the other courses would need room.

The meats and olives piqued his curiosity as did the different cheeses. By the time the pasta dishes arrived, he was mostly full. He made a half hearted attempt but came up short and asked for a dogie bag (oh the memories of my first dinner with Stephan). Stephan went to pay the check and removed a wad of bills and handed it to the maitre'd. He nodded and headed to the kitchen. We took our leave and headed to the apartment building. The rental agent greeted us and asked the preliminary questions such as, "Who will be living here, who will be responsible for the rent and will they be needing a parking space?" Stephan nodded and said, "This young man will be living here, I am his employer and I will be paying for the rent. He will need a parking space for his new Mercedes, under cover or a garage if available." She started to say that there was a waiting list but Stephan showed his capable hand and cut her off, "I perused your website and it said that you had penthouse accommodations available. Do you have them or not?" She backed down and allowed us access to the 'last one' she had at the end of the apartment. She opened the door and we stepped in. The view was panoramic and the space was an open design. The apartment took up about 25 percent of the footprint of the building. She took Joey on a tour of the spaces as we stood back and watched. She pointed out the amenities and the specialties that came with the space. She started again saying, "How would you like to pay, as it will be first, last month and security deposit. That will come to $15,000 payable before occupancy." Stephan simply said, "That will be fine, when will you have it ready for move in as it needs a good cleaning and new appliances for that cost. I wouldn't want Joey here to have to call you if they fail." She grimaced as she realized just who she was dealing with. Stephan turned to Joey and asked if it met his needs. "It's adequate sir. I think I could live here (playing along with Stephan, did he say the kid was like him). Stephan asked for the paperwork and followed her to the office to make it official. Joey looked around at his new place and asked, "How am I going to fill this place with furniture, I mean I have a bed and a couple chairs but that isn't going to cut it here." I reminded him, "Have you learned nothing today. Do you think that Stephan would let you live here in an empty apartment? Would I? Get with it Joey, your life is changing before your eyes. Just go with it, be loyal and you will live a life you couldn't have dreamed of."

We joined the agent and Stephan in the office and formalized the agreement. Stephan drove Joey back to his apartment to deal with the roommate and then we returned home. Caran ran to the door barking all the way with Bobbie in hot pursuit. "Sorry uncle Stephan and uncle Carl but Caran got away from me. I tousled his mop head and told him it was fine and that Caran would be a good watchdog. Bobbie's smile returned and they headed to the garden for a romp.

I told Stephan that I would oversee the new kid as he grew into his new role as gallery keeper. Joey seemed at ease and handy when handling the art pieces. He did however have Stephan's attitude and let me know when he thought I was micro-managing him. "I'm only trying to help you acclimate you little toad." Joey shot back, "I'm trying to keep you from falling. They don't make replacement parts for people your age." Touche'. My life now, caught between a man who controlled every situation with ease and a boy who thought he could. Oh well, I could have done worse or as they say, "It's easier to cry in a Bentley than a Civic" or something like that.

Johnny looked forward to attending college in the fall and tutored Joey, although Joey was just as insubordinate as he was with me. I decided that since Johnny was around until fall, Stephan and I should go on tour for a month abroad. I set the schedule, informed Stephan, and he assented to my agenda. We packed up and headed to Fiji first. Wakaya came into view, and we tendered into the dock where Allen met us to tend to our bags. Bruce greeted us as we entered the manse. We said our hellos and went in search of Declan and Tom. We found them near our 'tree' and, assuming from the sweat on their faces that it was now their 'tree', we giggled as they collected themselves. "We can take you on a tour of the new plantings and additions to the gardens if you'd like," said Declan. Stephan grinned and then broke his silence, "I think we've seen enough of the landscaping for today. Besides, you two look like you need a shower and a nap." The guys grimaced as Stephan and I continued to the house (can you say busted). Jaime waved to us from the kitchen, and the aromas coming from the oven and stove made my mouth water.

Jaime served up an early dinner of local favorites and cheeses from around the world. I was thankful that Bruce had requested wines from both Tonys' vineyards and had them stocked in the new wine cellar. Flat breads with local pork slices accompanied the cheeses and fruits (mango, papaya, and star). I ate with gusto, and Stephan picked as usual. Jaime prepared a tiramisu for dessert and

I all but inhaled that. Stephan tasted his and then actually ate his serving. I looked over at Jaime and saw him grinning from ear to ear, satisfied that he had gotten something right. Bruce and Tom created a fire in the new pit and we had our Bourbon and cigars around the fire and watched the sun set (light blue with white clouds turning pink, then a brilliant red and then a majestic purple before fading into dark blue punctured by small pinpoints of light set between the dark grey clouds). We finished the night by walking back to the house, holding hands, and off to the bedroom, and sweet dreams.

The week went by fast, and we said our goodbyes. Bruce saw us off and waved as we left for the airport. We flew from there to Russia. We landed, cleared customs, and went to the countryside where Stephan's beloved Svetlana was laid to rest. I let Stephan visit the grave and stood a few steps back (as a sign of respect for his relationship and his past wife). The village where we stayed was vintage Russian, meaning it had nearly no conveniences. The food was actually good, kind of like Bavarian, hearty, and mostly game meat. The Vodka was flowing, and I had daily hangovers trying to keep up with Stephan. He was treated like a king, and they tolerated me as though I were his footman. "Stephan, how come they treat us so differently? Is it because they don't like gay couples?"

Stephan burst out laughing, saying, "No, Carl, it's because you speak no Russian. There are actually two types of Russian, common and royal. Since I was taught royal by the monks (with Mikhail), they think I'm some sort of royalty." I was never so glad to get on with our travel plans. We left Russia and went to see Andreas and Vasiliki. We were greeted with open arms, and the family home looked much better. Andreas told us that they had sold some of the lesser artifacts and used the money to do the updates on the house and grounds. I told them, "If you need landscapers, call Fiji and ask for Tom and Declan. They do all our work, and I believe they would come if you ask." Andreas took their information and stored it in his wallet. Note that I didn't mention Lady Eddie; they don't have that much disposable income. Our week with them was quiet and relaxing. The food was great, and Vasi made sure that she made it from scratch: "No store-bought crap for our relatives." We extended our stay for three days because they were having a holy festival in town, and Andreas said we should accompany them. The Panigyria or local festival of the Orthodox Church started with St. John the Baptist on July 7th. It had music, dancing, food, and church services. All in all, it was quite impressive. It almost made me want to stay for the whole month (St. Marina – 7/17, Profitis Elias – 7/20, St. Paraskevi – 7/26, and St. Panteleimon – 7/27). The road called, and we said our heartfelt goodbyes and got driven to the hangar. Vasi accompanied Andreas and hugged us tight with tears in her eyes as she said to return home again soon.

Next stop, Rome and the Tonys'. We arrived at Elena's home and got another big welcome. She was delighted to have us and put out a huge spread. I asked her who on earth she was cooking for. I couldn't consume those quantities of food, and Stephan only picked. My question was answered in minutes as cars started showing up. Tony Sr. and Maria, then Tony Jr. and Dale. To my surprise, Bella, Davin, and the twins appeared from the house. Late to the party were Junior and Hunter (of course, they were fashionably late). Antipasto, seafood (raw, steamed, and fried), breads and cheeses, olive oil and balsamic vinegar, then pasta and red sauce with sausages and meatballs. Wine was poured by the bottle, and we all got to hand around the twins (under the watchful eyes of Maria and Bella, of course). Desert was fresh fruit and Prosecco. The twins got hard biscuits (as they were teething). We ended up staying with each of our hosts for two days. We didn't want to put them out or overstay our welcome. We also couldn't slight one for the other. It was exhausting, but we made it look good by staying packed and living out of our suitcases.

We ended our Italian experience and headed to France (France, you say, there are no relatives there), but Stephan requested that stop expressly because he wanted to visit Versailles and place flowers on his friend's (Louis XIV, the Sun King) grave. I made sure that we had time to spend there, as he had a special place in his heart for the king. We (or should I say I) ate our way through France for the week and did some buying and touring. It was calm and peaceful for a week. We made our way to England to visit the Duke and 'Duchess'. Lady Eddie was waiting as we approached the mansion and grounds. He was everything and a bag of chips in his finery. Silk, satin, brocade, and feathers (I began to wonder how Anthony could put up with this, but then remembered about our 'suits'). As soon as the door of the car opened, Eddie started his non-stop talking. I listened politely as Stephan gently walked past into the foyer, looking for Anthony. He was found in the den, working as usual. When Anthony saw his great, great grandfather enter, he ended the call and said, "Greetings, grandfather, you look well. Where is

Carl? Does Eddie have him hostage? Should we go rescue him?" Stephan calmed Anthony down with a wave of his hand. Carl is here, listening to Eddie. Let Eddie get it out, or we're all in trouble. How have you been?" Anthony poured two Bourbons and gave one to Stephan. "After you gave me a second chance in life, I've worked with determination to make you proud of me. I can say proudly but not pridefully that I believe that I've accomplished that." "That you have my boy, that you have." Anthony hugged Stephan lightly and noticed how thin he was, but said nothing.

Eddie led me into the house and stopped his speech when he saw the guys coming over to us. Stephan asked Eddie if he had made any more improvements to the house. "I've updated the plumbing, added a few more pieces of art from the warehouse, and worked on the landscaping some, but not too much, grandfather." I forgot that when Anthony married Eddie, he became a descendant of Stephan. Anthony let the staff know that we were ready to dine, and they mistakenly thought that we'd like an old-fashioned English meal. Bubble and squeak started the meal, and then a leg of lamb and artisan bread. Stephan picked at his, as did I. The blandness of the meal left us all rather peckish. I calmly said to Stephan, "Can we do some shopping while we're here?" Stephan nodded, and Eddie perked up. "I know all the good shops. Would you like me to go to show you?" Stephan shook his head no and simply said, "I think I can handle it from here. Thanks anyway, Eddie." Eddie said no more and felt a little diminished by the statement. He left us to our own and went out into his private garden. I leaned over and whispered into Stephan's ear, "That was a bit harsh. I think Eddie is a bit much myself, but we are his guests." Stephan, ever gracious, left me and went to talk to Eddie privately. They returned together, and Eddie was all smiles. I asked Stephan what he said, and he grinned and smiled while saying, "I told him that you expressly wanted him to join us. Have fun with him today, sweetheart." With that, he kissed my cheek and laughed all the way to the limousine. Well, chalk one up for my husband.

We spent the rest of the day in and out of stores and into the evening. The final tally was $15,000. My ear was ringing from Eddie's voice and Stephan's laughing. We stopped along the way and got some deli food to take back to the manse under the guise of not wanting to disturb the staff further. Breakfast was better as the staff was told we liked Eggs Benedict on toast points. Eddie was exuberant and wanted to continue shopping, but I told him that, as happy as I was for his guidance yesterday, today I needed to stay around for Stephan. Stephan literally threw me under the bus by saying, "That's alright, Carl, I'll be with Anthony all day, so you're free to join Eddie today." He chuckled as I side-eyed him with a "I'll get you for this" look. That made him roar with laughter as he waved me off and left me to Lady Eddie.

I made sure to ask Stephan for his black card before leaving, letting him know that this was his payback for the comments. This time, I smiled, and he grimaced, knowing I was going on a spree and letting the lady have at it. I thoroughly enjoyed the day with Eddie, more so than I expected. Letting Eddie lead me around and having his expertise shine, I saw why Anthony fell for him and was so accommodating to his eccentricities. This man was every bit the Lady of the house, and it fit him. We spent the whole day away from the manse. Stephan called my cell and asked if I needed help, and I just texted back to eat without us, as Eddie wanted to treat me to a special restaurant in town.

I got home late, saw that hubby had retired for the night, and left my hosts as I ventured to the guest bedroom. Stephan was fresh from the shower, standing in silhouette against the full moon in all his splendor. I disrobed, went to him, and wrapped him in my arms. He turned, pale in the moonlight, and kissed me with lust in his eyes. It seemed deeper and more urgent tonight. We turned in to reaffirm our commitment to each other and finally fell asleep in an embrace. Morning came too soon, and the lark called us to rise with the sun. I went to the shower and removed the scent of my sweat from the past night. Stephan was shaving as I emerged from the shower. We dressed and followed the aroma of fresh coffee to the kitchen and partook of the nectar of the gods.

Anthony and Eddie appeared from their wing of the manse, got their tea, and joined us on the island. I thanked Eddie for the past day, and he blushed. Anthony said, "I thought you were never going to bring back my wife. When you did, she couldn't stop fawning over the details of how happy you made her feel." Eddie stood, crossed to our side of the island, and kissed my cheek. "I thought you only tolerated me until yesterday. You showed me that I mattered, and I will always remember that with esteem." Stephan looked at me, and then I blushed. I whispered in his ear, "Wait till you get the bill," and then he blushed. The last few days went by at lightning speed, and Eddie was saying his goodbyes with hugs and kisses. Anthony shook hands, and Stephan did a surprising thing: he kissed Anthony on the forehead. I took note but said nothing. We left and headed home.

Our beloved Baltimore came into view, and we prepared for landing and our usual customs check-in. It took about an hour, as we had a lot of stamps from around the world. We arrived home to Caran barking, and the house in chaos (so situation normal). Elizabeth appeared in the foyer, yelling for Bobbie to get the dog. She almost got to us when Caran got tackled by Bobbie in front of me. I held Caran until Bobbie got the leash on her. Elizabeth hugged us, and Bobbie hugged me before wrangling the dog out to the garden. He didn't even wait for his presents. Elizabeth said that everything up until our entrance had been fine.

We sorted out the packages and let everyone have at them and retired for the rest of the evening in the den. Stephan seemed more mellow than usual and started the fire. I got the Bourbon poured and lit the cigars. We took our repose on the rug and cuddled as we watched the fire crackle and warmed our tired bones. When the fire became embers, we took ourselves upstairs for the night. A quick hug and cuddle, and we fell into a deep sleep. I awoke about three hours later to find that Stephan was standing in the moonlight again. I wanted to go to him and ask, but I decided he needed some time and rolled over to catch more shut-eye. Morning arrived, and Stephan was in the shower when I arose. I stepped into the shower as he was about to shampoo his hair. I took the bottle and lathered up his head. He rinsed off and repeated the process with me. He left me alone to clean myself and grabbed the nearest towel.

By the time I got out, he was dressed and ready to go to the kitchen for coffee. I asked him to pour me a cup, and he nodded as he left the room. My mind went into hyperdrive as I overthought all the possible scenarios as to why he was acting out of character. I threw on some clothes and literally ran downstairs to the kitchen. I caught him sipping his coffee at the island and joined him. I was about to start the conversation when he simply said, "I think my time is running short, Carl. I don't want to think about it, but the signs are becoming abundantly clear. I've been on this earth for 565 years and have seen many people slip away. I'm starting to show the same signs. That's why I wanted to downsize and then travel to see each of my descendants, all of them at least one more time. I want to spend what time I have left here with you, my dear Carl, you deserve it, and I crave it." Tears silently streamed down my face as I listened. "How much time do you think you have?" Stephan shrugged and said, "I don't know, but the days are all yours, if you want them." That made the tears flow harder as I nodded a 'yes, please and thank you' silently. I hugged my guy, my strength, my lover, my man, tight, hoping to give him myself, the two made one.

Halloween came, and I made it special as before, fawning over the costumes and asking Eddie to take over as event planner. "Spare no cost,

I'll personally underwrite it, Eddie." He took my black card and made it happen. Louis XIV himself would have been proud of the party Eddie threw. I

went downstairs, waiting for Stephan, and bore witness as he appeared above us all in all his regal splendor. It was a night to remember, which was what I wanted. Thanksgiving and Christmas were the same, overindulgence and intensely overdone. Christmas marks our 58th anniversary. I dusted off the old replica of his Batmobile and had it looking showroom new. I had him don his costume, and I mine, and we drove around town as the Dynamic Duo. We got stares and applause from admirers and fans. Then we returned to the 'bat-cave' aka the garage and raced upstairs. I didn't mind taking on the duty of the dry cleaner this time. Whatever my guy wanted, he was going to have.

The new year 2078 came, and we watched the ball drop as we toasted the night and the new year. I was trying hard to see what Stephan had been talking about as he didn't look as though he was failing. But as someone wise once told me, "It is easier to fake being healthy than to tell people about your real illness." Stephan kept all his health problems away from me and everyone else. The one thing that scared me was Stephan signing more and more deeds and titles over to me. Stock transfers were next, and then all the safety deposit boxes. I did whatever he asked, but it was emotionally painful to watch his wealth transfer out of his hands. The only thing I was happy about was that he had entrusted me with it. I wouldn't let him down.

Spring came, Tom and Declan showed up as usual, and tended to our gardens. I gave them explicit instructions as to how Stephan would like it. They bent to their work, and soon the gardens became resplendent. When they finished, I took Stephan out to see their work. His white roses, blue hydrangeas, and red trumpet vines cut a path, revealing little by little the entire back garden. New trees were also added. I put on a garden party for the Baltimore clan and all the newbies. The twins were a hit, having passed the teething period. Joey invited himself, as was his style, and Johnny was home from college. I stayed by Stephan's side, though he looked fine (was he just fooling around with me about his illness?). The food was superb, and the music was a mix of all the centuries that Stephan had lived. I couldn't believe that I was going to be 111 years old this year (or, as Bilbo Baggins would say, eleventy-one years old). Stephan still kept his looks and simply looked like an elder statesman with a fleck of silver hair. I asked Stephan about end-of-life requests, like where he would be interred, what service he would like, and the tomb design. He said, "Keep it simple, inter me here so you can be laid here also and maybe have Lady Eddie take care of the reception after the funeral." He said that so matter-of-factly that it stung a bit.

I decided to let it all go until the time came, and looked forward to any adventures that we might have left. I asked if there was anywhere he wanted to travel this year. "Maybe Fiji, or Greece. Italy is always a hit, and then there's England. Maybe not England as the food sucks." I looked at him and said, "So Russia then, right?" He laughed at that and decided on Fiji. I got everything ready and packed for a couple of weeks (and yes, the suits were coming). We left our beloved Baltimore and headed towards Fiji and our vacation home on Wakaya Island. Bruce and Allen were waiting at the dock and ferried us across the bay. We went to our room, and Tom and Declan greeted us. Jaime came around the corner and saw us, his face gleaming, and asked, "What would you like to have for dinner, bosses?" Stephan said, "Surprise us, Jaime," and with that, he turned and left us.

The surprise came in the form of a fruit plate with exotic cheeses and flat bread. The meat was prosciutto (Jaime had it flown in special, as he knew it was a favorite of ours). He paired it with Tony Jr.'s wine selection (again knowing our taste). Stephan picked through the plate as I devoured mine. I noticed that his appetite was getting less and less as time went on (which scared me more). Stephan rose, asked for a cigar, and went out to the patio for a smoke. I followed, not knowing what to say, so I blurted out, "Stephan, something is happening, and you're keeping me out. I can't help if I don't know how. It pains me to see you try to go through this alone." Stephan blew out a cloud of smoke and turned to me as he said, "It was never my intent to keep you out, but I don't understand it myself. I was so careful until the last couple of years. Somehow I have developed anemia of the blood, and it seems that doctors can't bring it around, even with injections of protein-based serums." I stood in absolute shock, trying to digest this new information. The only thing on my mind was to hold him tight and try to take away his troubles. I asked to see his medical records, to which he agreed, although he said that he didn't think it would be of any use.

I took the records, excused myself, and needed to clear my head. My guy was not about to go down without a fight, our fight. I did what I did best, research. I looked through his records, noted the therapies that the doctors had tried. Only one drug seemed to even try to help, and it was still in animal trials. I thought for hours before making a single call. It was a Hail Mary attempt, but it was the only card I was holding. I called Anthony in England. He answered the phone, and when he heard the urgency in my voice, he said that he would be on the next flight to Fiji. I told him that I'd send the bus for him, but he said he'd hire a private jet and would be here in the morning. With that, he hung up.

True to his word, Anthony (and Lady Eddie) were at the front door as we crossed the foyer in the morning. Stephan was excited to see them but didn't understand why. I hugged them both and had tears in my eyes as I couldn't keep my emotions in check like Stephan. Anthony went to Stephan and hugged his grandfather. Eddie came over to me and calmed me down. I told Stephan that after reading all the material, I noticed an experimental drug, but it needed tweaking. Anthony had the connections to help get it ready and do it quietly. Stephan told me that I shouldn't have bothered Anthony with it. Anthony interrupted Stephan (which was very unusual) and said, "Grandfather, you saved my life twice and put me on the path of a life I have now. I'll move heaven and earth to save you." Anthony set up an impromptu command center in the den. He had phones, laptops, and printers whizzing in no time. My job was transportation for the people Anthony called to the island. Bruce and Allen handled the ferry rides and accommodations. Tom and Declan handled cleaning and laundry with Darren (Allen's husband). Jaime had meal prep, and Eddie assisted as well as he could. The security guy rounded out the island team. The island started looking more like a resort than a private island retreat.

Anthony made copies of all the material I gave him and the team went over it in detail before developing a plan. Adam Sims, a fifty year old scientist who took lead on the project having worked at the forefront of new medicines, controlled the lab. He purposely left his college team behind as he wasn't sure about their allegiance. More people arrived and were added to the team. Adam started with the original formula and a sample of Stephan's blood. It didn't interface with Stephan's unique blood type. I asked if my blood could help but Adam, not knowing I was a hybrid, decided against it. I confided in him about me and Eddie and our hybrid blood with enhancements from Stephan's blood. That picqued his interest. I came clean and gave over my medical records as well. He immediately took samples from us and started over. It seemed that Eddie and my blood did interface with the formula. But would it work with Stephan. The new concoction did interface but didn't seem to affect him in any way to help. A baby step, but a way forward. Next, Adam tried adding protein substitutes into the mix, no go. I suggested legume based protein, still no success. Eddie came into the lab to call us all to dinner and spotted a lizard crawling on the wall. "Damn things, they're all over the place, I can't kill them no matter how I try to poison them." I looked at Adam and he at me. "It's worth a try." We asked Eddie where he saw them most and he said near the kitchen. Butterfly nets in hand, we bagged about ten of them. We stored them for later and went to eat. After dinner, I joined Adam in the lab and we took many blood samples and tried to match it together with my blood. My blood wouldn't interface with the sample but strangely enough, Eddie's did. Next we mixed it with Stephan's blood and unbelievably, it seemed to work. I asked Stephan to come into the lab. "We have to show you something." He looked through the microscope and didn't stop until called away. Adam finally said, "It's weird but it looks promising." Stephan was skeptical but with some of my convincing, he said to get a sample size made up and he'd try it. I smiled and kissed his cheek. We kept this new tweaked formula between ourselves lest it got copied. It took two days and another blood draw from Eddie to make it but we finally achieved our sample.

Stephan entered the lab looking pale, rolled up his sleeve, readied himself for the injection, and took a full dose. We had him sit so we could watch for any side effects. An hour went by, no problems appeared, so it was time to see if it had an effect. A blood draw from Stephan and a smear on a slide told the story. It did interface, and the anemia was lessened but not entirely cured. Adam grabbed me and shook me with both hands. "You what this means? We could develop a vaccine that could end anemia in older people. This is monumental, life-changing, a whole new way of looking at medicine." I looked at Adam and said, "Let's help Stephan first, then you can celebrate for the world." Adam nodded and stated that he thought he could enhance the formula to create a true vaccine. I took Stephan to the kitchen, and he asked for a sandwich (I would have made him anything but he asked for rare roast beef on rye with mayonnaise and horseradish). He actually ate the entire sandwich and asked for another. I ran to the refrigerator and made him another one. "I could do this all night, sweetie."

Stephan downed the second sandwich as quickly as he did the first. "I don't know what caused this spike in hunger, but I feel really frisky too (thankfully, the suits were in the room). Note to self, if this is what it does to Stephan, I'm going to be a happy pappy. Stephan left the table and grabbed me up, "Suddenly, I'm in need of a nap. Care to join me?" I arose, and he literally dragged me to our room. I got as far as putting on my mask before Stephan threw me on the bed. Let's just say my man was back. We stayed on the island for the better part of a month as Adam worked on the enhancement. I tried hard to be with Adam in the lab, but it seemed my guy needed me more. I was getting exhausted, but it was worth it. Stephan was getting stronger every day. Adam asked Stephan to try the new and improved serum. Stephan removed his shirt, showing off his restored physique. The injection went in, and I prepared for a long night. Adam took daily samples and saw that it was holding (that lizard did the trick). Eddie and Anthony got ready to leave, and so did the lab staff. Adam stuck around for another week as things got back to normal.

The last sample showed that Stephan was good to go. Adam left all his information and returned to the States. We decided to leave also and packed (or had the staff pack for us). We ferried over to Fiji and headed to the airport. We decided to stop in Sacramento and see Miguel again. We went back to the Firehouse Restaurant and then back to the hotel for the night. Miguel arrived at check-out time and got us to the hangar, ready for the last leg of our trip. He got his usual tip and smiled before disappearing. We boarded the bus and rested for the 6-hour flight. The captain told us that Baltimore was coming into view and to ready ourselves for landing. The bags were offloaded, and we headed to customs. Stephan went through, and I was asked to stay behind. I was taken into a separate room and questioned about my passport. "It says here your birth year was 1967. That would make you 111 years old. Care to explain?" I forgot that I hadn't updated my passport like Stephan and didn't know what to say. If I told the truth, they wouldn't believe me, and if I lied, I'd be in hot water for lying. Just then, Stephan opened the door with a middle-aged man whom I thought I recognized. The customs officer asked who and why they were interrupting an interview. "Well, since you don't recognize me, officer, let me show you my credentials." The officer took the ID and stared at the man for a few seconds. "How can we help you Senator Halstead (How could I forget Dahlia's son Jeffrey)?" Jeffrey turned to me and then back to the officer, "These two men work for me and they were supposed to be back to my office right after landing. What's the hold-up?" The officer showed him the passport and Jeffrey simply said, "It's a typo, thanks for pointing it out. I'll have it taken care of officer. Very observant of you. I'll let your superior know that you're doing excellent work." Jeffrey took the passport, pushed me out the door, and we headed to our limousine. "Jeffrey, thank you so much. How will I ever repay you?" "Really, Uncle Carl, after all you've done for the entire family and me. Rack it up to family helping family. But get it updated, okay?"

Stephan shook his head and said, "I swear you're becoming more like Lady Eddie every day. Sure, you don't need the vaccine?" I came back with, "Well, as long as you still love me, it's okay." He flashed that gorgeous smile, and I knew we would be fine. "How did you know why they took me away and know to call Jeffrey?" "Does it matter as long as we got your butt out of trouble?" I had to concede the point as Stephan was always two steps ahead of me. A cuddle session was in order, and we arrived at the manse and entered our beloved home hand in hand. Bobbie ran towards us with Caran in hot pursuit. "You didn't happen to bring anything back with you, did you, Uncle Carl?" I looked despondent because I had forgotten while handling Stephan's problem. Stephan said, "Of course, we did, Bobbie. Have we ever forgotten you and the others? I blushed as Stephan opened one of the bags and gave out the items. Note to self, if you start something, keep it up.

A month went by, and we got a call from Adam. He wanted to see how Stephan was faring. I told him that he was as healthy and as randy as a satyr. "He's only missing the ram horns." Stephan grabbed the phone away from me and took the call into the den. The call went on for an hour, and then Stephan emerged and handed me back my phone. "Care to share the conversation with me, lover?" Stephan took my hand, led me into the atrium, and said that he had invited Adam to Baltimore for a follow-up. "I want to make sure everything is still the same or better." I nodded, and we went in search of a meal. Harold whipped up a quick brunch, and Stephan ate his entire meal. I quipped, "Better watch out with that new appetite. You'll gain weight and have a dad bod by Christmas."

Secretly, I was enjoying that Stephan was eating so well. He whispered back, "I'll work it off, and you're in for a workout." I started to laugh and then remembered my part of the equation. Thoughts about Adam were put aside as the more urgent need was about to be addressed. I don't think we made it back downstairs until called for supper. Stephan began the table talk and asked Bobbie (who was now ten) if he knew how to ride a bike, and he said no. "We'll have to remedy that, won't we?" Bobbie looked at his mom to see if it was all right, and she nodded to him and turned and grimaced at her uncle Stephan. "Let's go tomorrow and get you a bike and maybe get ice cream on the way home." Elizabeth showed her disapproval, but Stephan shot back, "I said maybe Elizabeth." She broke up at that and just shook her head and left us. Bobbie called Caran, and they went outside to play.

Adam stopped by the next day, but Stephan was out with Bobbie getting his bike. I welcomed Adam into the atrium, and we talked. He seemed overexcited about telling me about the serum and its results. Stephan joined us as he left Bobbie's training to Bob. It was better that way, father and son togetherness. "I was about to tell Carl all about the results of the serum." Adam went on and on about the efficacy of the drug. "It looks like a single dose can fix the anemia. I want to see the long-term effects of the serum and then ask your approval to try and make it known." Stephan rolled up his sleeve and gave Adam another draw. We took the sample into the den where Stephan had a microscope, and we looked, one after the other, at the specimen. Adam was impressed, and Stephan and I were happy. "Well, it worked. Who would think that a lizard and a hybrid blood would create such a powerful serum?" Stephan told Adam that he could have the total credit for the 'discovery'. "I have to make it perfectly clear, Adam, that neither Carl nor my name ever gets cited in your work. That's the price I require for your fame and fortune." Adam swore it and offered to sign a contract to that effect. "That won't be necessary, Adam. I have other ways to keep people in line, as Carl has seen on several occasions." Adam's face paled at the unspoken threat. "Don't worry, Stephan, your secret is safe with me." Stephan smiled and nodded, knowing the message had been noted. The only thing I had to say was that the side effects were a hearty appetite and a strong sex drive. Adam noted it, and we all got called to dinner.

Harold presented a hearty stew, with artisan bread, hummus drizzled with extra virgin olive oil. A side salad of fresh greens with a green goddess dressing. We had Harold get some of Tony Sr.'s wine selections and allowed Adam to pick one. A crisp Sauvignon Blanc was tasted and poured. "It's a good selection, Adam. You must know your wines." Adam said he had actually heard of this vintage as he traveled to Italy and went to that vineyard. "We are partners with Tony Sr. and with his son Tony Jr. As a matter of fact, one of our security people, Davin, is married to Tony Sr.'s daughter, Isabella." Adam looked shocked, wondering how we were so affluent. Stephan explained our situation. "We have invested heavily and well over the years, and the return on investment has been fruitful as you can see." The rest of dinner went well, and we bade Adam goodnight.

We put him up in the Kimpton Hotel Monaco (one of the top 3 hotels in Baltimore). I had Davin drive him there and told him to take my Bentley. He jumped at the chance to drive the Bentley for a change, and soon they were off. Stephan said, "Do you think we may have been a bit too ostentatious?" I responded by saying, "As long as we didn't mention the original oil paintings, or the warehouse, or the villa, or the tons of other stuff we bequeathed to the family, I'd say no." I can't remember laughing so hard, and Stephan joining me in the absurdity of my statement. Speaking of the warehouse, I hadn't made a visit to check on Joey's progress. I decided to follow up the next day, now that Stephan was on the mend. Well, my day started fine, the bed was stripped of its covers, the master of the house was smiling, and I was feeling the afterglow of passion. We descended the stairs calmly and followed the aroma of fresh coffee in the kitchen. Harold was just finishing the Hollandaise sauce for our breakfast as we got ourselves coffee. The eggs Benedict looked heavenly, and the toast popped up as we sat at the island. Two sips of coffee, and the dishes were served. Stephan was given his usual one egg on toast, and I was served two (as was usual). Caran was at our feet, awaiting her share of Stephan's. Stephan finished before me and asked for another. Harold said okay, but then turned and looked at me quizzically. He served up two more, and Stephan ate most of that. Poor Caran got one toast point and some Hollandaise sauce. She took it nonetheless and went looking for her food. "Your appetite has greatly improved, Stephan. Kiss that 'modeling career' goodbye." He smiled and asked if I wanted a round two to work off the calories. "I would, but I said that I was going to check on your 'mini me' Stephan." He slapped my butt while passing by and said, "You could use some exercise too," and then kissed my cheek and left the room.

I really wanted to take advantage of his invitation, but duty called. I got to the driveway and saw that our Bentleys had been washed and polished. I grabbed my silver one and left for the warehouse. I was greeted at the gate and steered to the side of the warehouse. Arnie stepped out of the warehouse and said hello. I asked him how things were and if he was getting along with Joey. "he's really good at his job, but he's hard to control. He thinks he knows everything." I nodded and said, "I'll talk to him and let him know that he reports to you." Arnie thanked me, and I entered the building. I went to the gallery and saw that he had organized, cataloged, and created a gallery of sorts to display the works. I thought to myself, this kid is good. Joey saw me and came over. "Well, hello, do you like?" I had to say that he was good at what he did. I really didn't want to stroke his ego, but I couldn't deny the results. "It's okay, I guess." He took that as an opening salvo. "What's wrong, I can fix it any way you want. But you'll have to tell me what you don't like first." He had me, and he knew it, and sadly, so did I.

"Well, I'd have put some of the larger works in the aisle ends so you can get a better perspective." I was shooting from the hip, and I think he knew that too. "Well, I'll take that into consideration. When Johnny comes home, I'll consult with him as he knows more than I." I really thought I was talking to Stephan and had to remember that I was the boss, or at least the boss's spouse. In order to change the subject, I asked him to order lunch for the staff and us, and that I would be on the roof waiting for the delivery. He questioned, "How would you like to pay for it, or did you think I would foot the bill?" I handed him the black card and said, "Of course I'm paying for it. After all, I said to order it, not pay for it. You are a real toad, you know that. If I wanted someone to be snarky, I'd have brought Stephan." He smiled as though I had complimented him and turned to secure the purchase.

One hour later, the staff assembled on the roof for lunch. The toad had bought Mexican and got it extra spicy. The heat level was that of a ghost pepper. I had a couple of tacos and left the sauce off, after all, I had 'exercise' scheduled for later. Joey ate until he was stuffed and sauced everything. I chuckled to myself as I kind of knew the day he would have tomorrow. The staff took a more conservative approach to the food. I told Joey to take the leftovers home. I toured the rest of the facility and found nothing to complain about, so I took my leave and went home.

Home was quiet, a bit too quiet, so I went in search of anybody. The house felt ghostly, so I went to the kitchen, empty, then the atrium, again empty. I headed to the den; Stephan had to be there yet, but it was empty. I was getting scared by then, so I went to the dining room and opened the French doors. Everyone was there celebrating. "What's up, Stephan? I thought I was left behind in the rapture." Stephan came over, handed me a toasting flute, and said, "There was a special election, and it seems that Jeffrey won in a landslide. He's an up-and-rising star in the Democratic Party. They're calling him the new Newsome. You remember him, don't you? He won the election in 2028, taking down the Trump regime." I remembered that it has taken 50 years to get the world to forgive us.

I joined the merriment, and we continued the celebration the rest of the day. Stephan called Jeffrey and congratulated him. "If you need a backer, you can count on me, my boy." Jeffrey thanked him and said, "I'll keep that in mind, but I'm trying to run a grassroots campaign with all small donors." He was the preeminent politician. Stephan returned to me and whispered, "Don't you have an appointment to exercise, young man?" My face was grinning ear to ear as I grabbed Stephan and we excused ourselves and ran upstairs.

As promised, I 'updated' my passport and told Jeffrey so. "Thanks, Uncle Carl. I don't need a family scandal right about now." We both laughed, and then I went in search of Stephan. I got sidetracked by Bobbie and Caran, but after a fashion, got to the den and found my target. "I fixed my passport, and yes, I called Jeffrey to let him know." Stephan handed me a Bourbon and lit my cigar. I said, "The only thing missing is a roaring fire and a bear skin rug." Stephan pointed to the rug and bent in front of the fireplace. It did take about ten minutes, but he got the fire roaring and joined me on the rug (after refilling his bourbon glass). "You're feeling chipper, Stephan. I'm so glad that we found a cure, even if it meant that you now have Eddie lizard blood." I received a slap and tickle for that, but it was worth it. I had my guy back and in full health.

We decided to spend the end of summer at the camp, and of course, we called the staff and troops to join us. I added David and Jen as well. I quietly set up a party for Bob, after all, he was turning 77 this year. He had confided in me that he wanted to retire and let Albert take the full reins. I used his birthday celebration as an excuse to give him the party. Two days into our 'family' vacation, we set up the party and made sure that Elizabeth and Bobbie were kept in the dark (for surprise effect). The party started at 2 p.m. Tom and Declan came over with Jaime so he could assist Harold with the food. The cake was uncovered as Bob came forward with Elizabeth and Bobbie. Bobbie said, "It says 'happy birthday and happy re-tir-e-men-t daddy'. What does that word mean?" Bob picked up his son and said, "It means that I get to spend a lot more time with you and mommy." Bobbie smiled and got down so his father could cut the cake. Stephan stepped forward and began, "Bob, I know it's a surprise, but you had been hinting around about it. I'd like to thank you for all the years of loyal service. You have more than earned it. Carl and I would like to gift you a little something as a token of our esteem." With that, he handed over a rather large manila envelope.

Bob opened it, and car keys fell out (the emblem was a lurching jaguar). There was also a letter with a gold invitation to Wakaya at any time that Bob and Elizabeth wanted to go. Finally, a check of many zeros so that Bobbie could go to college and not burden his parents with debt ($5 plus six zeros to be exact). Bob's eyes glazed over, but he did manage to hold back his tears. He shook our hands and walked over to

Elizabeth to share it with her. The party went on into the night, and Stephan kept me up with him to enjoy it. I whispered to Harold not to expect us for breakfast, and he nodded.

The camp days lasted another week, and then we all returned to our 'normal' life. Tom, Declan, and Jaime returned to Fiji. The bills got caught up, and the house calmed back down. Stephan said he got a letter from Vasiliki. I followed him to the den, and he disclosed the contents. It said that Andreas was thinking of coming to America, and she was wondering if he could stay with us. Stephan said that he called her and let her know that he was welcome and that he would let us know when, so we could send the 'bus' to fly him here. "I also asked if she would need assistance during his absence, but she said she had taken on servants due to our generosity." It seemed that our gifts had enriched a lot of lives.

The date was set, and Andreas arrived at our hangar on the following Saturday. Stephan greeted him in Greek and helped him get through customs. Andreas was thankful for that as he knew less English. We took the limousine, and he got to ride in the back for probably the first time. Stephan asked him if he was hungry and said we could stop at a restaurant. Andreas begged off and said a good night's rest would be better. We went home and got him settled and said goodnight. Stephan was peckish, so we went to the kitchen and made up a charcuterie board for us. We went to the den, and I started a fire as Stephan laid out the feast. He was reclining on the rug and started enticing me with cheese bits. I laughed, knelt down, and was presented with my treat. We fed each other, and Stephan started using the food as foreplay. Needless to say, it wasn't long before the clothes were history.

Long story short, the rug had to be sent out for cleaning and stain removal. Breakfast came, and Andreas asked for a simple Greek one, which consisted of fruit, cheese, bread, and a cup of strong coffee. Harold asked Andreas something about Greece, and Stephan leaned over to me and whispered, "Greece, Na, you're finally loose enough for KY." I nearly spit out my oatmeal. Stephan let out a roaring laugh, and the others just looked at us as I blushed a new shade of deep red. Stephan decided Andreas needed some new clothes for sightseeing. We stopped at Hunter's old shop, now run by Edward Garibo. He greeted us at the door and waved the clerk away. Stephan shook his hand, and he asked what we were looking for. "Well, this 'young' man needs a new set of clothes. He's my cousin from Greece, and I'd like him to get some new things that he'd be more comfortable in. Edward asked his age, and Andreas quickly looked at me, and I nodded. "Well, 417 years as of last fall." Edward didn't bat an eye as he bowed and left to collect some items. Stephan spoke in Greek and said that this was Hunter and Harold's cousin and that he knew about the family. Edward motioned for Andreas to accompany him to the back, and we followed.

If you for one second thought that we were going to miss out on the fashion show, you would be mistaken. When Edward needed a translation, Stephan stepped in and let Andreas know. Edward was as eager to see this Greek Adonis in his underthings as we were. He handed over the silk briefs and nothing else. Andreas quickly caught on and took the underwear behind the curtain. When he emerged, Edward gasped, and we smiled. The 6-foot-3-inch god with curly black hair and a treasure trail that disappeared about 4 inches below his navel appeared. Muscles from years of farm work and a butt you could bounce quarters off of. Edward caught his breath and said, "Is anyone else hot? I didn't realize the thermostat was set so high." Andreas got the attention he wanted, and we certainly got the show we wanted. The show continued, and Andreas got lots of clothes. The black card was presented, and the packages were going to be delivered the next day. Edward said he would deliver it himself (I wonder why). Andreas said he could accept the meal he passed on the night he arrived. Stephan was all in, and we had the limousine driver take us to our Italian place. The Maitre'd led us to the booth in the back and ran to get us wine as we sat and relaxed. Andreas spoke to Stephan, and he laughed. The conversation went on for the better part of 5 minutes before Stephan spoke English again. "Care to share with the rest of us, or me to be more specific?" Andreas asked about Edward. I told him that I didn't know until the show began. Then it became blatantly obvious. Edward has the hots for Andreas, and Andreas is more like me, and thought it was cute to be fawned over. Is that enough, or should I go into details, nosey rosey?"

I responded, "If that's the case, have Andreas around when the clothes get delivered. I see Andreas in a speedo, in the atrium with a glass of wine. Edward won't need much more to swoon." The wine and the food arrived, and we munched the afternoon away. Per usual, Stephan paid the bill and gave out tips to the entire staff personally. He then turned to Andreas and said, "That's why we always get excellent service." Andreas took note, and we left. We, or should I say Stephan, let Andreas in on our plans, and Andreas agreed. "It will be a good surprise. I hope he's ready for me." He then said something in Greek to Stephan, and they laughed as Stephan said, "No problem, I'll get you some from upstairs."

I hated to be out of the loop and decided that I'd get conversational language discs. I sent away for Russian, Greek, Italian, Spanish, and French. Might as well tackle it all. I might need them over the next century. I so wanted to be a fly on the wall as Edward delivered the clothes, but I figured the date might not happen if too many people were there. Besides, I was married to the translator, so that was that. The doorbell rang, and Elizabeth answered (knowing the plan). She led Edward to the atrium and said to wait there. Enter Andreas, power blue speedo, muscles oiled, and sipping a good wine. Edward lost his ability to speak until Stephan appeared, and Andreas started speaking. Stephan nodded and turned to Edward. "He would like to know if this swimsuit comes in different colors. Also, he would like it if you could store the clothes in his room. If it's not too much trouble, of course." Edward said, "No trouble at all, please show me the way." Andreas motioned for him to follow, and Edward followed like a puppy.

Who would figure that it took sooo long to store clothes? And it must have been grueling work as Edward finally came down 3 hours later, sweating profusely. He took his leave, and Andreas appeared about 5 minutes later, a smile on his face and twirling a pair of white cotton briefs. "A token of his esteem." To which we all had a good laugh and knew we had made another connection. Andreas extended his stay to a month, and Edward became a regular guest (how often did those clothes need folding?). The last day of his stay, we threw a party to say goodbye, and Edward attended. He was sadder than Andreas. Andreas asked Stephan how to say something in English so he could get it right, and then whispered in Edward's ear. That perked him up a lot.

We sent his clothes on ahead so he'd have them when he got home, and then sent him off on the bus. Edward begged us to let him come to the airport, and we acquiesced. We said our goodbyes, hugged it out, and returned to the limousine so they could have a private moment. They hugged and kissed as they said so long. Edward walked back to the car as the cabin door was locked. We pulled to the edge of the tarmac and watched as the plane got its clearance and left the ground. Edward was quiet all the way to his store, and we went home. Stephan said that Edward was going to visit Andreas in Greece soon and that I had agreed to let him use our plane. I asked if maybe we should consider giving him some anti-aging pills. "If it goes there, then yes, we'll share." Stephan then quipped, "Great, now we're going to have two Lady Eddies, one in England and one in Greece." I fell over on Stephan as I hadn't thought of that, and it warmed my heart to pieces.

Back at home, I went into the den, and as Stephan poured the Bourbon, I lit the cigars and sat at the desk. Stephan brought over my snifter and looked over my shoulder. "Whatcha doing there?" I showed him the partial list of the people we had brought together and continued with the list. Stephan hugged me tight and said, "It looks like we've done some good work over the years. But I could not have done it without you, dear Carl. Life has been made more whole having you by my side. It's made the last 73 years seem like days or, better yet, hours. Time has flown and we with it. And to think of how we got together. You were looking for me, although at the time you didn't know it, and I was trying to find out what you were all about. I only have one regret." I looked at my Stephan and asked, "And what is that?" Stephan looked directly into my eyes and said, "I should have thrown away that damn bologna the day I met you." Tears filled my eyes as I laughed and put my face on his muscular chest.

I raised my snifter, and we clinked our glasses together as we toasted ourselves. "Here's to another century, Batman." "And to you, Robin, now where did you put those new suits?"

The end...